A Destiny Among Worlds
Book I

OVERTAKEN BY DESTINY

*Joseph Hale
with
Vanessa Hale and Ian Hale*

Copyright © 2015 Joseph Hale,
Ian Hale, and Vanessa Hale

All rights reserved.

ISBN-13: 978-1519779168
ISBN-10: 151977916X

In memory of Samuel Charles Snyder

(February 8, 1995-August 15, 2015),

whose rich and wonderful personality continues to be inspirational.

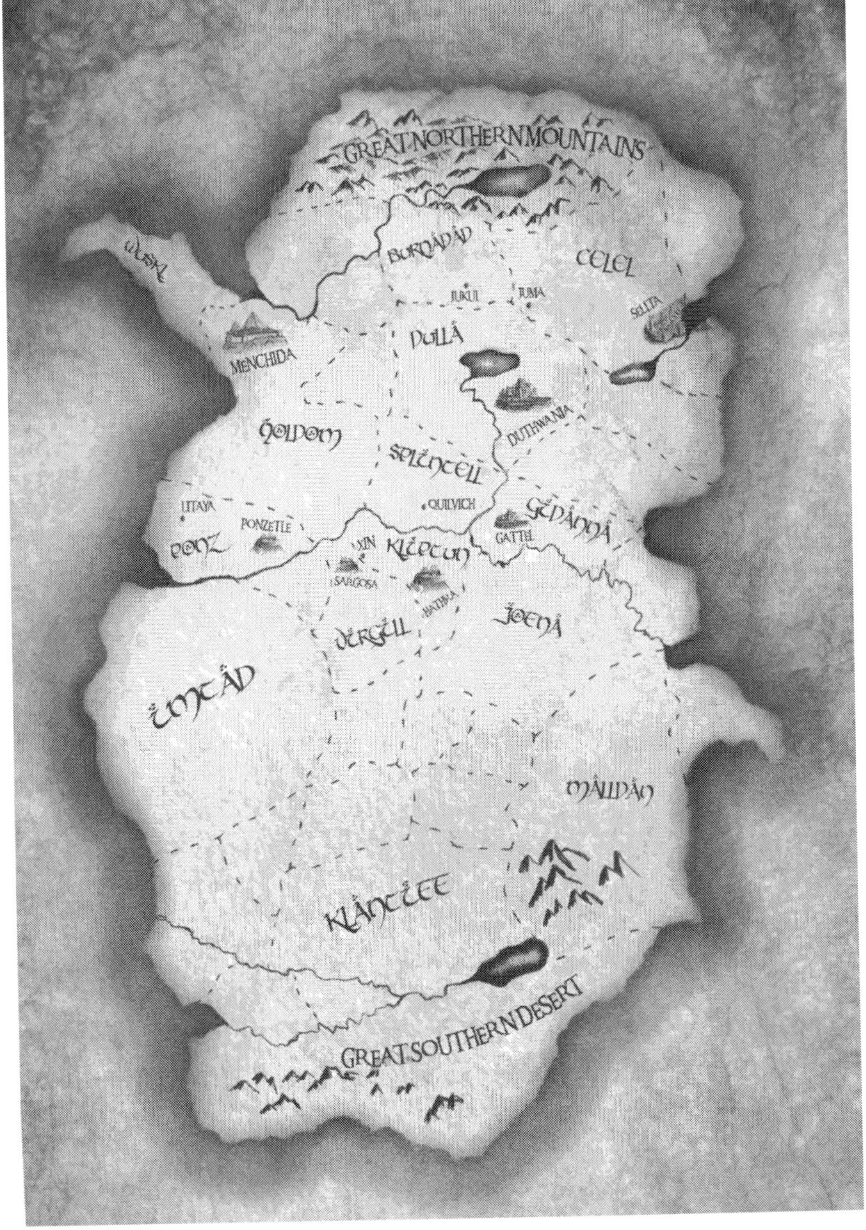
GREAT NORTHERN MOUNTAINS
CELEL
JUKUI
JUMA
MENCHIDA
DUTHWANIA
LITAYA
PONZETLE
QUILVICH
GATTEL
XIN
SARGOSA
GREAT SOUTHERN DESERT

Acknowledgments

We owe a debt of thanks to many family members and friends whose encouragement, experience, and advice brought this project to fruition. We offer special thanks to our parents, Alan and Julie Hale, for all of their support and encouragement throughout our lives. We thank our dear friends Samuel Sherrouse and Benjamin Snyder for helping to sculpt multiple characters' personalities within the book. We thank Katherine Scheiman Manning for the wonderful cover art and Brandon Fenty for creating the map.

I (Joseph) would also like to thank several college professors who helped expand my communication potential. Dr. Halsey Werlein provided the tools I needed to become a skilled writer, and Dr. Michael Hartman helped expand my creativity so that I could generate this captivating story. Also included are Drs. Scott Cook and Joseph Bean, who encouraged me to excel during their classes.

Prologue

"ALL RIGHT, DEAR, COME on. We have to get Jackson's classes settled today," urged Albert Ingle, a tall, athletic man in his mid-twenties.

"I know, I know," replied his wife, Jenny, picking up her pace. "It just seems so odd that we had to come down here to see the class coordinator. I thought we could just choose Jackson's classes online or something." Jenny was a petite blonde whose soft dimples and bright eyes bespoke beauty and intelligence.

The couple walked down the long hallway that ran through the center of Eagleton High School. Eagleton High stood at the cul-de-sac of the road that ran along the Eagleton Private Academy Complex. The complex also included an elementary school, where Jackson was currently a student, and a middle school. It was a rainy Saturday, and very little sunlight came through the windows lining the top of the hallway. The overcast atmosphere made the hallway appear dim despite its rows of overhead lights. The entire school appeared empty. Apparently, everyone except the class coordinator had gone home for the weekend. The couple's footsteps echoed down the hallway as they walked. Lockers lined most of the hall, but a gap allowed room for various school officials' offices, including the principal, vice principal, and class coordinator. The class coordinator's office stood on the hall's left side opposite the principal's office.

Albert knocked on the class coordinator's door, which seemed to give way under the pressure of his knuckles as it was swung open from the inside. As they entered, they saw a tall, slim man standing behind the door still holding the doorknob. The man had a round face and brown hair streaked with occasional wisps of gray. He wore a distinguished-looking suit even though it was Saturday, and he appeared surprisingly fit for someone whose job predominantly consisted of paperwork.

A desk stood at the far end of the room surrounded by bookshelves full of old books. Pictures of the man now before them standing with many of the high school classes attending Eagleton High School over the years covered much of the wall space not occupied by bookshelves. The wall also contained an empty place, where Albert guessed that the brightly colored flag neatly folded on the desk had recently hung. The flag was one that he did not recognize. It had a dark blue field, and he saw part of a red star at the edge of one of its folds. The desk also supported a laptop computer and a variety of notebooks, pens, and paperweights.

"Greetings." The class coordinator smiled warmly as he extended his right hand. "My name is Dr. Taylor. You must be Mr. and Mrs. Ingle. I've been expecting you."

"Yes, we are." Albert returned the professional-looking man's firm handshake. "We received your message about our son's classes."

"Yes, indeed," Dr. Taylor said, exchanging a handshake with Jenny. "Please have a seat. It's my job as the school's class coordinator to see to it that our students are matched with classes that best suit their personalities and potential futures." Dr. Taylor moved behind his desk and took his own seat.

Jenny interjected, "Yes, yes, but don't we have some say in Jackson's extracurricular activities?"

"Of course you do," replied Dr. Taylor, "but it's the school's sincerest hope that our students' parents will seriously consider professional advice in this matter. For the last decade—really after the Second Great Depression—schools have relied more and more on class coordinators to aid in directing students' learning and development. I have personally observed these children at the elementary school throughout kindergarten and kept detailed notes on exactly which activities they will not only excel in but also enjoy all the way up through the end of high school. For your son I also discovered that in the brief time he's been at the elementary school, he's already formed strong bonds with two other young boys. I've overlapped the majority of these friends' extracurricular activities because I believe that strong bonds developed in childhood can last a lifetime. Don't you agree?"

"Well, yes. That is a good point." Albert glanced at Jenny. "We don't have any particular problems with the classes you've chosen for our son," he clarified, glancing down at the coordinator's recent email the couple had printed and brought with them. "We just thought that we would have a little more input. When I was young, I didn't take very many extracurricular classes. I pretty much just played baseball and ran track, but you have a fairly extensive list here. Do you think the kids will be able to keep up with these extra classes and still do well in their normal credit courses?"

"Of course I do, Mr. Ingle. Jackson and his friends Benjamin and Charles are highly intelligent children. Like you, sir, I believe these boys need athletic and mental stimulation. Besides, this is a private academy, and higher standards should be expected. Isn't that why you chose this institution?" Dr. Taylor paused for a moment before continuing, "As you can see, I signed them up for the chess club and fencing classes several years down the road in order to build their mental fortitude. I have also placed them in wrestling and martial arts to turn these boys into athletes, just as you were, Mr. Ingle, when you were in school. After all, here in the South we believe in both physical and mental strength."

The Ingles were silent for a moment, and only a faint tap, tap could be heard as raindrops collided with and ran down the office window.

Jenny finally broke the silence. "They just seem a little bit violent—the classes you've chosen for Jackson. They don't seem completely normal."

Dr. Taylor responded, "Mrs. Ingle, these are normal classes open to every child in the school, and skills like martial arts or fencing also have many nonviolent aspects. These activities have a great deal of historical and cultural aspects that can deepen a young man's learning and imagination."

Jenny's features softened.

Dr. Taylor leaned back in his chair. "I've already spoken with Benjamin's and Charles's parents, and they agree that Jackson is a good boy. They would like these children to continue spending time together, and these classes will suit all three children well in the future. In addition, I would advise you as parents to befriend, at least on a cursory level, your son's friends in order to help solidify their relationships so that strong, healthy bonds can be built in their future."

Albert cleared his throat. "Well, these classes are agreeable to me if they are to you, dear, and I wouldn't mind meeting these other boys' parents."

Jenny nodded. "As long as he enjoys them, it's okay with me."

"Good." Dr. Taylor picked up a consent form from his desk. "I will make the final preparations, and you will need to sign here. Allow me to assure you that the principal himself has spoken very highly of my ability to effectively place young students in activities that help them grow most efficiently. My doctorate in psychology focused specifically on the development of young people. I would encourage you to read some of my essays on child development. I based much of my writing on my observations of children attending this school over the years, both while in school and after graduation. I can assure you that I have a good track record for guiding students toward success."

He placed the signed form on top of a stack of papers on his desk. "It was a pleasure to meet you both. You have a great son; I expect great things from him in the future. I'm excited about the possibilities."

"Thank you for your time, Dr. Taylor," Albert replied. "We'll be on our way. You have an excellent day, and maybe we will take your advice and look up some of your work."

The Ingles shook hands with Dr. Taylor again and departed.

As the couple once again walked through the empty hallway, Albert snickered. "I'm glad we got out of there before he started talking about how many research studies he has been involved in and his magnificent findings. Are all physiologists that eccentric?"

Jenny, apparently deep in thought, replied only with a slight smile.

"Don't be so worried, dear." Albert placed his arm around his wife's shoulders. "Jackson will do fine in school and grow up to be a great young man."

"I know," she replied. "I just worry about what kinds of things might happen in the future."

"Everything will be fine," he assured her. "This is America, a land of safety and opportunities. In all likelihood, Jackson will grow up, find a nice girl, get a job, live happily right here in Tennessee, and maybe even send his kids to this same school."

Jenny leaned into his embrace. "You're right. I shouldn't worry so much."

A Destiny Among Worlds

Chapter 1

JACKSON INGLE TOOK A deep breath. He could still hardly believe that he was here at the State Martial Arts Championship between Eagleton Private Academy and Harrison Private Academy. He had worked so long and hard to get here that the day seemed as though it would never actually arrive. His schoolwork had piled up as he and his friends approached their graduation and prepared for their competition. Eagleton Private Academy ran on a year-round school program, and the days grew warmer and warmer as spring ended.

The championship was held in a sizable gymnasium with several basketball courts. Six rings stood in the gym's center surrounded by bleachers full of excited parents, teachers, and friends. Each ring resembled a boxing ring with five thick strands of elastic around the edges and pads on the floor. Jack knew his parents were somewhere in the stands, most likely sitting with Benjamin's and Charles's families.

Ben Chambers and Charles Elston had been Jack's best friends for as long as he could remember, and it seemed as though they did everything together. His two friends were here beside him now with Ben on one side and Charles on the other—the way it usually was. For many years the other two had looked to Jack as the unofficial leader of their trio. All three of them had made it through the preliminary matches, and the competition was coming down to the last few fights.

The referees and their assistants were clearing away the extra rings because the final fights would take place one at a time.

It had been a bright, sunny day in Middle Tennessee, but Jack could barely tell from the sunlight streaming through the narrow windows that rimmed the walls at the ceiling. Jack ran his hand through his short brown hair. Jack had an athletic build like his father, but he got his brown eyes and thoughtful, contemplative personality from his mother. Jack usually bore a calm exterior and tended to analyze situations carefully before settling on a course of action. He glanced to his right and saw Mr. Thompson approaching them.

Keith Thompson had been the boys' martial arts instructor since high school began. He was a retired police officer who had developed a fondness for various types of martial arts. In his own training and in his teaching, he did not become overly wrapped up in one particular martial art discipline such as karate or taekwondo. As a result, he irritated many of the other instructors who believed that the artistic, cultural, and historical aspects gained from mastering a single, pure martial art discipline were just as important as combat training. Mr. Thompson, however, did not usually care what other people thought of him, and most people toned down their negative comments substantially when he was present. Mr. Thompson always maintained a laidback, calm exterior—except when he was in a fight. Ever since Mr. Thompson had retired from the police force and obtained a job at Eagleton High School, teaching martial arts had become his passion.

"Well, how are you doing, boys?" Mr. Thompson asked as he approached. "Are you ready for the last few matches?"

"Yes sir," they replied as one.

Mr. Thompson stopped in front of the boys. "Just remember what I taught you. These guys are good, but you three can take them. Ben, you'll be up against Clarence Coulter. Remember to stay focused. Pay attention when your opponent shifts his weight, and take advantage of your speed and agility. Charles, you're fighting Doug Mason. You've got height and weight on your side, so remember to try to close the distance quickly. If you can grab a hold of your opponent, don't let up, and don't let go. Jack, you're going to be up against their top guy, Edgar Tanning, based on your current ranking, so remember, you'll need to create openings in his defenses by faking your emotions like I taught you.

Now, spend a few minutes working out your strategies before the matches start."

Jack rummaged through ideas in his mind on how to throw his opponent off balance. The whole last year, Mr. Thompson had drilled into him the importance of controlling one's emotions during a fight. He reviewed which emotions his teacher had said were connected to which physical reactions. Display fear or uncertainty when you are trying to get your opponent to rashly attack, let down their guard, or just shift their weight, putting them off balance. Taunting or displaying pleasure provokes your opponent and makes them overconfident. Sadness or pain brings either pleasure or sadness to your opponent, depending on your opponent's personality and how they feel about you. Anger gives increased power and strength at the cost of defense and control. Concealing all of your emotions puts you in the best state of mind to analyze your opponent and discern their strengths and weaknesses.

Jack could still hear his teacher's words echoing in his mind, "Remember, a skilled combatant who lets his emotions control him is a relatively poor fighter, but a warrior in complete control displays and feels whatever emotion he wishes."

Jack's thoughts were interrupted by the ring of the bell.

"All right," yelled the referee. "Will the top five candidates of both schools line up on opposite sides of the ring? The rules state that the school with three out of five victories will win this championship. Based on how everyone performed in the preliminary fights, the lowest two for each school will go first, ending with the highest two."

Ben bumped Jack with his elbow and whispered, "Do you think we can take them?"

Ben was lean with a dark complexion and dark brown, almost black, hair kept slightly longer than a traditional buzz cut, which he insisted made him look cool. His dark complexion coupled with his piercing, dark eyes made him seem more serious than he actually was.

Jack replied, "Well, we only have to win three out of the five fights, so if you and Charles do your jobs, I shouldn't even have to fight."

Charles snickered. "But then all these people would miss out on watching you and Edgar Tanning go *mano a mano*."

Charles, a heavily built young man, would have seemed intimidating if he was not always so cheerful. His round face, short sandy brown hair, and ready smile fit nicely with his kindhearted nature.

Ten minutes later the scenario looked much worse for Eagleton Academy. Harrison Academy had won the first two matches, leaving just the three friends' fights remaining.

"Well," Charles concluded, "I guess all three of us have to win now."

The other two responded with words of encouragement as Charles stepped into the ring.

The bell rang, and Charles's opponent, Doug, began with a flurry of jabs and quick roundhouse kicks to Charles's left side. He was obviously trying to feel out Charles's defenses before making a serious attack.

Although Charles deflected the attacks, Doug closed the distance again as he shot two jabs and faked a right cross.

As Charles palmed the right cross aside, his opponent gave a straight punch to Charles's exposed midsection with his left hand.

Charles grimaced and exhaled rapidly as the punch made contact. He had not tightened his abdominal muscles enough and received most of the impact without resistance.

"One point," the referee yelled.

Charles tried to move in close for a series of rapid punches.

Doug, however, danced to the side and counterattacked with a roundhouse kick, forcing Charles to move back. Doug dodged to the right and attacked with a series of roundhouse kicks in an attempt to force Charles back into the corner of the ring.

Charles, clearly irritated, initiated another dash toward his opponent and spun, launching a back kick.

His opponent leapt backward to avoid the kick then jumped forward again, punching directly toward Charles's exposed head.

Although Charles partially deflected the punch, the referee yelled, "One point."

The bell rang again.

Doug came in quickly and jabbed twice, trying to catch Charles off guard.

As Charles palmed the second jab, he grabbed the other young man's fist with his hand and yanked him forward.

The combination of Doug already shifting his weight forward to make the punch and Charles jerking him forward pitched the Harrison High School hopeful forward so fast that it was not clear for a moment what had happened.

The two combatants collided with each other.

Charles's dazed opponent was unable to quickly dodge away, leaving him completely open.

Charles stood to his full height and dropped a right cross.

Despite the protective gear they wore on their hands, heads, and feet, the impact was so great that Doug dropped like a rock.

"One point," the referee yelled.

Doug staggered to his feet, still dazed and now very wary of going on the offensive again.

Charles rushed at his adversary but to no avail.

Although dazed, the other young man was still too quick. He closed in on Charles with a roundhouse kick in an attempt to push Charles back again, but Doug still moved slower than normal due to the collision.

Charles caught his opponent's kick in the crook of his left arm and backfisted Doug in the face.

The referee again called the point. After the standard break in combat, he cued for the fight to recommence.

Now, however, the match was essentially over because Charles's opponent was even more sluggish.

Charles scored twice more in rapid succession, and the time expired.

The referee yelled, "Winner," as he walked over to Charles and followed up with, "two wins for Harrison and one for Eagleton."

Jack smiled slightly as he mused about how many of Charles's fights looked this way. Charles usually had a slow start, but being 6 feet 3 inches and weighing 210 pounds usually brought him through in the end. Charles was much less aggressive than most big guys Jack had known, which sometimes made him slow initially when fighting. Charles was, however, very smart, particularly in mathematics, and he was good at designing and building things. Jack completely approved of Charles's plans to major in mechanical engineering in college.

Like Jack's family, Charles's family was middle-class and predominantly generous. The major economic depression that occurred just before Jack was born had changed almost everyone who grew up during that time, making people either very stingy or generous.

Jack's thoughts were again interrupted by the bell. Ben's fight came next.

"Don't worry guys; I've got this." Ben stepped into the ring. "This guy won't know what hit him."

Ben was always a little overconfident. He liked to boldly try new things just because he could, and when events took a negative turn as a result of his spontaneity, it usually did not bother him—it was simply expected losses in his mind. At least he usually tried not to bring down Jack and Charles with him. The two had certainly gotten him out of trouble on more than one occasion. That being said, Ben was the most loyal of friends and had a reasonable sense of morality, so the trouble in which he found himself was not something that would send him to jail; it was just rather unwise. He would buy something because it looked interesting but not know what it did, or as in this case, begin a match with a flying sidekick because he thought it would be fun and look cool.

Apparently, Ben's challenger did not know him as well as Jack because Clarence was completely surprised. He managed to bring his arms up in front of his chest, but the force of the kick launched its recipient backward despite the block. Clarence hit the elastic rim around the ring, and the spring-like bands pitched him back toward the ring's center.

Jack looked to the referee to see if he would call the point.

The referee shook his head and yelled, "Blocked!"

Ben, at 5 feet 11 inches and 160 pounds, was not necessarily as aggressive as he was reckless.

Ben swiftly approached his adversary and launched a series of full power attacks at his opponent's head.

The Harrison boy managed to block and dodge the punches but allowed himself to be pushed back into the corner of the ring in the process.

Ben paused for a moment to think then moved in with a series of jabs. As Clarence tried to counterattack, Ben sidestepped the punch and grabbed his opponent's arm, pulling him slightly forward and off balance. Then Ben twisted his body and struck Clarence in the back of the head with the bottom of his own fist. The coach had taught Ben the backfist and hammerfist techniques early in his training, and he had adapted them very well with his speed and agility.

The referee called out the point, and the two went back at it hard and fast.

Clarence now matched Ben's aggressive style, assuming that Ben was naturally always aggressive.

Ben stepped forward to deliver a front kick to his opponent.

Clarence saw it coming and spun, delivering a back kick into Ben's midsection that knocked him backward and onto the ground.

"One to one," the referee called.

During the brief break Jack overheard their instructor telling Ben not to get caught up in the extremely aggressive facade he had created. When a fight started, Ben was good at creating emotional deceptions, but when he acted aggressive and became frustrated, he would usually buy in emotionally to the facade he had just created, leaving his movements too predictable.

Mr. Thompson said, "Fight defensively for a minute to cool off; then turn your anger back on. Remember, the longer you stay calm, the more powerful your aggression becomes when you release it and the easier it is to control so that you won't do something you'll regret."

Taking his advice, Ben started fighting defensively, and Jack could see him becoming calmer.

When the bell was about to ring, Ben switched back to his aggressive style, coming at his opponent quickly with two roundhouse kicks to throw him off balance before driving a sidekick straight into his abdomen.

"Point and match," called the referee. "Another for Eagleton."

"It's your turn now, Jack," said Mr. Thompson. "Remember what I said: switch up your emotions to keep your opponent off balance."

This is it, Jack thought. *I have to win, or I'll lose for the entire school.*

Edgar loomed in the ring in front of him. Edgar was a good 6 feet 2 inches and 200 pounds in comparison to Jack's 5 feet 11 inches and 145 pounds. Edgar was strong, fast, and good at using his size and weight in an aggressive style.

The bell rang, and Edgar dashed forward toward Jack.

Man, that guy is huge, Jack thought.

Edgar came in with a roundhouse kick to Jack's left side.

I get it, Jack thought as he blocked. *He's trying to come in, hit me with a couple of jabs, and probably end the combination with a right cross.* Jack executed a front kick to force Edgar to back off and interfere with his planned combination. *I must look scared,* Jack thought. He definitely felt intimidated. *I need to portray a different feeling.* Jack smiled slightly while letting out a small chuckle. It had the desired effect.

Infuriated, Edgar ran straight at him.

Jack quickly jumped to the side and shot a roundhouse kick directly into Edgar's midsection.

Edgar growled, "You little punk."

The referee called, "Point."

Jack now changed his expression to one that was completely calm and unchanging.

Edgar did the same.

Apparently, he's taking this more seriously, Jack thought.

Edgar moved in slowly this time.

Jack quickly pushed forward and shot a couple jabs at him.

Edgar dodged backward just a little and returned with a front kick. He then jumped forward and leapt into the air, performing a flying sidekick.

Jack pivoted to the side at the last moment to avoid the kick. As Edgar landed in a slightly crouched position, Jack jumped upward so that he looked straight down toward Edgar's head and punched.

Edgar moved his head just in time and gave a straight punch to Jack's midsection.

The blow pushed Jack backward, but he still landed on his feet.

"Point, Harrison," called the referee.

Edgar's coach yelled at him to close the distance and hit Jack up close.

Edgar moved in, shooting a few jabs and trying to grab Jack's arm.

I can't let him grab me, Jack realized, *or he will get an easy score. I'll have to use roundhouse and front kicks to force him to keep his distance.*

This strategy worked for a time, but Edgar became bolder and started brushing Jack's kicks aside. Then Edgar caught one of Jack's roundhouse kicks and shoved his leg upward.

The force lifted Jack into the air, and he landed on his back.

"Point for Harrison Academy," yelled the referee.

As the bell rang again, Jack looked at the clock and thought, *I'm running out of time. I need to do something extreme.*

"Is that all you got, Jackson?" Edgar taunted. "Looks like I've got this match in the bag."

No, Jack told himself. He closed his eyes for a moment. He was calm; then he became angry. *Now, I have to feel the emotion just like it's real while still staying calm.* Jack opened his eyes.

Edgar started to close the distance between them.

Jack ran straight at Edgar, jumping toward his head and faking a punch at his face.

Edgar blocked the punch but was too slow to move out of the way of Jack's body as Jack soared through the air.

Jack's body collided with Edgar's upper torso, and Jack grabbed with his legs and left hand.

The force of the impact knocked Edgar backward with Jack still hanging on him. Edgar grabbed Jack, trying to pry him off.

Jack swung his right elbow into the side of Edgar's head.

Despite the headgear he wore, Edgar dropped to the floor with Jack still on top of him.

The referee said, "All right, get off. Point, Eagleton."

But Edgar didn't get up.

Edgar's coach yelled at him, "Get up, weakling! You're tired, but if the bell rings, and you're still down, you lose."

Edgar lifted and shook his head then pulled himself to his knees. He stood slowly but dropped back to one knee.

The bell rang.

"The win goes to Eagleton," the referee announced.

The crowd stood and cheered.

Jack looked into the crowd and caught sight of his parents in the stands. His mom hugged Charles's mom. They were both crying. *That's a good picture,* Jack thought. The three families were very close, and they had only grown closer when Ben's mother had passed away when he was a boy. All three fathers stood clapping with big smiles on their faces. Charles's little sister, Sarah, and Ben's older brother, Derek, also clapped energetically.

The next hour or so was a bit of a blur. The trophy ceremony took place. After that Mr. Thompson accompanied the boys to the bleachers around the building's edge. Jack thought both of his parents looked very proud, and he could still see a hint of tears on his mother's cheeks.

Mr. Thompson said, "All you parents have good reason to be proud of your children today. They fought hard and with honor."

Albert Ingle nodded and replied with a smile, "It's a good thing you boys won because there's a celebration back at Eagleton High just waiting for you to get there."

The students loaded onto their bus to travel back to the high school. Most of them were loud and rambunctious on the return trip after their victory, but Jack remained lost in his own thoughts.

Back at Eagleton High School, more students, parents, and teachers waited. Everyone ate and talked, and the party entered full swing.

Despite the fun of the party, Jack felt as though something were missing. When the party started to die down, Jack wandered through the school's main hallway until he neared the end. The principal's office stood on the right, and Dr. Taylor's empty office remained on the left just past the lockers, where it had always been.

Jack opened the door to Dr. Taylor's office and stepped inside. The room had been emptied of most of Dr. Taylor's personal belongings years ago. Only the pictures of him with the classes of which he had been a part still hung on the walls, and some of his old books still stood on the shelves. The new class coordinator had chosen to place her office in the school's new wing, leaving this little room purposeless. Dr. Taylor had been a mentor to the three boys until they were ten. *He would have been so proud to see me win the championship,* thought Jack. *He always believed that I could excel, and he pushed me to become better, and not just me, but everyone in our class.*

Dr. Taylor had essentially set the course of life for all of the students. He observed and befriended them in their early years, and since he was the class coordinator, it was his job to select all of the children's classes. Jack owed all the hours of training in martial arts and fencing to Dr. Taylor, and his time in the chess club held some of Jack's best memories. Charles and Ben also played chess well, but they were much less patient than Jack.

No matter what other people said about Dr. Taylor being an antigovernment extremist, no student, parent, or faculty member at the school would ever believe it was true. Supposedly, before Jack was even born, Dr. Taylor had recruited a group of highly skilled students and computer hackers to hack into the government's newly established DNA recording program for infants.

After the Second Great Depression, the government had instituted many more restrictions and requirements to cut down on crime. Registering a DNA sample for all infants at birth was one of the new requirements. The government apparently discovered fourteen years after the leak had been established in the DNA database that Dr. Taylor was the one responsible and sent a team to arrest him. The boys were only ten years old at the time. Jack still vividly remembered the night when he saw the reporter on the news standing in front of the charred remains of Dr. Taylor's residence.

The reporter had gestured over his shoulder at the rubble and said, "The police have just informed us that Dr. Isaac Taylor, the alleged head of a ring of hackers who had been under close police surveillance, was just pursued into his home by federal agents and was killed in an explosion of unknown cause. The police just issued a statement that, moments before they breached the home's perimeter, the suspect created a fire, possibly in an attempt to destroy incriminating evidence. The police speculate that the fire caused an unintentional explosion, which resulted in the utter destruction that you see before you. The police refuse to release any additional details at this time because of the ongoing investigation."

As a result of Dr. Taylor's untimely death, no one ever had the opportunity to discover what his reasons might have been for hacking into the DNA database, and no one ever found out whether he was even guilty since he never went to court.

Some people did not believe that he actually did anything illegal. Others thought he must have had a good reason for doing it since he had always seemed like such a good man. *Who cares what he did before he came to this town*, thought Jack. *Maybe he was a bad dude who changed and tried to start over, or maybe he did have a good reason that we will never know. Maybe the explosion wasn't an accident; maybe he was killed so he couldn't talk.* Jack shrugged. Dr. Taylor had always been there for Jack even though Jack was just a child.

When Jack was six years old, he fell asleep on the playground after school, and his teacher thought he had gone home. When Jack's parents called around to find out if anyone had seen him, Dr. Taylor volunteered to check the school grounds since he lived nearby. He found Jack under a large oak tree, which was part of the far side of the tree line bordering the playground behind the school.

"Jack, my boy," he had said upon waking him. "I found you all the way out here. Your parents are worried. Let's see if we can get you back to them." Then as they walked, he told Jack about the importance of the bonds of friendship and asked why he had been alone. "Why weren't your friends with you? Why didn't they know where you were?"

"I didn't need them keeping track of me," Jack had replied. "I can take care of myself."

"I see," said Dr. Taylor. "Well, I say always keep your friends close, even if it's not convenient, because almost nothing in this world is more important than your family and your friends. Treasure those bonds forever. I have given you a great gift today, son; you should always remember what I have given you."

"You're right, Dr. T. My friends are important and my family, but I don't see why they're as important as you say."

"Well, one day when you are older, you'll understand. Outside of the people close to me, the only other valuable thing in my life is my desire to make a difference."

"What do you mean you want to make a difference?" Jack asked.

"My boy, everyone lives life, and some people even become famous or wealthy, but only a few make a difference. It's easier than becoming famous or wealthy, and you can even make a difference in small ways. Sadly, most people are content with caring only for themselves, and they never make a difference for anyone else. Here come your parents; I called them when I found you. Your mother looks worried."

Jack now thought about what his old mentor had told him and said to himself, *I also want to make a difference. Did I make a difference today when I won the championship?* Maybe he had. But Dr. Taylor must have meant a bigger difference than that. *I need to find a way to make a difference for someone else.*

Jack's memories and thoughts were interrupted by the door opening behind him.

"Hey, Jack," said Charles. "Ben and I thought you would be here. Nobody else knew where to look, but we said we'd find you and bring you back to the party. What were you doing here anyway?"

Like Jack, Ben and Charles had each changed into jeans and a T-shirt. Charles had a scratch on his neck that he had earned during one of his fights.

"I was just thinking," said Jack. "Remember how Dr. Taylor always told us that we should stick close together and value each other's friendship more than anything?"

His friends both nodded.

"Well, I think it's because Dr. Taylor lost his family and most of his friends before he moved here. Remember how he always said, 'The people in this town are the only people I have left in this world.' He always seemed sad if we asked him about anyone he used to know. I think that's why he wanted us to value each other so much—so he could remember how it felt."

"Yeah," said Charles. "I don't think I ever saw pictures of him with anyone other than us kids from the school. I often wish that I could thank him for all the advice he gave me."

Ben nodded. "He was always ready to help me with my homework or any other problems I had when my dad was busy after Mom died."

"Well," said Jack, "enough memories. Let's rejoin the party. Mr. Thompson and our parents will want to see us. Today is supposed to be happy, so let's not think about the past."

"I need to stop by my locker to get my backpack," said Ben. "I'm too lazy to come in tomorrow just to grab it."

"All right, we'll wait for you," said Jack, "but hurry up."

******

Ben slammed his locker closed and ran down the hall to meet his friends. He was glad that the teachers were at the party since they would probably not approve of his rate of travel.

After Ben joined the others, the three boys walked down the hall side by side. As they neared the open double doors at the end of the hallway, they saw the party's lights streaming out into the hall.

Ben thought, *Wow, it actually looks like the light is reaching toward us ... and it seems to be getting brighter.*

Suddenly, the light became blindingly bright. Ben could barely see, but the light appeared to reach out and touch Jack, and his friend was gone.

Chapter 2

BEN YELLED, "GET BACK!"

He grabbed Charles's arm and tried to pull him sideways into a classroom, but it was too late. Charles was also gone. Ben could still feel Charles's arm, but now he could not see most of his own body. In fact, the only thing he could see was his right hand still clutching the classroom door's handle. Then Ben could not see anything. The light completely surrounded him. He was not one hundred percent sure that he could feel either. He thought he still held Charles's arm, but his whole body felt numb so he could not be sure.

From somewhere off to his right, he heard Jack scream as if in pain.

Ben tried to reach his right arm in that direction, but he could not find Jack.

Jack screamed again.

As Ben tried to reach this time, he seemed to drift away. He lost his grip on Charles and was not able to find him again. He thrashed in the surrounding light, desperate to find his friends, but he could not orient himself or detect Jack or Charles. After a few minutes he thought, *I'm not getting anywhere. I need to get a grip on myself.* He stopped and took a deep breath.

After a few moments he turned his head to the left and noticed a hole in the light. He thought he saw trees, and he realized that he was moving in that direction. Suddenly, the hole vanished, and everything became motionless. Light still surrounded him, and it was so bright that he could not see any of the features around him. It felt difficult to move. He heard Jack groan, but Ben could not feel his friend. Ben moved his legs, but he was not sure if he was walking or swimming. He tried to travel in different directions and found that he could move in the direction that he thought he had been originally moving. It was, however, difficult to travel sideways toward the sound of Jack's groans or backward in the direction from which he had come.

Ben was not sure how much time passed as he struggled in the blinding light. It felt like hours. He tried to call for his friends, but there was no answer. Suddenly, he saw the hole in the light again, and he felt himself moving toward it without an effort. Then in an instant he passed through it. He tumbled out of the light and sprawled onto the ground.

What happened? thought Ben. Charles lay on the ground next to him, and he was holding Ben's arm. Charles must have gotten out and pulled him in the same direction. But where was Jack? The light, consisting of a vertical oval, was still there behind the two boys. It resembled an upright pool of water with ripples on its surface traveling outward from the center.

Ben heard Jack call their names. The sound came from the light, which now seemed to be dissipating.

"Quick, Charles!" Ben yelled, "Give me a hand. We have to get Jack."

"You mean you're going back in?" replied Charles.

"Do we have a choice?"

"Okay, I've got you, Ben." Charles grasped his friend's waistband and planted his feet firmly on the ground. "Reach in and see if you can grab him."

Ben stepped back into the light, and his senses were again completely engulfed. He yelled, "Jack!" He could not hear Jack anymore. *Did he somehow drift farther in?* thought Ben. Just then, he touched something that felt like cloth and grabbed it.

"Okay, Charles, pull us out." Ben backed out, dragging Jack's limp form out behind him. "Thanks, Charles." Ben looked back where the light had been, but he saw only trees.

Jack lay on his side on the ground next to Ben. He bled from several puncture wounds—two on each arm and one near the middle of his chest.

"Help me turn him over on his back, Charles." Ben grabbed Jack's shoulders and turned him. Ben could not fathom who or what had stabbed Jack, but it was obvious now why Jack had been screaming. "Jack, can you hear me?"

"Yeah, I think so, Ben," Jack replied faintly as he seemed to come to himself. "What happened?"

Charles replied, "I have no idea! That was the weirdest thing ever." Charles was an even-keeled individual, but this experience definitely seemed to have his attention.

"Not only that," added Ben, "we *were* in a building in the evening, and now we're in a forest during the day! What in the world?" Although Ben loved adventures, he did not remember signing up for this one. "Whatever that light was, it's gone now."

"But since we don't know what it was," replied Charles, "we don't know how to prevent it in the future. It's obviously dangerous. We also don't know how to reverse it."

"Let's see if we can piece together what happened," suggested Jack.

"What do you remember about that light thing, Charles?" asked Ben.

"Well," Charles began slowly, "this bright light swallowed me up. Then I heard men yelling as though they were fighting, but I couldn't understand what they were saying. Then I felt something, grabbed it, and pulled it to me, but I'm not sure what it was. I felt numb all over, so I couldn't really feel anything. I guess it was Ben."

"What do you remember, Jack?" Ben pulled up Jack's T-shirt to assess his wounds.

"I was surrounded by light, and yeah, I felt numb, but something like a knife was driven into my left arm. The rest is kind of a blur."

They all looked around more carefully. They were in a small clearing with grass surrounded by trees. Burn marks streaked the ground, and one of the trees had split in half down the middle. Ben could smell burned grass, and thin wisps of smoke passed into the sky from the split in the tree.

"What could do that to a tree?" asked Ben.

"We had lightning hit a tree right next to our house one day," said Jack, "and it split right down the middle just like that. That's most likely what happened. It probably started some of the grass on fire at the same time. This could have happened days ago."

"It doesn't smell as though it happened days ago," said Charles. "It seems like it happened sometime in the last hour, but it's a sunny sky, so where did lightning come from?"

"Everything about this is odd." Jack stood, holding his wounds on each arm with his opposite hand. "Charles, you studied forestry for a while, right? What kind of trees are these?"

Charles examined several nearby trees. "Well, I would expect these red oaks in a northern hardwood forest type. These are pretty common where we live, so I expect that we are near a similar latitude as Tennessee. That should put us roughly thirty-five degrees north of the equator. On the other hand, I've never seen a tree like that one before, so it's hard to be certain. Even though we don't recognize this place, it could be near the school. But if that's true, we spent all night in that light thing."

"It's a little chilly out," said Ben. "It feels like it must be fifty degrees out here, but it's usually not that cold at the end of spring."

Jack cut in, "Ben, Charles, look over there. It looks like smoke, maybe from a chimney. Let's head that way. Maybe we can find someone who can tell us where we are."

"Hold on," said Charles. "You're not going anywhere until we bandage your wounds."

"Yeah?" Jack chuckled despite their predicament. "What do you plan on bandaging my wounds with? We don't really have anything with us, do we?"

Ben triumphantly pulled off his backpack and dropped it onto the ground. "Good thing I'm too lazy to leave this thing at school."

"Oh yeah," said Jack. "I'm sure I need bandages made from Ben's sweaty T-shirt and socks."

"That's not fair," Ben protested. "I just happen to have clean clothes, a flashlight, a half full water bottle, and some notebooks and pens. Oh yeah, and a bag of potato chips."

"Wow, at least we won't starve to death," said Charles.

Ben tossed Jack a T-shirt to replace his own bloody one.

Charles grabbed another T-shirt out of Ben's backpack, tore it into strips, and tied the pieces around Jack's wounds.

Ben suddenly exclaimed, "Oh, and—" He pulled his cell phone and a cigarette lighter out of his backpack's side pocket. "No signal." He sighed. "And the battery is almost dead."

Charles shook his head. "Well, I left my phone, my watch, and even my wallet with my karate gi when I changed. What time is it?"

Ben glanced at his cell phone. "It's 7:49p.m."

"That's funny." Charles scratched his head. "It was almost 7:00p.m. when we went to find Jack. So we lost almost forty-five minutes in that light tunnel."

"All I can say," Jack concluded, "is it's a good thing my wounds seem to have mostly stopped bleeding on their own, but this does seem to be helping a little bit too."

Charles examined Jack's bloody clothing. "The wounds don't look as bad as I expected with the amount of blood on your shirt."

"I'm carrying the backpack," Ben announced, "so Charles, you get to help Jack walk toward wherever we're going."

The three headed toward the smoke. Ben marveled at how he felt. The experience had, of course, been a little scary—the whole weird thing with the light and Jack getting hurt—but now that the three of them were hiking through the woods, it seemed interesting and maybe even fun. They had grown up in a small town where few exciting things usually happened. Ben thought he could enjoy a change for a while. Plus, he had just saved Jack's life, or at least it seemed like that, so it was turning out to be a pretty good day. *It's weird*, thought Ben. *This forest doesn't seem to have any trails. I didn't think forests existed anymore that didn't have trails running through them.* The forest was fairly sparse, so many small saplings and bushes filled in the areas between the trees.

"Look there." Jack pointed into the distance. "The forest ends. Those trees just beyond the edge look like they're planted in rows."

Sure enough, as they approached, the forest terminated, and they found themselves in an orchard. *Those don't really look like normal grapefruits,* thought Ben, *but a grapefruit is a grapefruit, right?* He reached up and plucked one off the nearest tree.

"What are you doing?" Charles said, "These obviously belong to someone. Look, there's a stone building over there on the orchard's border. Whoever lives there probably owns the grapefruit you just took."

"Okay. Fine, Charles." Ben shrugged. "I won't eat it until we ask the person if we can have a grapefruit. I mean, it's the South. Southern hospitality demands that they feed us. Who wouldn't?"

"We don't know that we are still in the South," said Charles. "I just said it looked like we were about the same distance from the equator as where we lived, and everyone doesn't share the same ideas about hospitality that you seem to have."

Ben inquired absently, "Isn't it kind of cold for fruit?"

Charles shook his head. "No, in warmer climates it's not uncommon for citrus fruits to grow through the winter and into spring as long as it doesn't get too cold."

As they approached the house, Ben picked up his pace. "Come on, I'll prove to you that I'm right about being welcome to eat the fruit." Ben dashed up the front steps onto the front porch and knocked.

The door opened, and a small boy stuck out his head. He wore a gray shirt and pants that looked like they were made from homespun wool. The clothing appeared worn and a size too small. The boy spoke very quickly.

Ben could not understand anything he said, but the way the boy chattered made Ben think he sounded sort of like a chipmunk. Ben smiled when the child stopped and introduced himself.

The boy just stared quizzically at him for a moment before slamming the door in his face.

Ben heard Charles chuckle behind him.

"You're right," Charles said. "That was some good southern hospitality right there."

"Oh, come on, both of you," said Jack. "Ben, why didn't you answer his question?"

"What question?" Ben held his hands palm upward. "I didn't understand anything he said."

"I couldn't understand him either." Charles shrugged. "I thought it was just because I was farther away. You understood what he said?"

Jack answered, "Yeah, he asked Ben why we were in his dad's orchard and whether we had seen his dad."

"No way," replied Ben. "That kid did talk really fast, but there's no way you could hear what he said all the way down there, and I couldn't understand him up here."

Jack and Charles came up onto the porch.

Jack called through the door, "We're just passing through, and we got lost. We haven't seen anyone else around."

The boy opened the door again cautiously and chattered away, but Ben still could not understand him. The boy was certainly not speaking English.

Ben glanced over at Charles, who had the same clueless expression on his face.

Jack, meanwhile, replied in English to the boy, asking where the nearest town was located.

The boy seemed to understand Jack and rattled off another garbled paragraph complete with hand motions.

Jack reached over, and taking the grapefruit from Ben, asked the boy if they could each have a grapefruit.

The boy shifted his eyes back and forth between the young men as if scared to answer. He glanced at Jack's bandages and nodded.

Jack thanked the boy and started to back away.

The boy chattered some more.

Jack paused to listen then replied, "Okay, no problem."

Ben heard the door shut again as they stepped off the porch.

"What was that all about?" Ben asked Jack. "Did you learn a foreign language in your spare time or what?"

Jack evidently did not get the joke, because he squinted and looked at Ben. "The kid spoke English, man. Sure, he talked a little fast, but he wasn't that hard to understand."

"There is no way that was English." Charles shook his head. "And he looked at our clothing as though we were the ones dressed strange."

"Regardless," said Jack, "he said we could have a couple of grapefruits, and if we find his dad somewhere around, to see if we can help him or bring him back here or something. That was kind of the gist of it. To be honest, it was also a little confusing for me to understand him, not his words but what he meant. The nearest town is that way, so let's go."

Little conversation took place on the walk to town.

Charles seemed to be constantly irritated by almost every tree or bush they passed.

Jack was still in some pain and not interested in talking.

Ben just was not in the mood for talking. Somewhere along the way, despite their many unanswered questions, he had become bored with walking through the woods.

Finally, Ben saw buildings up ahead. The majority of the structures consisted of stone with straw-like roofs. The houses had square or rectangular holes for windows with wooden shutters, many of which were open despite the chilly weather. A few people meandered through the town on a dirt path that served as a street, and several people stood with carts full of different types of fruit and vegetables. Most of the men wore either tunics or baggy shirts and plain brown pants. The pants either extended to the ankle or ended just below the knees. The women wore simple dresses that were mostly brown or gray. The clothing appeared to be made from homespun cloth. Some of the buildings had signs, but Ben could not read what the signs said, nor could he understand what the people standing near the carts said. They appeared to be advertising goods for sale. As the boys drew nearer, most of the townspeople seemed to shy away, and the merchants stared curiously at them.

Charles gestured at the surrounding buildings. "This place looks like it's from the Middle Ages. How is that possible?"

"Maybe someone's trying to trick us." Ben stared back at one of the townspeople.

"Ben, don't gawk." Charles surveyed the carts. "Should we try to buy some food here?"

"With what?" Jack replied. "I don't think I have much money with me."

"We could trade stuff in my backpack," suggested Ben.

"That sounds like a reasonable idea." Jack rubbed one of his sore arms. "Ben, why don't you try buying some food? Charles and I will look for a map or someone who can tell us where we are. Okay?"

"Sure thing," said Ben. "I'll stick right around here until you guys get back."

As the two others headed off, Ben approached the first man with a cart. Ben decided that vegetables would be best in case they did not eat them right away. It would take longer for them to spoil than fruit. Ben asked the salesman how much it would cost to purchase an assortment of vegetables.

The man just shook his head and shrugged as if he did not understand.

Obviously, Ben could not communicate with this man either. *No problem*, he thought, *I'll just barter with hand motions.*

Ben collected some carrots, potatoes, and other vegetables and laid them on an empty area of the cart that he presumed was a sales counter. Then he set his notebooks and pens down next to the vegetables. Over the course of a few minutes, he managed to convey what he wanted in exchange for the pens and paper.

The shopkeeper seemed to take a long time to decide but eventually agreed by nodding his head. Then the merchant gestured toward the mushrooms and pointed at Ben's backpack.

Ben figured, *Why not? I like mushrooms, and this guy seems really excited about selling me some.* Ben offered the man his flashlight.

After a little while the man agreed and handed Ben two bags of mushrooms.

Ben waited for several minutes, receiving more odd stares from passersby, until Jack and Charles returned.

"So what did you buy, Ben?" Charles asked.

He told them and showed them the man with the cart, who waved excitedly as they passed. The salesman had used Ben's flashlight to prop up a fruit basket, apparently not knowing its true purpose.

"Wait a second," said Jack, "you bought *those* mushrooms from *that* guy?"

"Yeah." Ben shrugged.

"The sign above those mushrooms says something about spirituality or happiness. It's a little confusing." Jack let go of Charles,

37

who still intermittently provided some support for him, approached the shopkeeper, and asked him about the mushrooms.

Again, the man looked excited and tried to offer Jack more mushrooms.

Jack rejoined Ben and Charles, looking very upset. "Man, are you trying to get us in trouble?"

"What do you mean?" asked Ben.

"According to that guy, those mushrooms are like drugs. They help you see your dead relatives. They're probably some sort of hallucinogenic agent. And you bought them? What if the law catches us with illegal narcotics?"

"I couldn't read the sign or understand the dude. I just figured they were mushrooms," replied Ben defensively.

"He's right, Jack," said Charles. "Unlike you, we can't understand anything these people say or read any of the signs in this place. It doesn't seem like anywhere in America that I've ever heard of, so hallucinogenic mushrooms might not even be illegal here. Of course," he added under his breath with a sideways glance at Ben, "we might have needed a flashlight."

"I suppose you're right," said Jack. "We're obviously not in America, because no one I asked had ever heard of America, and the map I found was completely worthless. I didn't recognize any landmarks or town names."

Ben noticed a man loitering to his left. The man had a dark complexion, shortly cropped hair, and a full beard. He was dressed like the other townspeople, but his mannerisms rather than his appearance made him stand out to Ben. The man scrutinized items on a sales cart, but he repeatedly cast covert glances in their direction.

"Hey," interjected Ben with a slight jerk of his head in the man's direction. "Is it just me, or does that guy seem really interested in us? I know a lot of people have given us strange looks, but he acts like he doesn't want us to know that he's watching us."

Jack glanced over his shoulder. "Yeah, he was in the building we went into when we asked for directions. We should probably get out of sight. We don't know what kind of consequences we might receive for being noticed."

The three friends stepped off the street between two buildings, entered the forest on the town's edge, and hid in the bushes among the trees.

Sure enough, the man snooped down the alley and looked around as though searching for something before turning to his right.

They stayed in the bushes until he was out of sight.

"Let's head out of town," said Jack. "According to the map I saw, there's supposed to be some sort of road going east to a bigger city called Gredune."

They made their way to the road and started hiking.

Jack had recovered remarkably quickly and was able to walk now without assistance.

Ben let out a small sigh. He had hoped this would be an interesting adventure, but it mostly consisted of walking on dirt paths. He thought about his father and how worried he probably was. He knew Jack and Charles were probably thinking the same thing. Finally, he piped up, "No matter what, we'll get home sometime."

Jack and Charles looked a little surprised.

Charles responded, "Oh, yeah, of course we're going to make it home."

They were all silent for a while.

Ben wondered if that was true.

As they continued walking, Ben grumbled, "This little adventure isn't nearly as much fun as it should be. I'm hungry, and my feet are killing me."

Charles nodded in agreement.

Jack commented, "It does seem like we've walked down this road forever, and we haven't seen anyone."

Charles glanced up at the sky. "It'll be dark soon. We should probably make some kind of preparations for the night since it doesn't look like we'll reach a town or village before dusk."

Jack pointed at a relatively clear section of ground on the road's right side in front of them. "That seems like a good place to make a fire."

"I'll get some firewood and get a fire going." Ben smiled. "Good thing I have a lighter. I always said it would come in handy one day." He leaned his backpack up against a tree and searched for deadfall among the sparse trees nearby.

Jack pulled the vegetables out of the backpack and examined them.

Charles commented, "With this cold we'll need something to separate us from the ground in order to stay warm. That large bush over there should keep the dew off of us. If we lay down a thick pile of leaves on the ground, it will hopefully be enough to keep us warm throughout the night."

Jack nodded. "The fire will also help us stay warm."

Ben laid down an armload of branches and kindling in a pile. "Let's get this fire going so we can eat." He leaned the smaller sticks next to each other in the shape of a teepee. Ben was confident in his ability to build a teepee fire because of the many weekends the three families had spent camping together over the summers.

Charles said, "Let's bury the potatoes in the hot coals after the fire dies down to cook them."

Jack nodded. "Good idea. Without aluminum foil the skins will burn, but they should be fine on the inside."

Charles finished gathering leaf piles and arranged them into a bed under the bush.

Jack and Ben collected more firewood. It took them some time to amass enough wood to last all night. As they returned with their final load, Ben noticed that the fire had burned down nicely, and Charles was banking the coals over the potatoes.

They munched on some of the carrots while they discussed their plans for the next day and waited for the potatoes to cook. They decided to save the rest of the food for the next day.

The fire began to burn more brightly as Charles added additional wood.

Ben suggested telling campfire stories.

Charles replied, "I'm not really in the mood. Let's just finish eating and turn in for the night."

Ben nodded and tossed another log onto the fire.

******

Jack awoke suddenly to the sound of pounding feet. He was cold and stiff from the chilly night, but he looked around and saw a faint glow as though torches were coming toward them. Jack glanced at where the fire had been, but nothing remained except for ashes and a few spent coals.

He bumped Ben and Charles, whispering, "Wake up guys; someone's coming."

Through the darkness they saw an old man running down the road, probably as fast as he could, but the torches belonged to another group following him.

"For a second I thought those people might have been after us," Ben whispered, "but it looks like they're after that old guy."

The man stumbled in front of them and crawled under a bush on the other side of the road just opposite where the boys hunched in the darkness.

The men with the torches arrived quickly. There were four of them, but only two of the men carried torches. They all had swords on their belts and light armor made from animal hides on their torsos and heads.

One of the men spotted where the old man had tripped and pointed at the bushes. "Search!"

The three boys watched as two of the men pulled their swords and jabbed them savagely into the bushes.

"What are we going to do?" whispered Charles.

"I don't see any kind of official insignia or distinguishing marks on their armor or swords," whispered Jack. "I assume that means that they're not any type of law enforcement. I think law enforcement would have some kind of distinguishing symbol."

"They all have their backs to us," said Ben. "I say while they're distracted by searching the other side of the road, we jump them."

Charles held up a hand in the darkness. "Let's just wait a second, and see what they do. We don't know for sure that they're bad guys."

One of the men with a torch looked at the man standing next to him and asked, "Why do we even care about the old man? He probably won't survive the journey anyway."

His comrade looked at him contemptuously. "You idiot! We're not chasing the guy so we can sell him as a slave; he's not worth that much. You seem to forget what else we did. We can't leave any witnesses alive."

Jack whispered, "It sounds like they're some kind of murdering bandits. I say we stop them. Ben, you take the first guy with the torch; Charles, you get the other guy with a torch. It should be easy to take the other two without the torches because their eyes won't be adjusted to the darkness yet."

Charles hunched more to conceal his large outline. "I can't understand what they're saying. Are you certain we should attack them?"

Jack replied quietly "I think so. They're going to kill that old guy, and it sounds like they did something really bad and don't want any witnesses. Also, one of them mentioned selling people as slaves."

"Got it. Let's go," said Ben.

The three young men jumped out of the bushes.

Ben sprinted to his man and drove a front kick directly into his back, launching the man into a tree in front of him.

Charles grabbed his man, picked him up over his own head, and threw him to the ground. A loud thump resounded in the darkness, and the man lay still.

The moment the torches hit the ground, Jack moved behind the man he assumed was the leader. While the man drew his sword, Jack shot a straight punch toward his right kidney. Then Jack grabbed the man's shoulders, bending him over backward. Jack brought his knee up into the man's spine. He heard a sharp snap. Surprised, he dropped the man to the ground.

The last man had drawn his sword. He swung it in front of him, yelling angrily.

Jack jumped to the man's right side and fired a sidekick into the man's knee.

The man let out a yelp and leaned forward, putting all his weight on his other leg.

Ben then popped a front kick into the man's face, knocking him onto his back.

"That went well," remarked Ben. "Since they're bad guys, it would be irresponsible of us not to go ahead and loot their swords and money. That way they can't hurt anyone else; it's a win-win."

Jack did not answer.

"It does look like we need a way to protect ourselves in this place, and we don't have any way to feed ourselves," said Charles. "I guess we should just take whatever they have that's valuable and leave them." He looked surprised as he bent over what had been the leader of the group. "Jack, this one's dead."

"I know," Jack said heavily. "I didn't mean to kill him, but I could tell when I heard his back snap." Jack added silently, *I'm not sure if I should feel horrified that he's dead or relieved that we're all okay. Either way, I'll think about it later.*

"Jack, didn't that hurt because of your wounds?" Charles asked, picking up a torch from the ground.

"Actually my wounds closed overnight, but I think I tore one of them open again just now in the fight." Jack touched a spot of blood that had seeped through his shirt.

The old man stuck his head out of the bushes. The man was short with mostly gray hair and a full, white beard. His back was bowed as if he had spent years in manual labor, but his eyes looked bright and intelligent.

The old man surveyed their faces and glanced down at their clothing. "Where did you come from? Who are you?"

In unison Ben and Charles both exclaimed, "Hey, I can understand you."

"Of course you can," said the old man. "Everyone can understand me. My name is Elton. I'm a traveling merchant."

"Where are your goods?" asked Jack.

"I used to have goods to sell, but the band of mercenaries that the other merchants traveling with me and I hired to protect us decided they could make more money if they commandeered our goods for themselves. The bandits are camped just a half mile or so from here with the other merchants and all of our goods in their possession."

Jack strapped on his new belt and sword. The sword was a great deal different from any he had ever used in fencing class. This one was longer and heavier, but he liked the feel of it in his hand.

"So," Ben asked suspiciously, "why is it that everyone can understand you?"

The old man considered the question for a moment before replying, "It's a secret I have carried for many years, and if you boys help me get my wares back, maybe I'll tell you. What do you say?"

"Isn't there any law enforcement around here?" asked Charles.

The old man shook his head. "The bandits would be gone by the time Gredune's town guard arrived, and I doubt they would come this far just to help some traveling merchants."

"How many bandits are left in the camp?" asked Jack.

The old man squinted one eye, tilted his head, and looked up as he mentally calculated. "Probably fifteen, and if these don't come back by tomorrow afternoon, they'll probably get suspicious."

Jack crossed his arms. "Well, we can't take on fifteen guys."

"I agree," said Charles. "Even with surprise on our side, we could probably only take care of two each. If they're alert and have guards posted, we wouldn't even have the element of surprise."

Ben gave them a sideways smile. "I have an idea, and I think you're going to like it a lot."

The other two boys grinned as he told them his plan.

Jack turned to the old man. "Fine, we'll help, but we'll need your help as well."

They reached the bandit's camp approximately one hour before dawn. The camp was laid out in a rough circle of tents within a small clearing. Several carts, probably full of the stolen merchandise, stood around the camp's edge. A large pot hung over a fire in the center of camp with a cook tending it intermittently.

Jack inhaled deeply, trying to pick up on the aroma coming from the camp. He felt hungry as he smelled the bandits' breakfast simmering, but he could not make out what was being prepared.

The cook periodically sat down on a nearby stone and closed his eyes as if resting before returning to stir his pot.

Two lookouts moseyed in opposite directions in a large circle around the camp. Every now and then one of these guards would lean against a tree then reluctantly pull himself away and start walking again.

The captives sat tied up on the camp's upper edge, trying to stay warm in a large huddle. The merchants' and bandits' horses stood staked out near the captives.

"All right," said Jack. "Elton, you watch the cook, and whenever he's sitting on the stone dozing, hold up this branch. Charles, you watch the guard on the left, and when he's walking the opposite direction, hold out your branch. I'll watch the guard on the right and hold out my branch when he's going the opposite direction. Ben will sneak into camp, hide by the center tent, and watch. When all three of us are holding out our branches, you make your move, Ben. Everybody understand the plan?"

They all nodded and moved into position.

They waited about twenty minutes before the guards walked with their backs toward them at the same time that the cook dozed. Finally, it was time. Everyone held up their branches.

Jack saw Ben steal out of his hiding place and up to the cooking pot, where he dumped both pouches of the mushrooms he had bought into the bandits' morning meal.

The three friends and Elton retreated back to a safe distance to wait.

"Are we sure this is going to work?" asked Charles.

"Not really," replied Jack, "but if it fails, we haven't lost that much."

They all grew quiet.

Jack kept thinking about earlier that night and the man whose sword he now carried. Jack knew that, logically, he had made the most safe and practical move possible. His training had taught him to escalate the level of force used based on the situation's degree of danger. Taking on two well-armed men definitely warranted the level of force he had used. *I wonder if everyone who is forced to kill someone feels this way*, he thought. *I wonder if everyone second-guesses their decision.*

His thoughts were interrupted by Ben asking Elton, "So, we're helping you, right? That must mean you can tell us why we can understand you."

The old man fidgeted. "There's no way you could take it from me even if you killed me, so there's no point in trying to kill me to take it."

Ben's eyebrows shot up. "Kill you? Why would we do that? What is it?"

Elton narrowed one of his eyes as he looked sideways at Ben. He seemed somewhat suspicious and confused. "My translation stone. Have you never heard of translation stones?"

Now all three boys were very interested.

"So," Charles asked, "you have a stone that makes it so you can understand other people's languages?"

"Yes," the old man replied, "translation stones are the most common type of gemstone. They don't actually translate words; they translate ideas and concepts and sometimes even feelings."

"How do we get our hands on one of these translations stones?" asked Ben.

"Any type of gemstone is very expensive. Usually you must kill whoever owns the stone and take it because few people possessing a gemstone are willing to sell it for any price."

Ben leaned forward. "Elton, you said that you have a stone, but we couldn't take it from you even if we kill you. Why is that?"

Elton settled back as if becoming more relaxed about the conversation. "Because I am an iconic blood mage. This happens when you insert a stone into your bloodstream. It dissolves there, and you can use it anytime. No one can take it from you. Even if you bleed, the stone's elements are heavier than blood and cling to the inside of the blood vessels so none of the stone will be lost—or, at least, that's my theory. There's also no way to put the stone back together once it has dissolved."

"So these are magic stones?" asked Charles.

"Yes, of course." Elton wrinkled his brow. "Each type of gemstone allows the user to perform a certain type of magic."

"What other kinds of stones are there?" asked Jack.

Elton replied, "Many different types of gemstones exist such as fire, lightning, earth, air, water, and some other rare types. I can't say that I know them all."

"Cool, so you could blast fire with a fire stone?" exclaimed Ben. "Could you burn a whole forest at one time?"

"No," replied Elton. "The gemstone's size and quality determine how far you can cast a spell and how powerful it is."

"Magic stones?" Jack snorted. "This is crazy. I want proof."

Elton gazed a Jack for a moment. "I've known many people who were not familiar with gemstones, but I've never known anyone who didn't believe that they exist." He narrowed his eyes. "You say you don't believe in gemstones, but aren't you using one?"

"What do you mean?" asked Jack. "I don't have any stones—definitely not magic ones."

"But I don't need my translation stone when speaking to you," said Elton. "Do you know the language Lavdoric? It's the most common language spoken across all the realms."

"What if he's right?" asked Charles. "You've been able to understand everyone here, no matter who they were, but Ben and I can't understand anyone except Elton."

"But I'm telling you, I don't have any gemstones," Jack insisted.

Ben held up his hand. "We'll put that on hold for a second. What's a blood mage?"

"There are three types of blood mages," Elton explained. "As I mentioned, iconic blood mages have dissolved stones inside their bodies, which can be used at any time. Inserting a stone into your body, however, is incredibly dangerous. I don't really know why, but usually people attempting this die. If you have a stone in your hand or embedded on your helmet, sword, or anywhere else, you can use the stone just as well.

"The only reason I have a translation stone in my bloodstream is because I was once a slave. My master was a warlord, and he was a cruel and terrible man. One day my master executed a diplomat from a nearby king. My warlord assigned me the task of disposing of the body. Before I burned the corpse, however, I went through the diplomat's clothing and found the translation stone.

"My master's guards were coming to check on my progress. Knowing the value of the stone, I couldn't part with it, so I decided to risk death by stabbing it into my own bloodstream. I became sick for weeks but eventually recovered. In a battle soon after this, my master perished, along with almost all of his soldiers. I escaped, and with no communication barrier, I decided to become a traveling merchant. I became very successful in kingdoms like this one, the kingdom of Vergill. Here in Vergill three different languages are spoken because this used to be multiple kingdoms. This variety of languages makes it difficult for the inhabitants to trade, even between cities. I also still have to be careful since I bear the slave brand on my ankle, so I could be recaptured and sold if someone saw it. I am only telling you all this because you are helping me, and I trust you."

Jack inquired, "What about the other types of blood mages?"

Elton thought for a moment before saying, "I don't know much about the other types of blood mages. Indeed, I've never actually met another blood mage or traveled to a city where someone claimed to be one. When a gemstone dissolves in blood, it can be very powerful, but it can never be returned to the form of a stone, so all types of blood magic are little more than scary stories. You asked, however, what the other types of blood mages are, so I'll tell you what I know even though I don't think they really exist.

"Parasitic blood mages are the most terrifying. According to the stories, they kill people, usually their slaves, and dissolve a gemstone in the fresh, warm blood. Supposedly, this enhances the gemstone's power temporarily, but I'm not exactly sure how. Hemorrhagic blood mages cut themselves open and dissolve the stone in their own blood to increase the gemstone's power. I think this is usually fatal, but I'm not sure."

"Going back to what you said before," interjected Ben, "you mentioned that you had a successful business. Does that mean you're wealthy?"

"I am fairly well off," Elton said slowly as if unsure where the conversation was headed. "But a great deal of my wealth is invested in my wares, which are currently in the bandits' possession."

"Not for much longer," said Jack. "Look, they're starting to stir in the camp."

The guard shift changed, and a bandit checked all the prisoners. The majority of the thieves lounged lazily. The leader did not seem to run a particularly strict crew.

The cook called out that the food was ready, and the bandits gathered around the cooking pot.

Charles bumped Jack. "Look there." He pointed at the trail.

The bandits they had attacked on the road, minus their leader, limped toward camp.

"Great." Jack rolled his eyes.

"What are we going to do?" asked Charles. "This could ruin the whole plan if they immediately go search instead of eating breakfast."

"There's not really anything we can do." Jack shrugged. "We just have to hope that they eat before searching or while they search."

The sentry shouted at the three men, but recognizing them, he called to the leader.

"Bring them to my tent," ordered their chief, "and someone get me some food ... but none for them. They obviously failed since they hobbled back like whipped dogs."

Some of the bandits dragged their injured comrades into their boss's tent while another brought their leader some soup.

Everyone else sat down to eat. The prisoners did not receive any food; they apparently had to wait until their captors finished.

Jack nodded slightly and allowed himself a small smile. "So far, so good. How long do you think it will take before they suffer side effects?"

Elton replied, "Based on the type of mushrooms you had, it shouldn't be long. Let's sit back for a while."

About fifteen minutes later the bandits seemed very relaxed.

"I think it's taking effect," said Jack.

"What are we going to do with them?" asked Charles. "Elton, would the law enforcement you mentioned earlier throw these guys in jail if we tied them up and took them to town?"

Elton nodded. "Yes, almost all of the larger towns have a place to detain criminals until they can be dealt with."

"Good," said Jack. "This should be easy. They may not resist at all."

Suddenly, one of the bandits pointed at a tree and shrieked. The sharp noise must have frightened the other bandits because many of them jumped up and scrambled around screaming as well.

"They're seeing hallucinations," remarked Ben.

"Yeah," said Jack. "I've heard that quick movements or loud noises near someone having hallucinations will often scare them. Let's just watch for a bit, and see what happens."

The three injured bandits rushed out of the bandit leader's tent. "What's ... wrong with them all?" one of them asked.

The one next to him said, "I don't know. I've been with you. First the boss and now everyone else has gone insane."

"Maybe it's some sort of magic," said the first one. "Let's just get out of here."

The three injured thieves hobbled off as fast as they could.

"Are we going to let them get away?" asked Ben.

"Yes," replied Jack, "they have nothing of value, and there are only three of us with fifteen crazy bandits still in the camp. Let's get in there and tie them up."

The three boys chased down the tipsy bandits one at a time until they had all of them tied together behind the carts.

"Who are you?" asked one of the bound merchants.

"Just a friend of Elton's," Jack replied.

After the boys and Elton freed the merchants, the businessmen hitched their horses to the carts and moved the caravan down the road toward Gredune, the nearest town.

The bandits seemed to sober somewhat and were able to walk in the caravan. Many of them sang happily while a few appeared to be engaged in conversations with nonexistent people.

The merchants had many questions, such as what was wrong with the bandits, where were the boys were from, and what were the boys' future plans? The language barrier, however, required Jack to speak for the three boys.

After a few minutes Elton pulled Jack aside away from the other merchants. "Jack, you have a translation stone, but you should be aware of it. Is it possible that it's in your bloodstream like mine?" He looked at the blood on Jack's shirt. "Were you stabbed at some point?"

"Yes," Jack admitted, "several times, not long ago."

"I see," replied the old man. "I will think on this. For now, enjoy chatting with the other merchants. I would like to give each of you a new set of clothes as a reward for your assistance. It may help you attract less attention."

The merchants told the boys many tales about the country, their own misfortunes, and the town to which they were going.

The boys finally excused themselves to change into their new clothes, which consisted of ankle-length pants with roomy pockets and baggy shirts made of homespun cloth. Then they lay down in one of the carts to get some sleep.

Chapter 3

JACK WOKE UP WITH a jolt as his cart hit a rock in the road.

"Ah, you are awake," said Elton. "We are near Gredune. We will head straight to the town guard. You will need to claim that you are a bounty hunter, and you and your friends captured these bandits while in the employment of our merchant caravan."

"Okay," replied Jack. "So the soldiers are responsible for enforcing the law in this town?"

"Yes, my boy, almost every town has a guard post in it. The guard post is important to the town because these soldiers enforce the law and act as the town's garrison."

"What happens to the criminals?" asked Jack.

"Murderers are executed, but other crimes usually result in the offender being sold into slavery. Just about every country has an agreement with one of the major slave organizations that allows enemy soldiers, rebels, and anyone against slavery to be taken as slaves."

"Slave organizations?" asked Jack. "What are they?"

Elton stared at Jack, blinking.

"We're not from around here," Jack offered.

Elton examined Jack closely with narrowed eyes. "Where have you been that you don't know about gemstones or the slave organizations?"

Jack replied in a low voice, "We sort of just found ourselves here. We don't know where we are or how we got here."

Elton stared into space for a few moments as though piecing together his interactions with the three boys. Then he started as if coming to himself. "There are three major and very powerful slave cartels," replied Elton. "Kings and warlords constantly try to stay in these organizations' good graces because the cartel leaders are more powerful than most rulers. Nations may have slightly larger standing armies than slave cartels, but the slave organizations are wealthy beyond imagining. If anyone moves against them, they can hire other nations or mercenaries to do their bidding. Also, if you're not a member of any of the slave organizations, you may be branded an international criminal who stands against slavery and have a bounty on your head in almost every nation. As a result it's important to stay in the good graces of at least one slave organization."

"Does anyone actually stand against the slave cartels?" asked Jack.

"Yes, powerful individuals with great wealth and influence will sometimes try to create their own slave organizations. If they can establish treaties with some of the existing slave organizations, they might be successful, but if they are not successful, they usually become slaves themselves. Knights of Celel also come against slavery. They are often hailed as the champions of the common folk, but I know little about them except that they come from the country of Celel, which is apparently against slavery. Many people expect that the three slave organizations will briefly unite one day to crush Celel, but this has gone on for many years, and so far, they have not been able to overcome their hatred and mistrust of one another long enough to challenge the country. Look there," Elton interrupted himself, "that building is the town guard. Good luck."

The guard post appeared able to house about fifty troops. The building was constructed from large square stone blocks, and more of these blocks covered the roof, probably to increase the building's defensibility in case of rioting or an attack.

Jack whispered for Ben and Charles, who had just woken up, to stay and led the bandits to the guardhouse.

He was met by a tall young man in chainmail with a spear in his right hand and shield on his back. Jack informed the soldier that he was a bounty hunter with bandits who had tried to rob some merchants.

The young man disappeared inside the guardhouse.

Soon a big brawny man in plate armor stepped outside. Jack thought the man looked sort of the way he would have imagined an ogre. He was huge and ugly with weathered skin and pock marks on his face, but his armor was bright and polished. He wore a neutral expression on his face, which seemed to fit the ogre stereotype well. He had dark hair, a long sword on his hip, and a shield on his back.

"I am Ogol," said the huge man. "I'm told you have proof that these bandits tried to rob some merchants."

"Yes, all the merchants will testify to that," Jack replied, forcing himself not to snicker at the man's name.

Ogol surveyed the bandits. "I will pay five coin per man and ten for the leader if you have him."

"Excellent. That's the leader." Jack pointed at the bandit chief. "They're all yours."

They quickly concluded their business transaction.

Jack turned and started to walk away with his payment.

Ogol yelled, "Wait. Did you know these men work for the Caishan slave ring?"

"No." Jack turned back to face the big man. "You do still want them, correct?"

"Oh yes," Ogol replied quickly. "My master, Warlord Acelet, recently sided with one of the other slave cartels. Now the Caishan cartel is sending men throughout the less populated areas of Vergill to kidnap citizens as slaves. Because of the increased hostility with our neighboring nations and the agreements we still have with the Caishan, I cannot legally stop them. Despite the fact that I cannot prosecute them for being slavers, I *can* prosecute them for stealing if there is adequate evidence proving that they are bandits rather than slavers.

"It states in the agreement our nation has with the Caishan that the slavers are not allowed to steal from the population. Most of the slavers do it anyway because they're already kidnapping our people, so why not also take anything valuable they have. Many more slavers are spread throughout this country right now. Even though I can't legally do anything about them as slavers, if some crazy bounty hunters brought them in with sound evidence of thievery, there could be a reasonable reward. I already paid you a bounty for these men, so you know that we will honor our bounty."

"We'll think about it," Jack replied. He returned to the merchant caravan and informed his companions of the offer.

Elton commented "I don't see where you boys have much to lose. I doubt the Caishan will forgive us even though we didn't know these bandits worked for them."

"Why would we want to hunt slave traders and frame them for stealing?" asked Charles.

"Because we want to get home," replied Jack, "and to do that, we will most likely need a lot of money. For the trip home we will probably have to buy information, travel places, and maybe even pay someone to take us back if we find someone at all. Until we are able to find a way home, we also need a way to support ourselves. I suspect the slavers make it a general practice to steal just about whenever they can, so we won't have to frame them. The flipside is that bounty hunting would probably be difficult and dangerous, so it may be better to find a safer way to make money if we can."

"I think it sounds like fun," said Ben. "I mean, we could never do anything dangerous and cool like this back home, and I like the idea of having lots of money in any place."

"Our caravan will sell goods in this town for a while depending how business goes," said Elton. "Then we'll move on to Sargosa, the capital of this region. We will probably spend one or two months there before moving on to another country. If you all are able to join me around that time, I'll pay you a fee to escort me out of this country."

"But what would we do in the meantime?" asked Charles.

"Well," Elton replied, "before you boys start chasing bandits, I suggest you go see a man in this town named Hal. He fought in many wars long ago and ended up as governor of this town. I know him well, and he knows a great deal more than I do about gemstones. Having been educated, he might know something about your home, or at the very least, may know someone who does. Here,"—Elton pulled a parchment out of a little sack—"I'll write a note for you boys. He lives in a large house near the center of town. His doorman will read this note and take you to see him if he isn't too busy. I should warn you, though, he is a little abrupt. It's just the way he is, so don't take it personally. Anyway, I must help the other merchants set up for our business. We have been delayed for several days and must get started. You boys have a good rest of the day."

The boys headed toward the area Elton had indicated.

Jack was surprised by how unfriendly the people in the town appeared, not just to them as strangers but to each other. The townspeople seemed to avoid making eye contact when passing others on the street, and they did not greet merchants with a smile or friendly welcome when making purchases. The wind picked up the dust off the dirt road and blew it around in a small swirl in front of them as they walked. Jack glanced at the wooden structures to his right and left. This part of town seemed to have more shops and businesses than homes. Most of the buildings consisted of wooden walls with thatched roofs.

Jack finally asked, "Have you noticed that most people in this place seem unhappy and suspicious?"

His friends looked at him.

Ben shrugged. "I didn't really notice." Ben never was a particularly empathetic individual.

Charles agreed, "Yeah, the people here distrust everyone. There seems to be very little freedom and a great deal of fear and poverty."

The three arrived at the house Elton had described and gave the note to the doorman.

The man disappeared briefly then returned and led them through a room full of bizarre statues of strange animals and mythological-looking beasts. The house had two stories, but the main room was located in the house's rear on the first floor, so they did not have the opportunity to explore upstairs.

Entering the room in which their host resided through a pair of double doors, the boys found an elderly man sitting in a chair that faced the window reading a book.

Bookshelves full of old books encircled the room. Several large glass windows allowed streams of light to slip in onto the floor despite the partially drawn curtains that provided just enough light to read. This was the first glass Jack had seen since they had found themselves in the woods. A few antique-looking trinkets rested on some of the shelves, and a neatly kept desk stood near the man's chair.

Their host turned as they entered and raised an eyebrow as though he were slightly curious. He had a scar running down the right side of his face. His right arm also bore scars as if he had been badly burned. His hair was white, and he had a bushy, gray mustache. He noticed Charles eyeing the windows and said, "Ah, do you like my glass? It's imported all the way from the capital of Celel. I'm a bit of a collector." He pulled his shoulders back with satisfaction.

"They are very nice. Are you Hal?" Jack asked, knowing that the man's explanation was lost on Charles.

The man leaned forward. "Indeed, and you must be Elton's friends whom he mentioned in his note. What can I do for you boys?"

"We want to know if you have ever heard of another ... place ... maybe very far from here ... a place very different from this one, perhaps on a different continent," Jack explained haltingly.

"What a strange question," Hal replied. "I have heard rumors of strange people occasionally claiming to be from other worlds. Everyone dismisses them as crazy, and few believe that their outlandish claims have any credence. I have heard, however, that the king of Celel is interested in other worlds, and rumors say that one of his knights is from some distant place. I presume you boys claim to be from another world by the question that you asked?" The governor raised his eyebrows expectantly.

"I don't really think that's relevant," Jack said quickly. "Let's just say we're curious."

"I see," Hal replied, "but if you wished to conceal things from me, you should have come alone. I can see that your friends cannot understand what I'm saying, so at the very least, they are foreigners to this region. Let me help." Hal reached into a box on the nearby desk and pulled out a small stone. The light glinted off the dark green stone as the man spoke. "Is that better?"

"Yes," replied Charles, "that must be a translation stone."

Hal glanced at Charles curiously. "Yes." He pulled a dark green ring out of the same box. He tossed the ring to Jack.

The ring glowed brightly in Jack's palm.

"Well, well." Hal absently rolled the green stone between his own fingers. "Let's see your translation stone, boy."

Jack was shocked. "What is this? How did you know I have a translation stone?"

Hal smiled. "Well, the type of crystal that you hold reacts with the crystals from which gemstones are made. I can't actually tell what type of stone you have, but I can tell that you have at least one. Because you could understand me while your friends couldn't, I guessed that the stone you had was a translation stone. However, I have never seen my ring glow so brightly, so I suspect that you have more than one stone."

I wasn't even sure I had one, thought Jack. Elton had said he must have a translation stone in his blood. *What if I actually have more than one?*

"You look surprised," remarked Hal.

"Yeah," said Ben, "We weren't even sure he had one stone, but more is awesome."

"How could you be unsure whether he had a stone?" Although Hal directed his question at Ben, he turned his piercing gaze toward Jack.

"They're in my blood," replied Jack. "I don't know how they got there, but somehow when we were brought to this place, I was stabbed multiple times. Elton thinks I'm some sort of blood mage. I think he called it an 'iconic blood mage.' I didn't want to trust you at first, but Elton trusts you, so I suppose we will have to tell you everything, or we won't get any answers. I was stabbed several times, and we found ourselves in the woods, but I don't know why or who was responsible for it."

"An iconic blood mage," Hal mused, stroking his mustache. "That is rare. Blood mages have a few slight advantages on the battlefield of which many people are unaware because blood magic is so rare."

"Like what?" Jack handed the green ring back to Hal.

As Hal returned the ring to its box, Jack noticed that it glowed faintly in reaction to Hal's translation stone.

Hal explained, "Most gemstones can only be used once every so often because every time you use a gemstone, the crystal heats up. If you reuse a stone too rapidly, it can shatter. Not only does this destroy the weapon but it can also potentially injure the wielder by shattering violently. It takes a while for a stone to cool down after it has been used, so a stone can only be used maybe four to six times during a battle that lasts from sunrise to sunset. I don't believe there is any way to tell whether your stone has cooled off enough to be safely used again. Most mages just ensure an ample amount of time goes by before trying to cast again."

The number of daylight hours depends on the time of year, Jack thought, *but it sounds like a stone could be cast four to six times in an eight to twelve hour period.*

Jack's thoughts were confirmed as Charles leaned toward him and said quietly, "That means it can only be used about every two hours."

Jack nodded slightly in agreement but did not want to interrupt their host.

"In contrast," Hal continued, "blood mages, because the stones are dissolved, can use the same stone again sooner, although I don't really know how much sooner. Unlike other types of blood mages, however, iconic blood mages still retain the blood inside their bodies, so they can actually boil alive by using their stones too frequently. Skilled iconic blood mages learn how to balance the stones they carry with the ones that flow in their blood.

"Parasitic and hemorrhagic blood mages, who use blood outside of their bodies, also heat up that blood when they cast spells. The reason this concept is so powerful is that they can cast the same stone in rapid succession until the blood in which the stone is dissolved evaporates. As a mage chain casts a spell, the blood heats up quickly and boils away.

"With iconic blood mages, there's roughly a forty percent mortality rate upon stabbing yourself with a gemstone. Some die immediately while others become ill very quickly and ultimately die within a few weeks. The chance of dying increases the more gemstones someone tries to insert into their bloodstream. Please take off your shirt," Hal instructed Jack abruptly.

Jack untied the strings in the front of his gray woolen shirt, and as he removed it, he looked around for a place to hang his shirt. Finding nothing, he resigned himself to awkwardly holding the garment while standing self-consciously for inspection.

Hal examined Jack's wounds, which had closed remarkably quickly. "It would seem that you were stabbed five times, although you also bear a scar here on your chest that isn't recent."

"I've had that scar for a long time—since I was a kid." Jack fingered the scar. "I don't remember how I got it. I have another scar on my left leg too from way back. I wasn't afraid to try new things when I was a kid. I also hung out with Ben, and he's always ready to try something dangerous."

Ben smiled and nodded with pride.

"I see," Hal replied. "Well, since one of these puncture wounds was apparently made by a translation stone, it would seem that, logically, all of your recent scars were probably caused by gemstones. This must mean that you potentially have five gemstones, one being a translation stone. I don't see how you could have survived that, though."

"That is *so* not fair," exclaimed Ben. "So he's going to be able to throw fire and stuff?"

"Perhaps," Hal replied. "It would, of course, depend on whether he has a fire stone. I have no way to identify the size, quality, or type of stones that you possess. You will have to discover what they are through trial and error, or find the person who put them in your body. Some stones are easier to use than others. I have a book I can lend to you that should help you understand how to safely use gemstones and how to activate each stone."

Hal walked over to a bookcase against the back wall, selected a volume, and handed it to Jack.

Jack examined the book. It was small enough to fit in his pocket and was written in a bizarre, ancient-looking language, but something about it was odd. As he looked at the words, they actually *felt* old. Jack thought aloud, "Even with a translation stone, I'll have trouble understanding these words and pronouncing them."

"In time with your translation stone, you will be able to read what is written in the book," Hal assured him.

Jack asked, "Why is it I seem to be able to use my translation stone automatically? Is it different from the other stones?"

Hal nodded. "Yes, translation stones are unique and are often referred to as the 'gateway stone' because you cannot become a mage unless you have used a translation stone to awaken another stone. Once you have awakened the stone, you no longer need the translation stone. The translation stone is unique in that it does not need to be awakened, and anyone holding it can use it. The stone also does not heat up like the other stones, and you cannot cast it the way you cast other stones."

Charles asked, "Can the translation stone convey the meaning for a term that may not exist in another language? Units, for example."

"Because the translation stone translates ideas rather than specific words," Hal replied, "it will convert the meaning behind the size or distance into whatever unit the other individual understands and would use. With the aid of a translation stone, two people could use different terms yet have the same meaning in their minds. The translation stone will also translate the meaning behind idioms."

Hal suddenly looked bored. He glanced at the light from the windows and then at the door. "Kids, I may have helped you because you're Elton's friends, but you boys owe me a favor. It's lucky for you that I'm a collector of rare, unusual, and sometimes even mostly useless gemstone artifacts." He turned back to the window and started reading again.

The boys stood for a moment, watching him.

Jack glanced at his two friends. "I ... guess we're done here."

The three young men showed themselves out of the house.

Once they were outside, Jack said, "I'm not really sure about hunting down the slavers in order to collect the bounty on them, but since we accidentally made ourselves their enemies, I'm going to try to gather some information about them."

Charles contemplated their predicament for a moment and observed, "We have to consider several problems if we decide to hunt these slavers. Number one is how to find them. Also, how do we plan to catch the slave traders, and how do we expect to get them back to town?"

"We can use Jack's new superpowers!" Ben chuckled.

"Yeah, I don't see that working very well," said Jack, "considering that I don't even know what powers I have or how to use them. Why don't you two hang out with Elton for a while? I'm going to ask around at some of the businesses. The people in this town have probably been, at the very least, inconvenienced by the slavers. By talking to random individuals throughout the nearby area, it shouldn't be too hard to get some of them to complain."

"We need to get some more of these translation stones," remarked Ben. "We can hardly do anything without them."

Jack nodded. "Maybe the two of you can get Elton to help you purchase some supplies. We all need some kind of bedroll, probably backpacks, and food. You guys know what I'm talking about. Just get some basic supplies, and I'll meet you back at Elton's camp tonight after gathering information in town."

Jack watched his two friends walk off, and he wondered what the three of them could really do against the slave cartels.

Jack first went to see the farrier, who was very happy to talk about all the people going in and out of town. He also informed Jack that if he planned to do any traveling, he should stay away from the Mangotten Marsh south of the town. "That marsh," he said, "is particularly active right now because it's spring."

Jack wrinkled his brow. "What's wrong with the marsh?"

"They say that two powerful mages fought there long ago. One mage had a powerful water stone, and the other had a powerful air stone. Now it's very difficult to survive if you fall into the water in the marsh, and strong, unpredictable winds blow through there from time to time. Even animals avoid that place unless they are water dwelling by nature. Such treacherous land supposedly can be created when powerful mages kill each other in battle, but that is all just a legend.

"Many people over the years have hunted for the stones that those mages possessed—some in order to use the stones and others in an attempt to return the land to normal. That area used to be fertile farmland, I'm told, and it made this town wealthy by allowing it to export food. Now the town is just a shell of what it once was. I also hear that some bandits are camped out near the old quarries outside of town, so stay away from there too if you're traveling."

Jack asked the innkeeper and a few other business owners questions, but no one had heard of any slavers. A few knew about the disappearances, but they theorized that it was only odd behavior from bandits or maybe wild animals. Jack reasoned that the townspeople were all too afraid to talk, which meant spies probably lurked somewhere within the town. Jack returned that night to the caravan and told his friends what he had discovered.

Ben frowned. "It doesn't sound like you got much useful information. How are we supposed to avoid the slavers that we apparently irritated?"

Jack thought seriously for a moment and replied, "I'm not sure. For now I think we should take a day to return to that place in the forest where we found ourselves when we arrived here. I think it seems pretty obvious now that this isn't anywhere in North America, and it may not even be on planet Earth. The technology here is far too simple. Even most Third World countries have traces of modern technology. This world seems to have no such knowledge, and it supposedly has some type of magic. I don't think a society like this could exist anywhere on our planet."

Charles grunted. "How did we get here if this is some other world?"

"I have no idea," Jack replied. "Maybe some type of magic. However we did it, we're here, and we're going have to deal with it."

Charles was silent for a while and finally said, "I agree. The place where we entered this world may have more clues about what happened. At the time we didn't try to understand exactly what happened because we assumed that we were still in our world. If we went back there, we might be able to find a way back home. The only other option seems to be finding the king of Celel and talking to him."

Ben sighed. "I guess it doesn't matter what we do—it's going to involve lots of walking, so let's get some sleep."

The three friends laid out their bedrolls underneath one of the merchant's carts in Elton's caravan.

Jack looked over the supplies that Ben and Charles had purchased and packed for their trip in the morning. Then he glanced up at the sky. "It's barely dark out. Do you guys want to hang out with the merchants by the fire for a while?"

"That does strike me as an opportunity to get in some intelligent conversation," Ben quipped, "since Charles and I don't have translation stones."

Charles shook his head and gave Ben a sideways smile. "Those merchants over there are playing instruments. Even if we can't understand the words to their songs, we can at least listen. Besides, I don't feel like sleeping just yet."

The three friends stepped over to the fire.

Ben and Charles sat down near the musicians.

One of the merchants possessed something that looked and sounded like a pennywhistle. Another played a harp. As the two men played, the other nearby merchants around the fire intermittently joined in song.

Charles found that even though he could not understand the words, he could still join in by clapping on occasion.

Ben was content to just sit back and listen.

Jack sat with Elton and two other merchants near the fire, who discussed their business that day.

One of the merchants, a man with a round face and large nose, shook his head. "I hate it when towns like this get caught up in political problems. It always interferes with business when warlords and cartels go after each other."

Elton nodded. "The townspeople are frightened of any strangers now, but they should warm up to us in a few days. I recall this town being much friendlier in the past although it has been some time since we've sold here."

The other merchant, who had deep-set eyes and sagging jowls that made him resemble a hound, asked, "Jack, my young friend, what's your take on how the region's politics affect the townspeople?"

All three men turned to listen to Jack's reply, making Jack feel a little uncomfortable. He thought, *Of everyone in this town, I probably know less about what's going on than anyone, yet they want my opinion on the subject?* Jack was not sure how to answer, and a long moment passed.

Elton must have sensed Jack's discomfort because he redirected the conversation to an experience he had earlier that day. The story Elton told was about a humorous customer, who thought that Elton should give him a discount on a new hammer if the man traded Elton his old, broken one. When he was done, one of the other merchants told a similar story.

Before long the group was laughing heartily and telling stories that become more and more outlandish until Jack was reasonably confident that the majority of the tales had no basis whatsoever in reality.

******

In the morning the trio woke up early and headed back toward the first village that they had found. They made slightly better time on their journey since they knew where they were going, but it was still late in the day when they reached the village.

"Hey," said Ben, "we have some money from the bounty we got on those bandits. Let's just stay at the inn tonight. We won't be able to gather any clues in the darkness anyway."

The other two agreed, and they entered the inn. In small villages like the one in which they stopped, an inn was apparently a house with an extra room or two that the owner was willing to rent out for the night. Jack kept telling himself that they must have missed something before, and there was probably an easy way back home. Other than a few optimistic comments, none of them discussed the topic. If they were wrong, there was no telling how long they might be in this place. Rather than addressing the subject, the three friends chatted with the innkeeper and his wife over dinner.

At some point in the conversation, Jack asked the innkeeper, "In a time like this when all the townspeople seem wary of strangers, why were you willing to take us in for the night?"

The innkeeper chuckled. "My wife and I are old and have no children. We're not really worth anything as slaves. It's true, they might kill us just because of our proximity to the village, but there's no real way to avoid that. We choose to just live happily day by day."

After the meal the boys retired to the room that they had rented for the night.

******

In the morning they headed out past the citrus orchard and did their best to retrace their steps. It did not take them long to find the clearing. As they remembered, they found burned grass and a tree split down the middle.

Jack watched Charles examine the tree and charred grass at its base. The initial point of contact for the lightning strike appeared to have been approximately five feet off the ground, and the tree split from that point along its length in both directions. The tree's two pieces were still attached to the stump at their base, but they leaned away from each other under the weight of their branches.

Jack stood in the middle of the little clearing and slowly scanned everything on the clearing's edge.

Charles walked over to Jack and said, "There's something very unnatural about that tree. It does look like a lightning bolt split it, but the lightning didn't come from the sky."

Jack thought about his words for a moment then commented, "Based on what I've noticed about the rest of this clearing, that's not surprising."

Charles placed his hands on his hips. "Not surprising that a lightning bolt actually traveled parallel to the ground, which completely goes against the laws of physics? Yet for some reason, the lightning automatically reverted to following the laws of physics at some point? After it struck the tree, it went straight to ground as it should have in the first place."

Jack glanced at his friend. "Come look here."

Charles and Ben both looked where Jack pointed. Two trees stood on the clearing's boundary, and from where Jack stood, the boys could see between them. Another tree stood between the two trees approximately ten feet deeper into the woods. This tree had a large burn mark on it about six feet off the ground.

Charles shook his head in disbelief. "No way! How is that possible? That tree is burned halfway up the truck, but it's not burned at the base, and nothing else around it is burned."

Ben declared, "And I know what's happening." As the other two turned to look at him, Ben smiled triumphantly. "Didn't you guys pay attention to what Hal said? If a person could use magic to create a type of element, why couldn't they create it halfway up on the tree? I suspect some kind of fight took place here between magic users. The real question is, did this fight have anything to do with us, or did we just happen to drop in right after it took place?"

"That does make sense," Jack replied. "I wonder if that guy we saw hanging around in the village was involved in this confrontation."

Charles raised an eyebrow. "What guy?"

Jack replied, "You remember when we were in the village after we asked around for directions, and that guy seemed interested in us? He started following us, but when we hid in the bushes, he passed by without seeing us. Whether or not the confrontation had anything to do with us, one or both sides probably had scouts or spies snooping around, and since we were so different, we would obviously look suspicious."

They searched around the clearing's edge and a little beyond it in the trees but did not find very much of interest.

"Let's head back to the town of Gredune," Ben finally mumbled. "I know a shortcut that will allow us to bypass the little village and hit the road that takes us straight back to the town."

"And how would you know a shortcut?" Charles challenged.

"Okay, I don't *know* a shortcut, but it stands to reason that if we just walk straight this way, we'll eventually hit the road to Gredune. If we head back through the orchard to the village, then we'll have to turn and head up to Gredune after that. Trust me, this is saving us a large distance, and it will be much faster."

Jack and Charles exchanged glances, shrugged, and followed Ben as he headed off through the woods.

They continued walking through the forest for a ways, but eventually the trees became more dispersed, and they eventually found themselves hiking through fields. The fields looked somewhat cultivated, and a dirt path ran along their edge. The boys headed for the dirt path and followed it in the direction that was supposed to take them back to the main road.

Jack looked up ahead and saw a few buildings and some smoke in the distance. He pointed at the area. "This village looks much smaller than the first one we found, but regardless, they should be able to tell us how close we are to the main road."

They picked up their pace and headed for the largest little clump of buildings.

As they approached, Ben suddenly stopped and grabbed his friends' arms.

Jack froze at his friend's warning. "What is it?"

Ben gestured at the building nearest them. "That smoke is coming from the roof, not the chimney."

The other two looked more closely. Sure enough, wisps of smoke rose from several places in the town. The entire area looked uninhabited.

Jack whispered, "There isn't anywhere to take cover on this path or in the fields next to us. Let's just try to stay low and get as close to the buildings as we can."

The three drew their swords and crept toward the buildings as quietly as possible.

When they reached the wall of the first building, Jack peeked around its corner and examined the town. He saw a broken cart and many wood fragments that could have belonged to tables and chairs. "It looks like the whole place has been ransacked."

They slowly made their way toward the town's center, but as they rounded a building's corner on the edge of the town square, they froze. Just around the corner to their left a man lay on his face with blood all around him on the ground.

Jack shook his head, trying to stay focused, and looked around them. Just inside many of the buildings' open doorways, he now noticed people in a variety of different positions. The one thing they all had in common was complete stillness.

Jack turned back to his friends. "I'm not sure what we should do next. Everyone in this place is dead. If we touch stuff, someone might think we had something to do with it."

Ben responded, "I don't think so. Unless someone sees us here, they shouldn't be able to connect us to this place."

Charles stroked his chin. "He's right. And what if someone is still alive? We may be able to help them."

"That's true." Jack glanced around the corner again before turning back to his friends. "Let me move in first to make sure the place is empty. Then you guys can come out."

They both nodded.

Jack stepped out into the open. He wanted to yell an offer of help in the hope that someone might still be alive to hear and answer him, but he held his tongue. He did not know if the perpetrators were still anywhere in the vicinity.

Jack finally whispered, "Hello, can anyone hear me? We're here to help."

Something moved on Jack's left.

He spun in that direction.

A faint voice murmured, "Please help." The voice was raspy, but it was loud enough for Jack to determine its direction.

Jack headed for the sound. As he drew closer, he realized that it came from inside one of the buildings. It was dark inside. Jack hesitated. Then he thought, *There's no reason for someone to set a trap for me. If the people who did this were still here, there would be enough of them to take the three of us out. They wouldn't need to resort to a trick.* Jack stepped boldly into the building's darkness. As his eyes adjusted to the gloom, he saw an old woman lying on the floor.

Jack rushed over to her and knelt down. "Are you okay?"

The old woman laughed or coughed—Jack wasn't sure which, maybe both. "I'm dying," she whispered.

"What can I do to help you?"

"There's ... nothing you can do for me," she said with an effort, "but please ... tell someone ... about what happened here. They took all the young people. They ... killed everyone else."

Jack's eyes widened. "They took all the young people? Like, to enslave them?"

The woman nodded and grabbed Jack's hand. "Please, they ... took my children and my grandchildren. I ... don't know you, but please ... tell the captain of the guard in Gredune. Maybe he can send ... out a ... rescue party ... I can't bear the thought of my ... family being separated and ... slaves for life. We just ... wanted to live ... in peace."

Jack looked into the woman's eyes. "Don't worry; I'll tell the captain of the guard. I'll make sure that your family receives justice."

The old woman did not seem to hear him. "We were so poor, but we ... were together, and we were ... happy. Why did this ... have to happen?" The old woman coughed up some more blood, lay back, and was still.

Jack held the old woman's hand for what must have been a long time because Charles stuck his head through the doorway and whispered, "Jack, you okay in there?"

Jack looked up and dropped the old woman's hand to the floor. "I don't know." Jack looked at Charles and saw a tear streak on his cheek. "What about you? How are you doing?"

Charles swallowed hard. "I feel so heartbroken for these people. They were just poor peasants, yet they got butchered like animals. I say 'butchered' because I can't think of any other way to describe what I see."

Jack stood and thought, *Get ahold of yourself, Jack*. He recalled how Mr. Thompson taught him to control his emotions to allow him to still function effectively in high-stress situations. *It doesn't matter what I feel. I choose what I feel.* Jack pushed all of his emotions down and out of his mind as he stepped out of the house.

Outside, Ben looked at his face and observed, "You look rather serious."

Jack replied, "Perhaps I am. How are you doing, Ben?"

Ben shrugged. "I'm okay. I'm not going to deny that this is upsetting, but there's nothing I can do for these people. It's not my fault they died, but it all seems so worthless, and I'm not really interested in seeing this happen to anyone else. So if you two are a little bit more open to hunting these slavers, I'm totally on board."

Charles clenched his fists. "I'm up for it if you guys are."

Jack thought for a moment and realized that horrible things occurred in this world, and no one did anything about it. He calmly looked around again. "As atrocious as this sight is, there is something else here. Even if I told the captain of the guard in Gredune, he already told me that his hands are tied. I can't just let this go."

Jack looked around him again. "Dr. Taylor once told me that he wanted to make a difference. I think now I understand what he meant. I could make a difference in our world, but here I see that the three of us are really needed. We may not be strong enough to rid this world of people like the slavers, but if we can rescue the kidnapped people from this town and bring justice to the murderers, then I say let's do it. We will make a difference in our own small way. We will make a difference to the people that we save, that we bring home. Come on; let's find our way back to the road. We can't do anything here."

The three followed a path that they were fairly certain led in the direction of the main road. Before long they did reach the main road, and they continued walking even after darkness fell. Finally, the scattered torchlight from Gredune was visible before them, and they rejoined Elton's merchant caravan.

Elton saw them enter camp and greeted them. "Was your trip informative? Did you find out what you wanted to know?"

Jack nodded. "We didn't figure out how to get home, but we did decide what we'll do until we get there." The three boys sat down as Jack continued to his two friends, "In the morning we'll go out to the rock quarries."

Charles asked, "Uh, where the bandits are camped?"

"Yes," replied Jack. "If anybody knows where the slavers are, it will be the bandits. Think about it. The slavers are cutting into their turf. The bandits must either hate the slavers or work for them. Either way, they'll know where the slavers are. We will head out in the morning."

Charles raised his eyebrows. "But how are we going to convince the bandits that they should help us instead of killing and robbing us?"

Jack leaned back with his hands behind his head and closed his eyes. "I haven't figured that part out yet, but we have until morning to come up with a plan."

******

Charles tossed and turned, unable to fall sleep. He thought about his parents and his little sister, Sarah. He imagined Sarah lying in bed weeping as she lost hope that her brother would ever return. He shook his head to clear his mind. He would return home. He thought, *We should be on our way to Celel to talk to the king of that land, not here chasing slavers.*

Suddenly, the image of a baby—dead in the arms of her dead mother—flashed through his mind. He had stumbled upon this scene in the village the slavers ransacked. The baby would not have been useful as a slave, and the mother either fit into the same category or had resisted the slavers. Both had been brutally slaughtered. The child's blond hair had reminded him of Sarah.

Charles realized that families everywhere in this world suffered just like the people in that village. *I can't stand idly by and ignore what's happening around me,* he thought. He wished that he could return home and that none of this had ever happened, but his sister did not need him as much as the people in this world. As he lay on his back, he reached his hand toward the sky and slowly closed his fingers into a fist. He thought, *Mom, Dad, it's going to be a little longer trip than I would like. Be patient; I will come home. Sarah, don't cry. What I'm doing here is more important than anything I've ever done before.*

******

The next morning as the three friends prepared the gear that Ben and Charles had purchased, Jack observed, "This is pretty much just a scouting mission. I'm concerned that with all our gear it will be harder for us to move around undetected."

Charles nodded. "It won't be a big deal. The rock quarries are only a few miles away right?"

Ben piped up, "Any opportunity not to carry our backpacks around sounds like a good opportunity to me. I say we leave them here."

They all agreed and headed out of town toward the rock quarry.

"So what's the goal of all this scouting?" Ben asked.

Jack replied, "We need to know how many bandits there are and how well armed they are."

The boys traveled on the main road for a while. When they reached the grown up remains of the once wide road that led to the rock quarries, Jack estimated that they were about a half mile away, so they diverted their path away from the road into the woods. The forest here consisted primarily of thick evergreen trees, which made it very dark.

"Some of these trees are really tall," remarked Charles. "We should climb one of them to look down into the rock quarry. We should be pretty well concealed and have an excellent vantage point."

The other two nodded their consent as they attempted to stealthily move through the forest.

"We should be getting close to the rock quarry now," whispered Jack.

Ben held up his hand to signal a halt. "Just hold on a second, guys. Be quiet."

The three stood perfectly still. Sure enough, a twig snapped behind them. They spun around and drew their swords.

They could not see anyone, but Jack spoke anyway. "Who are you, and what do you want with us?"

"I must say, I'm impressed that you noticed us," a man said, stepping out from behind a tree about twenty-five yards behind them. "I thought we had kept our distance."

The man was average height and wore a black helmet, which concealed most of his face. He also wore a dark green cloak loosely draped over light chainmail. He bore an insignia on the front of his helmet and sword hilt, which consisted of a single horizontal line with three vertical lines above it. His posture looked relaxed as though he planned to enjoy what came next.

"Then again," the stranger continued, "we've been following you ever since we recognized you in town this morning as the ones who turned in our recent hires at the guardhouse, so I shouldn't be too impressed."

"I assume you work for the Caishan cartel," replied Jack, "and you want revenge. I hope you're prepared to fight."

"Oh, we are." The man snapped his fingers.

Eight more men with the same insignia on their shields stepped out from behind cover around their leader.

"You see," the man in the dark helmet continued with a sneer, "my organization has to make an example of people and countries that disagree with its policies."

"So does that mean you paid off all the bandits in the entire country to help you?" asked Jack.

"No, that was actually the only group," said the leader. "Too bad they were such a disappointment."

"What are we going to do?" asked Ben quietly. "We can't fight all nine of them alone."

"Yeah, I have a crazy plan," whispered Jack. "Are you two ready?"

They both nodded.

"What are you talking about over there?" The man in the dark helmet signaled his men to walk forward.

"Now! Follow me," said Jack.

The three boys turned and took off running.

"This was your plan?" remarked Ben. "I kind of suspect that they were ready for this one."

As Ben predicted, their enemies were catching up quickly, and they all had their swords and shields ready.

Charles glanced over his shoulder at their pursuers. "I don't think I can outrun these guys much longer."

Jack replied, "We don't have to. Okay, guys, when I start yelling and screaming angrily, join in."

"Got it," they replied in unison.

They ran down a steep hill and jumped off a five-foot drop onto the little path that led to the rock quarry. Their pursuers were only about ten yards behind them now.

"Just give it up, kids," the Caishan leader yelled, apparently irritated that he had to chase his prey.

Someone else yelled in front of them.

Jack could not understand what the person said, but he could guess. "Okay now, guys, start yelling. Ahh! Die, you bandit scum!"

They rounded the last turn. The path ended, and the quarry opened up into a large open, rocky area. Bandits stood lined up in front of a collection of tents, brandishing swords, spears, and shields.

"Everyone attack! For the Caishan," yelled Jack.

The bandits did not try to hold a steady line, so the boys easily pushed through it. Several bandits turned and chased the boys, but the remainder engaged what the bandits presumed to be the remaining soldiers of the attacking force.

The man in the dark helmet yelled at the bandits, "Stop! We're not here to fight you. We just want those kids!"

His men, however, were already engaging the bandits who had attacked them, and the ringing of blades and flow of adrenaline made his words fall on deaf ears.

Jack glanced over his shoulder.

The Caishan leader growled and smote one of the bandits on the head with his sword. "Fine, kill these miserable dogs!"

Five bandits had followed Jack and his friends. One stabbed his spear at Charles's midsection.

Charles stepped to the side, grabbed the spear's haft, and pulled the bandit close to him. Then he straight punched the bandit in the stomach, forcing the bandit to bend over, and Charles kicked him to the side.

Ben successfully deflected another bandit's sword, and bashed the man's face with Ben's own sword hilt.

A second bandit grabbed Ben's arm and pulled him sideways.

Ben's foot hit a stone on the ground, and he pitched forward.

Two bandits ran at Jack, but he leapt to the left, dodging the swing of the bandit on that side and roundhouse kicking him in the stomach.

The bandit doubled over.

The other bandit shoved his comrade out of the way and swung his sword.

Jack deflected the weapon and swung his own sword at the bandit's torso.

The man turned sideways slightly and blocked with his shield. The outlaw swung three more times in rapid succession.

Jack blocked all three attacks with his own sword.

Before Jack could counterattack, the bandit lifted his shield and pushed the rim into Jack's shoulder, knocking him to the ground. The man raised his blade to finishing Jack off.

Jack hit the ground hard but swung his sword in a sideways arc at his attacker's ankle.

The bandit screamed and dropped to one knee, using his shield to prop himself up.

Jack rolled farther away and grabbed a rock with his left hand. He jumped toward the bandit and swung his sword in a downward arc.

The outlaw deflected Jack's sword off to Jack's right.

Jack pivoted to the right, turning his whole body that direction, and swung his left hand at the bandit's head.

As the stone made contact, the bandit crumpled to the ground.

Jack turned and saw Charles come up behind and slice the right arm of the bandit attacking Ben on the ground.

Seeing that he was outnumbered, the wounded bandit fell back to await reinforcements.

Jack turned to see more outlaws coming, and the one Jack had kicked had found his sword and was regaining his footing. Only about a minute must have passed; it had all happened so quickly. He gestured to Ben and Charles, and the three took off running.

Jack stole one more glance over his shoulder.

The man in the dark helmet saw the boys run but was unable to pursue them because even more bandits now barred his way. His men seemed to be more skilled than the bandits, but they were outnumbered. Jack was not sure how he thought the fight would end, but either way, they had made their escape.

A Destiny Among Worlds

Chapter 4

JACK AND HIS FRIENDS became rather frustrated after their daring escape because they had trouble finding their way back to the main road.

"I can't believe we got lost," said Ben.

"Don't worry about it." Jack lightly punched his friend's shoulder with his fist. "We'll find our way before too long. As long as nobody knows we got lost, we can just pretend that we were busy doing something else."

"So you don't actually mind that we're lost." Charles chuckled. "You would only care if someone found out about it; that is so typical."

They all laughed.

Jack said, "Of course, it's a little bit uncomfortable right now, but soon it will be just a memory."

"Besides," Ben added, "we're together, and for the moment, out of danger."

"Yes, although I don't know how long that will last." Jack glanced over his shoulder. "If that guy ordered his men to fall back immediately after we left, theoretically the bandits wouldn't follow him until after they regrouped, which means someone could be tracking us."

"Well, it's getting dark," said Charles. "Let's camp here for the night."

"Sounds good to me," replied Ben.

"I'll take first watch," said Jack. "We should sleep in shifts to ensure that we don't get killed while we sleep."

They created a bed with a thick layer of leaves like the one from their first night spent in this world. They decided not to build a fire since they were concerned that their pursuers might still be searching for them.

As the others lay down to sleep, Jack stared into the dark forest and thought, *I wonder if there's some grand purpose or plan behind us being brought to this world. Was it just destiny, just fate?* From what he had seen and heard, this whole world seemed like a war-torn, cruel land run predominantly by slave cartel leaders except for a few strong kings, and except for Celel, all of those kings and their kingdoms seemed evil as well. Then he laughed to himself, *Yeah, my two friends and I are going to change a whole world. That's rich. It's more like, I hope we live through the next couple of days and eventually get home.*

Jack tried reading the book Hal had lent to him by the light of the full moon. He was still not able to understand any of the words written in this ancient language, but he began to understand some of the concepts within the pages. Each type of stone apparently had some sort of poem or chant that awakened the crystal substance from which the gemstones were formed. Every time someone wanted to use a new stone, they had to repeat the words. *Great*, he thought. *Since I don't know what stones I have, I'll have to master all the different awakening spells, recite each one, and try to use the power that comes with it.* Jack was not sure if all of the writing in the book was awakening spells or whether the pages also contained instructions on how to use the stones and descriptions of what one could do with them. He reasoned that since one of his gemstones was a translation stone, he could have four other types, assuming that he did not have duplicate stones.

After considering the matter for some time, Jack finally woke up Ben for his shift, lay down, and drifted off to sleep.

******

Jack woke up the next morning cold and stiff. "I really don't like sleeping outside when it's this cold," he mumbled to no one in particular.

They all arose and started walking. After about an hour the trees became sparser, and the ground grew wetter.

Ben placed his hand over his grumbling stomach. "I'm starving."

"So am I," said Jack, "but talking about it isn't going to make it better." A few moments later Jack heard a crunching noise. He looked over and saw Ben munching on a bag of chips. "Where did you get those?"

"My pocket. They're the chips from my backpack," Ben answered. "Just because I didn't want to carry all the gear doesn't mean that I didn't take a snack. They're a little smashed, but don't worry; I'll save some for you and Charles."

Charles interrupted the conversation, "Have you guys noticed that the ground is turning marshier? And these are pumpkin ash and cypress trees, which tend to grow in wetter soil."

Jack thought for a moment. "Let's avoid going any farther this direction. I heard from the farrier that there's a marsh we really don't want get lost in. I think he called it the Mangotten Marsh. Let's go this way." He gestured with his hand toward his left. "I think the farrier said the marsh was directly south of the town, so we should be able to use it to get our bearings."

About one hour later they reached the forest's edge and saw the town in the distance.

Jack observed, "I guess that was the marsh the farrier mentioned—good thing too because that means we're close to the town."

It was afternoon by the time the boys finally rejoined Elton and the caravan.

"We need to keep our eyes open," said Charles. "Jack, you said that guy with the dark helmet had watched for us ever since we dropped off the bandits at the guard post. He recognized us when we passed through town earlier, so that means someone may be watching us again."

They ate a hearty meal and helped Elton and the other merchants with their business for the rest of the day.

Since Ben and Charles could not speak to the customers, they tended to the horses. None of the boys had much knowledge about horses, so this was an interesting learning experience for them.

One of the merchants sold salted fish from the coast. Two more carried fabrics, including silk, from other distant lands. The fabric merchants were the musicians who frequently played music in the

A Destiny Among Worlds

evenings. Elton's cart was full of tools such as hammers, picks, and axes. Elton apparently also had shared interest in a spice and clothing cart run by one of the other merchants. These two seemed like old friends. This spice merchant was a short, stubby middle-aged man with brown hair. He often bustled about examining and adjusting his wares, but he cooked well, so he was popular with Jack and his friends. There were several other merchants, but Jack did not have an opportunity to assist any of them during the course of the day.

That night after the merchants finished their business, a little boy approached the camp and asked to speak with Jack.

As Jack and his friends walked toward the boy, the child said, "This way," and darted into a dark alley.

"Are we sure we want to follow him?" asked Charles.

Jack replied, "I don't think the Caishan would try to kill us in the middle of town; otherwise, they would not have bothered to follow us out in the middle of nowhere yesterday. Regardless, we don't have much of a choice if we want to find out what he wants. Let's follow him and see what happens."

The boys followed the messenger into the alley.

A large shadowy figure loomed in the darkness. As the young men approached, the figure let out a deep chuckle and said, "It seems as if you boys got found by the Caishan instead of finding them, but your little stunt with the bandits to escape was quite brilliant. Despite your cleverness, I found it entertaining that you got lost in the woods on your way back. My informant was very unhappy about spending the night in the cold forest. Since you boys didn't take any provisions with you, he apparently didn't think he needed to either."

"Who are you?" asked Jack, "Why were you spying on us?"

The man, whose hulking shape surpassed that of Charles, stepped closer. "Perhaps I should put on my armor so you can recognize me."

"Ogol?" Jack gazed in surprise at the large captain of the guard. "Why were you following us?"

"I can't run this town with people like the Caishan snooping around causing trouble," the big man replied. "I thought I made that clear. If we can find their main hideout, I think they've committed enough crimes like murder and theft that I can take them down. I'll even pay you to accompany my men and me during the raid. Thanks to you, we've identified one of their leaders—that guy in the black helmet who tried to kill you in the woods. He definitely carries some clout around here. I received a report that three kidnappings took place all in the same area last night. It's on the west side of town, a little village. I want you three to go check it out. One of my men will watch you just like yesterday and today."

Ogol crossed his arms and leaned forward. "We want to find the group kidnapping the villagers. With any luck the group trying to kill you will contact the kidnapping unit in order to bolster their numbers before attacking you again. See, the problem we've had is that the slavers going around doing the killing are just here for a political agenda to punish the warlord. Those men don't usually go back to the main base. Only the kidnapping groups go back there to drop off their new slaves. We have theorized that at times, like when they need more manpower, the groups temporarily hook up. This contact will expose the unit that returns to the main base, and my men can follow them back when the groups separate again."

"The only problem I see with this idea," said Jack thoughtfully, "is that it involves two groups of our enemies joining together to kill us. How do we not die in this plan? Could you send some of your troops to back us up when the enemy makes their move?"

The big man shook his head. "Sadly, I cannot. The Caishan watch the majority of my men. I have only managed to keep a few of them secret, and my men being absent from town would, at best, make the Caishan suspicious. I'll pay you seventy-five coin if you pull this off, and another seventy-five for participating in the raid."

Jack consulted briefly with Ben and Charles before turning back to Ogle. "Fine. We'll do it, but give us tomorrow to prepare."

"The Caishan will probably have moved away from the village by then."

"Yes," replied Jack, "but they kidnap people every day, so I'm sure you'll have a new location for us by tomorrow."

"Fair enough," Ogol replied.

The three boys returned to the caravan.

"How are we going to prepare?" asked Ben.

"I happen to know a group of bandits who are very angry with the Caishan right now for attacking them completely unprovoked," Jack mused. "I'm sure that they would be interested in ambushing the Caishan and getting a little payback."

Charles inquired, "But how are we going to present this opportunity to the bandits without getting ourselves killed?"

Jack shrugged. "I guess we'll just go to the rock quarry waving a white flag and hope for the best."

"That's very encouraging—us at the mercy of angry bandits," said Ben. "You don't think any of them will recognize us, do you?"

"Maybe," replied Jack, "but I think we can conceal our faces with some black cloth from the caravan. As long as we don't remove our masks, no one could recognize us. Charles, do you think you can figure out how to wrap a cloth to conceal the entire head and face?"

"Absolutely. Just give me an hour or so. I'll figure something out."

After they returned to the caravan, Jack procured some black cloth from one of the fabric merchants.

Charles and Ben sat down near the fire where the musicians were playing so that Charles could experiment with the best way to wrap the cloth around Ben's head.

Jack smiled as he watched his friends. Seeing Charles wrap cloth around Ben's face in every conceivable pattern was actually rather comical.

As Jack sat down near Elton, the elderly man asked where the boys had been the previous night.

Jack briefly recounted his tale.

When Jack finished, Elton was silent for a long moment. Finally, the old man leaned back and smiled. "Be careful challenging these cartels. I've not heard of anyone being successful. On the other hand, I don't think I've even heard of anyone who really tried. Maybe it's because of my own past, but when I hear that someone is challenging the cartels, I feel excited and hopeful."

The two continued chatting for some time.

As Jack stood to retire for the night, he wished that he could stay up longer just to talk. This whole new world was so strange and different, but chatting with Elton around the fire was relaxing.

Ben and Charles arose as well, and the three of them crawled into their bedrolls by Elton's cart.

Charles announced, "I figured out a good way to cut and wrap the cloth, so we should be ready for tomorrow."

Jack nodded. "All right. Tomorrow we get to chat with some bandits."

******

The next morning the boys ate breakfast, packed some provisions, just in case, and headed out of town. Rather than following the main road, they retraced their steps from the last time they were in the forest. After reaching the marsh's edge, they turned toward the rock quarry. They were careful not to leave tracks, and on multiple occasions they stopped to hide, waiting to see if someone followed them.

The third time they stopped to hide, Ben doubled back and circled around behind the path they had just taken.

Jack and Charles came out of hiding and moved forward. Within a few minutes they heard someone cry out in pain. They turned to see Ben standing over a man dressed in black and green clothing with the Caishan cartel symbol on his sword and shield. A drop of blood fell from Ben's sword into the weeds.

The fallen man whimpered as he clutched his right leg.

"Well, it would seem we were followed," said Ben, "but I think we're good now."

"What should we do with him?" asked Charles.

"Please don't kill me!" The man bowed his head in submission and held his hands toward them.

Even though Ben and Charles could not understand the man's words, his posture spoke clearly.

The young men exchanged glances.

"We can't just kill him," said Charles. "He can't keep up with us with his injury anyway."

"The road is that way." Jack looked at the Caishan soldier and pointed to his left. "You can probably get some help or a ride there. The Caishan cartel is not very popular right now, so if I were you, I would leave the sword and shield here."

The group continued on, reaching the rock quarry and donning their masks.

"Remember, let me do the talking." Jack grinned.

"Yes, very funny," replied Ben. "As if we could talk even if we wanted to."

"Oh, we could talk," said Charles, "The bandits just wouldn't be able to get anything out of it. Here's the white cloth for the flag."

"Let's go," said Jack.

They walked down the path into the quarry until they saw a sentry standing above them on a large rock.

"That's far enough." The sentry fingered his sword hilt. "What do you want?"

"We're here to talk to your leader about a business opportunity." Jack held his voice steady although he felt his pulse rate increasing.

The bandit squinted his eyes in confusion but yelled for two of his comrades to watch the boys as he left to look for their leader.

Before long a man approached with six bandits behind him. He was average height but very muscular. He carried a sword on his belt and a shield on his back like the majority of his men, but he also had a quiver of arrows on his opposite hip and a short bow in his hand.

"Who are you, and what do you want?" The leader nocked an arrow onto his bowstring. "Actually, I think my first question should be this: Why shouldn't I kill you right now?"

Jack replied calmly, "We understand that you've had trouble with some of the same people that we have. These Caishan slavers seem to think that they can attack anyone and everyone and haul them all away as slaves without any repercussions."

The bandit leader grunted. "I wouldn't know anything about the Caishan."

"Really? So you wouldn't be interested in perhaps ambushing some of these men and robbing them in the next day or so? Because I think I can find out where some of them will be. Unfortunately, there are only three of us, and the city guard won't help. It seems as though no one is willing to give any retribution to these scum. If you don't do anything, they will continue to encroach on your turf and may attack you in an effort to enslave you and your men. You all must be rather wealthy in comparison to the peasants, so you would eventually become tempting targets. I imagine that the Caishan carry a good bit of money with them. Anyone who robbed them would certainly benefit financially."

As Jack spoke, the bandit leader's face developed a crooked grin. He removed the arrow from the bowstring and twirled it slowly between his thumb and forefinger as he considered Jack's offer.

Jack was surprised how easy this was. Based on the man's relaxed posture, Jack suspected that he had manipulated the bandit leader quite effectively with his smooth words. "If you're not interested, then I guess we'll just leave." Jack gestured to his friends to imply that they were leaving.

The bandit leader held up his hand to indicate that he wanted them to wait. A long pause ensued. "Fine. As long as we get to steal whatever they have on them, and we don't take the majority of the risk, we'll help."

"Excellent." Jack gave the bandit leader a location near the city to meet on the morrow.

As the three boys exited the camp, Ben asked, "How did you know that he would go for the deal?"

"Well," Jack replied, "for most people you just need to present a choice in such a light that it makes all other choices seem ludicrous in comparison. Really, the trick is to make all other choices look bad more than it is to make the one choice look good. Besides, they already wanted revenge on the Caishan."

On the long walk back to town, the boys found themselves talking about home.

Ben chuckled. "Charles, if your little sister could see you now, she would have to take back all those times that she said I got us into trouble and dangerous situations."

Charles shut his eyes and shook his head slightly in mock disapproval. "You just never had a younger sibling who needed you to look out for them. Jack or your brother, Derek, was always there to bail you out of whatever trouble you got into. Sometimes you even dragged me into it."

Ben smirked. "Yeah, but you can't tell me that you regret all of those times I pulled you into whatever I was doing. The life of excitement is always the best one."

Jack cast his gaze over the fields around them. The field on his left looked fallow with large weeds growing up in it. The land off to the right had shoots of wheat sprouting up out of the otherwise bare ground. Finally, Jack said, "Our families have to be worried about us. It's been about a week."

Ben mumbled, "They've probably called everybody they know trying to figure out where we are."

Jack nodded. "I'm sure my mother is worried sick. Neither of my parents ever really pictured me leaving our town long term for any reason."

Charles stared down at his feet as he walked. "I wish I could just grab Sarah's hand and tell her that I am safe and not to worry."

Ben laughed. "Yeah, but that would be a lie."

The time seemed to pass quickly until the town was in sight. They scouted the area where they had told the bandit leader to meet them before returning to the caravan.

Before long Ogol's messenger approached and told them another location from which people had disappeared that day.

The entire plan was falling into place, but the three young men were still a little apprehensive.

It seemed to Jack that he would never be able to fall asleep. He attempted to read his book again, trying to awaken the dormant stones within him, until he became drowsy.

******

The boys woke up early the next day, donned their black masks again, and strode boldly through the middle of town to ensure that no Caishan spy could miss them. They walked through the field where they were supposed to rendezvous with the bandits. Jack could only hope that the bandits were, indeed, there and that they followed the trio.

The village associated with the most recent kidnappings was close to the town, and the boys arrived before noon. The village's appearance was similar to the other towns they had seen—small stone or wood buildings along a dirt path. This village, however, had a large wooden building in the center with a deep well in front of it. Nothing appeared out of the ordinary.

"They must not want to attack us with witnesses." Jack adjusted his mask. "It will probably take them thirty minutes or so to gather their men together and get organized. Our bandit reinforcements can't get very close to us in the middle of the town, so let's circle the outside of the village and return to the road."

The other two nodded, and they all turned toward the village's edge.

"This is so annoying," said Ben. "I wish they would just attack already. I can't stand this waiting around, and this mask is uncomfortable."

"I know. The wait is bothering me too," replied Jack. "I thought that they would have been ready by now. Perhaps they're suspicious and think we have a plan. If they don't attack, I hope the bandits don't take out their frustrations on us."

After circling the entire village, the boys started back toward Gredune. On the road back to town, they came upon a man bent over a large handcart. It appeared as though one of the wheels had broken off the axle.

"Can you boys help me?" the man called.

"I guess we might as well help the guy," Jack said to his friends with a shrug.

They walked over and grabbed the cart's handles.

As they lifted the cart, Jack thought, *It's strange that this guy seems to trust three people who are obviously concealing their identities.*

Suddenly, the cart burst into flames.

The boys dropped the cart and jumped back, startled. The entire road in front of them became engulfed in flame, and the fire rapidly spread to the sides of the road as well, cutting off their route toward the town.

The man with the cart had drawn a sword. "The boss was right," he taunted. "He said you boys were easier to catch than random villagers."

From the direction of the town, two dozen men with swords and shields stepped out from behind the trees.

"Remember," one of the men said, pointing his sword at Jack, "the boss wants the head of that one intact for the glory of the Caishan. Apparently, he wants to kill him face to face."

The group laughed.

"He'll get his chance." Jack stared back calmly. He slowly drew his sword. "But I think that when he gets his chance, he will regret having given me the opportunity. Tell me where I can find your boss."

The group looked annoyed, and the one who had pointed his sword at Jack called, "Get him."

"If I can add a footnote for any future plans," mumbled Charles, "I say we don't center the plan around bandits."

"Yeah. I'm starting to agree," replied Jack.

Just then, Jack heard a twang and the sound of rushing air.

One of the Caishan soldiers fell onto his back, an arrow shaft protruding from his right shoulder.

Jack heard a yell, and bandits poured out of the woods and charged the enemy from behind.

The Caishan turned around to face the bandits, but they were too slow and badly outnumbered. A quick skirmish ensued, but it only lasted a few moments before the slavers tried to flee. Three of them managed to break through the bandits' charge and escape, but the rest were put to the sword.

After the fight the bandit leader approached Jack. "Were you worried that we wouldn't show up, my young friend?"

"Not at all," Jack lied.

"Ha! Sounds like you had more faith in me than I did. I wasn't sure that I was going to help you until I fired my arrow."

"Our business is done," said Jack. "I'd advise you to be cautious. The Caishan do not like it when people retaliate against them for the wrongs they've committed."

The bandit leader shrugged. "True, but I think they will be less eager around this area from now on. The men you see here are actually three bandit groups together. That's why there are over fifty men in all. The Caishan were foolish to make an enemy of us."

"Very well." Jack smiled and tipped his head cordially. "Enjoy your spoils. We must be on our way."

Although the three boys did not have anything that the bandits would consider valuable with them, they still did not think it wise to linger around the outlaws any longer than was necessary. The fires died down quickly. Apparently, the Caishan had laid down only a thin layer of pitch, so the boys were able to walk unhindered toward the town.

Jack chuckled as they walked. "What a day. We managed to turn three groups of bandits into a sort of guarding force for the people around this entire area. I'm sure the bandits will continue their pillaging, but at least they won't kidnap and murder large numbers of people each day."

"I was disappointed not to see the man in the dark helmet among the Caishan," said Ben.

"Yes, he was skilled with a sword," replied Jack. "It would have been nice to defeat him in a battle that was so slanted in our favor."

"I doubt that the next battle will be so easy," added Charles. "Even with the town guard on our side, if the Caishan were able to field twenty-five men on the outskirts of town, I'm sure a greater number will be garrisoned at their primary base."

Jack replied, "Look on the bright side: they have twenty-two fewer men than they did before."

The boys laughed. They stopped to eat a leisurely meal before returning to town since they had not taken the time to eat lunch when they were trying to set their trap. As they walked through the town gates, they were surprised to be met by Ogol.

The big man crossed his arms. "You boys have been busy. I don't think I want to know how you convinced the bandits to kill the Caishan, but regardless, the town of Gredune will always be in your debt. As promised, here is seventy-five coin. My scouts successfully followed the three men who escaped. We have the location of a temporary Caishan camp. If we sack the camp, they will hopefully leave us alone."

"I thought we were going to find their main camp and attack that," Jack protested.

"Based on how many men are at this site, I doubt that we would be able to destroy their primary base even if we found its location. Get some sleep. We leave for their camp in the morning."

Jack relayed this disturbing new information to his friends as they walked back to the caravan. "It seems we may not be able to drive the Caishan out of this land after all."

"Maybe we will think of something else after we destroy the camp," said Charles. "You shouldn't be so discouraged."

"I know." Jack sighed. "I just felt like we were doing something important, and now it may only be a minor setback, a financial irregularity, for the Caishan."

"Don't worry, we'll definitely find some way to get these guys," said Ben, "especially that guy in the dark helmet."

Back at the caravan, Charles assisted two of the merchants with the horses.

Ben sat down with several of the other merchants for a card game. After Jack relayed the rules, Ben picked it up quickly.

Jack turned away from the game and thought about the plan for the next day.

His thoughts were interrupted by Elton walking up and saying, "I heard there was quite a bit of excitement outside of town today. The entire marketplace was abuzz with news about the skirmish that took place. I can only assume that you all were a part of that."

Jack nodded unenthusiastically and mumbled, "Yes, it was a small step."

Elton grinned. "You almost sound disappointed, as though it weren't a success."

Jack replied, "I just don't feel like what we're doing is anywhere close to enough."

Elton gazed up at the night sky overhead filled with stars for a long moment. "My friend, I'm an old man, and I've seen a lot of people over the years in a lot of different countries. I have to say, sometimes a small step—even the smallest of steps—can encourage others to follow. What you did today just isn't done. It wouldn't take all that many people following in your footsteps before a real change took place."

******

The next morning well before the sun came up, a messenger from Ogol awoke Jack, instructing them to meet the captain of the guard at the town gate. At the gate Ogol had assembled forty men, all with chainmail and shields. About thirty of them had swords, and the others carried bows.

"Good to have you boys here," said Ogol. "We will approach the camp from the west. Our archers will take a position to the east behind the enemy. The archers firing their first volley will be our signal to attack. The Caishan will be crushed in the middle."

"What if the enemy sees our positions before we close in and attacks the archers in force?" asked Jack. "They would not be able to hold their ground."

Ogol snorted. "Nonsense. These ruffians won't know what hit them until it's too late. Let's move out the troops." He turned and marched through the gate.

In about two hours they reached the camp and set up their troops. The camp was situated in a small clearing surrounded by trees. The ground was level all around. Only a few men wandered about the quiet camp. Each tent had a weapon rack near it with spears, swords, and shields. Three sleek horses stood tied to a tree on the camp's southern end.

"Do you boys never carry shields?" asked Ogol.

"Well, we haven't found any yet, I guess," replied Jack. "Why?"

"I thought everyone knew to carry shields." Ogle shook his head. "Not having a shield makes you very susceptible to archers. It's also very difficult to block a blast of fire or lightning with a sword. Shields are standard issue for all soldiers in case you come up against mages. Even a poorly trained mage can decimate the ranks of a group of soldiers if they don't have shields, forcing the soldiers to break formation. In fact, there's a legend that long ago a great king armed all his soldiers with shields that had handles coated in a certain type of tree sap in order to prevent his men from being killed by his enemy's lightning mages. Now all sword and shield handles are coated in that sap, making sap expensive across all the lands."

When Jack relayed this information to his friends, Charles's eyes lit up with understanding. He explained, "That's very ingenious. The tree sap provides insulation so that the electric charge does not travel through the sword or shield and kill the defender. Some rubbers and plastics in our world originated with sap."

Great, Jack thought, *so now I have to learn how to use a shield.* Jack had not learned much about shields in fencing class. *I guess fencing is taught from a perspective after the invention of gunpowder, which significantly reduced the effectiveness of armor and shields.* He realized that in this new world it would probably pay off to learn about shields.

The archers opened fire on the camp. For their first volley the archers used flaming arrows lit by a brazier that two of the archers had carried on a pole between them. This volley successfully set several of the tents on fire.

Ogol roared, "Attack!"

They all charged into the camp.

It seemed like chaos to Jack. Men ran out of tents and grabbed weapons, and small battles popped up all over the camp.

Jack saw Charles lift an entire weapon rack into the air and throw it on a tent, crushing it to the ground. Jack saw movement under the collapsed tent and knew that Caishan soldiers were still inside it.

Ben had trouble breaking through his opponent's guard because of the man's shield, so Ben grabbed the shield and pulled himself next to the man, forcing them both to fall to the ground.

The Caishan soldier dropped his sword and shield and wrestled with Ben over control of Ben's sword.

Jack did not see how it ended because two men crawled out of the collapsed tent to his left.

Jack gave the first man a front kick in the stomach then added a left hook to the side of his head. Jack turned to see the other man stabbing a spear at him. Jack shifted his weight to his other foot, pivoting his body so that the spear narrowly passed to his left. Then he swung his own sword.

His opponent instinctively put his arm up in front of his face. The sword bit deep into the man's arm, causing him to scream in pain. The man dropped his spear and ran.

Jack saw Ogol cleaving his way through a group of Caishan that had managed to form near the camp's center.

Another man armed with only a sword came out of nowhere and dived straight at Jack.

Jack stepped to the side, dodging his swing, and thrust with his own sword. His sword punctured the man's left side, dropping him to the ground.

The bleeding man turned over as he gripped his side. "The boss will see you dead for this," he whispered weakly. Then he collapsed.

Jack thought, *Well, 'the boss' planned to kill me anyway, so I guess I haven't lost anything.*

Ben had apparently defeated his opponent on the ground and now stood next to Charles, helping him fend off rapid spear thrusts.

When the man with the spear saw Jack running toward him, he turned and fled rather than face three opponents.

The battle was essentially over now. Approximately fifty men lay on the field. Jack noticed that another dozen or so had grouped together and fled south, taking the horses with them.

"Not bad." Ogol wiped the sweat from his brow with his arm. "They outnumbered us about fifty-five to forty-five, but we totally caught them off guard. You boys have earned your second payment." He handed Jack a pouch of seventy-five coin. "You are welcome to march back with us. I've already dispatched a messenger to inform my warlord that a group of murderous bandits has been annihilated. There weren't even any slaves in the camp, so the Caishan can't claim that we breached international law by freeing slaves."

Jack's eyes widened with realization. "You found their main base didn't you? But it was full of slaves, so you couldn't come up with a way to justify attacking it legally. Instead, you hit this place."

Ogol suddenly looked very uncomfortable and ashamed. "We got to punish them for a little bit of what they did. That's something." He started to turn away.

"Wait," said Jack, "where's their main base?"

"It doesn't matter," Ogol replied. "Word came down yesterday that even if we found proof of other crimes, we would not be able to justify to our neighboring countries or the other slave cartels an attack of that magnitude."

"But they have dozens, maybe even hundreds, of *your* people there. At least tell us where it is," Jack pleaded.

"What do you three think you're really going to do?" The frustration was evident in Ogol's voice and his face looked tense, but then his features softened. "Fine, it's about a half day's walk northeast of town in a cave. It's on a mountainside, and although it's a defensible position, it's fairly easy to scout since many small caves lay scattered in the area. My scouts estimated that over one hundred fifty men were stationed there, including your dark-helmeted friend. Apparently, he's the leader for the cartel in this country."

Jack could tell the big man was furious that he could not do anything more permanent. Jack asked, "Ogol, did your scout have an estimate on how many slaves were in the cave?"

"He theorized about three hundred, but in case you're thinking of trying to free them and have them help you fight the Caishan, you can forget it. The slaves are mostly just children and some women. There are probably fewer than thirty men in all. The Caishan usually send the men out quickly so that there are never enough of them to rebel."

The group returned to Gredune.

Jack informed his friends of the situation and asked Elton and the other merchants if they had any advice or ideas on how they could take down the Caishan.

"You know that's crazy, right?" responded Elton. "There's no way you could pull that off. Plus, you probably already have bounties on your heads for meddling in their affairs as much as you have. I know that I've encouraged you all to stand up for others, but three people cannot possibly accomplish this idea." Despite Elton's negative words, Jack could see the excitement in his eyes at the mere prospect that someone might attempt such a task. Elton met Jack's gaze. "You're going to go anyway, aren't you?"

"We'll have to come up with a plan first," said Jack, "but we started this, and we have to finish it no matter what. I promised a dying woman that I would ensure justice for her family."

Ben and Charles nodded their agreement.

******

That night Charles and Ben joined the merchants around the fire while Jack focused on trying to develop a plan. Charles was tired from the day's activities and looked forward to some downtime.

Earlier that evening, Jack had confided in Elton that the boys actually thought that they were from a different world.

Surprisingly, Elton seemed to take the news in stride. He had nodded gravely then said, "Hal stopped by after his conversation with you three, and we compared the experiences we each had with you all. He felt that, as ridiculous as it sounds, you actually appear to be from another world. He said he recommended that you seek your way home by speaking with the king of Celel."

Ben joined in a card game, and several of the merchants were more excited about playing with him now because they said his beginner's luck from the previous night would certainly run out.

Charles shook his head as he watched Ben examine his cards. Charles was not even sure how the game worked, but Ben seemed able to win the majority of the hands.

Finally, Charles moved back to his bedroll and sat down. Although he felt sluggish after the tiring adventures of the day, he tried to think of a plan himself. Charles often preferred to analyze and modify one of Jack's plans than invent one from scratch.

The merchants who had been playing their instruments were immersed in the card game with Ben, and Jack looked deep in thought.

Charles shook his head as he thought about Ben gambling. Charles believed gambling was usually a great way to lose all of one's money, but Ben did it fairly successfully. Back home, Ben never gambled for anything big, but he often seemed to get the better of his classmates. Even so, his gambles did not always turn out perfectly.

Charles gazed up at the night sky. He missed home. A few dark blotches of cloud prevented the stars from shining through, but for the most part the night was clear and beautiful. Charles could not find a single constellation in the sky that he recognized, and he smiled to himself. Everything was different here, yet so much was still the same.

Chapter 5

THREE DAYS PASSED WITH the boys helping the merchants in their day-to-day activities. Charles had settled into a routine of feeding and watering the horses and moving merchandise from one place to another.

Ben usually assisted Elton with delivering merchandise to different customers throughout the town.

When Elton was away, Jack took care of his cart and sold tools to the customers.

The three days were relaxing and enjoyable, but none of them had thought of a solution to the Caishan problem.

At the end of the three days, the merchants prepared to leave Gredune. They had already stayed longer than they had intended and needed to travel to the capital.

Finally, Jack had an idea. "Ben, Charles, I've got it." He triumphantly slammed his right fist into his open left palm. "The easiest way to beat a small army is to have a small army. Now, it would be very difficult to get an army ourselves, but this army doesn't actually have to do what we say, it only has to do what we want. I think I have a way to get one of the other cartels to attack the Caishan. Basically, we'll con two different cartels at the same time, making them fight a battle with each other. While that's going on, we'll free the slaves and right a significant number of wrongs. If this is going to work, though, we will need the governor's help."

The three boys went to Hal's home.

Governor Hal sat in the same place in front of the same window but read a different book. He turned in his chair when they entered the room. "I hear I owe you boys a debt. I know I said that you owed me a favor, but I wasn't really serious. What you have done is much more than anyone could have required, and I find myself now owing you a favor. According to Ogol, you are quite a formidable trio. Of course, I would expect nothing less from a blood mage. Have you had any success with the book I lent you?"

"A little," replied Jack, "but I have a different question for you. If I had a plan to get rid of the Caishan, would you be willing to secretly assist me?"

"Secretly? Hmm. Well, I suppose it depends on what I have to do."

"First, I need you to tell us about the other two slave cartels and where some of them are causing problems in this country or even a neighboring country."

"All right." Hal leaned forward and took his translation stone out of its box on the desk for Ben and Charles's benefit. "There are two other major cartels: the Bendel and the Zangan. They don't really respect any kind of border with each other or any country. They typically do, however, have an uneasy peace, which is often broken and remade—usually when the person who broke it has been killed.

"All three cartels usually have at least one lower-ranking officer in every country at all times, but the number of troops under that officer's command can vary substantially based on the kind of activities in which the cartel is engaged within that country's borders. The Caishan, for example, have significantly increased their garrison in our country right now because Warlord Acelet sided with the Bendel cartel in some foreign matters.

"The Caishan blatantly kidnapping and murdering in our rural areas is in retaliation for our warlord's choice. It's impossible to please all the cartels, so warlords and kings are forced to act in fear. This means that whichever cartel a warlord fears the most at that moment is the one the warlord supports. When a cartel doesn't get their way, they sometimes burn whole towns or villages."

Jack asked, "Do you have an idea where the Bendel or Zangan officers are in your country?"

Hal nodded. "Yes, we've been on reasonably good terms with the Bendel officer, so he has not bothered to move his base of operations even though we are aware of its location."

Jack asked, "I don't suppose you could spare any of the armor, clothing, and weapons that Ogol captured from the Caishan? We'll need equipment that has the Caishan seal on it if we're going to look the part."

Hal narrowed his eyes in thought. "Even if you were able to go undercover in the Caishan ranks, how would you drive them away?"

"Leave that to me," replied Jack. "We also need you to write a letter to Warlord Acelet, informing him that you had nothing to do with the Caishan cartel's recent activity against the Bendel."

Hal wrinkled his brow. "What recent activity against the Bendel?"

"It doesn't matter," Jack replied. "Just write exactly what I told you, and send the message in exactly five days."

"I think you boys are a little crazy, but I'll write the letter. I'll also send a note to Ogol, telling him to let you have your pick of the supplies in the armory and to give you the Bendel camp's location. I don't know why, but for some reason I think you boys might impress me again."

The young men thanked Hal and showed themselves out again. They were excited as they went to the armory and picked out the equipment bearing the Caishan seal. They said farewell to Elton and the other merchants and left in search of the Bendel camp.

******

It took the three boys almost an entire day to reach their destination. Once there, Ben scouted the area around the camp, and Charles observed the day-to-day functioning that took place inside the camp. Jack monitored the path leading into camp, finalized his plan, and read his book. They did the same thing for two more days.

"It is as I expected," Jack said finally. "These guys have no purpose right now, so they're not on guard at all. They have one guy at a time patrol around camp, and most of them spend half their time lounging against trees."

Ben added, "This rocky hill we're on also provides easy concealment, so we can get right next to the camp."

Jack closed his book and put it in his backpack. "Okay guys, when it gets dark, we know where everybody is sleeping and how best to avoid getting close to any of them. All we have to do is get to the officer's tent, knock him out, and drag him out of there."

"You make it sound so simple," said Charles. "I agree that there's very little security. Obviously, nothing of importance has happened here in a long time, but we still need to be careful."

"Indeed," Jack said, unperturbed. "I will muffle his mouth. Ben, you'll hit him in the back of the head. Then I'll pull the sack over his head. Charles will grab his top half, and I'll grab his legs. The hardest part of this whole thing is that from the moment we grab him, you two cannot say a word in his presence, or else he might recognize that we're not Caishan soldiers. Also, whenever we give him food or water, never lift the sack up high enough that he can see our faces, only our insignias. He has to believe throughout this entire thing that the Caishan kidnapped him; otherwise, the Bendel cartel will come after us when this is all done."

The boys easily sneaked into the camp. As they wove their way through the tents, they heard a rustling in a tent on their left as someone emerged. Jack and Charles crouched low behind a nearby tent, and Ben slipped under a wooden bench near the fire pit.

Fortunately, the fire had died down hours ago so the man did not see Ben as he walked right past him. The man bore the now familiar Bendel seal, which consisted of two crossed swords, on his right sleeve. He sat down with his back to them and pulled a jug out of a sack on the ground.

"Great, just what we need," muttered Jack, "an idiot who wants to get drunk in the middle of our kidnapping."

They stole quietly behind the man and slipped into the officer's tent. The three crept up next to the man's bed as he slept.

The officer's loud snoring was interrupted as Jack shoved a wet piece of cloth into his mouth. The man struggled violently as he awoke.

Ben struck him in the back of the head with a club that the boys had brought. The only sound that had escaped was a little muffled growl.

After the officer's body went limp, Jack slipped a sack over his head.

They dragged the body to the tent's rear, waited for the sentry to pass by, and hauled their prize through a slit Jack made in the tent's back wall. They rotated which two of them carried the prisoner as they quietly left the camp. After about fifteen minutes they reached the sanctuary of the rocky hill outside of the camp.

Before long Jack could tell that the officer had woken up because of the constant muffled noise that emanated from within the sack. Jack signaled by pushing his open palms downward.

Ben and Charles set down their prisoner.

The three young men pulled the officer up onto his feet and did their best to force him to walk. To make their task easier, they had bound his hands but not his feet. Since he could not see, however, they did still have to guide him.

Time seemed to pass slowly because their prisoner dragged his feet at every opportunity, and they had to get off the main road each time someone approached. The trip was also boring because none of them could engage in any kind of conversation. About a day and a half later following Ogol's directions, the group eventually neared the Caishan caves.

As they approached their destination, Jack signaled with his hands to indicate that they should tie their prisoner to a tree and walk out of earshot.

"Okay," said Jack when they were away from their prisoner. "Remember, we can only talk now because he can't hear us. As soon as we finish this conversation, we can't talk anymore. We'll send Ben ahead to locate one of the small caves Ogol mentioned. Ben, look for one about a quarter mile down from the main entrance to the Caishan cave. We'll stash our prisoner there. If the Bendel don't have a spy in the area already, they will soon."

"How do we know?" asked Charles.

"We don't know if they already have a spy, but when Hal sends that letter to Warlord Acelet, he will inform the Bendel that something suspicious is going on here because he is on good terms with the Bendel. The Bendel, knowing that their officer was kidnapped, should be able to put two and two together. When a spy gets here, or if one is already here, he should notice me every day exit the Caishan main entrance with a plate of food. I hope this is suspicious enough for the spy to notice, but not so suspicious that the guard stationed at the cave entrance takes notice.

"As soon as the Bendel spy discovers that the Caishan abducted their officer, they will march an army over here to crush them. Thankfully, the number of people going in and out of the Caishan hideout is low because we destroyed their exterior camp. Until they get new orders, roughly three hundred slaves and one hundred fifty slavers are crammed into one cave, so they should hardly notice one extra person who looks like he belongs."

Jack reiterated the remainder of the plan. Then he said, "Guys, this is going to be intense, and we will probably have to personally kill some Caishan slavers in order to free the slaves. Are you both sure that you're on board with this?"

His friends both nodded solemnly.

Charles had a look of grim determination on his face. "We'll have to use force to rescue the captives. I'm okay with this plan."

As Jack expected, he was able to walk right into the cave with no problems. The guard did not closely examine anyone. The way the man halfheartedly glanced at people entering the cave made Jack suspect that anyone possessing the Caishan seal could probably pass freely.

Jack pushed deeper into the cave. A side passage immediately off to the left seemed to function as the base's armory. Farther in and to the right, a couple smaller passages connected to a large room, where the majority of the soldiers bunked. A smaller room deeper in on the right served as the kitchen. About four feet up the kitchen wall, a two-and-a-half-foot-diameter corkscrew passage led to the outside. This hole conveniently served as a chimney.

Opposite the kitchen on the left side, a large passage stretched a good way back and dead-ended. The slaves were all chained there, lined up all the way to the back of the passage. Past the slave holding passage and kitchen, the main passage opened up into a large room with a table that seated about twenty. A large ornately decorated chair stood at the head of the table. The whole room, in fact, possessed a good deal of decoration for a cave. A few paintings hung on the walls and a brightly colored cloth draped over some wooden pegs like a tapestry. Jack thought, *The man in the black helmet must really fancy himself to be kinglike with a room like this.* Six guards stood at attention in front of a narrow passage opening off of the decorated room's right side. *That must be where he keeps his valuable possessions,* thought Jack.

The first night, obtaining two plates of food was easy. The cook did not even look at people as he served them. All Jack had to do was go through the line twice. People lined almost every passage in the cavern.

As Jack left the cave, the entrance guard stopped him. "What are you doing with all that food?" the guard asked.

Jack hesitated for a second and replied, "I met a girl who lives across the creek south of here. I discovered that I could make it there and back before my shift starts at midnight."

The guard crossed his arms. "I see. You're one of those romantics who think you should give presents to a woman to win her heart. Let me give you some advice, kid. As soon as hostilities die down a little around here, most of us will get shipped out to other job sites in other countries. When you've been around as long as I have, you'll find it's easier just to abduct the girl and take her here than it is to win her heart. But you go on, kid; you'll learn."

Jack walked down to the smaller cave thinking, *Well, I guess I won't expect to get an invitation to his wedding.* It disgusted him. These people thought they could take whatever they wanted without consequences. Consequences, however, were on their way.

As Jack had hoped, he caught sight of a man sneaking out of the cavern behind him on the third night. *That must be the Bendel spy,* Jack reasoned. Jack scouted regularly around the cave. His plan would require some good timing, and he had to make sure that he was ready when the Bendel attacked.

******

After Jack left the small cave in which they kept their prisoner, Charles scanned the dark forest for danger yet again then stared up into the night sky through the cave entrance. Ben seemed about to go stir crazy in this cave under forced silence, but Charles was content with the quiet. He liked to have time to think. Charles was the careful one in the group, and he appreciated having an opportunity to examine situations from every possible angle. He marveled at how frequently Ben could shoot from the hip and actually hit his target.

Occasionally, kids at school had called Charles 'Jack's henchman' because he had the physique of a bouncer and the devotion of a subject. Charles, however, knew that his role was far more critical than one who simply carried out orders. Among the trio Charles was the rock of stability. What Ben might do at any given moment was anyone's guess, and Jack was a visionary and an idealist. Charles, in contrast, was an anchor. He was practical and consistent.

Whenever Jack set out to reach a lofty goal, Charles saw it as his duty to think of potential complications and bring those up for discussion. When they were growing up, Charles rarely experienced any type of power struggle with Jack. Instead, Charles usually encouraged Jack's leadership. He preferred to watch Jack's and Ben's backs rather than bask in the limelight. Jack and Ben, in turn, could boldly step out and take risks because they knew they could count on Charles to be in just the right place at just the right time. Although the long hours of waiting dragged on, Charles knew that he had to remain vigilant so that when the time for action came, he would be ready.

******

On the fifth day while scouting, Jack found several small groups of men camping in the woods. They were not using tents or fires. *It's finally time*, thought Jack. He rushed back to tell his friends.

Jack stepped into the cave where his friends and their captive resided. He tried to make his voice sound low and raspy so that the Bendel officer would not be able to recognize his voice if he heard it later. "I don't like this. Something is going on out there. Grab the captive, and bring him. We'll hide him with the slaves."

Overtaken by Destiny

They led, prodded, and half-dragged the tied, gagged, and hooded Bendel officer directly above where the kitchen inside the main cave was located. Ben and Charles waited with him there. This was the only other way in and out of the cave other than the main entrance. Jack predicted that if the base came under attack, the Caishan would choose to fight the battle on open ground in front of the cave. This strategy made sense because the Caishan, being a secretive group, would have important locations and plans for the organization inside the base. The cave also contained valuable items that they had stolen from all over the countryside.

About an hour later Jack rushed into the cave's main entrance and informed everyone there that he had just returned from a scouting mission, and enemies were camped throughout the woods below the cave.

Word spread quickly, and the Caishan dispatched several scouts to collect information about the enemy force's size and troop movements.

In the confusion that ensued, Jack managed to reach the kitchen.

The kitchen was empty; most of the soldiers gathered around the armory or front entrance.

Jack and his friends had no trouble getting their captive down through the hole in the kitchen wall.

Ben and Charles followed him down into the kitchen.

Jack peeked around the corner into the hallway. Several men bustled about, but only two looked directly in their direction. Jack gestured with his hands to Ben and Charles, telling them to take the captive across the hall when the coast was clear.

Jack approached and walked just past the two men. He then turned around and asked them, "Have either of you seen a short, stocky man come through here? He's supposed to be carrying maps of the surrounding area to the main room."

The two men turned to face him.

One of the men shook his head. "We haven't seen anyone with maps."

When the two soldiers turned away, Ben and Charles dragged their captive across the hall to the slave passage.

"Fine, thanks anyway," Jack said to the soldiers.

Jack joined his friends as they quietly chained their captive to the wall. They waited a few minutes in silence, trying to casually lean against the wall.

The two guards in charge of the slaves paid no attention to them and busily discussed who might be outside the cave.

A horn blew, and the hall outside erupted into a flurry of activity.

Jack thought, *One or two of the scouts must have confirmed an enemy presence outside the camp. Now to deal with the two guards here ... .*

Jack nodded to Ben and Charles and walked straight past the two slave guards, who now debated what they should do with the slaves. This time, Jack turned and sharply ordered the guards to attention.

Both guards spun crisply and faced him. Then they furrowed their brows and exchanged glances as if trying to determine Jack's rank.

Ben and Charles crept up behind the guards. Ben stabbed his guard in the back, and Charles smashed his guard over the back of the head with the flat part of his blade.

Jack grabbed the keys from one of the guards' belts.

They relocated their Bendel prisoner to the passage's farthest end out of earshot of the main hallway so he would not understand who freed the slaves.

Jack glanced into the main passage. "Okay, you two unchain the slaves. I'll keep a lookout."

By now the Caishan had filed out of the cave in ranks and prepared to do battle on the hillside just as Jack expected. A messenger ran down the hall toward the main room, and Jack heard him yelling orders from the front to evacuate the slaves and valuables. It took several minutes for the guards in the main room to collect everything of value and start transporting it toward the main entrance.

Jack turned around. All the slaves were now free and huddled together behind Ben and Charles.

Jack said, "Ben and Charles, you should probably go over against the wall." Jack turned and glanced down the hallway again.

The guards were coming, dragging a large cart full of the valuables they were supposed to save.

Jack knew his timing would have to be perfect. He turned back to the slaves. "Okay, directly across the hall is a room with a hole leading to the outside. When I say 'go,' I want all of you to run straight across the hall. There are going to be a few men and a cart full of stuff there. Ignore the men—just get them out of the way—and everyone grab one thing from the cart. Don't get greedy or try to choose something. Just grab one random thing as you run by. I also need five men to volunteer to go out last."

Five men raised their hands.

"All right, good." Jack continued, "You five are in charge of getting the smaller children up and out of the hole. I need all the smaller children in the back of the group so they don't get trampled. If the young kids have mothers here, the mothers can stay back with them. The remaining men other than these five will lead the way." Jack turned back and peeked down the hall again as the slaves arranged themselves.

The guards were almost there.

Jack stepped back out of the way. "Go!"

One of the guards in the hallway gave a cry that was barely audible over the pounding of feet from three hundred slaves. Then his cry was silenced as the slavers were literally trampled to death.

Jack pressed his body against the cave wall as the slaves streamed past him. "Ben and Charles, you two cover the passage coming from the main room. Make sure no guards come up and start killing slaves. I'll take the passage that leads to the main entrance."

The three stepped into the hall, which was full of slaves. The kitchen had not been large enough for all of them to fit inside at one time.

"Just keep going steadily and be patient; wait your turn," called Jack. To Ben and Charles he said, "I suspect we have about twenty minutes before we encounter serious resistance. There shouldn't be more than half a dozen men left in the main room and probably about the same number at the main entrance. Until someone notices that the treasure is running late, no one should come check on things here. I hope that the battle will keep everyone focused on what's happening in front of the cave."

After about ten minutes Jack heard shouts coming from the hallway near the main room. Then there was a clanging of weapons followed by silence. *It sounds like Ben and Charles had a little excitement,* he thought.

More time passed. It seemed like hours to Jack as he waited in the hall for someone to discover his plot, but Jack knew that it was more like another ten minutes. All of the remaining slaves fit in the kitchen now. It looked like about fifty people, but these were the small children. Jack hoped this would not slow things down too much.

Ben and Charles now joined Jack. They all fell back to the shadows just outside the kitchen's entrance.

Jack saw several men coming from the cave's entrance. "Get ready, you two," he whispered. "We're going to have to stall these guys for a few minutes."

Just then, Jack recognized the man in the dark helmet.

The Caishan officer had three men with him. He stopped cold when he saw and recognized Jack. His face turned red. "What are you doing here? And in a Caishan uniform!"

"New recruit, sir." Jack cast him a sideways smile. "I was just escorting the slaves and treasure out of here."

The man's mouth twitched. "You have something to do with this, don't you? You are a Bendel spy." He ordered his men, "Kill the other two, but the middle one is mine. You should know better, kid. You don't challenge Delger the Cruel."

"Wow," Jack replied in a mocking tone, "You must've really worked hard to get a title like that."

Delger squared his shoulders and lifted his chin. "It's the title that goes with a Caishan of my rank."

Delger and Jack moved closer to each other, circling.

Jack thought, *What a weird organization that dubs its commanders 'Whoever-another the Cruel' instead of something like 'Captain.'* Jack's Caishan shield felt slow and clumsy, and he suspected that Delger the Cruel was skilled with both his sword and shield. Jack would have to come up with an out-of-the-box idea to best him.

Delger swung his sword.

Jack deflected the blow with his shield.

They exchanged three more rapid blows, but neither weapon came close to hitting its target.

"You're very slow with your shield," remarked Delger. "What a pity. I had hoped you would make a better opponent than this."

Jack tried to focus to drown out the clanging of swords near him.

Charles had adapted quickly to his shield. He used it as a battering ram to knock one of his opponents to the ground, but he had his hands full with the other soldier.

Ben seemed to be experiencing a similar shield problem as Jack. The shield was large and clumsy to him, and these soldiers were more skilled than many of the others they had faced previously.

Jack tried to push with his shield and bring the rim up to block his opponent's vision.

The strategy partially worked, but Delger managed to move to the side at the last second. Delger countered with his own shield, forcing Jack's sword hand back. He kicked Jack's shield to the side. With a quick follow-up attack, he knocked Jack's shield out of his hand and shoved with his own shield, throwing Jack against the wall.

Charles pushed one of his own opponents back, grabbed Jack, and hurled him across the hall out of Delger's immediate range and into Ben's opponent.

Ben quickly took advantage of his opponent's weakness and moved in, stabbing him in the gut.

Jack barely had a second to recover before Delger was on him again.

Delger grinned maliciously as he thrust his shield forward again.

This time, Jack jumped aside and saw Charles pinned between his two opponents. Ben was already on his way to help Charles, but it was too late.

One of the men's swords slipped past Charles's shield.

Charles jumped back to avoid the thrust.

The slaver swung his sword down toward Charles's head.

Charles saw the attack coming but could not dodge in time. He kicked his attacker in the leg, throwing his opponent off balance.

The man's sword came down, but because he was off balance, the blade turned. The flat of the blade struck Charles's forehead.

Jack saw blood trickle down Charles's face from the gash on his head. Charles stumbled backward and gasped for air.

Charles's other opponent easily knocked Charles's shield aside and swung toward his head.

Ben caught the soldier's weapon with his own sword.

Charles was now too dazed to fight effectively, and it was two on one for Ben. Jack had to somehow beat his opponent, or it was all over.

Delger let loose with a flurry of sword strikes then lifted his shield straight up and swung it down.

Jack jumped backward and out of the way. *This is ridiculous,* thought Jack. *I have one weapon, and he has two. Maybe I could pick up a shield, but I don't think it would do me much good.* Then Jack saw Charles's sword lying on the ground. Jack jumped to the wall, leaping and rolling past Delger.

As Jack grabbed the sword, one of Ben's opponents turned to face him.

While still on the ground, Jack rolled onto his back and swung both swords at the man's legs.

His opponent deflected one with his own sword, but his shield was too slow. The man yelled in pain as he dropped to the ground.

Jack finished him with one swift blow and leapt to his feet, deflecting another attack from Delger. Jack smiled; this felt better. He let loose with a flurry of attacks.

Delger stepped back, and his eyebrows lifted in surprise.

Jack moved in and attacked with frightening speed. He swung his right sword high and his left sword low.

Delger deflected the blows and prepared to counterattack.

Jack swung both swords downward toward Delger's head.

Delger raised his shield and sword to block, but Jack's swords were not his primary attack.

With his opponent's weapons in the air above his head, Jack drove a front kick directly into Delger's chest, knocking him backward into the wall. Jack closed the distance between them and swung his right sword at the edge of Delger's shield. The shield swung outward. Jack struck the shield's back with his second sword.

The shield flew out of Delger's hand and clattered to the floor. Fear now gripped the cruel man's features.

Jack pressed in with a rapid series of attacks.

On the fourth block, Delger was too slow.

Jack's sword bit into his opponent's shoulder.

Delger gave a cry and tried to run at Jack with one final attack.

Jack shifted his weight and swung his right sword with all his might, taking Delger's head off in one swing.

As blood spread across the hallway floor, Jack turned to see Ben finish off his own opponent.

"Quick," said Jack, "grab Charles! Let's get out of here."

They rushed to the kitchen, supporting Charles, who was still dazed.

Fortunately, one of the freed slaves had stayed behind at the top of the hole to wait for them. "Hand him up to me," he called.

Jack and Ben lifted their huge friend, and the three of them managed to pull Charles out of the cave.

"What are you still doing here?" asked Jack when they were all safely at the top.

The man grinned. "I just had a feeling that you might need something, and since you just saved my life, I figured I owed you one."

The man was a little smaller than Charles but broad shouldered and thick necked. He had a dark tan that must have been earned through hours in the sun.

They bandaged Charles's head as well as they could and helped him away from the battle taking place below in the valley.

Charles's wound was not as severe as it had initially looked. After a few more minutes, he was more aware and able to walk around with only minor assistance.

"I think he just got a concussion," observed Jack. "He should be a lot better in a day or two."

The group guided Charles away from the battle's remnants before stopping to rest.

"So, what's your name, and where are you headed?" Jack asked the man who had joined them.

"My name is Fenha," he replied. "I left my home to try to help some family members living in the city of Xin. My relatives were being threatened by a group of men trying to force everyone in the city to pay a religious tax. A temple was built there to the demon god, Gultten, and the priests bribed the governor to allow them to collect religious taxes. People who refuse to pay have their property seized or animals taken to the temple and sacrificed to Gultten.

"My relatives were particularly worried because servants of Gultten have been known to escalate their activities and start demanding human sacrifices once they gain enough power. The Gultten priests apparently also bribed the local Caishan officer. When I arrived with a group of other people from our country, all interested in preventing the spread of this religion, the Caishan abducted us and sent us to this place."

"Where do you live?" asked Jack.

"My son and I live outside a small village near the town of Gredune. I own an orchard there."

Surprised, Jack asked, "How old is your son?"

"He's twelve."

"Interesting ... I think we met him," said Jack. "I suppose you'll head back to him since you have been gone so long."

"I should, but I still don't know what to do about my family. My sister and her husband in Xin also need my help."

Jack informed his comrades about what Fenha had just told him.

Ben responded, "If these people sell slaves and collect money from locals, they must have some wealth. Remember, we are trying to earn money to get home. Since these guys don't deserve it, I say that it would almost be a crime not to commandeer some of their ill-gotten booty for ourselves." He chuckled. "After all, even though we relieved the Caishan cartel of a huge amount of wealth, I think we were the only ones who didn't get anything."

"I know," said Jack. "But you have to admit, it was awesome. We conquered the enemy, freed the slaves, and stole everything of value from the cave."

"And somehow we're still poor." Ben smiled.

"True, but the most important thing is that we freed the slaves. Fenha," Jack continued, turning back in the recently freed man's direction, "We'll take care of these Gultten priests."

Fenha's eyes grew large. He stammered, "But ... why?"

"Let's just say we have a score to settle with them. Any chance your relatives could put us up while we are in Xin?"

"Yes, absolutely," replied Fenha. "I'll write a letter for you to carry that explains the situation."

"One more thing," asked Jack, "where is Xin, and how do we get there?"

Chapter 6

THE THREE BOYS STAYED at Hal's house for a couple days while Charles recovered and they resupplied.

Jack frequently sat in the library reading the book Hal had lent him. As he read now, the book seemed to have meaning; in fact, he could understand more of the language every day. The letters on the page almost seemed to change as he read. He also tried speaking the words aloud.

"I see you're making progress," said Hal.

Jack looked up, startled. He had not heard Hal enter. "Yes," Jack replied, "it makes more sense now, but I still don't understand all of the words."

Hal examined the bookshelf as if seeking a particular title. "It is an ancient language with no name. In fact, it cannot be read without a translation stone. It's believed to be the language of the makers of gemstones. Ancient texts are rumored to still exist that tell stories from the beginning of time, but I've never had an opportunity to read one of these. A few other records from long ago not written in this language, however, tell of a great war some two thousand years ago. Apparently, mages became so powerful that when war broke out, they almost destroyed the world. Anyway, my point is that the ancient language, or the 'tongue of angels' as it is also called, takes time to understand. It cannot be taught by one who already knows the language. It must be learned by studying a book like the one I gave you."

"This book must be worth a great deal," said Jack.

"Yes, it is. Hundreds of them exist, but they are rare and expensive, nonetheless."

"Thank you. Without this I wouldn't be able to learn anything about the circumstances involved in our arrival here. I'm not sure if learning how to use the gemstones will help us get home, but it's possible."

"Yes," said Hal. "There are many gemstones. I don't believe anyone knows how to use all of them, and it's possible that there are some that no one knows how to use. Why don't you keep it?"

"Keep what?" Jack asked, confused.

"The book," Hal said, employing his usual abruptness. "It will take you a long time to master this language. I consider this a small price to pay for the peace that you have brought to our people."

"Thank you," Jack said, honored by Hal's gesture. Jack paused for a moment before changing the subject. "May I ask you another question about the translation stone?"

"If you wish." Hal did not look up from the book he now perused.

Jack asked tentatively, "I've heard of an iconic blood mage with a translation stone who can tell if someone else has a translation stone, but I'm not exactly sure how it works."

Hal scratched his chin. "Yes, it's actually a rather rare skill because, as far as I know, I've never met anyone who teaches it. It seems more like something that you develop after years of experience. Most mages don't need to figure out how to not use their translation stone because they can just separate the stone from themselves, but a blood mage cannot do that. Elton is very good at controlling his stone's use, probably because he's talked to so many diverse people of different languages. Because he's a blood mage, he isn't able to simply set down his stone."

"I see," Jack replied. "First, you have to figure out how to *not* use your translation stone when speaking with someone. Then you have to simply see if you can understand them after you have turned off your stone." Jack thought for a moment. "So in order to do this, I have to figure out how to speak without using my translation stone."

"That's just a guess." Hal shrugged. "But it seems to make sense to me."

Jack leaned back in his chair. "It's been two days. We plan to leave in the morning. Thank you again."

"Don't thank me," Hal replied. "Apparently, I run one of the safest regions for quite a distance, and it's because three young men showed up at my door one day. I still don't entirely understand what you did, and I don't want to, but it worked. That's good enough for me."

******

The next morning the boys departed after trading their weapons and shields for equipment not bearing an insignia. Jack now carried two swords rather than a sword and shield.

"I hope we brought enough food," said Ben. "We have quite a bit of walking to do. After all, this job you signed us up for is across the border."

"Yeah, I didn't exactly know that at the time." Jack adjusted his new swords on his belt. "Besides, this was partially your idea."

Ben lifted his backpack and slung it across his shoulders, grimacing in mock discomfort. "I think on the last hike we should've made the prisoner carry my bag. I would have made an argument on the subject then except that we weren't allowed to talk."

Charles raised an eyebrow. "The prisoner was blindfolded and had his hands tied behind his back."

Ben shrugged. "So?"

Jack studied the map he carried of Vergill and the surrounding countries. Xin was just across the border in the country of Kliptun. Jack tried to focus on the map as Ben continued to chat.

Ben said, "Charles, I noticed that back in the cave you didn't kill one of the guys guarding the slaves. You hit him with the flat part of your blade, didn't you?"

"Well," Charles replied, "he had his back to me, and it seemed different from killing someone who is trying to kill me. I don't want to kill anyone unless I have no other choice."

Jack stopped studying the map; the conversation now intrigued him. "I pretty much agree with that, Charles, but it seems like I should feel guiltier than I do because of the things I've done since I came here. I hope I'm not broken, like I don't have a conscience."

Ben said, "When I fight, I just feel alive, and it's fun ... not the killing, just the intensity of the moment. I get that awesome adrenaline rush. It's amazing."

"Don't worry, Jack," Charles said, "you're definitely not broken; you're just doing what needs to be done. But Ben, I'm not sure about him."

The three laughed.

It felt good to laugh together. It had not been all that long since the three of them became stranded here, but Jack felt like it had been forever.

The hours of traveling to Kliptun turned into days until they finally stood outside the city of Xin. The city was larger than Gredune, and it had a crude stone wall about ten feet tall built around it. There were also four gatehouses, one each facing north, south, east, and west. The gatehouses were about fifteen feet tall and contained two guards each. Additional guards patrolled the walls. The primary purpose of the relatively short walls seemed to be simply keeping out bandits and rogue slavers. If an actual army arrived, Jack doubted the city would hold out for more than an hour. The city gates remained open during the day, allowing people to pass in and out as they pleased.

The city's southern and western portions were filled with narrow streets and cottages all clustered closely together. The eastern side was filled with shops and merchants, and the northern district was where the governor's mansion and all the other important structures in the town stood. The newly constructed stone temple was in the northern section along with a few old buildings that looked as though they once had significance. The guard post was also in the northern section, along with two large buildings that functioned like barracks for the town guard.

The boys had no trouble following Fenha's directions to his relatives' house. The house was located on the city's southern side.

Jack knocked on the cottage door and heard stirring inside the house.

A man of about thirty opened the door. He held a long knife in a threatening posture. The man's hand looked callused and rough, and he had sun-bleached blond hair that hung just past his ears. He was a little shorter than Jack with muscles that appeared to have been earned through hours of hard labor. The man pointed the blade toward them. "What do you want?"

Jack calmly extended his hand with the letter from Fenha. "This will make our purpose clear."

The man looked suspicious, but he took the letter and read it without taking his eyes off of his visitors for more than a few seconds at a time. "How do I know you didn't force Fenha to write this letter?"

"Oh my, I'm afraid you caught us," said Jack. "Since the three of us were unable to overpower one man with a knife, we kidnapped another man, transported him to another country, forced him to write a letter of introduction, and then used that letter to infiltrate the home of his relatives."

The man smiled and lowered his knife. "I think I like you. My name is Hrot. Please come in." He led them through the entryway into a large main room. Only a partial wall separated this room from the kitchen. Hrot gestured toward a woman in the kitchen. "This is my wife, Fenta."

Fenta did not closely resemble her brother. She had light red hair down to her shoulders and fair skin. Her soft eyes and small delicate mouth made her appear naturally trusting. Like Hrot, she seemed to be about thirty and was dressed in plain clothes. She looked at them curiously as she wiped her flour-covered hands on her white apron.

Jack inhaled deeply as the aroma of baking bread wafted toward them from behind her. Jack introduced himself and his friends.

Ben and Charles simply nodded when they heard their names mentioned.

"I'm afraid my friends don't speak the language," Jack explained, "but such a thing is not necessary for our task here."

Hrot said, "My brother-in-law simply wrote that he sent you here to deal with the city's problems. What is it that you do exactly?"

Jack smiled. "As far as anyone in this town is concerned, we are simply friends visiting. This should cover the expenses that you may incur because of our presence." Jack reached into his cloak, pulled out a small sack of coin, and handed it to their host.

Hrot felt the weight of the pouch. "How long do you plan to stay?"

"Hopefully, not very long," Jack assured him. "As for what your brother mentioned, it's better that you don't know about such things. We'll do our best to stay out of your way. If you have a room where we can stay, it would be appreciated."

Hrot gestured toward the main room. "We don't have any kind of furniture to assist with your sleeping arrangements, but you're welcome to the floor."

Fenta stepped over to the table and placed one of their two chairs there before saying, "You can put your belongings here in the corner."

A small stone chimney stood behind the table, and the three boys sat down on the hearth.

Their host invited the travelers to join them for the evening meal, which the boys gratefully accepted.

The boys enjoyed some vegetable stew and freshly baked bread.

With the aid of Jack's translation, Charles politely observed that the vegetables seemed very fresh.

Hrot replied, "I work as a farmhand on a large farm outside the city, and a portion of my pay comes in the form of produce."

Hrot and Fenta were gracious hosts, and the three young men felt at home despite their meager accommodations.

******

The next morning Jack asked Charles to explore the area outside the city walls and sent Ben to explore the town itself. "I'll go to the temple in the northern district and see for myself how big of a problem this is going to be."

Jack strode down the street to the northern district. The houses on either side of the street were of a Tudor construction. The large timber frame pieces had an adobe spread between them to form a hard, dry mud wall. Jack could tell that the quality of the homes and cleanliness of the streets improved the closer he came to the northern district. *It's humorous,* he thought, *how people actually consider streets in American cities to be dirty. Come to a place like this, and your entire perspective changes.* The street now consisted of a crude cobblestone with packed dirt between the stones, and the town apparently even had people who were supposed to remove manure from and maintain the streets because Jack passed two of them on his way. The roads were busy with other people on foot and horseback.

When he arrived in the northern district, Jack walked directly to the temple. The building was a simple rectangular structure formed from stone blocks. Steep stairs about ten feet wide without rails led up to the temple entrance.

Inside the temple, there were no chairs, only mats, and people knelt on the mats chanting quietly. Many candles burned around the room's edges, and on first glance the scene did not even seem all that unusual. Jack thought the structure resembled buildings and temples that he had seen in pictures of ancient Greece. Decorative tapestries hung on some of the walls and two large stone columns rose near the room's center. The front wall had once been very thick, but large quantities of it had been chipped away to form a great bear-like head protruding toward the worshipers.

The stone alter in front of the head had a recess carved out of it. The depression was about eight feet in diameter and two feet deep with chains embedded in the stone along its edges. *Man, this is creepy,* thought Jack. *Well, what did I expect? Fenha said these people escalate their game until they're conducting human sacrifices, so of course it should be creepy.*

A student in Jack's school had asked him once in debate class what made one religion better than another. At the time Jack had not really known how to respond, but at this moment, basic morality seemed to be a good place to start.

Several priests walked in wearing orange, robe-style cloaks with yellow hems and collars. They talked excitedly in hushed tones.

Jack held his breath to hear the conversation.

One priest said, "I hear the great coopa is coming to this temple in order to declare it officially holy to Gultten."

The other priest responded, "Yes, his envoy arrived yesterday, and he read from a book here in the temple. Listening to him read in the tongue of angels was amazing. I understand he's staying in the most prestigious inn here in the city's northern section."

That's fantastic, thought Jack. *What a find. That means the envoy has a translation stone. Ben and Charles will be overjoyed.*

The priests walked up to the front and clapped their hands twice to gather the worshipers' attention.

"Everyone!" one of them called. "In preparation for the great coopa's arrival, the temple will close for two days while we prepare it to become even more holy."

As Jack hurried back to their hosts' house, he went over in his mind how to steal that stone.

Back at the house, Jack patiently listened to Charles's report of Xin's outside. Major landmarks included a very rocky area to the west that would be good for ambushing someone coming down the west road. Trees lined the northern road for miles.

"I didn't find any particularly easy ways in or out of the city," Charles said, "but the walls are short and have few guards. As long as they don't increase the number of guards, it shouldn't be particularly difficult to climb the wall and leave undetected if necessary."

Ben explained that he found what appeared to be slave cartel members with a different seal than either the Caishan or Bendel cartels going in and out of an official-looking building near the temple.

"We only know of one other major slave cartel," said Jack, "so you must have found members of the Zangan cartel."

"Yeah, probably," replied Ben. "I checked out the governor's house too, and it looks a lot like the other buildings around here, just a good bit larger. Pretty much all of the buildings in the northern district are much nicer than the cottages around the city. Some of the cottages look like mud splattered on a wooden frame, but the buildings in the northern district actually look nice. Oh, and there was an inn in the northern section that seemed to cater toward a wealthy type of clientele.

"I also scouted the eastern section of town. That area seems to be mostly merchants, and the streets are wider, so there's plenty of room for carts on either side of the road. Lots of people were buying and selling goods. Some of the merchants seemed to live in the city. Others, I suspect, travel like Elton's caravan. That section of town had a lot more activity as well."

Jack leaned forward. "I'm particularly interested in the prestigious inn in the northern section."

"It's like a high-end bar or pub that allows people to sleep upstairs," Ben explained. "I only saw wealthy-looking people go upstairs, but from the appearance of the people I saw inside, I think anyone is allowed to drink there. It also provides meals for the people who stay there, and I think anyone can order food."

"Excellent." Jack told his two friends about the traveling priest and his translation stone. "Is there a lot of security, Ben?"

"Not at all," Ben replied. "It's just a business. There's one big guy, who is sort of like a bouncer. If you start a fight, he'll probably throw you out."

Jack could tell that Ben and Charles were even more excited than he was about the translation stone.

The three traveled immediately to the northern district. They passed a barracks for the town guard and could see the temple spires behind it.

As they continued on, Ben pointed to a building on the left. "This is where I saw the Zangan members hanging out, and that's the symbol they wore there on the hitching post."

The Zangan seal was a ship with its sails unfurled.

Continuing on, they arrived at the inn.

Jack said, "I'm going to go inside to see if I can identify the priest and determine which room is his. I'll also watch him speak and try to determine if he has the translation stone on him or keeps it in his room. This may take some time. Why don't you guys meet me back here after you get some food?"

Inside the inn, Jack ordered food from the innkeeper. Apparently, they only served one dish. Jack glanced around the room and saw four rows of three tables each. An assortment of benches and chairs surrounded the tables. The tables only had four occupants, two of whom sat together talking in hushed tones.

Colorful stones set in the walls formed mosaics depicting picturesque images. One of these scenes portrayed a mountain range, and Jack wondered if a traveling artist had designed the work since the land in this area was relatively flat.

Jack waited about an hour until a priest entered. He wore an orange cloak with a blue collar and hem. Although the priests Jack had seen earlier possessed different color hems, they wore the same style orange cloak as this man.

The priest sat down and ordered a drink.

Jack was fairly certain that the priest was not using his translation stone to speak, because there were now a few travelers in the inn talking about him. He either did not want any trouble or did not understand what they said.

After another fifteen minutes or so, the priest stood and went upstairs.

Jack followed quietly behind him and saw him enter the second room on the left. Jack casually walked back downstairs and outside the inn.

On the way back to Hrot's house, he relayed all that he had seen to his friends. "Tomorrow night," he concluded, "we'll sneak into his room, get the gemstone, and search for information on this coopa guy."

******

The next day Ben and Charles went out again to explore.

While they were gone, Jack studied his book. For the first time he could understand whole paragraphs at a time. The first paragraph he could fully understand was for lesser stones of earth, which let one create soil and rock. Jack read aloud the words for awakening the lesser earth stone, but he could not seem to make the magic work. *Perhaps I don't have a lesser earth stone,* thought Jack.

At this point Jack realized that the section he had been studying was actually two separate awakenings. Realizing that the page contained two distinct paragraphs, Jack focused on the second segment. This awakening was for a lesser stone of air. This time, Jack repeated the awakening words for a lesser air stone.

He stood, extended his hand and said, "Air," while trying to imagine air.

Nothing seemed to happen.

He wondered, *How would I even know if I've created air?* He imagined air moving toward the table in front of him.

He felt a strong breeze. The table suddenly lifted a few inches off the floor, flew across the room, and crashed into the far wall, throwing his book to the floor.

Shocked, Jack dropped his hand, ran to the table, and inspected it for damage. Finding none, he thought, *I should probably practice these outside from now on. This is incredible, though. I can pull air to me or push it away, essentially creating wind.*

After returning the table to its original location, Jack returned his attention to the book and turned the page. The next page contained many words that he did not recognize, although he knew some of them. *Fascinating,* he thought, *the translation stone is teaching me this tongue of angels. Before too long I'll be able to read the whole book with no problem.*

Jack apparently studied for hours because around midafternoon Ben and Charles returned.

"Are we ready to get that translation stone?" Charles asked excitedly.

"Of course I'm ready," replied Jack. He wondered if he should tell them about awakening his stone, but he thought, *It will be more fun to let it be a surprise, and I need more practice before I can demonstrate it.*

They headed toward the inn. Once there, Jack ordered some food for Ben to eat while he kept a lookout.

Jack and Charles went upstairs.

Wow, Jack thought as he turned the knob on the door to the priest's room, *it isn't even locked.*

The two stepped inside and searched for the stone. Only a few items in the room seemed to belong to the priest: a sack with clothes, some food, and a jug of water. They also found a leather binder full of parchments with a leather strap to keep it closed. The parchments included building designs for the temple and schedules for several different men.

Jack had brought some parchment and a quill, which he was woefully unskilled in using, to copy any interesting information. *How did people ever write anything with this stuff back in the Middle Ages?* he thought.

Charles fiddled with a container that resembled a jewelry box. As soon as he tried to open the box, however, it became clear that it was, in reality, a type of puzzle box. Charles was skilled in solving mechanical types of puzzles, and he had the box open in a few minutes. Inside was the translation stone.

Charles's face broke into a broad grin. "I want to call it Rosetta Stone."

Jack smiled. "Nobody here would have a clue what that means, and that has been way overdone in our world."

"I guess you're right, Jack. What should I do now?"

"Why don't you go back down and help Ben keep a lookout? If the priest comes back, you two can distract him. I need to copy as much of this information as I can. There are schedules for five different guys here, but 'coopa' is apparently a title, so I need to figure out which one of these people is coming and when he's going to get here."

"Okay, Jack. See you downstairs." Charles headed for the door.

******

Ben was impatiently picking at his food on the inn's ground floor when he saw Charles coming down the stairs.

Charles casually walked over and joined Ben at the table. "We got it," said Charles quietly, "but Jack is still trying to copy more information about the important guy who's coming."

"Why didn't Jack just take all the information so we could leave?"

"Because," replied Charles, "we want to make sure the priest doesn't realize he's been robbed. He kept the stone in a special locked box, and he probably doesn't open the box every night just to make sure it's still there. Most likely, the priest only uses it during special services, so he won't notice it's missing for days, maybe weeks."

After a while Ben began to wonder what was taking Jack so long. It had been close to ten minutes since Charles had come downstairs. He looked over at Charles, who also appeared nervous.

Then the inn's front door opened, and in walked the priest. He sauntered over to the innkeeper and asked him a few questions before heading toward the stairs.

Ben looked at Charles and held out his hand. "Give me the translation stone. I'll stall him until Jack is finished."

Charles nodded and handed him the stone.

Ben cringed for a moment because he could suddenly understand all of the conversations around him. Refusing to be distracted, he stood and walked directly to the priest.

"Hey, priest," Ben called. "Where I come from, we have great respect for you people."

The priest pursed his lips, looking annoyed. "Thank you," he said in a patronizing tone as he turned back toward the stairs.

"You don't understand," Ben continued, "It's considered good luck in my country to beat a priest at a drinking game. Won't you do me the honor of drinking with me? The governor and I drink here all the time, and he says you priests can hold your liquor like champions."

At the mention of the governor, the priest's ears twitched. "You have a room here at the inn?" The priest lifted his eyebrows and tilted his head up in surprise.

"Of course," replied Ben.

The priest hesitated for a moment as if trying to decide if this young man was important and whether he could risk offending him. "Fine," the priest finally said, "the first one to pass out loses. As the challenger I assume you're paying?"

Ben nodded confidently and turned to the establishment's owner. "Innkeeper, get us some beer. We will start with a mug each."

The two started drinking rapidly. As they drank their first mug, Ben was not sure if he could drink long enough to stall the priest. On the second mug, however, it became clear that he would not only delay the priest but also possibly even beat him.

On the third mug the priest started chattering happily about the glorious temple and how much time had been dedicated to constructing it. Apparently, he was in charge of the temple's construction.

As they drank, Ben discovered that the temple was a magnificent work of art, and these priests were not really such bad men—just a little different. After the fourth mug Ben realized that everyone in the inn was a great guy, so he bought a round for the house.

The priest, deeply moved by Ben's gesture, also bought a round for the house.

Ben and the priest moved on to discussing how glorious the city was and how funny the governor looked. When the sixth mug was down, the two decided to inform the world that the slave cartels were heathens and should start worshiping at the temple.

After the seventh mug, Ben was confused because the entire world became dark. Then he realized that he had just shut his eyes for a moment, and he laughed at his good fortune in discovering that he should not keep his eyes closed so long when blinking.

******

Charles was pale and felt sick. He had two untouched mugs of beer in front of him, which he was not sure why the bartender had brought him.

Ben and the priest were singing. Charles had not been able to understand much of the conversation that had taken place between them because he could only understand Ben, who was becoming rather incoherent. He hoped that Ben did not say anything that would give away their robbery.

Finally, Ben fell over, and the big guy who worked at the inn came over, picked him up, and threw him out the front door.

Charles was not sure whether it would look suspicious if he went out and checked on Ben or not.

As Charles deliberated, Jack came down the stairs.

The drunk priest stumbled up the stairs past Jack.

Jack came over to Charles and asked, "Where's Ben? Why is the priest so drunk?"

Charles replied somewhat tentatively, "Ben decided to stall him, so he somehow convinced the priest to drink with him. To be honest, I don't know much about what happened other than the innkeeper kept coming over and collecting money from both Ben and the priest, and they sat there drinking until Ben passed out."

Jack chuckled. "Well, Ben stalled him long enough. I got everything I needed. Let's go see if he's all right and get him home."

Charles took the translation stone out of Ben's pocket, and they picked him up and started carrying him back to Hrot and Fenta's house.

Chapter 7

CHARLES WOKE UP EARLY the next morning, but when he looked around, he saw Jack already up studying the documents that he had copied from the priest.

Ben, still sound asleep, snored loudly.

Fenta heard Charles stirring and called from the kitchen, "There's some food left over from last night on the table if you boys are hungry." She draped a plain woolen shawl over her shoulders. "I need to pick up some things from the market; I'll be back soon."

The rest of the house was empty. Charles assumed that Hrot was already out in the fields working.

Jack stopped reading and flipped through the pages in his hands.

Charles stood and looked over his friend's shoulder. "What are you looking for, Jack?"

"I'm trying to discern which one of these guy's schedules corresponds to the great coopa, but I believe I need to discover some portion of his schedule another way and compare that to these documents. My other option would be to discover who the priest calls the 'coopa' because he never refers to anyone in these documents by title, only by name.

"I'm also trying to determine when they're going to start human sacrifices and how they intend to get the people to sacrifice. Perhaps they planned to kidnap random people here in town, or maybe they're going

A Destiny Among Worlds

to buy slaves from the slave traders. If we're going to come against these guys, we need more detailed information."

"Yeah, you're right," said Charles. "Jack, are you going to need me for anything?"

"No, I'm just going to be sitting here studying, probably all day. Did you have something in mind?"

Charles shook his head. "No, I just wanted to leave for a few hours. I'm going to take the translation stone with me to see if I can understand the city better by reading signs and talking to people. When do you think Ben will wake up?"

Jack glanced at Ben's limp form. "I'd say Ben is going to be out for quite some time. If you find anything interesting while you're out and about, let me know."

"All right." Charles headed for the door.

Outside, Charles looked around at the small buildings. The street was quiet and mostly deserted. *Everyone must be at work now*, he thought.

Charles started walking although he was not really sure where he was going. He just wanted to think. *We all say we want to get home, but that doesn't seem to be what really drives Jack and Ben now*, he thought.

Charles wandered among the cottages in the city's southern and western areas. He lost track of time, but his stomach finally reminded to stop at an inn to eat. He turned north, meandering through the city in a general clockwise direction. His thoughts brought him back to his friends. *They seem happy here*, Charles thought.

Jack always excelled in developing plans, and although it rarely happened in America, he always seemed most alive when standing up for someone else. Ever since coming here, Jack seemed excited and vibrant. Even if Jack didn't realize it, he was in his element when fighting slave traders, rescuing people, and devising deep plans to baffle his enemies.

Ben also seemed happy. New experiences were one of his favorite things. What better place to try new things than in a whole new world?

All three of them enjoyed sparring with each other, but this fighting was different. Charles did feel invigorated when he fought, and he enjoyed helping people. It just seemed as though no matter what he did, all he could think of was home. Unlike Jack and Ben, nothing tied Charles to this world.

Charles looked up to discover merchant shops around him. All sorts of different food and clothing carts lined the street, and a cart selling weapons sat off to his left. He continued to wander on past a fortuneteller shop.

Charles noticed a girl to his right selling some sort of rings and bracelets, but something about this jewelry intrigued him. He walked over to get a closer look.

As he approached, the girl smiled and asked, "What kind of merchandise are you interested in?"

"Just looking," he murmured in reply.

Charles briefly examined the girl. She wore a simple shawl over a wool dress. Her clothing was overall very plain, so Charles guessed that she probably did not actually own the merchandise. Most of the merchants had at least one nice set of clothes to wear while selling.

Charles recalled Elton saying, "When selling to a customer, it's always important to make a good first impression. If merchants look poor, it must mean people don't buy much of their merchandise. If people don't buy much of their merchandise, there's probably a good reason."

Charles guessed that this young woman did not usually interact with customers, but he decided to peruse her wares anyway.

The girl had a bright smile that ended in dimples and a kind tone to her voice. She was about his age and had blond hair down to her waist. She was slim and a good bit shorter than him, but then again, so was almost everyone else. She had shining blue eyes and several light brown freckles on her cheeks. Her appearance reminded Charles of one of the popular girls in his class back home, except this girl seemed more quiet and shy.

Charles asked the salesgirl about the price of a couple different items. Then he asked how she obtained her merchandise.

The girl looked down and shuffled her feet a little. "These are gathered from soldiers who have fallen on battlefields all throughout the central realms."

Charles jerked his head up in surprise. "You gather the belongings of the dead on battlefields and resell them?"

The girl recoiled slightly and replied somewhat defensively, "There's no point in leaving the stuff there in the wild."

"I suppose you're right," said Charles. "It just seems like someone should send the belongings back to the soldiers' families."

The girl's features relaxed. "All the families of fallen soldiers would probably agree with you, but there is no way for that to happen."

Charles noticed a bracelet that appeared to have sockets for valuable stones, but the depressions were empty.

"What is this?" Charles asked.

"That's a mage's bracelet," answered the girl. "See the gaps for the gemstones? You can set three in this bracelet."

Jack would be very interested in this, thought Charles, *and we have a stone that, right now, I have to carry in my pocket. It may be beneficial to have such a bracelet.*

Charles asked how much the bracelet cost and purchased it. He slipped the bracelet on his wrist. It fit well. Without thinking, Charles pulled the translation stone out of his pocket to attach it to the bracelet.

The young woman gasped. "You're a mage! Please forgive me, my lord. I had no idea."

Charles was surprised for a moment, but then he thought, *Mages probably have the power and wealth to do whatever they want in this world.* The young men had not encountered a mage with a combat stone yet, but it made sense that the average peasant would fear mages.

"Don't worry. I'm not a real mage." Charles smiled reassuringly. "This is a translation stone. I'm just a foreigner."

The girl's expression changed from fear to curiosity. "Where are you from?"

Charles forced a laugh. "A place very far from here. I doubt you would have heard of it." He quickly changed the subject. "How do you mount the gemstone on the bracelet?"

She took the bracelet from him, and with dexterous fingers, lifted a thin metal bracket from each side of the bracelet, wrapped them over the gemstone, and secured them to one another on the band's underside before returning it to Charles.

Two rough-looking men approached the cart.

The girl looked down nervously again.

"What do you think of her?" asked one man.

The other shrugged. "I don't know." He looked at the girl and demanded, "How old are you?"

"Seventeen, my lord," she replied.

"Excellent," said the first man. "You'll be coming with us."

The girl shook her head. "Please forgive me, my lord, but my master will not allow me to leave the cart."

"So you're a slave?" the second man asked. "Even better. Where can we find your master?"

She pointed at a small building behind her.

"Good. Call him out," said the first man.

The girl went inside and came back out a few seconds later followed by an elderly gentleman with gray hair and a long gray beard. The man wore a brown, full-length cloak that looked like wool.

"What can I do for you?" asked the elderly man.

"We want to purchase your slave," said the first man. "Name a fair price."

The old man shook his head. "I'm sorry, but she's not for sale. She has been with me many years now, and I doubt that I could replace her."

"Do you defy servants of the demon god, Gultten?" The first slaver leaned forward menacingly. "They need this girl for the two-day ceremony taking place after the great coopa arrives."

The old man cringed then clenched his fists as anger flashed in his eyes. "You want to purchase my slave so you can sacrifice her to your god? I will not sell her to anyone—certainly not the likes of you."

The two thugs reached for their swords, and the first man said, "We'll just take her then."

Charles had stood by listening quietly, but now he took a step forward, reaching for his own sword. "Make this choice, and I will give your god two sacrifices this day."

The two men immediately halted as if startled by his declaration.

Even Charles was a little surprised by his statement.

The thugs glanced at each other then slowly removed their hands from their sword hilts. They studied Charles. He was definitely larger than them, and he had a sword on his hip and a well-used shield on his back. Apparently, the two decided not to trifle with someone who would fight back.

As they stalked away, the first man said, "Don't think this is the end of this."

The old man gave Charles a grateful smile. "Thank you, young man. But why did you stand in their way? Those men will be on the lookout for you for what you've done."

"Don't worry about me," said Charles. "I got more from those men than they did from me. He smiled and thought, *Now we know there's a two-day celebration taking place after the coopa arrives, and that is when they will perform the sacrifices.* "It was a pleasure to bump into you both." Charles turned to leave.

The old man raised his hand. "Wait a moment, young man. I need my slave to pick up some supplies from a merchant caravan just outside of town, and I'm afraid it's not safe with those ruffians about. I'd be willing to pay you a small fee to escort her to pick up my goods and bring them back here."

The girl's eyebrows raised, and she cast a sideways glance at her master. "I can do it myself. I'll be fine."

The old man smiled but otherwise ignored her. "What do you say, lad?"

"Fine," replied Charles. "I'm not in a hurry."

"Excellent then," said the old man. "You two better get going."

Charles and the girl set out at a brisk pace toward the nearest city gate.

Charles asked, "Well, what's your name anyway?"

"Vennel," replied the girl.

"And you're a slave?" asked Charles.

"Yes," she replied, "but old Dunnel treats me very well. He bought me when I was a child. The slave traders couldn't find a buyer for me because I was so young. As a result they were going to kill me. Dunnel, however, made them an offer, and I've been with him ever since."

"How did you become a slave?" Charles asked.

"The slave traders came and kidnapped me from my village in a faraway country. I don't even know which one."

"Will Dunnel free you when he dies?"

Vennel gave Charles a quizzical look. "No. It isn't legal anywhere to free a slave for any reason. When he dies, I can try to run, but anyone who finds me and discovers that I still bear the slave mark on my ankle will know that I belong to the Bendel cartel and send me back." Vennel pulled her shawl tightly around her and set her jaw. "I'll probably end up sold to some rich, greedy person like a warlord, and I'll have to do whatever pleases him. Slaves who don't do as they're told are tortured. Either that, or I'll be placed in a brothel somewhere. That's what happens to most slave girls my age." A glint of sunlight reflected off a tear in the corner of her eye. She angrily brushed the tear away. "Why do you ask so many questions?"

"I'm sorry," Charles nervously glanced down at his hands. He had been rather insensitive with his questions. *What can I say to comfort her?* he thought. "Look on the bright side," he finally said. "Maybe some kind person will come along and purchase you from Dunnel."

Vennel immediately calmed down, and her face lifted.

Charles realized that she had interpreted what he said to mean that he was offering to purchase her. No, no, that would not do at all. He did not want any ties to this place. Charles could just see himself returning to Hrot and Fenta's house and saying, "Hey, Jack, look what I picked up while I was out and about on the town. Oh, and by the way, I still plan on going home." *Yeah*, he thought, *that wouldn't be awkward at all.*

Vennel was apparently not daunted by his silence. "I would work really hard," she assured him. "I would do whatever you wanted. Surely an important person like you could use a good slave."

Charles felt a drop of sweat form on his forehead and roll down the side of his face. "I'm sorry, but I'm not an important person, and my friends would not be interested in adding another member to our group."

Vennel bit her lower lip. "You're saying you don't even care what happens to me?" Her eyes became misty.

Charles replied defensively, "Well, of course, I ... ." He stopped as he realized that she was manipulating him. "I'm sorry, but that isn't going to work on me. No more talking," he added somewhat harshly. Charles thought, *She was just trying to make me feel sorry for her.* He could not blame her. The horrible possibilities she had mentioned probably were her future. Charles felt terrible, but he told himself, *We can't save everyone.*

They picked up the supplies from the merchants outside of town, and carried the goods back to the old man.

Charles said farewell a little awkwardly and turned toward his current residence. *I'm glad I was able to help them in some small way,* he thought, *and that's all I could do.* As he walked, however, he found himself thinking about Vennel. He tried to shake off the thoughts. *Seriously, Charles, get your head on straight,* he told himself. *It's not like I could have a relationship with someone in this world, no matter how pretty she is. And she's a slave, so none of the countries would recognize a marriage between a free man and a slave.* Then he thought, *Whoa, she just wanted me to buy her; where did that marriage thing come from?*

Charles entered Hrot's house, where Hrot and his wife welcomed him.

Jack, still studying in the main room, looked up when Charles entered.

Charles surveyed the cottage. "What happened to Ben?"

"He woke up sometime around midafternoon, I think, complaining of a headache," said Jack, "so he took a walk." Jack's eyes narrowed as he looked at his friend. "Is something wrong, Charles?"

Charles was not really surprised anymore by Jack's uncanny ability to notice when he was bothered. He told Jack about his interactions with the slave girl and asked what Jack thought.

Jack was silent for a moment before saying, "I think you are a little wrong in your perspective on helping people. You're right that we can't save everyone, but we should be willing to save anyone we can. Even for people like these priests or the slavers, if we could change them for the better, then that would be a superior answer to killing them. As difficult as it is to see, there are some good people in this world just like in our world. Look at Hrot and his wife or Hal. If there are good people here, it means everyone in this world must have the same choice to be good or evil as do the people in our world. That means we should be able to help them. I just haven't figured out an effective way to save them yet."

"I know," said Charles. "That's exactly what I think."

"Ah," said Jack, "but you wanted to help her, and you rationalized your desire away by deciding that Ben and I would not approve. Part of that is good. We have to stick together, and it's important what the other group members think. But be honest; you like this girl, don't you?"

"Of course not. I just met her today!" said Charles defensively.

Jack placed his hand on Charles's arm. "Calm down. I didn't say you should go propose to her right now, but I think tomorrow morning you should head back out there and see if you still feel the same way as you did today. If so, even if you don't want a relationship with someone in this world, at the very least we should be able to find someone decent like Elton or Hal who would be willing to take her in if we make the purchase."

Charles thought for a moment and sighed. "You're right, Jack. I'll go out there tomorrow and see what happens."

"As for the information you got from the guards, it's good to have a rough idea of when they will make the sacrifices. That will help me plan our countermoves. It sounds likely that the human sacrifices could begin as soon as the day after the coopa arrives."

Charles lay down on his mat on the floor. He hadn't realized until now how tired he was, and he quickly went to sleep.

******

Charles awoke early the next morning. Again, Jack was already awake and studying his plan. Sometimes Charles wondered if Jack ever slept at all. Charles heard Hrot helping Fenta in the kitchen on his day off work.

"So, Jack, do you have a plan yet?" Charles asked.

"Yes, I do. According to the priest's documents, the coopa may arrive today. That means tomorrow or the next day should be when they start the sacrifices. I believe I have a way to take care of this quickly and quietly. My objective is to avoid getting the entire kingdom, all the slave cartels, and everyone who believes in this religion hunting us."

"Well, I'm taking your advice and heading back to the market district."

"Let me know how it goes," Jack said a little absently. "I would go with you, but I'm too busy with my work."

Charles left the house and breathed deeply of the early morning air. He felt uncharacteristically excited the nearer he came to the market district, but as Charles approached Dunnel's place of business, something seemed wrong. Vennel was not at the cart, and the door to the small building behind it was ajar.

Charles ran the last few steps to the door and entered. He heard a groan.

"Help," a raspy voice whispered.

Charles saw Dunnel lying on the ground. A pool of blood surrounded him. Charles quickly grabbed a piece of cloth and started tearing it into strips. "What happened?"

"Those men came back early this morning," Dunnel whispered. "I tried to stop them, but they took her. Leave me; I'm … going to die soon. You … must … rescue her."

"I can't leave you even if you're going to die. I have to at least try to save you."

"There's … no time," the old man said in a barely audible voice. "They said the sacrifices would … begin today. You must get to her before they sacrifice her. I am … old and have lived … a good life. My last wish is that she … could have the same."

Charles gripped the man's hand and nodded. "So be it."

He stormed out of the building and sprinted toward Hrot and Fenta's house. *I have to get her back*, he thought, *but I'll need Jack and Ben's help*. With every step Charles's blood seemed to boil. Rage filled him, and he burst through the door, startling Fenta.

Charles ignored her and went straight to Jack. "They *took* her, and they stabbed Dunnel!" he bellowed. "I'm going to kill them all!"

Ben furrowed his brow and looked from Charles to Jack and back to Charles. "What on earth are you ranting about? Who are these people?"

"They're people he met yesterday," said Jack. "Now I need you to calm down, Charles, and tell me exactly what happened."

"The men from the temple kidnapped Vennel," Charles said between breaths, "and they're going to sacrifice her today when the coopa arrives!"

Jack quickly stood. "The sacrifices are happening today?"

"Yes, today!" Charles repeated.

"I'm going to have to come up with a new plan," said Jack.

"We don't have time!" yelled Charles. "I have to save her—to go in there and smash their heads and make them pay right now! Jack, what's the plan? I need a plan right now!"

Jack held up his hands to quiet his friend. "You and Ben go to the temple and smash some heads. I'll be along soon."

"Wait a minute." Ben lifted a hand. "I'm going with Charles to the temple to attack people in retaliation for them kidnapping people I don't know, and Jack might have a plan to keep us all from getting killed? Am I making sense? This sounds rash even to me. Shouldn't we be worried about this?"

"Do it," said Jack, "and yes, it's a bit rash, but go."

"Okay." Ben shrugged. "I just wanted to make sure everyone knew that I am completely lost as to what's going on."

Jack grabbed Charles's shoulder as Charles started to turn. "One more question, Charles. You said Dunnel was still alive, right?"

"Yes, but not for much longer."

"Okay, you guys go."

Charles ran toward the temple so fast that Ben had trouble keeping up with him. Ben was normally the faster of the two, but Charles possessed great motivation. Charles did not know how many priests in the temple would be armed or whether they had guards. All of those questions just seemed like unnecessary details right now. Besides, Jack had said to go, so no matter what happened, Jack would figure something out.

Suddenly, the temple bells started ringing. That surely meant that the great coopa had arrived at the temple or possibly the city gate, Charles was not sure which, but either way, they were running out of time.

The temple loomed just ahead, and walking up the front steps was a short, fat man in an orange cloak rimmed in black. *That must be him*, thought Charles. The coopa had four men guarding him, two in front and two behind. The four guards wore black armor and carried black shields. A row of ten priests stood at the top of the steps facing their leader.

Peasants were gathered around, but they were not celebrating. Instead, they collected in little clusters on the street and murmured among themselves.

Charles ran straight up the steps.

The guards apparently did not expect anyone from the crowd to cause any trouble and were not paying attention.

Charles grabbed the two guards in the procession's rear simultaneously by their armor between the upper torso and the neck. He pulled back hard and shoved both men, one to the right and the other to the left. He pushed them so hard that the guards actually fell off the steps on both sides, and Charles heard a loud clattering from their armor.

Charles drew his sword and grabbed the coopa around the neck, demanding, "Where is she!"

Ben also drew his sword and intercepted the other two guards in black before they could strike Charles.

"What are you blathering about?" asked the fat, little man.

Charles hoisted the great coopa up on his shoulder and walked straight through the temple doors.

Ben set his back to Charles and followed him through the temple doors, walking backward.

Charles, heedless of any danger, essentially ignored everyone. He walked directly to the sacrificial area, where two priests with knives knelt next to two frightened girls, who looked like they were about sixteen years old.

"Neither of them is Vennel!" roared Charles. "Where is she?" He dropped the coopa to the floor.

The ten priests rushed into the temple behind them and drew small daggers from their cloaks while the two guards in black drew their swords.

The two priests by the altar stood and held their knives ready.

The servants of Gultten exchanges glances and whispered words for a few moments. Then they moved forward.

Ben shook his sword in the air and pointed the tip at the two guards. "Move back, or my friend will kill your precious leader!"

For a moment the guards hesitated, but since Ben did not have a translation stone, they did not know that he had just threatened their leader's life.

"Charles, I don't think they understood me. Can you repeat that?" Ben asked quickly.

Charles turned to face their enemies. "Back off, or I will kill your leader!"

The guards and priests hesitated; then one priest asked, "What do you want? Tell us, or we'll attack."

"I want the girl you kidnapped—the one who lived in the market district with the old man you murdered."

"We didn't murder anyone," replied the coopa. "We just hired the Bendel and Caishan to capture people of a certain age group. Then we bought those people. It's completely legal."

The other two guards in black had apparently managed to get up and climb the steps. These two circled around behind, forcing Charles to turn.

Now Charles and Ben faced two guards each.

"You are criminals," said one of the guards. "We'll throw your corpses to our god."

The guards rushed in.

Charles used the coopa as a shield and viciously attacked.

Ben managed to bring his shield up in front of him and was trying to hold off the two guards when several of the priests dived at him with their daggers.

Charles threw the fat coopa at one of the guards, knocking the soldier over. Then he closed the distance with the other guard, pushed the man's sword aside, and grabbed him. Charles picked him up, threw him back to the ground, and ran his sword through him.

Ben lost his shield when five priests grabbed it and pulled it away from him.

Suddenly, a loud voice yelled, "Enough!"

Everyone froze.

Twelve archers stood in the doorway with arrows nocked on their bows ready to fire. A tall man, whom Charles presumed to be the governor from his attitude of command and expensive apparel, stood behind the archers. The governor was stout and muscular as well as tall. He had a long black beard and a black, bushy mustache. He wore light chainmail and did not seem like the kind of person who would take nonsense from anyone.

Charles was vaguely aware that a dark figure in a hooded cloak slipped into the temple and remained in the shadows behind the governor's men.

The governor demanded, "What is the meaning of this!"

Charles did not know how to reply. He did not think he had any legal grounds to be there, at least not according to this world's laws.

The shadowy figure stepped out from behind the governor's men and pulled the black cloak away from his head. It was Jack.

"Pardon me, Governor," Jack began, "I believe I can shed some light on this subject. These two men work for me. Perhaps they were a bit overzealous in carrying out their task, but I assure you, it is completely legal." Jack addressed the governor with a poise and confidence that almost made Charles believe him.

"You are the reason behind this?" asked the governor. "Why should I not just have my archers shoot? The security of this building is my responsibility."

Jack lifted both hands palm outward. "Yes, I'm aware of your responsibility. These priests bribed you to look the other way while they hired the Bendel and Caishan to kidnap citizens from your own town and sacrifice them. I have a ledger here containing a list of payouts to you, the Bendel, and the Caishan, proving this to be the case."

The governor suddenly looked very nervous. He cast furtive glances around the room and gave a weak chuckle. "Well, aren't you a busy little pain. Thankfully, there are only a few people inside this temple who just heard your declaration, and the majority of them are the ones who paid me. I think I'll just kill you and anyone who doesn't promise to keep their mouth shut about this, and I'll take that ledger for myself."

"That would be most unwise," countered Jack, "because all I have to do—"

The governor did not let Jack finish his sentence but signaled his archers to fire.

A dozen arrows whizzed straight at Jack, but Jack calmly raised his right hand, lifted his head, and said, "Push."

Charles heard a loud whistling sound, and a massive gust of wind struck the arrows, hurling them to the floor.

The entire room fell silent.

The governor's eyes were wide and his jaw slack.

The archers also stared wide-eyed and several inhaled sharply.

"As I was saying," continued Jack, "you would be very unwise to trifle with me."

One of the governor's guards pointed at Jack and said, "Did you see that? The colored part of his eyes turned light blue! How is that possible? What is he?"

The governor had obviously seen it too. After regaining his composure he asked, "Who are you, and what do you propose?"

"I am Jackson the blood mage, and this man"—Jack pointed at the coopa—"stole my property."

Charles was not sure what was happening, but he figured he should just stay quiet and let Jack handle this. After all, he seemed to be doing well.

"I have a bill of sale," Jack continued, "stating clearly that I, Jackson the blood mage, purchased a slave called Vennel from the man named Dunnel. This coopa and his priests, however, recruited the Bendel slave cartel to abduct people from your town. I believe they actually only bribed you to allow them to sacrifice people here and not to look the other way while they kidnapped your own citizens, but I will let that rest for now. My slave was brought here to this temple to that man." Jack pointed at the visiting priest whose translation stone they had stolen. "He decided that they only wanted girls sixteen and under and gifted my property to the Bendel as a bonus. As you are aware, it's illegal for anyone, even a member of the slave cartel, to steal slaves once they have been sold by a cartel. This bill of sale that I hold in my hand has your seal on it, Governor.

"Now, I believe they paid you in a lump sum, Governor, and these priests broke their word as to where they would obtain their sacrifices. If I may be so bold, I would suggest that you have nothing to do here, and you should simply march your guards outside that door and allow me to seek justice in whatever way I see fit. No great loss to you; no great loss to me. I won't tell anyone about your bribery, and you can simply order the crowd outside to disperse and return home. But I warn you, if you try to stay, Governor, not only will you be in violation of your own laws and your warlord's laws but I will also be forced to kill you."

"Oh, that sounds like a reasonable agreement." The governor nodded vigorously. "But I have a request. These priests, who started this temple, breached their contract with me, so I would like to have my men arrest them. You can keep the coopa, the visiting priest, and their three remaining guards."

Jack tipped his head graciously. "Agreed."

The governor ordered his guards to arrest the priests, and they hauled them out before the townspeople. Charles heard the governor declare that he had uncovered a plot by the priests to kidnap people from the town and sacrifice them.

While the governor's men had been taking the priests' weapons, Ben and Charles had also relieved the three remaining guards in black armor of their swords.

Jack freed the two girls chained before the altar and discovered that the Bendel had not actually marked them as slaves, probably because they were scheduled to be sacrificed. Jack sent the girls out of the temple.

As the temple doors shut with a resounding thud, Jack remarked to his friends, "Nice to know politicians are the same everywhere. Apparently, it isn't just our world that is cursed with crooked politicians. Anyway," he said, turning to the traveling priest, "tell me, where did the Bendel take my property?"

"To the west," the priest replied, "that's all I know."

"So be it," said Jack.

Jack walked over to the edge of the room, opened the temple's side door, and let in another man. The tip of the man's nose was slightly upturned and he had large bushy eyebrows. His dark brown eyes looked cold and his jaw line was sharp and hard, making him appear cruel by nature. He had long blond hair and was dressed all in brown with a curved sword on his hip and ship insignia on his shield.

"I see you didn't break your word," said the newcomer. "These five will do nicely." The man handed Jack a pouch of money and opened the side door again, letting in four more men with chains.

The five Zangan men chained the three guards, coopa, and traveling priest and led them outside the temple using the side door.

When they were alone, Charles shook his head several times to relieve some of the tension in his neck. "What on earth just happened?"

"Well," replied Jack, "you said Dunnel was still alive when you left, so I ran straight to the market district and found him. I told him who I was and asked him if he had a prepared bill of sale for Vennel. Just as I expected, he did. He knew he was getting old and that he would have to sell her soon, so he had a bill of sale prepared and sealed by the governor of this town. The only things he needed were a buyer and two witnesses from the town to sign the document. I called in two random people who owned shops nearby to witness the document, making it legal, and asked them to take care of Dunnel as well as they could.

"Then I went to the building where Ben saw the Zangan seal and I suspected that I could find cartel members. Apparently, this is

Zangan territory, and the Bendel have encroached on their turf with the help of these priests. The priests evidently only hired the Caishan to ambush people coming to the town, and that did not actually breach any territory agreement. One of the Caishan members was carrying out a deal with the Zangan when I arrived. For a small price he provided some information that he had picked up from the priests. That's how I knew they were only sacrificing girls under sixteen and that the Bendel rather than the Caishan must have Vennel. Once I informed the Zangan that the Bendel had stolen my slave, they were more than happy to pay me a finder's fee for the conspirators assisting the Bendel, whom they just took away and are going to sell into slavery."

"Yes, yes." Ben waved his hands. "Okay. I got all that, but you must've figured out how to use one of your gemstones in order to make that wind appear."

"Yes, I did." Jack chuckled. "I have to say, though, I didn't know that my irises would change color when I used the stone. I have not heard of mages' eyes changing when they cast spells. It must only happen to blood mages since they are so rare that most people wouldn't know about it."

The young men emptied the temple treasury of everything valuable, and Jack retrieved the old book written in the tongue of angels from which the traveling priest had read.

"I think I'll hang on to this," he said. "After I finish the book from Hal, maybe I'll read this one."

Charles leaned heavily against the temple wall and sighed in frustration. "Okay, we did what we wanted to do here, but I want to go after those guys who have Vennel."

"And that is just what we're going to do," said Jack.

Charles tiled his head and squinted one eye. "Jack, did you have this plan all worked out when I started running for the temple? I really was acting recklessly, wasn't I? Why did you let me go?"

"I had the initial idea," replied Jack. "The details I figured out as I ran from place to place. This was obviously important to you, Charles. I knew that if I told you to wait until we came up with a plan, and something happened to Vennel, you probably wouldn't be able to forgive yourself and might not even be able to forgive me. I just had to let you run on your feelings and gamble that I could get you out of whatever trouble you got into."

The boys discovered a basement in the temple full of young boys and girls, who were scheduled for sacrifice in the next two days. Most of these children were also unmarked as slaves. The three friends released everyone from the temple to return to their homes.

Jack tied the mouth of a sack containing the coins he had found in the temple treasury. "We now have the money to accomplish any moderate goals we set, but before we try to find our way home, we have to rescue Vennel. We need to catch up to her, and we've already lost a good bit of time. Let's stop back at Hrot's house to pack our belongings and supplies and head out as quickly as possible."

Ben nodded as he slung his own sack of loot over his shoulder. The temple's gold implements clanged against each other in Ben's bag as he walked.

The boys soon arrived at the cottage where they were staying.

As they entered, Jack said, "Ben, we need to travel light. Let's just leave that sack on the table and only keep the coins."

Ben shrugged. "I should've known we would only be able to keep half the loot."

The three quickly began packing their equipment.

Chapter 8

WITHIN THE HOUR JACK and Charles had packed all of their belongings, and Ben had returned from the marketplace with fresh provisions. Jack hoped that the Bendel cartel members traveling with Vennel were not in a hurry.

Hrot and Fenta had been out, and they returned home as the boys prepared to leave.

As Ben and Charles stepped out the door, they nodded cordially at their host and hostess.

Jack swung his own equipment onto his back and turned to Hrot and Fenta. "Our work here is done, and we have a new task. We really don't have time to talk, but we're grateful for your hospitality." Jack pointed at the sack on the table. "What's in that sack is yours. That should be enough for you to get some land of your own to farm."

Hrot opened the sack and stared with his mouth agape. "We can't accept this," he stuttered. "It's way too much."

Jack smiled. "If you feel that way, that's fine. Maybe you'll have an opportunity to do one of us a favor one day." Jack turned and waved his hand over his shoulder as he walked out, shutting the door behind him.

The three young men passed through the city gate in pursuit of the Bendel, but even after walking all day and late into the night by the light of the moon, they still had not caught up.

Charles seemed discouraged, but he was usually an exceedingly patient individual, and Jack was confident that Charles would become settled before too long. This was not like Charles at all. *This girl must really be something*, thought Jack, *and to think he only met her once*. They had been in this world long enough already; it was not as if a few more days and a little side mission would cost too much time. *We'll just chase this trail wherever it leads*, Jack told himself. *We will get the girl, and Charles can go back to normal*. Then Jack had a thought. What would happen if Charles or all three of them developed roots here? By the time they could go home, Jack wondered if they would all still want to.

In the morning they rose early with the dawn and continued to travel until they came upon a village.

Jack asked around and discovered that about six men had come into town, stolen food and other supplies, and moved on that morning. Villagers confirmed that they had a young woman in tow.

The group decided to continue moving in the hope that they would catch up.

Jack studied his book as they hiked. He found that he could make progress understanding it by looking at a word or phrase and then picturing it in his mind while he walked. He figured out the awakening for the next three lesser gemstones; these were for lightning, water, and fire. He would have to test himself sometime under controlled conditions to see if he had any of these three stones.

"You know," Jack said, "you two really should take turns studying this book with your translation stone. Who knows, we might run across more of these gemstones, and you guys could use them."

"Definitely," replied Ben. "I'm first." After about a half hour of studying, however, Ben said, "Charles, it must be your turn. This is way too much like school, and I'm considering this experience to be like a field trip—no school allowed."

Charles frowned. "Come on, Ben. We're seniors; you're going to graduate soon. It's not like it would hurt you if you spent a little more time on school."

"I get decent grades. That's all that matters," countered Ben. "Nobody said that I had to get an A plus on everything like you do, Charles."

"I don't think I could focus on anything right now," Charles admitted.

"Fine, if you're done with the book, I'll read it some more," said Jack. "There's no reason to have these stones if I can't use them, and the first one turned out to be pretty handy." Jack continued reading and recited the awakening for the three stones. "If I have one of these," he said, "I should be able to use it now."

"Well, that's good," replied Ben with a laugh, "because I'm sick of listening to you jabber on in that weird language."

"It is interesting," said Jack, "that the translation stone teaches the user the tongue of angels rather than simply translating it to a known language."

"Look up ahead." Charles pointed urgently. "Several men are walking on the road. It must be them! Let's go!" Charles drew his sword and took off running.

"Yeah, imagine that," Ben called after him, "men walking on a road; that does sound downright suspicious!"

"Oh, come on," said Jack. "Let's go after him."

Much to Charles's dismay, these men were not the slave traders for whom they searched but just ordinary travelers. After Jack convinced the men that they were not going to rob them, the travelers did admit that they had seen some other men just up ahead, but they did not remember seeing a girl with them.

The boys moved on at a brisk pace.

Ben leaned close to Jack and whispered, "What is it with this girl? Is she, like, a supermodel or something? Charles has really gone off the deep end."

"I'm pretty sure it's mostly guilt," Jack whispered back. "He kind of liked her and felt sorry for her. That, combined with the fact that he had a chance to help her and didn't take it, probably makes him angry, mostly at himself."

"I guess that makes sense," replied Ben quietly.

Eventually, they did come across a group of men bearing the Bendel insignia camped on the side of the road.

"Don't just go running in there this time, Charles," said Jack. "I don't see a girl anywhere, and we don't want to give away the fact that she's important to us, or they could use her as a hostage."

Charles slumped his shoulders. "I suppose you're right."

It was getting dark as the three crept slowly and quietly up to the camp. Even though the trees were sparse, there was a lot of underbrush. The boys listened from the bushes for a while, but the men did not seem to be talking about anything important.

Then one of them said, "At least we got a little extra spending money. I wish to propose that we don't tell the boss that we found a runaway slave. That way, we don't have to share any of the money we got."

"Do you think the boss will find out anyway?" asked one of the other slavers.

"Not unless one of us tells him. As long as we spend it before we get back to base, he won't notice anything to be suspicious about."

"They sold her," growled Charles quietly. "I am so sick of the people in this world kidnapping each other, selling each other, sacrificing each other ... and I thought our world was bad."

"Quiet." Jack placed a steadying hand on his friend's shoulder. "I'm going to sneak back to the road, walk up to them, start a conversation, and try to get information out of them. You two stay here, and if things go badly, back me up."

Jack sneaked back to the road and casually strolled along it.

As he approached, the men sitting around the fire noticed Jack and began to whisper.

Jack guessed that he was the topic of their discussion. When Jack was even with the men, he turned off the road toward camp.

As Jack came near, he heard one of the slavers say under his breath, "Leave him alone. We have an agreement with the warlord here not to trouble the people."

"Hello there, fellow travelers," Jack called, pretending not to notice their insignias in the darkness. "Mind if I stay for a few minutes and warm up by the fire?"

"Not at all," replied one of the slavers.

Jack sat down and started an ordinary conversation. "Did you hear about the trouble in Xin?" he asked. "The governor arrested all these priests. Apparently, they were involved in some kind of backdoor deal, and he found out about it."

One slaver glanced at his associates and raised an eyebrow. "Really? Tell us more."

As Jack continued his tale, he intentionally varied the details to imply that the governor figured everything out by himself. Jack's intent was to set the slavers off guard, and he knew that they would want to hear about what happened since they were involved in the story. Jack asked a few meaningless questions to help them relax and let their guards down even more.

Then Jack turned his face away, and a strong wind blew the fire, which had been calm. The flames readily licked at some dry leaves nearby.

"Careful there," said Jack. "The fire is spreading toward your supplies." He jumped up and started stamping it out.

Several of the slavers quickly joined him.

"That was a close one," said one of the slavers.

Jack turned, looked at the slaver, and casually asked, "So what was the fellow's name you sold the girl to?"

Without thinking or hesitating, the slaver answered, "Warlord Abgot."

Then all the slavers turned and looked at Jack.

"How did you know about the girl?" asked one.

They all reached for their swords as another asked, "Who are you?"

"I'm the owner of the girl you kidnapped and sold," replied Jack, "and I intend to reclaim my property. Here is a legal contract guaranteeing that what I say is true."

One of the slavers examined the parchment. "This appears genuine."

"Indeed," replied Jack. "I have a proposal. I have the information I want, so all you have to do is give me what the warlord paid for my slave, and I will forgive you."

The slavers all looked at each other.

"Legally, he has the right to demand what he's demanding," said one under his breath.

"But he was foolish to come alone," said another. "We don't have to do it. We could just kill him, take his money, and burn the contract."

More discussion like this took place for a minute before the slavers turned back toward Jack.

"Sorry, kid," one of them said. "Under normal circumstances we would honor the contract, but what we did in Xin wasn't really legal by the rules of our organization or Warlord Abgot. So we can't let you live to tell this tale to anyone."

"I see," said Jack. "That was a foolish decision."

The Bendel slavers drew their swords, but even before Ben and Charles could rise and dash to Jack's side, Jack lifted his hand and repeated, "Foolish answer, indeed."

"His eyes!" yelled one of the slavers. "They're purple; I can see them even by the firelight!"

"Get him now," cried another slaver.

Two of them ran straight at Jack.

There was a flash of light and a loud crack, and suddenly the two attacking slavers' corpses lay smoldering on the ground.

Everyone except Jack froze for a second, and Jack slowly drew both of his swords.

Ben looked over at Charles. "Did those two guys really just get hit with lightning? Because that's what it looked like to me."

Jack answered him over his shoulder, "Indeed. Apparently, I have a lightning stone. I actually tried to use fire first, but I evidently don't have a lesser fire stone. Will the rest of you surrender?"

The slavers all dropped their swords without saying a word.

"You will walk in front of us," Jack commanded. "We're going to see this warlord to whom you sold my property. When did you sell the slave?"

One of the slavers, eyeing his fallen comrades, answered, "Right after we left the last village. We ran into a group of Warlord Abgot's soldiers. The man leading the soldiers said he was an advisor to Warlord Abgot, and he purchased the slave as a gift for his warlord."

Jack and his companions gathered the supplies from the camp.

Charles said, "Hey, we'll need another bag for Vennel to carry later. Let's just keep one of these."

Jack nodded in agreement.

The young men marched toward the capital city of Hathra, taking their captives with them. It took the rest of the night and half of the next day to reach the capital.

Once there, they turned in the four slavers to the guard post. All three of the boys were extremely tired and even a little irritable. Despite this drowsiness, Jack politely asked the guard at the post what they would have to do to obtain an audience with Warlord Abgot.

"I doubt there's anything you could do," replied the guard. "It seems war broke out sometime last night, and I doubt the warlord will receive any visitors."

"War?" inquired Jack.

"Yes. Malldan, one of the most powerful southern nations, has long been expected to start conquering their smaller neighbors. In truth, no one's actually sure why they haven't started yet, but tensions are high, and smaller countries and slave cartels are trying to position themselves in preparation for a major conflict. The slave cartels spread across the entire world are requiring every country to pick a side. One of Warlord Abgot's rival kingdoms is trying to gain influence and appease the slave cartels and great southern nations by conquering this country. It's a nasty business. Every time something important happens, all the slave cartels take different stances on it, and everyone suffers."

"I see," said Jack. "Thank you for your time."

Jack conveyed the details of what he had learned to his friends, and they decided to continue heading toward the keep in the city's center.

At the keep Jack again conveyed his wishes to see the warlord about a legal matter.

While they waited for the messenger to return from inside the keep, Jack gazed over the city and noted the same Tudor structures that the peasants possessed in the surrounding area. The road system was different here, though. The roads were wider and laid out like spokes on a wheel toward the walls at the city's edges to facilitate troop movement to the walls or other needed areas. Regardless of the potential impending danger, the streets were full of people and activity, and the general mentality of the citizens was not one of fear.

Jack glanced back at the keep's interior and noticed the austere environment inside with few decorations and simple furniture designs.

Jack sensed that, like the layout of the city itself, the warlord intended his accommodations for function rather than comfort.

Jack's thoughts were pulled back to his mission as he heard footsteps approaching.

The messenger returned and informed them that they would not receive an audience.

"Please take a message to your warlord one more time," said Jack. "Tell him that I am respectfully requesting an audience, and if I'm turned away, I will disrespectfully ask."

The messenger looked at Jack blankly for a moment then turned and dashed up the keep stairs a second time.

"Don't you think it might be a little bit too bold and arrogant to demand an interview?" whispered Ben.

"Yes, I do," replied Jack, "but if we want an audience, this is the only way we are going to get it."

"How do you know they won't just try to arrest us?" Ben asked.

"I don't, but when three lone travelers walk up to a door inside a fortified city filled with soldiers and threaten the warlord, he has to assume that they are either very powerful or very crazy. Whichever is the case, it pays to treat them with a little courtesy."

This time when the messenger returned, he waved for them to enter the keep.

The two soldiers guarding the entrance allowed them to pass.

Just inside, about a dozen more guards sat around a large table; four of these stood and began to follow them as an escort.

They ascended several flights of stairs. The only light inside this portion of the keep came from a few scattered torches and the murder holes built into the keep's walls.

At the top of the stairs, two more guards stood on either side of two large ironclad wooden doors. As the group approached, the two guards opened the doors and allowed the boys to enter a small throne room.

A dozen guards stood along the throne room's walls, six on each side, with torches on the walls between them. At the room's far end, several other men stood near a short, skinny man sitting on a large throne. The man on the throne was clean shaven with brown eyes and hair. Jack guessed that this young man, who was probably only in his mid-twenties, was Warlord Abgot. Two of the men near the warlord appeared to be advisors, and they scowled unhappily. The final man in close attendance was tall, broad shouldered, and covered in armor.

"Who walks up to my keep and threatens me in my own house?" demanded the young man.

There was a line drawn on the floor at which Jack presumed visitors were supposed to stop, but he ignored it and walked straight toward the man on the throne.

The big man in armor reached for his sword, and all the guards brandished their weapons.

Once Jack was within a few feet, however, he stopped, extended his right hand palm upward in an expression of respect, and dipped his head. "Thank you for granting us an audience, your lordship. I apologize for the way I requested, but I am traveling, and it was imperative that I see you within the next few days. I realize that with war breaking out you must be very busy and cautious. An injustice has occurred in which some of my property was sold to you by thieves, and I have come to offer the money you paid back to you in exchange for my property."

"What is this property?" asked the warlord a little wearily.

"A slave by the name of Vennel."

"Do you have proof that this slave belongs to you?" asked the warlord.

"I do." Jack proceeded to lift his right hand into the air and drop to one knee to imply nonaggressive behavior as he reached into his cloak with his left hand and pulled out the document.

The man in armor took a few steps toward Jack and grabbed the document. After examining it he said, "It is, indeed, legal and signed by one of our governors."

Jack said, "I understand this is an inconvenience for you, my lord. My companions and I are prepared to carry out a task for you in order to compensate you for giving us your time on such a menial matter."

The advisors whispered frantically to the warlord, one in each ear.

The young man waved them off with his hand. "I rather like this fellow," said the young warlord, "and I believe he means what he says." The warlord leaned forward. "The task I give you is to bring me two gother heads within a week. If you can do this, I will return your property to you and pay you the normal bounty for both gother heads."

The eyes of the warlord's attendants grew wide, and the advisors murmured softly.

Jack heard the guards along the room's edges shift their weight as if they were exchanging looks behind him.

Jack had no idea what a gother was, but the term seemed to startle everyone. He guessed that the warlord had not selected an easy task, but its completion was now their only option for rescuing Vennel.

"Very well," said Jack, trying to sound confident. "That sounds fair. Is there anyone in the city who can provide information on gothers: the best ways to kill them and where we can find them?"

"I will have my captain of the guard take you to the only retired gother hunter in the city." The warlord gestured toward the broad-shouldered man in armor by his side.

"Excellent," replied Jack, "and I would request that no harm come to my property until our task is complete."

"Of course," replied the warlord. "She will be treated as a slave belonging to a foreign dignitary."

Jack again bowed his head. "Thank you." He turned and strode out of the throne room followed by his two friends.

The large captain of the guard walked with them. Once they exited the keep, the man said, "The retired hunter is down this way."

He took them to a rather impressive residence. The house was big and colorful with large open wooden shutters and a small garden in front.

"I will take my leave here," said the captain. "He will answer any questions you may have."

The boys walked up the stairs and knocked on the door.

After a moment an attractive girl opened the door. "May I help you?"

"We're here to speak to the retired hunter," answered Jack politely.

"He's in the library; right this way." She turned and led the way deeper into the house.

They passed through several rooms until they reached the library, but for a library there were not a particularly large number of books. Jack decided that it was perhaps more akin to a study. A desk sat in the corner, and the open shutters allowed sunlight to stream into the house. A soft breeze riffled the curtains. A slim, hunched old man sat in a chair by the window near a small table. His skin was wrinkled and appeared to have been weathered by the years. He had a skiff of white hair encircling an otherwise bald head and a white beard.

The old man looked up when they entered and smiled broadly. "Visitors, how nice. What can I do for you young men?"

"Warlord Abgot sent us to you. He said you could teach us about gothers," Jack explained.

"Ah," said the old man, "young hunters. Where should I begin?"

"First, why don't you tell us what a gother is exactly," Jack replied.

The old man raised his eyebrows. "You mean when you were a child, you never heard stories about gothers swooping in and grabbing you?"

"No," said Jack, "what are they?"

The old man seemed flustered for a moment as if not sure where to start. "They are like large flying lizards. Their whole bodies are covered with scales, and they have a long, slim body with a long tail. They have four legs with claws made for climbing, and their mouths contain several rows of small but razor-sharp teeth. The adults are larger than the average human, and their wings make them appear even bigger. As a man who killed many of them, though, I can tell you that they're not actually that heavy; in fact, they're less than half the weight of a normal human.

"No one really knows where they came from because gothers don't live anywhere else in the world. There are many rumors and legends about their origin." The hunter chuckled. "There is even a legend that hundreds of years ago a mage in this area was experimenting with unique ways to use his gemstones to increase his power. Legend says that his young assistant saw him using multiple stones at one time, and the mage somehow created four fully mature gothers, which viciously killed him and ultimately inhabited the area. No one knows how he could have done this because many have unsuccessfully tried to reproduce this scenario under safer conditions, but the child did not know what his master's strategy had been. Some say the mage used to live in the tower, the remnants of which can still be seen, at the top of the mountain on which the gothers live. I don't believe any of this, of course, but the other legends are even more outlandish.

"Gothers hatch from eggs and bond with whichever parent is present at the moment. Their bond will either last a lifetime or continue until they find a mate. They often do not find a mate, and they remain bonded with their parent. They know how to fly almost immediately. Because of their strong bonding, they travel in groups. This makes it difficult to attack one of them because even if you shoot one down with an arrow, the others will try to return it to the nest dead or alive. They also cannot be separated from each other for very long. No matter how far away they are, they always seem able to find their way back to their nest and the other members of their bonded group. Because of this ability, many people believe them to be a magical beast.

"They don't usually target humans when hunting. They tend to have a natural fear of humans, but they will attack if provoked. This behavior has caused them to attack people who tried to stop gothers from taking their calves or sheep. If someone ran up to a gother that swooped down after some livestock, the other gothers in the bonded group would consider that a threatening act and attack the person. Although different family units do not appear to defend one another, gothers are fiercely protective within their own family unit. Gothers are extremely intelligent and used to people setting traps for them and hunting them. The best hunter was never able to kill more than fifteen in his lifetime, but the bounty on their heads is high, leading to many young men like you trying to get rich by hunting them.

"I warn you, most gother hunters either die or give up. I, myself, have only killed twelve, but it was enough to provide me with a comfortable retirement, which is good because I can't hunt them anymore. The last one I killed took my left leg to the grave with him."

The old man stood and grabbed a crutch leaning against the wall.

The boys saw that his left leg was missing from the knee down.

"Thankfully, it takes them years to grow and mature," the old man continued, settling into his seat again. "In fact, if you go out to Nesting Mountain, as it's called, you'll see many very small gothers flying around among the adults. They'll be about a foot long and have a two-foot wingspan when they're a few months old, but it will take them another twenty years to reach full size."

"What methods did you use to hunt them?" asked Jack.

"I mostly used animals as bait while I hid in a tree with a bow. I tried a few other things like snares, but nothing had a high success rate."

"Where is this Nesting Mountain?" asked Jack.

"To the north of town, less than a quarter day's walk," replied the old man.

"You mentioned that they swoop down on their prey like a hawk or an owl?" Jack clarified.

"Yes." The old man shifted his weight a little. "I don't think they are very good at fighting on the ground. I've never even seen them try. They always try to swoop down, grab their prey, and pull it into the air with them."

"Thank you so much for your time," said Jack. "We will be on our way."

"If you have any more questions," the old man said, "feel free to return. I'll be here, and I always enjoy visitors. I don't get to see too many people now since I can't get out much."

As the boys exited the house, Jack asked, "Charles, if we found a blacksmith, do you think you could design a snare? That seems like the safest hunting method I heard."

"I'm sure I could come up with something, but it will probably take most of a day to forge the pieces we need."

"We need some sleep anyway since we walked all night," said Jack. "Let's find an inn."

*****

The next morning Charles stayed at the inn designing a snare while Jack and Ben set off to scout out the region around the city and determine which areas were likely to have higher gother concentrations. As they walked, they noticed that the gothers did fly in groups. When one gother swooped down onto its prey, the others spread out but did not swoop down after their own quarry.

Jack crouched down and peered out from under the trees. Several gothers circled over a field of sheep. Jack sat patiently watching the creatures circle until one of them dived down onto a sheep. The creature grabbed the sheep with all four of its feet, sinking its claws into the animal's back, and lifted it into the air. The sheep kicked and flailed, but the gother reached its head around and slashed with its teeth. The teeth sliced through the sheep's neck, and it stopped struggling.

"Fascinating." Jack ran his hand along his face. "These creatures ... their strength relies on diving onto their prey and taking it into the air where it's weaker. The one diving is exposed to any kind of attack that could come from the side, so the others basically set up a perimeter around it in order to deal with any danger that comes to the first gother. The method of one-on-one combat is also interesting. I believe these creatures could hunt other predators very efficiently. Did you see the way the gother stayed behind its prey the entire time? That means that even if the prey had teeth or claws, it would be unable to bring them to bear on the attacker. These creatures have several obvious strengths, but we may still be able to exploit some kind of weakness. Theoretically, if we could get them to perceive a false danger, we could make them all swoop down at one time, giving us the advantage. If the snare doesn't work, maybe we could try that."

Jack and Ben found a path to Nesting Mountain. Even from a distance they could detect the remnants of the ancient stone tower that the retired gother hunter had described.

"The slope doesn't look that difficult to climb," remarked Ben, "yet the old man didn't say that anyone hunts these creatures by going straight to the nests."

Jack nodded. "That's probably because there are so many nests. If any of the creatures saw you climbing up, they would attack. It would be almost impossible for us to defend ourselves while scrambling up the slope."

"Do you give any credence to the idea that gothers are magical beasts?" asked Ben.

"No," replied Jack. "So far, the only things in this world that seem magical are the stones. Everything else seems to be ruled completely by the same scientific laws and principles that exist in our world. I suspect that there's a scientific principle behind how gothers find their way back to the others, much like homing pigeons. Many animals can detect things like changes in barometric pressure and the planet's magnetic field, and we know that gothers are highly intelligent."

Ben crossed his arms over his chest. "They'd probably be considered to be some species of dinosaur in our world."

******

On the way back to the inn, Jack discovered how to use his lesser water stone. "This is fascinating," he said. "I can actually create water from nothing."

"Well, unless we're dying from thirst in the desert," remarked Ben, "I don't see that one being particularly useful. I think you missed out by not getting fire."

"I don't know," said Jack thoughtfully. "There must be something I'm missing, some way to use this stone in an effective manner."

As they walked through the city on their way to the inn, they paid more attention than when they had passed through originally. This city clearly possessed more wealth than any city they had visited previously. They noticed many large impressive houses, which must have belonged to important people. Even the small cottages, although still tightly packed together, looked well maintained. The city had three barracks in different locations so the soldiers could respond quickly to problems throughout the city. In addition, the city walls and gates were actually somewhat formidable, standing over twenty feet high. Climbing them would be difficult without a rope or ladder.

Along the way Jack also purchased three bows and quivers of arrows from the town fletcher.

Charles was very excited when they returned. He had successfully worked with the blacksmith to manufacture the appropriate materials to create a trap.

"The way it's designed," explained Charles, "we can put a sheep or goat here in the middle, and when the animal is lifted, the trap will snap shut."

"Then we'll test your invention in the morning," said Jack.

******

The next morning the boys headed out to their selected gother hunting area. Jack and Ben had identified the field where, according to the locals, the gothers hunted almost every day. The land was fertile and provided excellent grazing pasture. Any shepherd brave enough to guard his flock there could expect a great return. As a result there was always plenty for the gothers to eat, and like most animals, the gothers returned to areas in which they were constantly fed.

The boys purchased a small sheep that had died and placed it on the trap.

"Don't you think live bait would work better?" asked Ben.

"Yes," admitted Charles, "but it would be very difficult to keep it on the trap. If it moved much, it could activate the trap by itself."

After about an hour the boys were pleased to see a group of gothers flying their direction.

Ben scratched his head. "What do you think the people around here call a whole group of gothers?"

"What do you mean?" asked Charles.

"You know," Ben insisted, "a group of birds is a flock, and a group of dogs is a pack."

"They do have names for a group of planes, like a squadron," said Jack. "Something like that would be cool."

"I think we should call a group of gothers a horde," Ben stated conclusively.

The boys smiled.

Just then, the conversation was interrupted when one of the gothers noticed the lone sheep. It dived straight toward the sheep, but at the last second it changed course and flew slowly back into the sky.

"What do you think happened?" asked Jack. "Do you think the gother noticed the trap?"

Charles lightly punched his left hand with his right fist in frustration. "They must be so used to seeing odd contraptions by now that they're wary of them."

The horde of gothers descended slowly as if examining the sheep. Another dived at it, but this one also pulled up at the last second. Then the largest of the gothers flew in low circles around it.

"He's easily within bow range from the ground," observed Ben. "If we could come up with a way to get into the middle of the field without the others noticing us, we could fire arrows at him."

"This is interesting," said Jack, observing the gother's movements. "Look at the way the beast approaches the situation. The gother is smart enough to understand that there's a problem, and it's trying to come up with a way to get around it. It's like the way a parrot watches its owner insert a key into the cage lock and attempts to shove nuts into the lock to open it, sometimes even being successful."

Finally, the gother swooped down again, but this time it grabbed the metal trap on its edge and tried to fly off with the entire trap. The sheep fell off, and the trap activated with a loud snap. The gother dropped the trap and dived after the sheep, which was now on the ground.

The horde then flew off toward Nesting Mountain with its prize.

"I think these things are too smart for traps," commented Jack.

They pulled out their bows and arrows and positioned themselves just inside the tree line on three sides of the field. The gothers, however, had apparently been hunted enough that they never came near the tree line. The boys practiced some with their bows, but their skill level made them wonder if they would even be able to hit a gother if it came within range.

That night the boys returned to the inn a little frustrated.

"Do we have a plan for tomorrow?" asked Ben.

"I was contemplating a couple of ideas," said Jack, "but I think the best one is to attack the nests on Nesting Mountain."

"But didn't we decide that would be very dangerous?" asked Ben.

"For most people, yes," replied Jack, "but I may have an idea."

******

They woke on the third morning well before dawn, packed a few supplies, and set out for Nesting Mountain.

"Look." Jack pointed at the mountain. "It's not particularly steep, so we should be able to move up it quickly. There are plenty of large rocks to hide behind and small crevices and caves we can duck into. We won't have to make the journey to the top in one push."

"But how do we avoid being seen and attacked between those locations?" asked Charles.

"These creatures are used to man-made things being dangerous," Jack replied, "and they know to attack or outmaneuver these foreign objects, but naturally occurring phenomena could also be threatening. What we need is a naturally occurring phenomenon that they want to stay away from. Stay close to me, and we'll head for that first cave."

Jack pulled a cloth out of his pocket and used his water skin to douse it with water before wrapping it around his nose and mouth.

Ben and Charles both followed suit.

The boys started hiking up the mountainside, and Jack lifted his hand. Air began to circulate around them. Dust, leaves, and small branches became caught up in the wind and created a swirling dust cloud that moved wherever Jack moved. They began rapidly ascending the mountain.

"This is cool." Ben plucked a passing leaf out of the swirling cloud. "It's like those dust clouds out west except we're in the middle, where it's calm."

"The eye of the storm usually is calmer," said Jack, "but because this dust cloud is artificial, I've enlarged the eye. The entire thing is fairly small and just powerful enough to hold the debris in the air. This way the gothers won't see us behind all the dust."

Without warning, the wind and dust began to settle.

Sensing impending exposure, Jack desperately extended his hand and focused intently again.

The wind suddenly rejuvenated, and the dust swirled again.

Jack frowned and picked up his pace. "Oh, this won't work; I probably can't maintain my dust storm much longer. It doesn't seem as though we can walk up the entire slope this way. The rocks and caves have too many breaks between them."

"Look up and to the right." Charles pointed through the cloud. "That looks like a gully, maybe from water runoff. See how rocks are piled up on either side with bushes growing along the gully? It probably doesn't go all the way to the top, but it should get us fairly close if we can reach the trench's beginning."

The three friends ran for the gully within the dust storm.

As the wind slackened again, Jack focused and maintained the dust in suspension.

As they neared the deep trench, the rocks became sparser, and they dived into it just as the dust storm died down again.

"Wow," Jack exclaimed, "I feel hotter after trying to extend my air stone. I need to let my blood cool before I make another dust storm."

"That's okay." Charles dusted himself off and removed the cloth from his face. "We have some walking to do before we'll need it again. It also looks like there are several empty caves in which we can hide before we reach the nesting area."

The large rocks and bushes on either side of the gully provided excellent concealment as they continued to hike upward. When they reached the trench's termination, they could see the lower nests and gothers coming and going.

Several hours passed as the friends maneuvered their way through the trench and from one cave entrance to the next.

Jack examined the surrounding area. "All right, I doubt we can approach the nest in the dust cloud without spooking the gothers, so we'll wait here until we see a group of them leave their nest. Then we'll use the dust cloud to get into the empty nest and hide. We're taking a bit of a risk, but the other nests hopefully won't attack if just one group is threatened. As tightly bonded as these creatures are to each other, the gother hunter said this allegiance is only within small family groups. Since the nests appear to be mostly within small individual caves, the other gothers won't be able to see us well once we're in a nest."

After thirty minutes or so, the gothers in the nearest nest went out hunting.

Jack produced his dust cloud, and the three walked up to and entered the gother den.

The nest was surprisingly large, about the size of an eighteen-wheeler, and it was built into one of the small caves. The sun could still shine into the nest for a portion of the day, but the cave provided enough shelter to prevent rain from entering the nest. Two areas were filled with piles of twigs, and eggs nestled in both of them.

Ben fingered one of the eggs. "Should we destroy the eggs?"

"No," Jack replied. "We want everything to look normal when the horde returns. Besides, it won't do us any good for our mission to destroy the eggs."

The three boys lay quietly, covered in as many twigs as possible, for what seemed like an eternity. Ben and Charles had their swords drawn and placed under their bodies with their shields over their backs. Jack had both of his swords drawn and lay on them as well. The nest was very hot, but then, Jack figured it would be. Gothers were reptiles, after all, so they were cold-blooded.

I hope these creatures don't have a particularly good sense of smell, thought Jack. *Otherwise, they might detect us before they enter the nest, but there's a reasonable chance that they wouldn't be able to tell where the smell was coming from until they landed.* Four gothers had left the nest to hunt. They only needed to kill two in order to fulfill their mission, but Jack had no idea if the other gothers would retreat just because they were at a disadvantage. *Their eggs are in here, so they may attempt to defend them at any cost.*

Jack heard a faint crackling noise. He could not tell from which direction it came, but it was close. *Some little animal must be burrowing nearby,* he thought. Just then, Jack heard the sound of flapping wings beating the air. Jack flexed a little to get the blood flowing back into his muscles. The gothers were coming.

The largest gother landed right at the entrance with a sheep in its mouth and sauntered deep into the nest. Jack guessed that this must be the alpha male. Two smaller gothers landed next. This was probably the younger couple that owned the second set of eggs. One more gother was still outside, but it was time to strike.

Jack launched himself off the ground and swung his right sword straight down.

His gother target, which Jack guessed was the younger male, shrieked loudly.

The beast jerked his head to the side and reared up on his hind legs.

Jack pivoted, twisting his body and swinging his other sword up in an arc.

This time the creature reacted too slowly and acquired a large gash in his neck. He gave a cry and flopped against the wall.

The smaller female shot her head forward at Jack.

Jack brought a sword up in front of his head, but the force behind the blow was so great that it knocked him onto his back.

As the gother tried to strike again, Ben leapt onto one of her hind legs, and shoved his sword between two of her ribs.

She bellowed and tried to swing her head around at Ben.

Ben blocked the attack with his shield and struck her head with his sword, finishing her off.

Initially, Charles had also come after the smaller female, but the larger female landed in the nest entrance and rushed at him.

Charles managed to place his shield in front of her sharp teeth, but the power behind her strike slammed him into the ground.

The gother clamped down on Charles's legs with her forelimb claws and pulled him under herself, where she could reach him better with her teeth.

Ben turned around and swung his sword, cutting into one of the creature's front legs.

She growled and snapped at him but still maintained her focus on Charles.

Charles managed to bring his shield up over himself, preventing the gother from sinking her teeth into his body.

Jack sat up just in time to see the large male charge straight toward Ben's back.

Jack lifted his hand and pointed it directly at the creature.

There was a loud crack. For a few moments the cave filled with light. The creature lay sprawled in a twisted heap against the far wall.

Jack looked over to see Charles finish off the last gother with an upward thrust into her belly.

Except for the boys' faint panting, silence filled the cave. They remained wary, wondering if other gothers might have heard the battle. As time passed, however, nothing else entered the cave.

Jack exhaled sharply and looked around. He sat sprawled among one of the sets of eggs. "All right," he said, "I guess that takes care of these things."

Then Jack heard a quiet croaking noise. He looked down and saw a little lizard head poking out of one of the eggs. "Oh man, this egg is hatching."

He leaned in about a foot from the creature to get a better look while Ben and Charles also approached.

The little gother slithered out of the egg and opened its small wings.

"Wow, they're really cute at this age." Jack stood, went over to the dead sheep the alpha male had brought, and dragged it over to the hatchling. He used his sword to cut off a sliver of meat and offered it to the little gother.

The gother gobbled it up and looked up expectantly for more.

"What are you doing?" asked Charles. "We were tasked to kill these things."

"Well, we did." Jack carved off another slice of meat. "Two more than necessary. We don't have to kill this one too. They probably wouldn't even give us a bounty for this one's head."

"I'm with Jack," said Ben. "Let's leave it here. It's got enough meat to take care of itself for a few days. It should be able to learn how to hunt after that."

"Come on, Charles, you're already covered in blood," said Jack. "Let's just let this little fella be." He gave it one last piece of meat before standing up. "Well, let's get their heads and get out of here."

They cut the heads off of the four slain beasts and put them in a sack.

Jack put his hand to his forehead. "You know, I think I need to wait awhile longer before I make another dust cloud. I think it's been less than two hours since I last cast the air stone. I'm concerned that if I raise my body temperature too much, I'll give myself a fever and the possible negative side effects that go with it."

"You mean like brain damage?" said Ben.

Jack smiled. "Leave it to Ben to come up with the worst possible thing that could happen, but essentially that's correct."

"At least we have some entertainment," commented Ben. "Look, the little gother is trying to figure out how to fly."

"It amazes me," said Jack, "that something could learn how to fly so quickly."

The three boys watched and laughed as the little lizard jumped from one rock to another and landed, unsuccessful in getting its wings to move correctly.

"All right, let's go," said Jack finally.

The three made their way down the mountain the same way they traveled to the top. They made better time on the return trip because they traveled downhill and were less concerned about the gothers attacking them since they already appeared to be retreating.

They reached the mountain's base around midafternoon and carried their prizes back to Hathra. As they walked through the market district on their way to the keep, a grubby man, who had obviously been drinking too much, stopped them.

"What do you boys have in that sack?" he slurred. "Young folk like you shouldn't be allowed to carry anything valuable. Let me see. Maybe I'll take it off your hands for you."

Jack could tell that the delay annoyed Charles. "It's none of your business," said Jack. "You best just move along now, friend."

"I'm not leaving until I have a look in that sack." The man planted himself firmly in their path.

Several other men, who were at various stages of drunkenness, came over to join him. "We all want to see what's in there," one demanded.

"Fine," said Jack.

He reached over and took the sack from Charles. Then he grabbed the first man by the back of his neck and shoved his head into the sack.

At first the other men looked as though they would attack, but the shrill scream that came from inside the sack seemed to deter the group.

Jack pulled the man's pale head out and simply pushed him to the side as the boys started walking again.

Jack heard everyone around ask what the sack contained.

"Heads!" was all the drunk man could sputter. "Lots of heads!"

A couple of people screamed, and the onlookers all scrambled to get inside any available nearby building as the boys continued on to the keep.

The keep guards recognized the boys as they approached and ordered the messenger to inform the head of the keep. Within a few minutes the well-armored captain of the guard joined them.

"Show me the contents of the sack," he said in the tone of one accustomed to being obeyed.

Jack opened the sack and allowed him to see.

The man's eyes widened. "Four heads. There are men who cannot bag four gothers in their entire lives, yet you've done so in less than a week. My name is Keyvin. It's an honor to meet such great hunters. Please, follow me to the warlord's throne room."

As they walked up the stairs, Jack asked, "So Keyvin, why is it that you waited until now to tell us your name?"

"I'm the guardian of the keep, and it is not the privilege of foreigners to know my name. Your deeds, however, have made you more worthy than many who have been born even within this keep."

At the top of the stairs, Keyvin opened the doors and walked boldly into the warlord's throne room with the boys following.

"How dare you enter the warlord's presence uninvited and unannounced," cried one of the advisors, angrily surveying Jack and his friends.

Keyvin ignored him, walked directly to the warlord, and positioned himself on his leader's right side. Keyvin then declared, "My lord, I announce the success of the great hunters."

Jack and his friends approached the throne, again disregarding the area where peasants were supposed to stop.

One of the advisors gasped and stabbed an accusing finger toward Jack and his friends. "My lord, these boys have disregarded the line of peasantry. I say on this ground alone we should refuse to hear them."

Warlord Abgot leaned forward. "No, I like his bold attitude. This man could stand in any king's presence, and at least in his own mind, would not be the lesser. Yet he still manages to convey respect, as one king would when meeting another."

With a slight dip of his head, Jack said, "I apologize to the advisor. I am from a land where there is not a very strong split in the respect a man should receive based on title or position alone. In my land people are what they make themselves to be. Even if individuals are born with certain titles or positions, that is not what makes people great."

"It sounds like a very strange land indeed," mused the warlord, "but I understand that you have heads to show me."

Jack motioned with his hand.

Charles stepped forward on Jack's right with the sack and dumped its contents onto the floor.

The two advisors stared at the heads with their mouths agape.

Jack wondered if they were more surprised at the hunters' success or offended by the bloody heads on the floor.

The guards on the room's edges craned their necks to see the spectacle.

The warlord was more reserved in his expression, but Jack could read the surprise on his face.

Keyvin simply grinned.

The warlord clapped his hands together sharply and ordered that the slave girl be brought immediately. "And an appropriate bounty for each head," he added. "I must say," the warlord continued as his messengers rushed off to carry out his orders, "you have completed twice what I required in half the time. With a few men like you three, I could run this kingdom smoothly, but alas, I only have one." He gestured toward Keyvin.

The two advisors behind the warlord directed angry and hateful expressions toward Keyvin.

"In fact," continued the warlord, "war is brewing, and my army needs great commanders."

The two advisors inhaled sharply and immediately whispered frantically in the warlord's ears.

Warlord Abgot brushed them off with a wave of his hand.

Jack smiled. The advisors were clearly trying to gain power and resented anyone who might stand in their way, but the warlord, young as he was, did not appear to be too easily swayed.

"Unfortunately," said Jack, "we have our own task to complete, so we must depart. I thank you for your generous offer."

"I don't suppose an offer of money would change your mind?" The warlord leaned forward.

"You would suppose correctly," replied Jack. "We have significantly more money than we need for our journey, so any more is not tempting for us."

At that moment a side door opened. A young maiden escorted another young woman, who Jack assumed was Vennel, through the

A Destiny Among Worlds

doorway and brought her before Jack. Both girls knelt in front of and to Jack's right side, facing him.

The warlord asked Vennel, "This man claims that you are his property. Is that true?"

Vennel looked up and squinted at Jack as though trying to place him. She turned her head to the side as if about to shake it no.

Jack smiled and gestured to his right.

When Vennel saw Charles, she burst into tears.

From the way Charles shifted his weight, Jack could tell he was uncertain whether he should approach or not. Actually, Jack did not know either, but so far, he had been fairly successful with this warlord by acting bold and in charge, so he decided to stick with that. "Charles," he said confidently, "would you please retrieve my property?"

"Of course." Charles walked over, took Vennel by the hand, and gently lifted her to her feet.

Vennel started to say something.

Charles put his finger to his lips and shook his head.

They both stepped behind Jack and waited quietly.

The warlord furrowed his brow, shook his head, and stared at the floor. "I spent all morning poring over the battle plans, but my army just is not strong enough to win against my southern neighbor, who has joined forces with another warlord farther south. Even now, his armies march into my land, attempt to burn my villages, and with the help of the slave cartels, enslave my people." The warlord raised his eyes to meet Jack's gaze. "When I saw you walk in, something about you made me wonder. I gave you a giant task, and you completed it as though it were trivial."

The warlord stood and walked straight toward Jack. "I do not ask you as a warlord but as a humble man who is in need. You are a strange man that you have gone through such lengths to save a lowly slave. Based on what I've seen of you, it would be impossible for you to turn me down as long as I ask you as an equal to lend me your help." With that, Warlord Abgot bowed his head before Jack.

"My lord!" his advisors screamed in unison.

"This peasant man deserves no respect," cautioned one desperately.

"How could you even stand in his presence much less bow to him?" demanded the other in an appalled tone.

All the guards turned their faces away, and even Keyvin was shocked beyond words.

"I won't lift my head until you promise to help my people," said the warlord. "I don't know why, but I feel that you can save my kingdom."

Jack himself was rather speechless. "We ... will help," he finally managed to stutter.

The warlord raised his head and placed his hand on Jack's left shoulder. "Then please return tomorrow. We will discuss the rest of our battle plans. Any accommodations you require while you are here are yours. I will have you on my left with your friends and Keyvin on my right when we go into battle. After our victory you may carry on with your journey."

"We will return tomorrow as you have bidden." Jack dipped his head again in respect.

******

As soon as the throne room door shut behind Jack and his three companions, Keyvin said, "My lord, how could you do such a thing?"

Warlord Abgot smiled. "That man only respects strength and humility and perhaps compassion. His kind is rare. I have never met his like before. If I wanted him to join me, I had to show him that I was similar to him. In his land men seem to be created equal." The warlord stared into the distance. "I would love to see a land like that, even for just a day."

******

Jack and his companions made their way to the inn.

Charles introduced Vennel to his two friends and explained to her that Jack had purchased her from Dunnel before her owner's death in order to gain the legal right to protect her from the slavers. Then they had followed her to Hathra to rescue her.

As the three young men chatted, however, Vennel stayed silent.

After a few minutes Jack drew his eyebrows together in a serious expression. "I must apologize to you both. We are finally ready to begin our journey home, and I pledged that we would assist this kingdom in some battle without consulting either of you. That was wrong."

"Don't give it a second thought." Ben waved his hand dismissively. "You were put on the spot, and as it turns out, you said what was in my own mind. I'd also like to help this kingdom. The warlord seems to be one of the few decent leaders we've run across, and if given the opportunity, I think he could make this into a great kingdom."

"As for me," said Charles, "I agree with Ben, and I have slowed us down quite a bit myself, so I must thank you both for backing me up in this whole ordeal."

"What do you think, Vennel?" asked Jack as he turned his head to look at her.

She hung back behind the three of them, keeping her head down. When Jack spoke, she looked up, startled. "What did you want of me?" she asked timidly.

"Your opinion," said Jack. "And don't hang back too far. We came quite a ways to get you, and we wouldn't want you to get lost within the first hour of finding you."

Charles and Ben chuckled, and Charles said, "You saw what the warlord did, didn't you? How he treated Jack as an equal? It may take some time, but try to think of yourself that way."

"I know that you've had a lot of changes in your life recently." Jack stopped and turned to face her. "But you are welcome to go whenever you like."

A terrified look came upon Vennel. She suddenly cast herself onto her knees before him. "Please don't send me away! If anyone finds me, I'll be treated as a runaway slave. Please keep me!"

"Okay, okay," Jack assured her, a little taken aback. "You can travel with us until we find a better arrangement for you."

The young woman seemed a little comforted, but as they continued walking, she did follow more closely.

Chapter 9

WHEN THE INN CAME within view, Jack felt a touch as though someone tapped on his shoulder. He turned but saw no one. Vennel walked behind Charles and could not have reached Jack.

Jack looked at his three traveling companions. "Did any of you see someone walking right next to us just now?"

They all shook their heads.

"It's late," said Charles. "Hardly anyone is even out on the street."

"Strange." Jack stroked his chin. "I have this apprehensive feeling ... you know like when you hear a noise in your yard at night, but you look, and there's nothing there?"

"You're probably just tired," said Ben. "We did have quite an interesting hunting trip. Let's buy some supper at the inn and get a hot meal instead of our normal tasteless supplies."

The whole group nodded their agreement and stepped into the warm building.

The three boys sat down, but Vennel remained standing.

"What should I do?" she asked. "Slaves are not allowed to eat in public places."

"Sit down," said Charles. "No one can see the mark on your ankle, and if anyone tries, we'll throw them out of the inn."

"I suppose we would ask them to politely leave us alone before we threw them out," said Jack.

They all laughed.

Beef roast was for sale that night. The innkeeper brought four large chunks of meat over to their table. Only a few other people sat in the inn. Two men in the corner drank beer and talked, another man sat by himself at the center table, and a group of guards clustered together around another table, drinking happily.

Jack carved off a sliver of beef roast and took a gulp of water. When he looked down again, the slice of meat was gone. He immediately looked across the table at Ben. "All right, very funny, but stick to your own food."

Ben smirked but then seemed to realize that Jack was serious. He raised an eyebrow. "What are you talking about, Jack?"

"I just cut off a chunk of meat. I glanced away, and it disappeared."

"And you immediately assumed that I did it? I'm hurt." Ben placed his hand over his heart in mock emotional distress.

"Well, if not you, then who?" Jack looked back down at his plate. It was now empty. "What just happened?"

Charles started laughing as he took a drink, and his laughter turned into a cough. "I'd say you were just really hungry." He coughed again.

"This isn't funny. Someone stole my food, and I want to know who it was right now."

Jack heard a faint scratching noise, and a little gother landed on the table's edge with Jack's beef roast in its claws. The lizard began tearing the meat into pieces and devouring it.

Everyone at the table was too shocked to say anything for a moment

Before they could react, one of the soldiers walked by and glanced at the table. He suddenly screamed, "Gother!"

Within a few seconds everyone in the inn was on their feet except for those at Jack's table.

The little gother spread its wings and jumped off the table onto Jack's shoulder.

Instinctively, Jack tried to move back, but he was still sitting. Jack tripped over his own chair and barely managed to catch himself on the edge of the table before hitting the ground.

The little gother had no difficulty holding onto Jack's shoulder with its claws, but the little lizard did spread its wings for balance.

Then screaming erupted within the entire inn, and several of the patrons ran out of the building.

The soldiers drew their weapons, approached Jack, and surrounded him.

Ben and Charles stood and reached for their own swords.

Jack put up his hands. "Everybody, just hang on for a second."

"Where did you get that thing?" demanded the tallest soldier, who Jack guessed was the group's leader.

"We did some gother hunting earlier, and we apparently picked up a straggler," Jack answered. "He's very small, nothing to be alarmed about."

"That means he knew about it," concluded one of the soldiers.

"You brought that thing here inside the town," accused another.

The tall soldier said, "You will have to answer to the authorities for this. Please come along peacefully."

"Don't worry guys. I'll be all right," Jack assured his friends. "I'm sure we'll have all this sorted out soon."

As the soldiers approached Jack, the little gother jumped into the air and flew out the window.

******

While the soldiers escorted Jack outside, the innkeeper walked up to the remainder of the group with a red face and tight jaw. "You have ruined my business for tonight and perhaps my reputation as well. I want you three out of here. You cannot stay in my inn any longer."

Ben, Charles, and Vennel quickly retrieved the group's belongings from their room in the inn.

Charles tossed Vennel a backpack. "This is yours. We picked it up from some of your traveling companions a while back."

She did not answer but simply slipped the bag onto her shoulders.

Ben impatiently punched his left hand with his right fist several times in rapid succession. "Let's go find Jack."

******

The soldiers marched Jack directly to the keep. When they arrived, Jack was pleased to see Keyvin just in front of the doors with the two soldiers guarding the entrance.

Keyvin recognized Jack immediately and asked the soldiers what was wrong.

The tall soldier briefly recounted the tale.

Keyvin burst into laughter and turned to Jack. "You have an explanation for this, I assume?"

"We destroyed a nest of gothers," Jack explained, "and one hatched while we were in there. I gave it some food, and we watched it for a while. It apparently decided to find us."

"You were right next to it when it hatched?" Keyvin clarified.

"Yes."

Keyvin laughed even harder and slapped his thigh with his hand. "I have never heard a tale of a gother hatching in proximity to a person, but it has somehow bonded to you. I doubt there's anything you can do to make it leave you alone."

Jack shut his eyes for a moment and shook his head. "Hang on one second, that old hunter said these things bond for life with whichever parent is near when they hatch. What am I supposed to do with this thing?"

Keyvin shrugged. "I suppose you'll have to kill it." He was still chuckling when he dismissed the soldiers.

The little gother suddenly popped out of the darkness and landed on Jack's shoulder again.

"Just what I need," said Jack, "a strange flying lizard that is emotionally bonded to me and wants to go with me wherever I go."

Just then, Ben, Charles, and Vennel caught up to Jack, and Charles informed him that they had been kicked out of the inn.

Jack looked over at the little lizard on his shoulder. "You've caused me a lot of trouble tonight." He turned back to Keyvin. "Is there, perhaps, another place we could stay tonight?"

"Absolutely," Keyvin replied. "I'll take you to a city barracks that is currently empty."

As they walked, Keyvin went on and on about how he would tell the retired hunter this crazy story. "And beware, brave hunters," he said, laughing, "the greatest danger in attacking a gother nest is that you might find yourself a bizarre and unexpected child."

The group finally arrived at the barracks.

Inside, Ben asked, "What are you going to do with that thing?"

"I'm not sure yet," said Jack, "but tonight I'm going to sleep."

The rows of bunks inside the barracks were rather hard, but they were softer than the ground on which the boys were used to sleeping. The wooden bunks were covered in straw wrapped in cloth.

Keyvin stepped over to the back wall and lit a torch with his own torch.

The light danced across the edges of the building, revealing a long empty weapon rack along the back wall. Several walls made of roughhewn timbers separated the barracks into rooms, but the building's interior had no doors.

Keyvin explained, "The majority of the army is marshaling outside the city, so this building will remain empty until the conflict is resolved." He bid them farewell and departed.

Jack noticed a fire pit along the back wall. He gestured toward it and asked Ben if he would get a fire going.

Charles commented, "On our way in, I think I saw wood stacked out front. I'll show you."

Vennel quickly followed the two boys outside, and all three returned with firewood.

Charles then helped Jack unpack their bedrolls. They placed the bedroll that they had obtained from Vennel's captors on one of the bunks in the next room for Vennel.

Meanwhile, Vennel started arranging the wood in the fire pit.

Ben liked building fires, and Jack noticed that he seemed slightly annoyed that Vennel had taken over his job. At first Ben sat quietly and watched. Before long, however, his patience ran out, and he gestured toward Charles's arm, where the translation stone rested.

Charles pulled the mage bracelet off his arm and handed it to Ben.

After receiving the stone, Ben walked over to the fire pit. "I'll take it from here." The wood was ready, and Ben pulled the torch from the wall and held it close to the tinder.

Vennel seemed surprised by his actions, but she stepped back and sat on one of the cots without saying a word.

The fire began to crackle, and light filled the room.

Jack nodded in approval. "That should keep this and the adjacent room warm throughout the night."

Jack plucked the little lizard off his shoulder, dropped it onto the ground, and crawled under a blanket.

Within a few seconds the little lizard had jumped up on the bunk and slithered under the blanket with him.

At least it's not an amphibian, thought Jack. *Then it would be slimy.*

Jack rolled onto his side so that he could see the fire, and he felt the gother's frantic little scurrying as it tried to stay on top of him.

Vennel asked awkwardly, "Am I dismissed for the night?"

Jack replied, "Of course."

Vennel stood, retrieved her bag and the torch on the wall, and walked into the neighboring room.

Jack did not really pay much attention to Vennel's demeanor, but Charles commented quietly, "She looked a little uncomfortable. I think it will take her a while to get used to us."

Ben shrugged and sat on a cot near the fire.

Jack thought for a moment before whispering back, "She already commented that slaves weren't allowed to eat in public places. I wonder if she's used to a particular protocol when interacting with those in authority."

Even in the dim firelight, Jack detected Charles's concern. Jack said, "Don't worry about it. I wouldn't expect her to change overnight. Give her some time. If we treat her as an equal, she will probably naturally start to think of us as peers."

******

Jack awoke the next morning because something moved. He opened his eyes and found the little gother curled up on top of the blanket in the center of his chest.

The little creature's tail flicked back and forth as it dreamt.

Annoyed, Jack decided to get a little revenge. He lifted his head so his face was right next to the gother and cried, "Ahh!"

The little creature leapt into the air before it even had time to open its wings and fell headfirst toward the floor. At the last moment it managed to open its wings and slow itself down just enough to land on its feet. It looked around, jumped right back up onto Jack's chest, and laid its head down again.

Jack laughed as Ben and Charles walked over because of his yell.

"What are you doing, Jack?" Charles asked, rubbing the sleep from his eyes.

"Just having a bit of fun at my little nemesis's expense," Jack replied.

Ben laughed. "Wow, out of all the scary, evil guys you could've picked for a nemesis in this world, you picked a lizard."

Jack looked to his side as he heard the fire crackle loudly.

Vennel knelt by the fire with an iron skillet cooking something. She flipped a pancake in the pan, and Jack noticed that his pack was open next to her.

Jack scratched his chin and thought for a moment. He finally called, "You know that you don't have to make breakfast for everyone, right?"

Vennel looked in his direction and dipped her head slightly before returning to her work.

Ben said, "I think it's a great idea. Thanks for breakfast." He sauntered over to a bunk adjacent to the fire, where several pancakes already sat neatly stacked on a wooden plate. "Hey, I wonder what they call pancakes here."

Jack smiled. "Technically, with the translation stone they call them the same thing that you just did. The only way you could say something they wouldn't understand is if they didn't have a term for it in their language."

Charles leaned over and said quietly to Jack, "I don't know if this is healthy. I'm not sure we should continue to let her act like a slave."

Jack paused before answering and finally whispered back, "I think it will be okay. As long as we don't treat her like a slave, I think she'll get tired of acting like one. Besides, I would be behaving as her master if I commanded her to stop."

Jack walked over toward Ben. "Remember, we need to go see the warlord this morning, so everybody eat up quickly."

Vennel's head jerked up. She said respectfully, "You cannot take me to an audience with the warlord. It just isn't appropriate."

Jack thought for a moment. "You can stay here if you like. We'll be back after we speak with the warlord."

After breakfast the three boys headed to the keep.

The keep guards were at first hesitant to let them past because of the gother on Jack's shoulder, but they had their orders, so Jack and his friends were ultimately allowed to enter the throne room.

As the double doors opened, Jack noticed that this time a table rested in the room's center. The warlord, Keyvin, and the advisors were all gathered around the table, which had many parchments spread across its surface. Jack suspected that most of these were probably maps, and some were probably lists of the number of men under each commander.

As the boys approached, the two advisors looked shocked and offended; by now this seemed to Jack to be their natural state.

"How dare you bring a beast such as that into the warlord's presence," one of the advisors said.

"Actually he's quite docile," said Jack casually, "unless I order him to eat someone."

Just at that moment, the baby gother looked at the advisors and opened his little mouth, hissing.

The two advisors took a step back.

Jack thought, *Way to go. Those advisors needed a little hissing in their direction.*

Warlord Abgot smiled broadly and pointed at the little gother. "I hear you recruited another warrior for my army last night."

"That certainly wasn't my intention," Jack replied. "He's actually a bit of a pain, but I haven't figured out what to do with him yet or how to get rid of him."

Warlord Abgot nodded. Then his face grew serious. "Now, down to important matters. The armies of Warlord Gaekkin have already crossed our southern border, and scouts came in this morning, informing me that he has burned several of our outlying villages." The warlord indicated a particular area on one of the maps. "My army will be finished gathering by tonight, but our expectations suggest that our enemy's force will be somewhere around five hundred and our own only around four hundred."

"You're forgetting a key piece of information, my lord," interjected Keyvin. "Apparently, Warlord Gaekkin has hired a mercenary who calls himself 'Felter the fire mage.'"

"Yes," continued Warlord Abgot, "I looked into this man's past, and supposedly Felter can wield fire. He is not considered to be a very powerful mage, but he is still powerful enough to charge a great deal of money for his services."

"I, my lord, will personally guard you from this menace," said Keyvin loyally.

"It does not appear as though we have an effective way to defeat an enemy this large as well as a mage," said Warlord Abgot. "I don't believe we can risk an all-out confrontation, but if we stay here in a defensive position, they will burn the outlying villages and perhaps even the towns near the border as well."

"We must challenge him," said Jack. "Hiding will only delay the inevitable. What we need is something that will surprise them." Jack began studying the maps.

One of the advisors rolled his eyes. "Peasants and battle strategies? Ridiculous!"

Jack ignored him and shifted several maps to the side.

Charles and Ben joined him at the table.

Jack pointed at a canyon on the map and whispered, "There wouldn't be enough room for both armies to go head-to-head in the canyon."

Charles nodded in agreement.

They studied the maps for several more minutes, mumbling possibilities among themselves.

Finally, Jack looked up and smiled. "I think we have something. Here is a canyon. There's no effective way for either side to get their army to the top, yet they need to pass through here if they're going to continue on this route along your border."

"But how does that help us?" asked Keyvin.

"By forcing both armies into a narrow gorge, we essentially eliminate the fact that they have more soldiers than we do. Only about one hundred of our men will be able to face about one hundred of their men. The entire battle will be decided based on a few soldiers. Are your soldiers more skilled than theirs?" Jack inquired.

"I would say, all in all, our soldiers are pretty even with theirs," answered Warlord Abgot.

"All right. Can you defeat the enemy commander one-on-one?" asked Jack.

"I'm not sure," replied Warlord Abgot. "But even if I can defeat their commander, and Keyvin can defeat his guard, we could never hope to win because they have a mage."

"My friends and I will handle the mage," replied Jack confidently.

"Have you ever fought a mage in battle before?" asked Keyvin.

"Actually, none of us have fought in a battle before," replied Jack, "but you asked me here for my advice, and this is the best course of action that I can see."

"Preposterous," cried one of the advisors. "Please, my lord, ignore this raving lunatic. He has no idea what he is proposing. He will be the death of us all!"

Warlord Abgot stood in thought for what seemed like forever to Jack. Finally, he said, "I don't know why I have such confidence in a complete stranger, but we will do what you suggest—predominantly because no one else can offer me any other choice that doesn't end in complete disaster."

Jack smiled. "Very well, when do you want us to be ready to move out?"

"The army leaves when the sun sets," replied the warlord.

It took some time to finalize additional details. Then Jack and his friends departed.

As they left the throne room, Keyvin followed them. On the stairs he stopped them and said quietly, "I don't know how you have so much influence over the warlord. He usually ignores my advice and does what those two advisors say, but with you it's as if they were not even there. Those advisors are greedy men, and all they have sought is more power and wealth for themselves for as long as they've been here. I'm glad someone is able to reach the warlord's ear, but if you abuse your influence, I will kill you."

"No need to be so serious." Jack held up a hand. "After we win this battle, my friends and I will be on our way. You won't have to worry about me exerting my influence over the warlord anymore. I'd like to ask you for a favor, though."

"What is it?" Keyvin replied, visibly relaxing.

"Is there a way that my slave could travel with us in the army camp?"

Keyvin replied, "There's always plenty of work to be done in an army camp. It's actually rather common for wealthy or important army members to take slaves with them."

Back at the barracks Jack sat down, and Ben and Charles joined him on nearby cots.

Jack said, "I believe the enemy mage will try to kill the warlord during the battle. If he's successful, it will break the army's morale and give him an easy victory. I need you two to stay next to me and keep most of the enemies occupied. When the enemy mage makes his move, I must be ready, so I can't be distracted during the fight."

Ben and Charles both nodded in agreement.

"After the mage is dead," Jack continued, "the three of us will move in on the enemy commander. I suspect he will call a retreat when the mage goes down in order to fall back and regroup."

When Jack informed Vennel that she would be able to accompany them to the battle camp, she dipped her head and replied simply, "As you wish."

Just before sunset, they gathered their equipment, and headed out to where the army was gathering. They found the warlord and Keyvin at the warlord's tent.

Keyvin pointed to a nearby tent being dismantled for travel. "That one will be yours. Your slave will stay in camp while you are in battle."

Jack and his friends began inspecting troops with Keyvin.

"I noticed that there are only about fifty archers in the entire army," said Jack. "More would be better if we could get them."

Keyvin cast his gaze over the soldiers. "There are very few skilled archers for hire in this area, so it would be extremely difficult and expensive to procure more archers. The enemy probably won't have very many either, so we won't be at a disadvantage."

The warlord rode toward them on a large chestnut horse with plates of armor on its neck and rear.

They finished their inspection and reported to the warlord.

"Good," was his only answer.

When the army was ready to depart, the warlord ordered the march to begin.

After a few hours the army rested for the night. They marched all the next day. When they reached the gorge, they made camp and dispatched scouts to determine the enemy's position.

"How do we know they will not try to place archers at the top of the gorge?" asked Keyvin.

"It would take them an extra day of preparation to get their archers in the correct locations," said Jack. "That terrain is very unforgiving, and it would be difficult for them to do it without us knowing. They believe they have the advantage, so they won't risk scaring us away by trying to get an even bigger advantage. Since we were here first, we might have been able to get our archers to the top of the gorge, but it's unlikely that they would make it there in time for the battle, and we would risk splitting our forces."

Warlord Abgot placed Jack, Ben, and Charles in charge of picking the best two hundred men to position in front. Jack was extremely grateful for the years of experience that the three of them had gained in fencing. They organized duals among the soldiers to select the most skilled fighters. How well they believed the soldiers fought determined whether or not they placed them on the frontlines.

Jack, Ben, and Charles participated in several matches to personally test some of the soldiers. During all of Jack's duals, the little gother just sat contentedly on his shoulder. At first Jack had tried to pluck him off, but within a few minutes, the lizard would be back. After Jack finished his fights, he decided to go for a walk. He grabbed the little gother, set him down, and took off in the other direction.

I'm going to go be alone for at least a few minutes, thought Jack. He made it to some trees and hid in a bush. *Let's see if that little reptile can find me now.* He sat down and tried to read his book, but the light in the sky was diminishing, and he was fairly unsuccessful. Jack put his book down and wondered what would happen in the battle the next day. He acted so confident, but he had never been in a battle previously. *I wonder if I'll be too afraid to fight. I have to be strong,* he reminded himself. *I must get Ben and Charles back home no matter what it takes. I will fight to my dying breath to protect my friends. We need to win this battle and travel to Celel. We will hopefully find the answers that we need there.*

Jack heard rustling next to him and looked to his left. Sure enough, that pesky lizard had found him. *I wonder if he found me through his sense of smell,* thought Jack.

Jack stood and walked back to camp with his little companion on his shoulder. His friends sat by the fire outside the warlord's tent, eating stew that Vennel had prepared.

Jack walked over to the pot and served himself some. Then he looked at the little lizard on his shoulder and said, "You go find the carcass of whatever animal they slaughtered to put in this stew because I'm not sharing."

As if on cue, the little gother spread his wings and jumped into the sky.

"He's actually rather impressive." Jack sat down by his friends. "He manages to hang onto my shoulder very tightly without digging his claws into my skin."

"I see," said Ben. "Charles, I think he's finally warming up to his little friend."

"Forget it." Jack shook his head. "I'll find a way to ditch him, just you wait."

A scout ran up to the warlord's tent, panting. "I have news."

Keyvin emerged from the tent. "What have you found?"

The scout replied, "The enemy is camped on the other side of the gorge, and we found a few refugees who managed to escape from the villages before they were sacked."

"Feed the refugees; they will stay here tomorrow with the slaves when we march into battle," ordered Keyvin.

The scout gave a small bow and ran to carry out his orders.

Keyvin turned toward the fire and noticed the boys. "Do you boys not wear any armor?"

Jack and his friends glanced at each other.

"We haven't really needed it until now," said Charles.

"I'm sure there's some chainmail that would fit you in the armory tent. You should check there," Keyvin told them.

Jack and his friends finished their supper and went to the armory tent. The armorer provided all three of them with a set of chainmail that fit their torsos.

Much to Jack's dismay, the gother seemed able to hold onto his shoulder just fine with the chainmail. *I need to get some plate armor*, he thought.

The three returned to their tent, which stood next to the warlord's tent, and retired for the night.

******

In the morning after breakfast, Keyvin called the troops into formation.

Before joining them, Jack said, "Vennel, you stay here in the camp until after the battle."

She looked at the three of them and bit her lower lip. Her eyes became moist, but she bowed her head in acknowledgment.

Noticing her reaction, Ben chuckled. "Don't worry about us. Worry about them."

Charles rolled his eyes at Ben then turned back to Vennel. He started to say something, glanced at the translation stone on Ben's arm, and held his tongue."

The army traveled to the gorge in traditional marching formation. Jack had selected the gorge's narrowest place to stop.

When they reached the area, Jack looked around. It was tighter than he had predicted. Only about fifty men could stand abreast.

The troops reorganized themselves. Several ranks of foot soldiers stood shoulder to shoulder followed by the archers and more soldiers behind them. Then half of the men in each rank of the most forward lines took a couple steps backward in an alternating pattern so that each rank formed a zigzag using two lines of twenty-five men. This arrangement allowed ample room for the soldiers to swing their swords without leaving holes in the ranks.

Jack and his friends positioned themselves just to the left of the warlord and Keyvin in the most forward layer of the frontline.

"This is perfect," said Jack. "If they force us to retreat, it will widen slightly, allowing more of our men to become involved in the fray."

"They will hold the majority of their forces back," said the warlord. "This fight will truly be decided by a few men."

I hope I'm up to the task, thought Jack as he drew his swords and waited.

Charles had chosen a slightly larger shield that he claimed fit him better.

Jack rapped the shield with his knuckles. "If they give a volley of arrows before they charge, you'd better have room for both of us behind that thing."

Charles laughed. "You were the one who didn't want to carry a shield."

"I don't really know how to use a shield," replied Jack, "but I can use two swords, so I'm going to stick with what I know. Besides, it's really powerful in one-on-one combat."

"True, but it's not as good when facing multiple opponents," countered Ben.

"Don't worry," Jack assured them. "We've got this."

The enemy army approached, but they halted just out of bow range.

A man stepped out of the enemy formation and called, "You have no chance. Simply surrender, and we will let you live."

"As slaves," muttered Ben. "Let's teach these guys how to really fight."

Warlord Abgot yelled back, "I could say the same thing for you."

The enemy soldier returned to the ranks, and Warlord Gaekkin's men started marching forward again.

"Archers ready." Keyvin lifted his hand and held it suspended as the enemy marched closer. Then he dropped his hand. "Fire!"

The enemy army halted and hunkered behind their shields. The arrows landed without doing much damage, and the enemy army continued marching.

Jack asked, "Do you have the archers separated into two groups?"

Keyvin nodded.

"Then have the two groups fire at different intervals," Jack recommended. "We'll make them march toward us while the arrows come down."

Keyvin gave the order, and the archers were slightly more effective. The enemy archers, however, came quickly into range. Neither force's archers carried shields in addition to their bows, so both groups of archers begin firing at each other, allowing the enemy hand-to-hand units more freedom in approaching.

Here they come, thought Jack.

They were twenty feet away, then ten. A man sprinted directly toward Jack.

Jack attacked with his left sword. As his enemy deflected the blow with his own sword, Jack stepped to his right side next to Ben, allowing the man's momentum to carry him forward. Jack then stepped back in on the side with his opponent's shield and rammed his own body into him, causing his opponent to continue forward into the soldiers standing behind Jack, where he was quickly dispatched.

Charles had dug his feet in and braced for the impact of the man charging him. The enemy soldier bounced off Charles's shield, fell to the ground, and was trampled by the other soldiers running forward.

Ben launched himself at his opponent, and they both tumbled to the ground. The outcome looked uncertain for a moment, but Ben used the hilt of his sword to smash his opponent's ribs. Before Ben could finish him, however, more enemy soldiers pressed in from every side.

Warlord Gaekkin had not taken the initial precaution of spreading out his soldiers, and some time passed before his men gained enough space to fight effectively. The lines on both sides, however, were essentially broken by now, and men fought and scurried everywhere.

Jack rushed at two enemy soldiers.

One of them saw him coming and raised his shield, but the other did not react in time.

Jack yelled and swung one of his swords upward. It bit through the enemy soldier's chainmail, causing him to slump and fall to one knee.

The other soldier swung his sword at Jack.

Jack deflected it and counterattacked with three quick jabs.

Jack's opponent raised his shield to deflect the attacks.

Jack thrust with his other sword, ramming it through the man's chest.

Judging from the number of enemy soldiers at their feet, the warlord and Keyvin also seemed to be making a fairly good account of themselves.

Ben had just kicked another soldier to divert his attention before swinging his sword down on the man's shoulder.

Charles swung rapidly at a very large opponent, who seemed to deflect Charles's attacks rather easily.

Jack ran toward another enemy soldier who was engaged with one of Warlord Abgot's soldiers.

The enemy forced the warlord's soldier to the ground and swung his sword down at the man's head.

At the last moment Jack caught the sword with his own. Jack then spun and planted his sword in the enemy soldier's back. Jack grabbed his wounded ally and helped him to his feet.

Jack glanced to the right just in time to see several more enemies closing in on them. Jack and the wounded man fell back to where Charles had just finished dealing with his large opponent.

Ben and Charles positioned themselves between Jack and the advancing troops, giving Jack enough time to glance around. Jack saw the warlord take the head off an enemy soldier. Another man moved toward Warlord Abgot but maintained a little distance.

Jack drew closer to the warlord, cutting down an enemy soldier on the way.

Jack saw the man who was keeping his distance open his hand so that his palm was visible even though he still held his sword.

Keyvin noticed him now as well and yelled, "My lord, look out! It's the enemy mage!"

Jack had also guessed that this man must be the mage. Jack had not been sure, but he knew that when he cast magic, it came from his palm.

The enemy mage thrust his hand forward at the warlord, and a fireball hurtled directly toward him.

Keyvin leapt between the warlord and the fireball, but he was too slow to bring his shield up in time to protect himself.

The enemy mage smiled broadly and ran toward the warlord, assuming that he could finish them off easily after his fireball struck.

Jack, however, had raised his hand as well.

The fireball collided with a wall of water that appeared in front of Keyvin.

The enemy mage stopped and turned. He looked straight at Jack and hurled another fireball.

Jack saw the fireball coming but also noticed an enemy soldier running at him from the right. Thinking quickly, Jack waited until the fireball was right on him, and he could feel the heat. He then shoved his hand forward, knocking the fireball off course with a mighty gust of wind.

The fireball flew to Jack's right and slammed into the approaching soldier, who screamed and squirmed for a moment before lying still.

The enemy mage's mouth hung slack, and the color drained from his face. He turned to run.

Jack thought, *Now you're mine.* He raised his right hand, and a loud crack echoed through the canyon.

The enemy mage heard the sound and tried to jump out of the way, but he was too slow. The lightning bolt passed completely through his left shoulder blade, splitting him in two.

Jack breathed and looked around. The warlord and Keyvin looked dumbstruck by what they had just witnessed. Apparently, they had not expected the fight with the enemy mage to go like that.

Ben and Charles rushed to Jack's side, ready to move on the enemy commander before he could retreat.

To Jack's surprise, however, Warlord Gaekkin called for a full charge.

For a moment Jack was uncertain what to do. Then he realized that the enemy commander was heading toward the mage's corpse. "Of course," said Jack aloud. "He's trying to get the gemstones before he retreats. We have to get there first."

The three friends charged through the enemy and reached what was left of the enemy mage.

Jack yelled, "Ben, search the body while Charles and I hold off the enemy. I'll stop the commander."

Warlord Gaekkin moved in, brandishing his sword.

Jack doubted whether he could take the enemy warlord one-on-one. *I've already used all three of my gemstones,* he realized.

A soldier grabbed Jack's arm.

Jack twisted his arm up and sliced the soldier's arm with his other sword before running him through.

The enemy commander reached Jack, but Ben still had not found the gemstones.

Jack attacked the commander with a fury, but he could not puncture through the man's defenses.

The enemy warlord swung his shield forward as if trying to push Jack back.

Jack dodged to the side, but the shield maneuver was just a fake.

Warlord Gaekkin swung his sword at Jack's now exposed right side.

Jack twisted his right sword down, deflecting most of the blow, but the enemy's sword still caught him under the arm and split his chainmail. Blood trickled down Jack's side, but he did not slow his attack.

Ben found the stones and yelled, "Burn!"

Nothing happened.

Ben looked at the stones blankly as if they were defective.

"Fall back," yelled Jack. "We have to get the stones to safety."

Warlord Gaekkin knocked both of Jack's swords out of the way, and before Jack could bring them back up to defend himself, the warlord kicked Jack in the abdomen.

Jack doubled over. He could not think straight. *Come on, lift your swords,* he told himself, but his body would not obey.

Before the enemy commander could finish him, Warlord Abgot arrived and positioned himself between the enemy and Jack.

Charles grabbed Jack and pulled him after Ben.

Jack gasped for breath. He was not sure whether he had ever been kicked that hard.

The enemy commander apparently decided that since Jack was out of magic, there was no reason to retreat. He and Warlord Abgot went head-to-head.

Keyvin arrived at his warlord's side a moment later and fended off other attackers.

"I'm all right," said Jack.

Charles let him go.

"We have to get back in there," Jack continued, catching his breath. "The warlord needs to win this fight. We need to hold the enemy soldiers off of him. Ben, you hang back with the gemstones; we can't risk letting them fall into the enemy's hands."

Jack and Charles rushed to the warlord's left side and held off the soldiers who were trying to move in while Keyvin held the right side.

Both warlords were very skilled, but Warlord Abgot successfully knocked the other man's shield out of his hands.

Warlord Gaekkin, perceiving that he was now at a disadvantage, called for a retreat.

The entire army fell back.

Warlord Abgot and his army pursued for about one hundred yards, but they did not dare follow their opponents out of the gorge because the enemy army could turn and bring their entire force upon a small number of their men.

Warlord Abgot roared above the battle, "We have victory!"

A great cheer arose from his men.

Ben jerked his fist down. "These stupid gemstones don't work. What a letdown."

Jack said, "Didn't you listen to anything Hal told us about gemstones? You have to awaken a gemstone to a new user before it can be used. Also, if you had been successful using them, they would have shattered because the enemy mage already used both of them before he died."

"Oh yeah," Ben replied. "I forgot about all that. Can you blame me? We were in the middle of a battle."

"That's interesting," said Jack with sudden realization. "I don't think I even noticed it before, but the gother must have flown off right before the battle. At least I'm rid of him."

Warlord Abgot's army fell back out of the gorge.

Warlord Abgot dispatched scouts to see where the enemy army would stop, and the wounded were assessed and cared for.

Later, as Jack and his friends walked through the camp, Jack realized that he was the primary topic of discussion. All the soldiers discussed the mage on their side, who obliterated the enemy and saved the warlord.

Jack told his friends, "I'm not sure if letting the world know about my gemstones was a good idea, but I think it was worth it since we got two more."

Ben asked, "Are you going to awaken the fire stones right away?"

"No," replied Jack. "I'm going to teach both of you how to awaken the fire stones, and you both will be able to carry one. It's time you started studying my book with me."

Ben groaned in mock protest. "I suppose if I have to study in order to throw fireballs, it's a worthy trade, but just barely."

The three laughed. Ben could always lighten the mood when he tried, and his humorous personality helped Jack relax. They walked through the camp toward the warlord's tent.

The warlord saw them coming and called, "Well, if it isn't our three heroes. Jack, you didn't tell me you had any gemstones when we met, but I do understand now why you walk around so boldly. Be careful, though. You have kept them a secret until now, but the whole world now knows that you have gemstones. People will seek you out to either hire you or kill you."

Jack nodded. "Thankfully, we are traveling north. I doubt that word will spread that far."

"I personally owe you my life and the victory today," said the warlord.

"In all fairness," Jack replied, "I also owe you my life, so we will call us even on that score."

Warlord Abgot said, "Some of the men claim that your eyes changed color during the fight. I've never heard of mages' eyes doing that."

"Well, my secret is out; I might as well show you." Jack walked over to a horse trough and moved his hand.

The trough suddenly filled with water.

"Incredible, your eyes do change." The warlord dipped his hand into the trough. "I noticed that you used water in the fight and just now."

"Yes, why?"

"Well, depending where in the north you're headed next," continued the warlord, "there may be a place you should stop."

"We're going to Celel."

"Good," replied Warlord Abgot, "there is a mage who is a prince in the country of Dulla, which is not too far off track from where you're going. This mage may be willing, for a price, to teach you how to use your water stone to create ice instead of just water."

Jack could not resist a slight smile. "Interesting, I can think of many more applications for using both ice and water."

"I'll show you which country and city he lives in on a map when we get back to the capital."

Jack, Ben, and Charles returned to their tent for the night.

Vennel looked up as they approached, and her countenance brightened when she saw them. She was stirring a pot of stew sitting over the fire in front of their tent. Their bedrolls were draped over the tent lines as though they had been washed and were now drying. When Vennel saw Jack notice the bedrolls, she looked slightly flustered. She said quickly, "Don't worry; I'll have everything put back in its place in a moment." She rushed over and pulled the bedrolls off the line.

Jack said, "It's fine; we'll grab them. Thanks for washing them."

Vennel nodded in acknowledgement, but she still picked up the bedrolls and carried them into the tent. She came back out a moment later with some bowls and spoons and began scooping out the stew. She stepped toward Jack and offered him a steaming bowl of stew.

A little uncertain what else to do, he smiled and accepted it. "Thank you." As the aroma lifted off the food, he realized that he was starving. Jack shoved a large piece of meat into his mouth and chewed aggressively. *Apparently, fighting in a battle really takes its toll on a person*, he thought.

Jack and his friends sat down with Vennel around the fire.

As they ate, the little gother appeared with what looked like the hind leg of a pig. The creature viciously stripped the last bits of muscle and sinew off the bone.

Jack shook his head as he thought, *This little one is a survivor.* As soon as his hunger was satisfied, Jack realized how tired he was.

Although the sun had just barely set, the boys retired for the night soon after finishing their meal.

******

The scouts returned the next morning, informing them that the enemy was retreating back to their own land.

"You have not seen the last of them," said Jack, "but right now they believe that your army and their army are fairly evenly matched."

"Yes," replied Warlord Abgot. "I know when they get the advantage, they will return, but for now let's return to the capital and celebrate our victory. We lost only a little over half of the soldiers that they lost—about fifty men in all."

At the capital the warlord showed Jack and his friends where the countries of Celel and Dulla were located relative to one another.

"The water mage I told you about lives in the capital city of Duthwania in Dulla. I know it goes without saying and with as much power as you apparently have this is probably true wherever you go, but you are always welcome in my kingdom. I consider you a friend and will miss you."

"You never know," replied Jack, "maybe we will meet again. If I may, I will leave you with some parting advice. I suggest that you rely on Keyvin's counsel rather than that of your advisors. I could be wrong, but he seems trustworthy, and they don't."

The warlord smiled. "They were my father's advisers, and they know much about running a country."

Jack's eyes shifted upward as he thought. "They probably do. But they probably know enough to take over a country as well, and they have no loyalty to you."

The warlord tilted his head in acknowledgement of Jack's words and clasped Jack's hand tightly. Warlord Abgot similarly bid farewell to Ben and Charles.

Jack, Ben, and Charles picked up Vennel, who had been waiting for them with the supplies, on the way out of town and headed for Celel.

On the road just outside of Hathra, Jack said, "I enjoyed my time here more than anywhere else we've stayed since leaving home."

Ben and Charles nodded in agreement.

"In fact," Jack continued, "I can hardly think of a downside to this place."

Just then, they all heard a quiet screech overhead, and the little gother landed on Jack's shoulder.

Jack sighed. "Never mind. Forget everything I just said."

They all laughed. This really was turning out to be quite an adventure.

Chapter 10

THE GROUP TRAVELED NORTHWARD toward the country of Celel. It rained more often now, making traveling on the road rather unpleasant.

"Why does it always have to rain?" Ben flicked several drops of water out of his hair.

"It's early spring," said Charles, "or at least, that's what we theorize, so rain should be more common now."

"Of course it's spring," said Vennel. Although her tone was respectful, she looked confused by Charles's uncertainty regarding the season.

Ben did not understand her comment since Charles had the translation stone.

Jack and Charles exchanged glances.

Jack thought, *If she plans to stay with us, we'll eventually have to tell her that we're leaving so she can look into other options in this world. She and Charles seem close, so she would probably take it best from him.* Jack could not blame Charles for not wanting to tell her about their world. A few of the people they met early on sort of believed them, but the majority of people would just think that they were crazy.

Jack grimaced as four tiny feet landed on his head. *Apparently, gothers hate rain,* he thought, *because this little guy runs around like crazy whenever it rains.* So far, this had proved to be very inconvenient when passing other travelers. Jack had never heard of people in America walking around town with large iguanas on their shoulders. The gother was about the size of a small iguana now. Although they supposedly did not reach full size quickly, the lizard had still grown noticeably in a week and a half.

The group arrived at a small town along the road. A merchant caravan stood in the town's center, which gave Jack an idea.

Ben grunted and ran his hand through his hair before slinging the water off to the side. "Oh great. Another inn that will kick us out if we try to stay there. I'm really tired of sleeping outside just because you can't control your pet."

Jack smiled and shook his head. "Don't worry. I've got an idea. You guys go ahead to the inn, and I'll catch up."

They moved on without him.

The rain subsided, so the reptile stopped running frantically and instead placed himself on Jack's shoulder completely still like a gargoyle.

As Jack approached one of the merchants, the man took a step back.

Jack said quickly, "It's okay. He won't bite."

The merchant seemed to relax a little. "What can I do for you?"

"Do any of the merchants in your caravan sell cloth?"

"Yes," replied the businessman. "We have a variety of different types of cloth."

"Do any of you know how to sew a custom sack?"

"Yes, we could manage that."

"I want you to make a sack out of your strongest material that this little guy can fit in with maybe a little extra space for him to grow. The sack will also need some type of clips or strings so that I can tie it onto my backpack or use it as its own backpack. If you could waterproof it somehow, that would be good as well."

"We could sew a sack like that," the man said hesitantly, "but we would need to take measurements of your ... uhm ... pet."

Jack contemplated for a moment how he would get his gother to stay still while they wrapped him in cloth.

The man laid out some cloth reinforced with leather strips on his cart.

Jack looked over at the lizard and said, "Lie down on the cloth," in a joking manner.

To his surprise, the little gother jumped onto the cart and lay down on the cloth.

"Wow," said the merchant. "When you said he wouldn't bite, I wasn't really sure I believed you, but he's obviously very well trained. You must've spent months working with him."

"Oh, yeah," Jack answered, but in reality Jack was trying to figure out why it had obeyed him. He thought, *I haven't trained this thing at all. It was only born a week and a half ago, but it's as if he actually understood what I said.* Then Jack had another thought. *I have a translation stone. I wonder if animals can understand me. I wouldn't be able to control the animals because a translation stone doesn't force anything to obey me. But if, under rare circumstances, an animal wanted to please me, perhaps I could convey my desire to it with a translation stone.*

While Jack thought, the merchant finished his measurements and said, "I'm all done. I will have it for you in the morning."

"Thank you." Jack looked down at his little reptile. "Let's go."

Immediately, the little gother returned to Jack's shoulder. *This may not be so bad after all,* thought Jack. *If he will do what I say, it won't be nearly so inconvenient to have him around.* Then Jack had a disturbing thought. He remembered that the translation stones did not provide a direct, word-for-word translation; they could also sometimes translate emotions. *I hope this guy doesn't attack anyone just because I'm irritated with them or don't like them,* he thought. *This probably means I shouldn't say anything negative to him about not wanting him around either if he can understand me and pick up on my feelings.*

"Well, for now," he said aloud to the gother, "I need to go into the inn and eat with my friends, so you fly about for a bit. When I open the window to our room, you can come inside."

With a little screech the reptile leaped into the air.

While they ate their supper, Jack relayed his interesting discovery to his friends. Jack also saved a small portion of his meal, which he brought upstairs. He then opened the window shutters.

Within a few minutes the little gother flew into the room, ate his meal, and curled up on Jack.

"I suppose I'll have to name him now," said Jack, "since I think I'm actually okay with him staying around."

The next morning Jack picked up the sack that he had ordered from the merchant and attached it to his backpack. Jack said, "All right, little fellow, from now on when we are around other people, unless I say otherwise, you either fly around out of sight or stay in the sack. This should keep you dry when it rains as well."

The reptile darted into the sack, and stuck his head out the top.

Jack smiled. "I suppose I'll tolerate your head being out."

******

The group left the village and continued north. As time went by, Charles looked repeatedly at the same scenery that they had passed for the last several miles. Trees sporadically lined the road's edges, and thick undergrowth occasionally grew in large patches. Small bright-green leaves emerged from many of the bushes and smaller trees. It had been chilly in the morning, but a warm breeze now blew through the trees.

It was nice, but Charles became bored. He surveyed his companions. Jack was busy studying his book. He glanced at Vennel, who walked a little behind himself and to his left. Charles slowed down slightly until he walked beside her.

Charles asked her, "So, do you have any family?"

She jerked her head slightly as though startled. "Not anymore."

Charles was silent for a moment. He mentally kicked himself, thinking, *I should have remembered that.* In an effort to change the subject, he asked, "When we first met, you said you were from a faraway country, do you know what region that was?"

She shrugged. "Somewhere in the central kingdoms. I'm not really sure where to be honest." She looked down at her feet. "I was taken when I was very young, so Dunnel was the only family I ever really had."

Charles noticed that her voice quivered slightly as she spoke Dunnel's name. He was not sure how to respond, so he nodded for her to continue.

A tear rolled down her cheek. "We traveled all over the central realms together. Jofna was my favorite place to visit. When I was little, Dunnel would take me around the cities in Jofna and show me different historical buildings. Since the country is so old, it has a lot of history. Some people even say that it used to be the trade hub of the world. It still is the hub for the central kingdoms, but apparently, its glory days passed long ago.

"Dunnel used to love to show me things that were different or interesting wherever we traveled. He always used to say, 'There's something interesting anywhere you go.' He liked to explore. I think that's why he chose the business he did—because it required so much travel."

Another tear rolled down her cheek, and she bit her lower lip. "He even taught me how to read in the common tongue. I remember how many hours he spent teaching me, and when I got old enough, I helped him run the business. I was always legally a slave, but he treated me like family."

Charles replied, "I can only imagine what it would be like to lose someone that close to me. I've always looked after my little sister, and now I haven't seen her in weeks. I'm not even sure that I'll ever see any of my family again." Charles scratched the back of his neck with his left hand and tilted his head forward to give him an excuse for not making eye contact. "But I hope I will see them again."

Their conversation was interrupted by the little gother diving out of the sky and assaulting a stick lying on the ground. The little lizard carried the wood up into the sky then flew back down toward Jack. He dived into his sack, still carrying the stick. His head emerged a moment later, and he looked around. He hopped out of the bag onto Jack's shoulder, and launched himself into the air again. Then the little gother let out a triumphant screech as though he had successfully taken down an exceptionally difficult opponent.

Jack shook his head. "Well, someone's awfully cocky."

Ben chuckled. "Behold, the vicious hunter."

Jack commented, "He's like a little dragon. Ben, I need a good, fierce dragon name."

Ben thought for a moment. "Garthong."

"Then that shall be his name," said Jack.

******

In another day and a half, they neared the country of Dulla. Jack still had not uncovered his fifth gemstone because one of his friends frequently had the book. During the journey Ben and Charles took turns carrying the translation stone since Jack was trying to teach them how to awaken the lesser fire stones they now carried.

Rather than wasting his time, Jack decided to try to read the other book written in the tongue of angels that they had taken from the temple to see what it was about. Try as he might, however, Jack was predominantly unsuccessful at translating the book since it had many words in it that he had not yet learned.

The group entered another village, where they purchased more food and refilled their water skins at the town well.

Ben asked Charles if he could use the translation stone for a while to explore and talk with the locals.

Charles handed him the stone. "When we get back on the road, I'd like to have it back so I can continue to talk with Vennel."

Ben shrugged. "Okay, whatever."

A band of soldiers marching through the village had also stopped to resupply.

Jack decided to ask the soldiers some questions while Ben haggled with the shopkeepers over the supplies. He walked over to the leader and asked, "What are soldiers doing in a small village like this?"

The soldier replied, "There was a clash between two neighboring warlords near us a week or so ago. The battle didn't go well for either side, and deserters all along the roads have turned into bandits. We received orders to clear some of the roads of troublemakers. If you're traveling north, I strongly suggest that you wait or travel east first because we're not clearing the north road."

"Why not?" asked Jack.

"Our warlord is punishing some of the landowners in the region because they didn't send as many reinforcements as they should have. They are a vile and treacherous lot."

"Thanks for the advice," said Jack.

After rejoining his comrades, Jack informed them of the situation.

"I say we just continue north," said Ben. "It's not like some deserters are going to scare us away."

Charles rubbed his chin. "I agree, but it doesn't hurt to be cautious."

"Maybe we can help some of the locals on the way," said Jack.

When consulted, Vennel simply said, "Whatever Jack decides is fine."

The group decided to continue north.

Before long the road became very rough as if it had not received regular upkeep. As they continued, they came to a rickety bridge over a little creek.

Charles examined some of the wood then stepped onto the first few boards. "I don't think this is actually stable enough for us to cross safely."

The entire group climbed down into the creek bed and walked downstream until they found an easy place to cross and climb up the other bank. Back on the road, they walked for a while longer until they finally reached a town, which looked very poor in comparison to the towns they had seen recently. Splinters of wood lay scattered across the streets. Charred remains of many buildings dotted the town. Several roofs had partially collapsed, leaving piles of old thatch on the ground underneath where the roofs had been.

The few people on the street ran inside buildings when they saw Jack and his friends coming.

"How strange," observed Charles, "the people here seem terrified of strangers." Charles walked over to one of the wrecked buildings. "Look how the wall fell so far away from the house and in the street's direction. I suspect someone attached ropes to the supports and used horses to pull the wall right out of the building."

Jack's group approached what appeared to have been an inn at one time but was now mostly a broken-down building. As the group entered the inn, a man came down the stairs and asked in a shaky voice, "What can I do for you?"

Jack replied, "We need some rooms."

The man's gaze flitted back and forth between the newcomers as if he thought they might be lying. "Any rooms you want except number two."

Jack replied, "We want accommodations for three men and one woman."

The innkeeper nodded. "I'll set that up for you."

Jack and his friends sat down at one of the old tables and chatted amiably.

Before long a man in a black cloak came down the stairs and seemed to hesitate when he noticed them. The man then casually walked over to a table near them and sat down.

Jack discretely examined the man out of the corner of his eye. He had a strong, upright bearing that suggested self-confidence. The hood on his cloak obscured most of his face, but Jack could still make out a short black beard. Black strings kept the front of his cloak fastened tightly, and dust clung to his cloak and boots, making Jack suspect that he had traveled for some time without stopping.

Jack interrupted their careless conversation by observing quietly, "That guy seems to be paying a lot of attention to us."

Ben nodded. "It is weird that he would come over and sit at the tablet next to us when so many free tables are available."

"I'm going to try to find out who he is by just being friendly," said Jack. He stood, walked over to the other man's table, and took a seat.

The man lifted his head but did not change his neutral facial expression.

"Hey," said Jack. "Are you a fellow traveler? I'm Jack. It's good to meet you." The other man did not respond, so Jack continued, "This town doesn't seem to get very many travelers. We're on our way north. What about you?"

The man rested his left arm on the table and leaned forward. "What do you really want, traveler?"

"Okay, straight to the point," said Jack. "I actually didn't want anything. My friends and I just thought you were kind of suspicious because you sat down all by yourself within earshot of our table. When you came downstairs, it looked like you were heading for the door but changed your mind when you saw us."

"You're very observant." The man leaned back again. "But I'm not sure that I believe you." Jack could see a grim smile on the man's face even under his cloak's shadow.

"Whatever." Jack casually looked at the ceiling and rubbed his finger across his lower lip. "We were told to be on the lookout for suspicious people taking this road. I'm not going to start a fight just because you want to eavesdrop on our conversation, so have a good day."

Jack stood and walked back to his table. To his companions he simply said under his breath, "I don't know what his deal is."

The mysterious man continued to watch them for about ten minutes.

Suddenly, a scream interrupted their conversation.

The innkeeper obviously heard it too because he hid behind his counter.

Jack, Ben, and Charles jumped to their feet in unison and drew their swords.

"Where did that come from?" asked Jack.

"I think it came from out on the street." Charles jerked his head toward the inn's front.

As they rushed out the door, Charles half turned, held up his hand palm outward, and shouted, "Vennel, stay here." He said it in English, but she seemed to understand.

"Keep an eye out for that dark-cloaked guy," Ben told Jack and Charles. "This may be a trap of some sort."

Outside, about ten men with swords and shields were hauling townspeople out of their houses and into the street. The men stopped when they saw Jack and his friends holding weapons.

"Who are you?" demanded one of the men. He was tall and wore some sort of tattered uniform, as did most of the other men. The man who spoke held a young girl, whom he had just dragged out of a nearby building, by her hair.

Jack squared his shoulders and met the man's gaze. "I suppose we are the guys who are here to put a stop to this."

The man and his friends laughed. "We have a rebel," he called.

Several more men came out of alleys and nearby buildings at their leader's yell.

Charles bumped into Jack slightly and whispered, "We can't take on twenty guys. We should retreat for now and come up with a plan."

"I agree," whispered Jack, "but I'm not sure that we could successfully retreat at this point."

The enemy deserters began closing in around Jack and his two friends, leaving their prey in the middle of the street, where they had previously dragged them.

The leader sauntered toward them confidently. "I've stolen from this place for a long time, but thanks to the recent battle, I got some new recruits. I decided to take everything I wanted from this place and burn it to the ground." He sneered. "You look like travelers. Why don't you just leave after giving me all your money? If you resist, we'll kill you."

Jack glared at the man. "Even if your men kill us, I'll make sure that I take your life before I die so that at least in some small way, these people can receive justice for what you've done."

Their adversaries rushed toward the three boys, who positioned themselves back-to-back.

The tall man in the tattered uniform hurled himself at Jack.

Before Jack's adversary swung his sword, however, Jack felt a strong heat touch his skin and saw the man in front of him become completely consumed by fire.

Jack realized that a fireball had just passed right next to his head, and it was much hotter than the fireball he had deflected in his last battle.

Another fireball struck two more of their enemies, consuming them instantly.

Jack turned to see the man in the black cloak slowly walking toward them. The man raised his hand, and another fireball erupted from his palm.

The enemy retreated at full speed.

Jack and his friends turned to face the man.

Jack asked, "Who are you?"

The man looked at Jack and simply shook his head. "No," he said finally, "*that* is not the question. First, you have to tell me why the three of you thought that you could take on a group of twenty?"

"We *were* a little outmatched," Jack admitted, "but we're used to being a bit outmatched when we fight."

Ben mumbled under his breath, "We could've taken them."

The townspeople in the street nearby stared wide-eyed.

"I already told you my name," said Jack. "What else do you want?"

"Fine," the cloaked man said. "Are you actually interested in helping these people?"

"If it's possible, we don't mind," said Jack.

"Then return to the inn with me, and we will discuss what will happen next." The man turned and strode back into the inn.

"I say we go chat with him," said Jack. "He's a mage, so maybe he'll know some useful information. He also seems interested in helping these people."

His friends shrugged their shoulders.

Ben said, "What have we got to lose?"

The three young men returned to the inn and joined the man in the dark cloak at his table.

As they sat, the mysterious man said, "I don't know your faces, yet your desire to help seems genuine. I don't know for what reason you're interested in helping either, but I suppose I'll let that rest for now. After all, a man's reasons are his own, but you really shouldn't have left the girl in here by herself with a suspicious stranger."

Jack almost countered the man's statement, but then he remembered how timid the innkeeper was when they first walked in and how he had hidden behind the counter at the first sign of trouble.

The three young men turned and looked at Vennel.

"Sorry about that," said Charles. "We just didn't want you out there where it sounded dangerous."

She just shrugged as if it were not important and sat down with them.

The man in the dark cloak continued, "Those were not mere bandits or deserters; the truth is much worse. The reason these townspeople live in such a state of fear is because of something that happened in this country four hundred years ago. The warlord of Splintell had two sons; both married young and had many children. The boys' father gave both of them great power and influence. When their father died, the older son became the new warlord, but he was terrified of his brother's power and influence.

"As time passed, he became paranoid. As a result the new warlord eventually murdered his younger brother, and this created a civil war because the younger brother's oldest son discovered that his father had been murdered and retaliated by trying to take the position of warlord for himself. He marched his father's armies on the capital, defeating the current warlord and slaying him. Before he could take control, however, the dead warlord's sons arrived with their armies, and another great battle ensued. Many soldiers died and some family members on both sides as well."

The sound of a wagon passing on the road outside made the cloaked man pause and glance out the window before continuing in a more hushed tone, "After that, Splintell was in a sort of constant civil war until about five years ago. The current leader of the older brother's family rose to power as the current warlord, and he ordered his soldiers to capture the leader of the younger brother's family—an old man who wanted to bring peace. Now these captors threaten to kill the old man if those in his political sphere resist them in any way.

"To prevent any backlash, they disguise their soldiers as deserters, which allows them to rob and pillage the villages and towns. Over the last five years, they've taken almost all of the wealth from this section of the country. Then they became even greedier, so they started kidnapping and selling their own people as slaves. I've come here to rescue the patriarch of the younger brother's family in an attempt to create at least some semblance of peace."

Ben commented, "This sounds like an ordinary feud except among the descendants of warlords."

"Yeah," said Jack, "I'm not sure how you intend to bring peace, but we'll gladly help you rescue the old fellow." Jack added silently, *It will give us an opportunity to learn more about this mysterious mage.*

Both Ben and Charles were able to understand the stranger in the dark cloak, which meant that he had to carry a translation stone.

Jack's curiosity finally got the better of him, and he asked, "Are there more people like you?"

The man in the dark cloak just smiled grimly. "Perhaps you'll find out one day. The man we're going to rescue is locked in the top of a tower surrounded by three barracks. This complex is inside a small city with a weakly fortified wall around its perimeter. Getting into the town should be easy because the gates will be open. The barracks are not open to random citizens, so approaching the barracks and tower will set off the alarm, and the soldiers will close the gates. It will also probably result in more soldiers being placed on the walls. Before you three came along,

I wasn't sure how to hold the gatehouse and rescue the man from the tower. If you all have reasonable skills, two of you should be able to hold the gatehouse for a few minutes at least."

"I'll accompany you," said Jack. "You'll need an easy means to get a rope to the top of the tower unless you want to run up all the steps and take out all the guards inside the tower."

"How are you going to attach a rope to the top of the tower?" asked the black-cloaked man.

"Leave that to me. Just get a rope with knots in it so that we can climb up and down quickly. If my idea fails, it will only cost us a few seconds, and we can still fight our way up and down the tower if needed. Where is the old man being held?"

The stranger replied, "He is in the town of Quilvich. It will take us half a day to reach there by foot."

"Well, let's get started then," said Ben impatiently.

The man in the dark cloak shook his head. "We will leave at first light so we can work in daylight. Since we will be conducting a rescue mission together, I suppose I should tell you my name. I am called Sumbvi."

******

At first light the three young men and Vennel met Sumbvi downstairs in the inn. They all shouldered their equipment and traveled east toward Quilvich.

As they traveled, Jack looked around for Garthong, who had been out hunting.

Just as Jack started to become concerned, his little friend flew up and landed on his shoulder.

Sumbvi glanced suspiciously at the creature but did not say a word.

The terrain, even on the roads, was very rocky, but it became somewhat smoother as they neared Quilvich.

Jack commented, "Everything seemed flatter when we were farther south, but now that we've traveled northward, it seems like there are a lot more hills and rocks."

Sumbvi replied, "All the lands of the north are hill country. If you continue north far enough, you will encounter the Great Northern Mountains."

"Well," said Ben, "it's good to know that they have very original names for their mountain ranges."

"Is it really less original than the Rocky Mountains?" asked Charles. "As if mountains could be made of something other than rocks."

The boys all chuckled.

Sumbvi furrowed his brow. "I have not heard of these mountains; where are they?"

"It doesn't matter," Jack replied quickly.

The town of Quilvich now stretched out before them.

Vennel hid on the side of the road about a half mile outside the gates to wait with the extra gear.

The rest of the group passed through the town gates without any problems.

Ben and Charles stepped off to the side in order to claim the gatehouse when the alarm sounded.

Jack and Sumbvi continued toward the barracks near the town's center.

The town was constructed much like Xin with distinct peasant, merchant, and wealthy districts. Jack was not surprised; it was common that the wealthy wanted to separate themselves from the common folk, and it made sense for all the businesses to cluster together. Jack noted increased security in comparison to Xin. Patrols actually traveled along the streets here.

Jack suspected that there was more to this town than just keeping a political prisoner. "Why is there so much security?" Jack asked.

Sumbvi replied, "I have no idea, but I didn't expect there to be this much. I hope your friends can hold the gate as we planned."

"Don't worry about them," said Jack. "I'm more worried about us making it through the middle of town with an old man in tow. Unlike the cowards we faced earlier, I don't believe these guys will run just because we throw a few fireballs at them."

Sumbvi pursed his lips. "I could do this part of the mission on my own if necessary. I just couldn't be in two places at one time. That's why I need help to hold the gate. Feel free to return to your friends if you're worried about our success."

Jack raised both his hands. "Okay, I'm sorry. I didn't mean to offend you. I was merely commenting on security and saying that we should be careful."

They approached the barracks. Each one was a wooden building with one entrance toward the road.

Sumbvi explained, "Each barracks has a set of stairs leading to the roof, where a single archer patrols."

Jack commented, "If we want to sneak onto the roof, we'll have to come up with a quiet way to deal with that archer and somehow avoid being noticed by the other two."

"We're not sneaking anywhere. We are going right through the barracks door."

A little surprised, Jack said, "But what if there's a whole squad of soldiers in there?"

"Then we'll have to take them out."

Jack was not sure he liked this guy's mentality. *He's definitely brave, but come on*, he thought, *why not implement a detailed plan or a little strategy to avoid unnecessary risk*. Jack felt himself longing for a cool, levelheaded partner such as Charles.

Sumbvi interrupted Jack's thoughts by running straight for the door.

Jack took off after him. They rocketed through the door and encountered three guards, whose lack of weapons indicated that they were off duty.

As soon as the guards saw the intruders, they rushed to the barracks wall and grabbed weapons. The barracks was lined with weapon racks and apparently doubled as an armory.

Sumbvi was so fast that he surprised Jack. He had drawn his sword, pulled his shield off his back, and run his sword through one of the three men before the man could get his shield in a defensive position.

Jack drew his own swords and assaulted one of the guards with a massive flurry of attacks, overwhelming the man's defenses and slicing a massive gash down his torso. Jack looked over to see that Sumbvi had already finished off the other guard.

Sumbvi surveyed Jack's work. "Not too bad, but two swords? Really? You obviously haven't fought many mages." He dashed out the back door.

The three barracks' back walls formed a small triangular courtyard with the buildings' back doors opening into the courtyard. The tower, which was approximately forty feet tall, stood imposingly in the courtyard's center.

"All right," said Sumbvi, "you have a way to get a rope to the top?"

Jack found the rope's middle, which he had previously marked by tying a piece of thread tightly around it. He coiled half of the rope, looked over his shoulder at the sack on his back, and said, "Wrap this around one of the supports up there, and drop the rope."

The little gother rocketed out of the sack, wrapped his feet around the coil, and flew to the top of the tower. Four large wooden supports emerged from the stone tower's corners to support its wooden roof. Jack's little friend wrapped the rope around one of the supports and released the coil, allowing it to fall along the tower's side.

Jack tied the rope's other end to one of the barracks' supports, and grasped the end that had just fallen.

Sumbvi used a spear he found inside the barracks to bar the outside of the tower door.

Then they quickly climbed up the rope to the top of the tower.

Two of the rooftop archers could not see Jack and Sumbvi because the tower itself blocked their vision.

The other archer was not on the roof. Jack guessed that he had heard the ringing of swords from their battle inside the barracks and crept down the stairs to the barracks' first floor to investigate.

As Jack and Sumbvi reached the top of the tower, the archer on the barracks facing them emerged from below and blew his horn.

They smashed the latch on the trapdoor and dropped inside the tower.

The two guards at the jail cell's entrance had heard the archer's horn and drawn their weapons.

Jack and Sumbvi dropped onto the guards from above and ran them through. They collected the key from one of the dead guards and opened the cell.

"Who are you?" asked the startled old man.

"It doesn't really matter right now." Sumbvi gripped the old man's arm and helped him to his feet. "We're here to rescue you. Come on."

Jack climbed back to the top of the tower through the trapdoor.

Sumbvi hoisted the old man up to Jack, who pulled him the rest of the way up.

Then they started climbing down the rope. The previous captive seemed remarkably capable given his age and recent inactivity.

Jack made it to the ground and heard the guards inside the tower pounding on the door's interior, but they were unable to break the spear.

The archer who had sounded the alarm earlier saw the three of them climbing down the rope and blew his horn again.

The archers on the other two barracks rushed toward the first archer, giving them a clear line of sight, and all three archers fired arrows at the intruders.

One arrow whizzed right past Jack, but he grabbed the old man by the arm and darted into the barracks.

Sumbvi entered right behind them.

They rushed out the barracks' front door, but a group of soldiers had already gathered. Apparently, one horn blast sounded the alarm and any blasts after that signaled the enemy's presence in that location, so all of the guards on patrol were on their way to the barracks.

Sumbvi used his shield as a battering ram to push through three guards, clearing a path.

Jack sidestepped an enemy attack then twisted and rammed his sword into his opponent's side.

The old man ran immediately behind Sumbvi.

Jack took up the rear, preventing the guards from flanking their little trio.

Some of the guards followed them while others ducked into side passages as if planning to cut them off up ahead.

They were about halfway to the gate when the plan fell apart. In the middle of the road in front of Sumbvi, a man stood with two guards behind him.

Sumbvi stopped and clinched his fist. "How did you find me?"

Jack also halted.

A Destiny Among Worlds

The four guards still keeping up with them also stopped running and slowly formed a semicircle behind the group.

Jack surveyed the man in front of them. He was actually fairly small, much shorter than Jack, and his shield was smaller than any Jack had seen in this world. The man had a scar, which Jack suspected was from a burn, on his left arm. He wore very expensive-looking clothing and armor.

"Hucklee," Sumbvi hissed.

"You know this guy?" asked Jack.

"Oh yes." Hucklee laughed with glee. "We've run into each other at least twice since we first met. I've hunted him for a long time. Sumbvi, I can't believe that with all the extra security, you didn't think that there might have been a trap here waiting for you."

Jack glanced at Sumbvi. "We have to take this guy out and go. The longer we stay, the more soldiers will come."

Sumbvi whipped around so that he faced the road's edge and shoved his hands straight out to his sides, launching a massive fireball along the street in both directions.

The three or four town guards behind them were completely caught by surprise. Two were essentially disintegrated, but the other two brought up their shields and were simply knocked backward by the impact.

Hucklee lifted his hand and calmly created a wide wall of ice in front of him.

The fireball hit the ice and burned deeply into it before dissipating.

"So bold," said Hucklee in a mocking tone. "You only have two more." He laughed.

Sumbvi rushed at Hucklee and attacked him fiercely with his sword, but despite his skill he was no match for Hucklee and two guards.

While the two guards behind them struggled to their feet after the fireball's impact, Jack leapt at one of them, kicked his shield to the side, and ran him through.

Jack saw at least another two dozen guards running toward them, but they were still some distance away.

Jack turned his attention to the other guard and unleashed a flurry of strikes. Jack's swords moved so fast that the guard could not react in time. On Jack's fifth strike, one of his swords bit into the soldier's hip, and Jack gave a strong front kick to the man's shield, knocking him to the roadside. Jack thought, *Well, that guy is wounded and won't be able to follow us. Now I've got to help Sumbvi.*

Sumbvi rammed one of Hucklee's guards with his shield, pushing him back a little.

The other guard came in behind him and rammed Sumbvi with his shield.

Sumbvi dropped his sword due to the shield's impact, but he grabbed the top of the soldier's shield with his right hand and lifted his fingers. Fire erupted from his palm, consuming the soldier. Sumbvi quickly spun and planted his shield's rim into the other guard's face, laying him out on the ground.

Hucklee moved in and struck Sumbvi's shield with his own, knocking the shield out of Sumbvi's hand. Hucklee said, "Well now, Sumbvi, here you are with no weapons except one fireball. And me? I'm just fine and have dozens of men on the way. Do you want to try your luck with that last little spit of fire?"

Sumbvi raised his hand, but he was too slow.

Hucklee brought his palm up first and encased both of Sumbvi's hands and arms in ice. Hucklee continued, "Now I pronounce you finished." He swung his sword straight down at Sumbvi's head.

At that moment, a loud crack resounded, and Hucklee's body split into three pieces.

Sumbvi looked at the place where Hucklee had been a moment before.

Jack stood about eight feet behind Hucklee's body. He flashed Sumbvi a triumphant smile. "I thought you could use the help," Jack said offhandedly. "Let's see if we can find his stones before we take off."

"He only had two water stones, and he kept them on some kind of necklace." Sumbvi smashed his hands against his own shield to shatter the ice.

Jack looked down at a half-melted, smoldering necklace on the ground. "You mean like that one?"

"Yes, but I don't see any stones on it anymore."

The old man, who had been crouching next to a nearby building, now joined them again.

"We only have a minute before all those guards get here." Then Jack realized that the guards had stopped and pulled out bows. "On second thought, I think we have less than twenty seconds."

"Here's one." Sumbvi slipped a blue gemstone into his pocket.

"Let's go," Jack urged. "We'll have to leave the other one. More soldiers are trying to cut us off up ahead."

The guards released their arrows.

"There are too many arrows!" Pulling the old man to him, Sumbvi picked up his shield and tried to make himself as small as possible behind it.

"Not for me," whispered Jack. He turned, looked up at the arrows raining down on them, and said, "Push."

Dust, wood fragments, and even small stones flew into the air, and the arrows scattered.

"Let's go!" Jack yelled.

They sprinted for the gate.

Two ranks of enemy soldiers barred the way. They lined up in formation with their swords and shields ready, but the gate, which stood open, lay just beyond them.

Well done, my friends, thought Jack. He glanced over at Sumbvi. "You still have one fireball, don't you?"

"Not for much longer." Sumbvi hurled flames at the men in formation.

The soldiers all had their shields up, so none of them were scorched alive. The impact, however, knocked the soldiers backward and opened a hole in their formation's center.

The three fugitives slipped through the gap and out the gate. Ben and Charles were already on the other side of the gate. They all ran down the road with Sumbvi and Jack each holding one of the elderly man's arms to assist him.

When they reached the place where Vennel waited, she joined them.

Sumbvi placed a hand on the old man's shoulder. "Now we just have to get this gentleman back home before the guards catch up."

The old man seemed to suddenly realize that he was free. He did a little dance in the road and offered very sincere thanks to them all.

Charles asked Sumbvi, "What stops the warlord from using his entire army to crush these people? It doesn't look like they have much of an army to stop him."

"The kingdom is actually in the middle of a border clash," Sumbvi replied, "and it recently suffered a massive troop loss. The warlord will not be ready to march his army out for some time. After that, if he does decide to march on his people, I'll probably be sent back here again."

"You'll be sent back here again?" clarified Jack. "So you're not working alone."

"And you're not just a couple of kids with swords," countered Sumbvi. "I don't have a clue what you are. You obviously had more than one gemstone, and you are far more powerful than I had originally anticipated, but I don't know what your goal was here."

"We didn't have a goal," said Jack. "We were just passing through."

"You were just passing through, yet you managed to save my life, kill my nemesis, and complete my mission. Did someone send you all to keep an eye on me for this mission?"

"No," replied Jack.

The two argued like this for much of the way back to their destination, but neither of them gathered any useful information. They parted ways just before reaching the town in which they had met Sumbvi, and Jack's group turned north toward their original destination.

The first night after their adventure in Quilvich, they stopped in a small clearing on the roadside. Tall weeds grew up and formed dense underbrush along the clearing's edges.

Jack dropped his backpack on the ground and meandered through the tall weeds in search of firewood.

Charles followed him. When they were alone, Charles said, "I think Vennel still acts like a slave. I've tried talking to her, but even though she'll discuss any subject, she still doesn't like to share any kind of opinion."

Jack nodded. "I agree, but I think you should be patient with her. She's not used to sharing her opinions, and she may not even be used to having them. As far as the extra work goes, I think she's just grateful and trying to do her part."

They both had an armload of firewood now, so they turned back toward the camp.

Charles pushed a tall stalk of some plant that Jack did not recognize out of the way. Flowers budded on some of the branches amongst the shrubs' and trees' bright-green leaves.

They stepped out of the brush into the clearing, where they planned to set up camp.

Surprisingly, Vennel had already set up the tent, which was little more than a few tarps made of strong, oiled cloth. She was currently clearing a place for the fire.

Several of the bushes shook on the clearing's other side, and Ben emerged with more firewood. As he approached the place for the fire, Vennel pulled cooking utensils out of her bag.

While Ben started the fire, Jack cast his gaze over the surrounding bushes to see if he could locate Garthong.

His little friend had attached himself to the bark of a small tree within the dense underbrush. A few moments later Garthong dived to the ground.

Jack could imagine a huge scuffle with a bug or mouse taking place behind the leaves and branches. He turned his attention back toward his friends at the fire, which was starting to crackle cheerfully.

******

The next morning Charles woke up, stretched, and stepped outside the tent.

Vennel knelt by the fire, cooking breakfast, and Jack was nowhere around, leaving only Ben snoring inside the tent.

Charles approached the fire and sat down near Vennel. He absently poked the coals with a stick. "Something has been bothering me. When we were in the village before Quilvich, we all rushed out into the street to help the people out there. When we left you in the inn, we didn't know whether Sumbvi was a bad guy." Charles scratched his head. "I guess I'm just worried for your safety."

"You shouldn't be worried about *me*," Vennel assured him humbly.

Charles set his jaw. "It's not a trivial thing. When we get to another town or village, I'll buy you a dagger or something so you can protect yourself."

She replied, "If Jack wishes me to carry a dagger, then I will."

Charles stared into the fire and watched the flames slowly lick up toward the top of a stick that was holding out longer than he expected.

Jack, with Garthong on his shoulder, emerged from the underbrush, shaking the leaves and branches as he stepped through the gap he had just made. He did not look particularly pleased.

Charles broke a stick in half and added the pieces to the fire. "What were you doing out there?"

Jack rolled his eyes. "Well, *someone* jumped on my head and woke me up then flew out of the tent as though something were wrong. I got up and followed him. Finally, he stopped on a bush, and as I walked up, three or four rabbits ran out in different directions. Obviously, I didn't catch any of them with a sword. I'm not really sure how to read this little guy's noises and screeches, but as near as I can guess, he wanted me to hunt with him."

Charles laughed and slapped his knee with his hand. "Did you actually try swinging at any of them with your sword?"

Jack shook his head. "No, I was nowhere near fast enough to draw my sword before the prey had escaped. I suppose I could've shot one of them with lightning, but then there wouldn't have been anything left to eat."

After they rousted Ben and ate their breakfast, they broke camp and stepped back onto the road.

Chapter 11

BEN WAS RATHER PLEASED. It had been a long journey, but they had run into some merchants a few days after parting company with Sumbvi and were able to hitch a ride with their caravan. This made it so they did not have to walk, which satisfied all of them a great deal. Charles had purchased a knife from one of the merchants, which he gave to Vennel. Despite her claim that it was unnecessary, Ben could tell that she was pleased with the gift. Now, they were finally crossing the border into Dulla.

"Wow," said Ben, "the roads here are very high quality in comparison to anywhere else we have been."

They reached the first village, and the difference was even more apparent. *The people seem fairly happy, and the cottages are nice and well kept for stone buildings*, thought Ben. *Everything is so much richer*. This was the only way he could think of to explain it.

Ben commented, "The people here aren't necessarily wealthy, but the standard of living is exceptional in comparison to what we've been used to seeing."

Jack nodded in agreement.

In the village there was even a shop sign that read, "Mail." *There's no way people actually deliver mail from country to country*, thought Ben. He did not usually care what most of the travelers they encountered had to say, so it did not usually bother him when it was Charles's turn with the translation stone. For once, Ben was glad he had the translation stone.

Jack detoured to the building with the mail sign for a few minutes before returning to the caravan.

"What were you doing?" asked Ben.

Jack explained, "I wrote a letter to Hal, informing him where we are and asking him to pass our regards on to Elton the next time he sees him."

They left the village, and on their way to the capital city of Duthwania, Ben found himself wondering what kind of food they had in Duthwania and whether he might be able to try a new dish. The meals in, well anywhere, had been a great disappointment to him so far. The various countries must have had signature dishes, but up until now everyone, except the governors and warlords, was so poor that the only new dishes he had opportunities to taste were simple and bland. Ben thought, *Vennel is a better cook than any of us, but face it, the few herbs she gathers on the side of the road to season flour and jerky aren't a culinary delight.*

They passed a huge lake off to their left, which resided northwest of the capital. Ben decided that before they left Duthwania, he should find an opportunity to sail on that lake.

"Jack," he said casually, "we have to go north after this, and that lake is mostly north. Let's sail across it to reach Celel."

Jack glanced at the body of water. "I don't think that lake is really in our path, Ben. We should probably just stick to the road."

"But it would be so much more fun," countered Ben, "to sail across the lake. Plus, talk about the romantic experience for Charles and Vennel."

Charles reached over and shoved Ben off the path.

Vennel gave no perceivable reaction.

Ben smiled. It was easy to tease the two of them. Charles always responded in the same shy or offended manner, and although Vennel never showed an emotional reaction, Ben suspected that he affected her too. And it was important work; after all, if Ben did not lighten the mood, no one would. It was particularly fun to tease Charles when he did not have the translation stone because he could not defend himself in any way to Vennel without sounding like a babbling idiot. Ben got a real kick out of listening to him try to tell her in English not to listen to Ben and to completely ignore him.

In his frustration Charles did attempt to learn some of the common tongue from Vennel, but he made little progress. The learning process was complex since it required Charles to constantly pass the translation stone back and forth to Jack or Ben so that Charles could hear Vennel's language without the gemstone automatically translating it. Based on some of the comments that Elton had made and his own conversations with Hal, Jack theorized that with practice using the translation stone, one might eventually develop the ability to sense when the translation stone was in use, know what language it translated, and even turn it off. The three young men, however, did not yet have the skill necessary to turn off the translation stone while it was in their possession. As tiresome as handing the stone back and forth was, Ben suspected that the learning process would have been almost impossible for Charles without the translation stone.

They finally approached Duthwania. *Wow*, thought Ben, *This is a sight to behold!* Despite huge stone walls and massive gatehouses, the city somehow appeared bright and shining rather than old and gray. It had been several weeks since they had rescued the old man, and they still had not stopped anywhere for more than one night. The capital city was so large that Ben thought they could spend days walking around and still see only a portion of the city.

After they parted ways with the caravan, Ben asked, "So how do we find this guy we're looking for?"

"I'm not exactly sure," replied Jack. "I believe I'll go to the royal court, ask for a water mage, and see what comes up."

"I'll go with you, Jack," said Ben, "just in case you run into trouble. Since this is official business, I'd better take the translation stone."

Charles briefly protested, but Ben reminded him of their deal. When they traveled, Ben did not really care if Vennel could understand him, so he let Charles have the stone. Whenever they entered a town or village, however, he wanted to be able to read the signs and listen to people, so it was his turn now.

Charles reluctantly gave him the stone.

"You two can find a place to stay," said Jack. "We shouldn't be long."

Jack and Ben wandered through the city, trying to get their bearings.

Garthong soared high in the sky, and they soon lost sight of him.

Off to his left Ben saw a stable and blacksmith shop. A little farther down he noticed a large stone structure with a patrol of soldiers marching through the front door. The building's front was solid stone, but the second floor had several small windows. The roof possessed the same defensive arrangement of stone blocks as a wall or gatehouse. Ben guessed that the structure was either a barracks or a type of police station.

Jack and Ben traveled until they came to several more large buildings with huge stone columns. Some of the buildings reminded Ben of courthouses. They asked several nearby townspeople and discovered that one of the buildings was reserved for mages. *Wow, a building that large reserved specifically for mages*, thought Ben. *The city must have several mages.*

Jack walked up the large stone steps and into the front door with Ben following close behind him. The building was composed of several rooms opening off of the entryway. The room on the right looked rather official as if it were intended for teaching. The room had tables and parchments in it and reminded Ben way too much of a classroom. The room on the left had the medieval equivalent to couches and chairs and seemed to have no specific purpose. Ben guessed that it was a break room. The room directly ahead contained no furniture or anything on the floor except some painted lines. It actually reminded Ben of their martial arts dojo. They walked to the room directly ahead, where several people were gathered around talking.

As they entered, the group in the room took notice.

One of the group members, a short middle-aged man, walked over. "I'm sorry, only mages are allowed in here." The man had a prominent goatee. He wore black pants, a white shirt, and a red vest with gold buttons down the front and spiral designs embroidered in black thread.

Jack replied, "I'm looking for a man who can teach water stone wielders how to use ice."

The man frowned. "So you found a water stone, and you think that makes you a mage? Kid, you are in way over your head here; go home."

Jack did not move.

The man restated, "Only mages are allowed in here. Is that not clear to you? Get out."

"Fine." Jack shrugged. "What do I have to do to be allowed in the building?"

The whole group laughed.

The short man with the vest said, "There's not a person for miles around who could become a new member here since all of the mages in this region have already been identified."

"I've traveled quite some distance to find you," Jack said, identifying this man as the group's leader. "Warlord Abgot seemed to think you would help me learn how to use my water stone."

The short man raised an eyebrow. "Fine. Split the target with any magic spell, and you can stay in the building."

He pointed to the other end of the room where six small white balls hung, three on each wall. The man crossed his arms and smiled. "Strings are attached between the walls at angles so that each ball travels on its string to the opposite wall. Each time a ball touches the other wall, one of the balls on that wall starts moving to the opposite wall. You don't get to know which ball will start moving next. You have to hit one of the balls in motion with a magic spell. You are not allowed to hit either of the side walls or any of the strings. You have to split the ball without breaking the string. The balls move very quickly. If you fail, you cannot try again for at least a week. I'll warn you, kid, it takes reasonably skilled mages one to two months to succeed at this challenge."

Jack stepped up to the mark on the floor. "Whenever you're ready."

The short man frowned. "So cocky. All right, release the first ball."

Ben watched the first ball travel to the opposite wall.

It moved fast, but Jack did not move or even twitch. Then the second ball went to the opposite wall, and still, Jack did not move.

Four more chances left, thought Ben. *I hope he knows what he's doing.* Then he reassured himself, *It's Jack. If anybody is going to come up with a plan, it's him.*

The third ball started, and Jack slowly raised both hands, palms outward. Then the fourth ball began moving. Jack twitched his left hand, and wind swept into the room. The ball collided with the wind, which arrested the ball's movement and pushed it very slowly toward the wall from which it had originally come. Then Jack twitched his right hand, and a bolt of lightning leapt forward and struck the ball, splitting it into dust.

Jack turned around calmly. "Can we talk now?"

The short man in the vest raised his eyebrows, but otherwise his face remained stiff as if he did not want to show his surprise. He examined Jack closely for a moment as the wide-eyed mage group around him whispered back and forth. Finally, he said, "Fine, you can stay in the building, but I won't teach you how to use your water stone."

Jack turned his hands palm upward. "Why not?"

"You're not a mage from my country, so I have no motivation to help you."

"I'll pay you the normal fee," insisted Jack.

"I won't do it for money either."

"You must want something," Jack said, somewhat exasperated.

"There is nothing I need or want."

Just then, a tall man in extremely expensive clothing strode in with several guards behind him. He wore a deep blue tunic over a crisp white linen shirt and had a black cape draped over one shoulder. His face was hard like a warrior's face, which contrasted strongly with his extravagant clothing. Ben immediately noted a resemblance between this man and the shorter man's facial features; they even had the same style mustache and beard.

The newcomer turned toward the shorter man and said, "Daggoth, how dare you use the training room without permission! You know as well as I do that the training room is only to be used when the Advising Oversight Committee gives its express permission."

The short man, who was called Daggoth, replied, "Calm down, Dagder. It's not that big of a deal. We just had a mage test; that's all."

"I don't care." Dagder stood to his full height and looked down upon Daggoth. "If you do anything other than scratch your nose in this room, you must have my permission. You are not even supposed to talk in here."

Daggoth replied, "Dagder, seriously, it isn't that big of a deal."

"You think it's not a big deal. You mages are always warmongering and trying to blow things up. I'll tell father, and we'll see what he has to say about this." Dagder spun on his heel and walked out at a brisk pace with his guards in tow.

"What was all that about?" asked Jack.

Daggoth replied, "That is my younger brother. Our father is the king of Dulla." He turned to the other mages. "Well, apparently, we have to talk in the other room."

The whole group filed out.

"What about the new mage's companion?" asked one of the other mages.

"I don't care. We can't test him, so I'll give him leniency for today. You two can stay here," continued Daggoth, "but I'm not teaching you anything. Apparently, even if I wanted to, I couldn't."

"What is the Advising Oversight Committee?" asked Jack.

"By my father's decree, no one is allowed to use magic without the committee's approval. The law was designed to prevent mages from abusing their power, but unfortunately, it basically means we can't use our power. I'm leaving," said Daggoth. "You all enjoy yourselves as much as possible."

After he left, Jack asked the other mages, "So what's the story behind all this?"

They all looked grim, and one of them, a middle-aged man with cheery, round cheeks, brown hair, and a waistline that made Ben think he looked as though he had swallowed a watermelon, started telling the tale. "When the brothers were young, they were both skilled at using swords and shields. Their ages are not particularly far apart, and as a result the younger brother actually surpassed his older brother in fighting skills. The king became concerned that the people would not respect his heir to the throne simply because he was older, so when the head mage became old and died, the king gave the mage's gemstones to his oldest son, Daggoth. Daggoth quickly became skilled in using the gemstones and became a powerful mage, but his younger brother became insanely jealous because he was no longer stronger than his older brother in battle.

"The king did not want his younger son to start a civil war when he died, so the king did not give Dagder any gemstones and created a law stating that no one within the kingdom could give or sell Dagder a gemstone. Now Dagder holds Daggoth responsible for his inability to become a mage and seeks ways to punish him. The king does love both of his sons, and in an attempt to keep them from fighting, he formed the 'Advising Oversight Committee for Mages' and placed Dagder in charge of it. The two brothers are constantly at odds on almost every issue."

"That's unfortunate." Jack scratched his chin. "On a related topic, does anyone in the city sell gemstones?"

"It's illegal here to sell a gemstone to a foreigner," said one of the mages.

Jack politely thanked the mages, and he and Ben left the building.

Ben asked, "What are we going to do now?"

Jack thought for a moment. "I believe we need to find a way to get Dagder to order his brother to teach me what I want to know. Resolving the situation between them seems unlikely at the moment, so we have to figure out what Dagder wants and offer it to him in exchange for what we want. I'm going to need to do some research on this. I'll ask around and find out what kinds of things interest him."

"If you don't need help," said Ben, "I'm going to explore the town."

"All right," replied Jack, "but be careful not to get lost; this is a huge city."

Ben watched as Jack walked off. *Jack will probably come up with something clever*, Ben thought. Ben noticed that four other mages from the building were also leaving, and decided to follow them.

The mage group seemed to move with a purpose, but Ben kept up with them easily. After a little while the group split into two pairs. The two youngest went to the left, and the others turned to the right.

Ben decided to follow the younger group. *They usually do more interesting things*, he thought.

An hour passed, and the two young mages went out through one of the city gates. They continued down the road for about half an hour before turning off to the road's left side, hopping over a small wooden fence, and walking through a field. They climbed a fence on the field's other side and ducked into some trees.

Ben entered the trees and discovered a small clearing just a little ways into the forest. Here, the two mages he had followed met four other young men. The grass inside the clearing was badly burned, and many of the trees around the edge were also damaged. *This must be where they come to practice,* thought Ben. He waited for about ten minutes, but all the young men had sat down and were not talking about anything interesting. *I guess the only thing left for me to do is simply walk in and introduce myself,* he decided.

Ben stepped into the clearing and waved. "Hey."

The group all whipped their heads around and stared at him for a moment.

One of them smacked one of the two Ben had followed on the head. "I told you to make sure you were never followed. Every one of us needs to be careful. If Dagder finds out about this place, we'll all be in trouble." Then he looked at Ben and demanded, "Who are you, and what do you want?"

"I'm Ben, and I don't really want anything." Ben smiled broadly and an attempt to relieve the tension in the air. "I don't know anyone in the city. I met those two earlier in the mages' building and thought I'd see if you guys were up to anything interesting."

"How do we know you're not a spy for Dagder?" one of them asked suspiciously.

Ben thought for a moment. "You didn't know I was here, and you have obviously already broken the rules." Ben gestured at the burned ground. "So if I was a spy, I would have already told my master, and he would already be here with men to enforce whatever decision he has authority to make."

"That's true," said one.

Another interjected, "He's a foreigner. How do we know we can trust him?"

"Come on guys," said Ben. "Are you really going to say that I have to get lost because Dagder doesn't like foreigners? Daggoth is your actual boss, and he already said we could hang out in the mages' building. Those two were there; they know what I'm talking about."

The group of mages discussed the matter for a moment.

Finally, one of them said, "I suppose you can hang out with us. Anything that goes against what Dagder wants that we can get away with is a sure thing."

Ben stayed with the group of mages for the rest of the day and discussed a variety of topics. Apparently, many of them liked to hunt and fish, and they all loved practicing with their gemstones. Near the end of the day, that is what they all decided to do.

The two youngest mages, whom Ben had followed, went first, and both let loose very impressive fireballs.

Then one of the other mages took a turn.

After that, one of the mages Ben had followed said, "Hey, Ben, you were in the mages' building with your friend, the one who blew away the training test. That must mean that you have a gemstone as well."

Ben inhaled sharply and glanced around self-consciously. "Yes, I do have one, but I don't really know how to use it. I awakened it a few days ago on the trip here, but I haven't used it yet."

The oldest mage asked, "What kind of gemstone is it?"

Ben answered, "A fire stone."

"Does your friend know anything about fire stones?"

"Not really. He gave it to me without awakening it himself, so he has never used one."

"We'll teach you how to use it then. The first thing to remember is that the blast comes from your palm, so your hand has to be pointed at least in your target's general direction. You fire by focusing your mind on the target. The crystal will try to hit what you're aiming at in your mind. That means it's very difficult to shoot a fireball in a direction that you are not looking. It's also difficult to shoot two fireballs in different directions at the same time. Some people don't believe you can shoot more than two gemstones at once, but there are rumors of mages who were able to master this art in ages past. The most important thing, though, is if you can focus well enough on your target, you can actually adjust the temperature and some other small details about the fireball, or whatever else you're firing, before you cast it or even while it's in flight. These details are easier to control in some gemstones."

Ben asked, "So if I focus well enough, I can make my fireball hotter? What other details can I affect?"

"Yes, you can make it hotter. You can also make it colder, which would be less damaging, but some mages have used this as a form of torture. You can spray fire very lightly, causing small burns all over your victim's body. This technique can also be used to capture someone you are fighting without killing them. Other things you can affect include shape and, to some extent, duration—meaning, you can make your fire linger."

Ben formed his first fireball and sent it sailing against a tree.

"That wasn't too bad," said one of the mages.

"Yeah, but I was actually aiming at that tree, not the one I hit." Ben pointed at his target.

"It still wasn't that far off. We will meet here again around midday tomorrow. Come join us, and we'll show you some more."

The group broke up, and its members headed their separate ways.

The night at the inn was relatively uneventful.

Ben relinquished the translation stone that night with the understanding that he would get it back in the morning. They discovered that the best communication came when Vennel held the translation stone because she could then converse with both Ben and Charles.

Charles had spent several hours that day watching some villagers work on a house, and he was fairly confident that he could reproduce the thatching technique he had seen if he ever needed to repair a roof. Toward evening, Charles had become terribly bored because he could not talk with anyone. He had found some metal scraps and built a puzzle with another in the works.

Vennel spent the evening mending a rip in her dress. She had explored a little but was not comfortable wandering too far alone.

Charles asked Vennel, "Would you like to explore with me tomorrow?"

Vennel nodded shyly. "If I wouldn't be a bother ... ."

"Oh, not at all." Charles reassured her.

The two of them spread out a map and made a list of the sites they wanted to see.

Jack also studied a map to determine where he should gather information the next day since he had been very unsuccessful thus far.

******

The next morning Ben woke up early, which was unusual for him, but Jack had already left to work on a way to change Daggoth's mind.

Ben returned to the area where he had met his new friends, and the days passed like this for a week. On a couple of the days, Ben let Charles keep the translation stone, which worked out fine since the mages with which Ben spent his time possessed translation stones. Ben and Charles agreed that it would attract less attention if only Ben met with the mages, and Charles could learn about his own fire stone from Ben at a later time.

Charles and Vennel spent their days exploring the city. They also watched more building construction. In the evenings Charles excitedly described some of the designs and methods they had witnessed. He told them that he had many ideas for improving upon the building techniques using more modern ideas. "Don't worry, guys," he told them one evening. "If we ever need to earn a living here, maybe I could become a contractor."

At the end of the week, Ben was out with the mages again, and this time he actually successfully cast an extremely powerful and hot fireball.

"Careful," said one of the mages, "with fireballs like that, you'll burn down all the trees that keep us concealed here."

The group laughed and started talking about their arch nemesis, Dagder. According to the mages, Dagder was willing to do almost anything to impede, or even inconvenience, his brother. Some of the mages even thought that he bribed the other members his father appointed to the mage council.

This conversation gave Ben an idea. When Ben returned to the inn, he explained his idea and told Jack that the two of them needed to find a way to speak to Dagder, even if it was brief.

"Well, I think I've pretty much nailed down his schedule," said Jack, "but I still haven't identified anything he wants badly enough to give us the leverage that we need to convince him to let Daggoth teach me."

"No problem," said Ben. "I've got this."

Using the information Jack had gathered, they located a place on the street where they could meet Dagder.

"He should pass this way soon," said Jack.

Sure enough, Dagder and his four bodyguards were coming down the street. The man kept a very strict routine.

Jack and Ben stepped out in front of him and bowed at the waist.

Ben said, "Excuse me, but I have a proposition that you will want to hear."

Anger filled Dagder's eyes as he gazed at the two foreigners in his way. "I'd better, or I'll have you thrown in prison for impeding my path."

Undeterred, Ben smiled broadly. "We're offering an opportunity for you to inconvenience your brother, and we'll even pay you to do it."

The look on Dagder's face changed to curiosity.

Ben continued, "Your brother has refused to teach my friend here how to cast ice with a water stone, and he was somewhat embarrassed by my friend's very successful passage of the mage test. Traditionally, a mage will pay a fee to learn something from another mage. I propose that we pay you that fee and that you order your brother to teach my friend what he wants to know."

Dagder stood for a moment as if deliberating then named a price.

"Perfect." Without hesitation, Jack pulled the money out of his pocket, counted it, and handed it to Dagder.

Dagder said, "I like ordering my brother to do things that he hates. Go to the mages' building, and I'll have him teaching you whatever you want."

Ben and Jack bowed at the waist again and headed for the mages' building.

As they walked, Jack commented, "I did all that research to find something that he wanted. I even researched his father, the king, and read the king's life's story in that library-like building near the palace."

Jack smiled. "Apparently, what he wanted most was just to force his brother to do something he didn't want to do."

"Exactly," replied Ben. "Plus, a bribe never hurts during a negotiation."

Jack laughed. "Well done, Ben. I trust your new friends had something to do with your idea?"

Ben raised his eyebrows in surprise. "How did you know about my new friends?"

"Oh, come on," replied Jack, "according to Charles, you've been getting up early every day and rushing off. You come back at night with a smile on your face. You have either been having a lot of fun with some new friends, found a restaurant that serves truly divine food, or met a beautiful young woman who's madly in love with you."

They both laughed.

Ben said, "How did you know the exact order of importance of that list?"

Jack replied, "In all honesty, I thought the restaurant would actually be number one on your list."

The two friends were still laughing when they reached the mages' building. They entered and found several mages. Daggoth was also present.

Within moments a messenger arrived and spoke briefly with Daggoth.

Daggoth turned to Jack with a sideways smile. "I don't have any idea how you convinced my brother to make me teach you how to use ice, but I suppose I'll be grateful that I get to use my gemstones for any purpose."

Jack offered him a fee for the teaching as well, which Daggoth accepted.

They went into the training room, and Daggoth explained the principles behind ice.

Ben recognized most of the principles because both fire and ice casting involved altering the temperature before casting the spell. In Ben's case he heated fire, and in Jack's case he cooled water. There were some minor differences with which Ben was not familiar, and he suspected that every gemstone involved slightly different methods for focusing. A skilled mage could probably utilize all of the principles without even thinking.

Jack cast his water stone and froze the water against the wall.

"Not too bad," said Daggoth. "In a day or two, I think you'll have it."

"It's not quite perfect yet." Ben hurled a fireball into the ice, shattering it. "The ice should be able to stop my fireball."

Jack raised an eyebrow. "I see someone's been busy."

Ben smiled. For the first time since they'd arrived in this world, he felt as though he could really do something.

Daggoth glanced at Ben. "You might give some warning next time before you go around spitting fire." He returned his attention to Jack. "You almost have this. You were already altering some aspects of your spell casting by focusing through your gemstones when you passed the mage's test. I watched you hurl your air into the ball and then slow it down and reverse its direction to allow you to more easily strike the ball with your lightning. It takes a more skilled mage to alter the speed of a spell after it's cast."

Over the next few days, although he was slow to admit it, Daggoth actually became fairly fond of Jack and their conversations on gemstones. According to Daggoth, Jack was a prodigy, and any opportunity for Daggoth and his mages to demonstrate their gemstones was a rare pleasure.

Jack also learned many more paragraphs in the book that he received from Hal because he could only practice one time every two hours, giving him a great deal of time to study.

One night when they were all gathered at the inn, Jack exclaimed excitedly, "My fifth stone is a stone of illusion." Jack pointed at the book. "See, I can change aspects of my face or make it look like I'm wearing armor. It only seems to last for a couple minutes, but it apparently has the longest duration of all the gemstones." Jack cast the spell and created two duplicates of himself.

"I can totally tell that those aren't real," said Ben. "I can kind of see through the images. Of course, if I was farther away, it would probably be more convincing."

Jack frowned. "That means I may be able to make an image of myself running to distract some archers, but if I was fighting soldiers hand to hand, they would easily be able to tell which one was fake."

Ben was very interested in this concept. He leaned forward. "Can you create smoke or mist to cloud your movements or conceal you?"

"According to what the book says, I think I can," said Jack. "I think I can create an image of almost anything."

Charles asked, "How come your irises don't change color when you use the illusion stone like they do with other stones in your bloodstream?"

"Actually, they do," Jack replied. "According to the book, they turn yellow, but part of the illusion is that I make my eyes still *look* normal."

******

After Jack mastered ice casting with his lesser water stone, they joined a merchant caravan traveling north. Jack was relieved that they were finally on their way to Celel. At first the caravan had been thrilled to take on free security. Within the first six hours, however, Ben had managed to char much of the foliage growing along the roadside, and each time the fires erupted, the horses spooked. Once, Jack even had to put out Ben's fire with his water stone to prevent the forest from burning.

Ben had also been teaching Charles about his fire stone, and all three of them practiced their spells at every opportunity. By the second day Ben and Charles were working on controlling the amount of heat their fire produced, and Charles quickly picked up on how to control his magic.

Despite the uneasiness a few of the merchants seemed to feel, none of them made any negative comment to the young mages.

Charles also continued practicing Lavdoric, the common tongue, with Vennel, and he became more proficient every day. To the young men's surprise, Vennel actually possessed a fairly extensive knowledge of several languages other than the common tongue because of her broad traveling. Despite his interest in these other languages, Charles decided to stay focused only on the common tongue for the present.

Three days passed like this, and the young people's supplies started to dwindle. This was not really a problem because one of the merchants sold a variety of foods. Jack opened his pack and examined the last of their food. Then he had a thought. *Vennel has worked extremely hard ever since she joined our group. The slave mentality she has may dissipate over time, but if I gave her more trust, maybe she would start to see herself as more of an equal.* Jack pulled some money out of his pouch. Based on what he normally spent on food, he decided on an amount and approached Vennel.

Jack said, "Vennel, since you do a lot of the cooking, I thought it would be a good idea if you picked out the supplies we need. You're also a far better cook than the rest of us, so you know what foods go together. Here's some money for you to keep so that you can purchase supplies."

She simply replied, "Of course." She took the money and walked over toward the merchants.

As Jack watched her walk away, he contemplated whether he had been successful. *Actually,* he thought, *that sounded a lot like I just gave her an assignment, which is what masters do with slaves.*

His thoughts were interrupted by an unpleasant odor. He looked around but did not see anything wrong.

Garthong wiggled in his pouch on Jack's back and emerged. Once Garthong climbed all the way up on Jack's shoulder, Jack realized that the odor came from a half-eaten rat that Garthong clenched tightly in his mouth.

Jack raised an eyebrow at the little lizard. "Eat that smelly thing somewhere else."

With a little screech of annoyance, the gother jumped down on the ground to finish his prize.

Jack shook his head and thought, *Well, at least he can reliably catch things for himself now.* Jack chuckled as he thought, *A couple weeks ago that rat probably would've killed him if they had a confrontation.*

Another week and a half passed, and the boys' continued practice with their gemstones was yielding results. Charles, in particular, had made great strides in learning from Ben how to control the temperature of his fireballs. As they traveled one day, they passed a large field off to the east.

Jack suggested, "Hey, let's test how far we can all cast our gemstones."

Ben stepped forward and hurled a fireball at a forty-five degree angle into the sky. It finally came down a little over a hundred yards away. "That seems to be as far as I can throw mine," said Ben.

Charles was a little less practiced with distance casting, but he could hurl his fire almost as far as Ben could.

Jack raised his hand and cast a sheet of ice. He discovered that he could not make it travel beyond fifty yards. Irritated, Jack raised his other hand and let loose a bolt of lightning. It rocketed over the field and struck the trees on the other side, splitting one in two.

"Fascinating," said Jack. "With some skill, you can make the spells go farther, but there's no denying the marked difference in distance between these gemstones. Lightning can travel over twice the distance of fire, and fire seems to be one of the longer-range spells."

Jack tried creating an illusion out in the field; he conjured up the image of a merchant they had seen in the previous village and sent the image walking.

Ben commented, "It becomes fuzzier as it goes away from you."

Jack replied, "I think all of the spells get weaker as they travel, which makes sense because we're creating something from nothing, so the farther it gets from the power source, the weaker the spell should become."

"Theoretically," added Charles, "the greater the distance between you and your opponent, the easier it will be to block the other mage's element with one of your own. For example, water has an advantage against fire, but if someone casts water or ice from a distance, you may be able to create a wall of fire to block the attack."

Their practice continued until they crossed over the border into Celel. They had all learned much on their journey although Ben still expressed disappointment that he had never been afforded the opportunity to sail on the great lake.

Chapter 12

CELEL'S CAPITAL WAS ALL the way on the coast, but they arrived at one of the country's larger cities located near Celel's border with Dulla. This city was called Juma. Like the cities and roads in Dulla, all of Celel seemed to be bursting with wealth and prosperity. The people seemed happy, and even in the smaller villages, appeared to walk the streets without fear.

The boys asked around the city, and at least according to the people with whom they spoke, none of the slave cartels had bases inside Celel's borders.

Jack stopped by Juma's barracks and asked the captain of the guard a variety of questions about the law and whether there were any laws that foreigners typically unknowingly broke.

The captain of the guard informed him that the most common laws broken by foreigners involved their slaves. "Slaves are not recognized here to be slaves," explained the captain. "They must be treated as an indentured servant or peasant."

Jack's eyes grew wide. "Wow, so everyone is actually equal here."

"Oh, not exactly." The captain laughed. "It's illegal to have slaves, but some treat their servants better than others, and the nobility still imagine themselves to be above the peasants. Wealth and a family name still hold significant sway in people's minds even though the law no longer recognizes a difference."

Jack spoke with the captain at length and discovered that the country actually possessed some form of justice system. The city guards collected information about a person's guilt or innocence regarding a crime and arrested them. The captain pronounced guilt or innocence after hearing the information, as in most countries of this world. In Celel, however, convicted people could appeal decisions to the governor if they could convince another town's captain that there was just cause to do so. In addition, if they were convicted by the governor, individuals could appeal their case to the chief of justice at the capital if they could convince another town's governor that there was just cause. Jack and his friends decided that this was the freest country they had heard of in this world.

Jack also discovered that he could make an appointment to meet with the town's governor by submitting a request with the captain of the guard. Jack decided to submit a request for the next day to see the governor.

They stayed that night at a nearby inn and waited for the next day.

"All I have to do," said Jack, "is ask the governor how to get an audience with the king. With any luck the king will have heard of our world like the rumors say, and perhaps he can even get us home."

******

The next afternoon as Jack left the inn to meet the governor, a messenger approached and gave him a letter from Elton. Jack was surprised that a messenger found them, but the man explained that foreign travelers were rare, so searching for them was not difficult.

After skimming the letter Jack rushed back into the inn and handed it to Ben. "This is great news. Apparently, Elton got our message, and he is going to be here in Celel within the next month or two. Well, you guys can read the letter for yourselves. I have to get to my appointment"

With that, Jack rushed out again. He thought, *I definitely don't want to be late for an appointment with the governor.* As he walked, he thought, *I actually need to ask Elton for his advice about Vennel.* Jack believed she would naturally change, but it seemed to be taking longer than he had expected. As he walked, he considered the conversations that she had shared with Charles on the road. She had been interacting more with the entire group and Charles in particular, but she had not changed her attitude. Jack decided that Elton must have come up with a way to shake off those old ideas from his past, and he would probably have some good advice on how to help Vennel do the same. Then Jack shook his head as he considered, *Who knows, this country doesn't even recognize slavery, so maybe she will just catch on by herself.*

When Jack arrived at the governor's office, a maid answered the door and escorted Jack into a large well-lit room with a desk. Behind the desk sat a middle-aged man with a bushy, brown beard and mustache. The man had reddish-brown hair, a round face, and narrow eyes. He appeared to be about Jack's height, although it was difficult to tell since he sat behind the desk. The man carried a little extra weight and lacked the calloused hands of a laborer, giving him the appearance of one accustomed to luxury.

"What can I do for you, young man?" The governor leaned back in his chair and made a tent with his fingers under his chin.

"My friends and I need to speak to the king, and I thought that you would know the proper way to do that."

The governor remained silent for a moment. Then he burst into laughter.

Jack gave no reaction and simply sat looking at the governor until the man finished.

"You want to see the king, do you?" the governor said, catching his breath. "Because we let any random foreigners have an audience with his Royal Highness. Who do you think you are, kid, that you could get an audience with the king of a country, any king?"

"I understand it's a little unorthodox." Jack calmly rested his hands on the desk. "But it's very important. What types of people are allowed to see the king?"

The governor snickered again but replied, "People who work in the castle get to see the king, but foreigners are not allowed to work in the castle except under special circumstances because we've experienced so many problems with spies over the years. His lords and governors get to see him ... and the Knights of Celel. The Chief of Justice, a few of his other royal appointments who aid in governing, and perhaps, emissaries from a powerful foreign king also see him. I can't actually think of another way at the moment, but there might be another. Why do you need to see the king so badly?"

"My friends and I are trying to return home, and we heard that the king of this country was the only one who might know about our homeland."

The governor smiled slightly. "So you came all this way on a little rumor?"

"Yes," Jack replied. "Out of the possibilities you mentioned, it seems like a knight would be the easiest thing to become. How would one go about becoming a knight?"

The governor started laughing again but then seemed to realize that Jack was serious. "Okay." He sighed as if resigning himself to the reality of more conversation with this ignorant foreigner. "To become a Knight of Celel, you must get a recommendation from a current or retired Knight of Celel, you must possess at least one gemstone and know how to use it, and you have to gain the support of one of the prominent wealthy families in Celel. Important governmental appointments are made based on the merit of the individual and the wisdom of the family. The wisdom of the family is determined by the skill and heroic deeds performed by knights the family has previously recommended. I'm sorry, kid, all three of these tasks are extremely difficult, but good luck to you."

Jack remained sitting. He thought for a moment then asked, "Are there any prominent wealthy families that are currently in great need?"

The governor thought for a moment before saying, "Yes, actually, the family of Celshen had a daughter kidnapped several weeks ago. The Celshen family is one of the weaker prominent families in Celel, and they only have two knights appointed. Apparently, one of their knights, a man named Sir Meekah, cost the Bendel a great deal of money, so in retaliation they hired a group of assassins to kidnap the Celshen family's only child.

"The Bendel demanded that the knight surrender himself in exchange for the girl in the next two weeks. The slavers also gave a meeting location and a drop point. Presumably, the knight is supposed to go to the drop point and leave a parchment indicating the day he will turn himself over at the meeting location. Then on the designated day both the slavers and the knight are to arrive at the meeting location and conclude the deal. Unfortunately, I heard that the knight in question has been on tour for the last four months at least, and no one has been able to find him or reach him."

"On tour? What's that?"

The governor glanced out the window as if he were tiring of the conversation. "Knights of Celel must help a certain number of people every five years in order to remain a knight. If they fail, they must go into retirement, and if they do not reemerge from retirement within five years, the crown asks them to relinquish their gemstones so that the stones can be loaned to new knights. When a knight is approaching the end of his five years without having completed enough great deeds, he tours the countries of the world, helping whomever he can. It often takes a knight months to complete a tour."

"Do any of the knights refuse to give up their gemstones?" asked Jack.

"No one has ever done that because it's considered a great dishonor. Retired knights can be called to battle in times of dire need, but that has never actually happened either." While the governor spoke, he retrieved a parchment from his desk. He quickly wrote down a few details, including the drop point and meeting location. "Here is all of the information that you should need to find the kidnapped girl. I wouldn't recommend bothering the Celshen family about the matter—no need to give them false hope if your mission fails."

"Thank you for your time." Jack took the parchment from him. "I must be on my way."

Jack exited the governor's study and thought, *There must be an easier way to see the king, but if there is, he certainly didn't tell me.*

When Jack arrived back at the inn, he related his conversation with the governor to his friends.

"I don't think I mind," said Ben. "It would be totally cool to be knighted in any world, even if no one back home ever found out."

"I kind of have to agree," said Jack. "In our world most countries don't have any type of honor like knighthood, and the ones that do don't necessarily knight people who deserve it. They knight random famous people."

Charles thought for a moment. "I have to agree. I'd like to be knighted. That's something that essentially never happens anymore."

"Besides," added Jack, "the job is basically just going around helping people in need, which is what we've done since we came to this world anyway. I can't just turn my back on all the people who need help in this world. Even if I eventually return home to a normal life, I want to have made a difference here." Jack smiled. "Let's go get knighted. The best place to start seems to be saving this girl from those slavers. If we win her family's support, that's step one."

Ben looked upward as though thinking through the scenario. "But how are we going to fool the Bendel into thinking that one of us is the knight that they are after?"

Jack sat down on one of the beds in the room. "I don't think it will take much. I doubt any of them have ever seen this Sir Meekah, so I could easily claim to be him. They certainly won't expect some random person to impersonate their victim."

Charles commented, "You know it's going to be a trap."

"Yes, I do." Jack put his hands behind his head and fell backward on the bed. "That means we're going to have to think of a way to outsmart them. First, we will need to scout the meeting location and try to determine how they plan to trap us. Then we need to devise a way to use their trap against them."

For a moment there was silence. Then Jack looked across the room to see Vennel packing the last of their bags.

Jack smiled slightly. "It looks like we are already ready to go."

Vennel smiled shyly as she fiddled with one of the backpack straps. "I knew that you would decide to go save her as soon as you started the conversation, so I went ahead and packed."

Charles chuckled and grabbed his backpack.

Jack sat up and glanced at Vennel, "You can come along as we scout the area if you want."

She nodded eagerly and grabbed her already packed bag.

They traveled to the meeting location under the cover of darkness. They searched the entire area thoroughly to ensure that no one watched the meeting location. Then they gathered together on a tall rock that overlooked the entire region.

Jack gazed over the surrounding area and thought for a long time. From this point their enemies would be able to see a great distance, so it would be impossible to take extra soldiers to the meeting location without the Bendel being aware of it. In addition, the specific area for the meeting was not flat, empty land. Jack knew this rough terrain could allow the Bendel to conceal themselves in many different locations. The rock on which they stood rested on top of a tall rocky hill, and a gorge about twenty feet deep cut through the hill.

After surveying the area for another long moment, Jack pointed at the hill's base. "They will most likely position the girl at the bottom of the gorge with a group of hand-to-hand soldiers and station archers up here on both sides of the gorge. Anyone who walked into the gorge could be fired upon by the archers while still engaged with men on the ground. We'll have to approach across that open land, but we could temporarily conceal ourselves in those few trees and big rocks at the base of the hill. We could attempt to climb the hill and attack the archers directly, but we would have no way to prevent them from killing the girl. They probably would let me take you two"—he pointed at Ben and Charles—"to that little wooded and rocky area, but only I would be allowed to walk forward into the gorge without them killing the girl." Jack thought for another moment before saying, "I think I have a plan. Let's tell them to be here tomorrow at noon."

Jack explained his plan to his friends. "If all goes well," he concluded, "they won't know what hit them."

"Indeed," said Ben with a sideways smile. "I like it."

"The only problem," added Charles, "is the plan requires them to allow Ben and me to approach the base of the hill with you."

"It's not that high of a risk," replied Jack. "If people are holding a hostage, they only have leverage as long as the hostage is alive. They can't actually force the person that they're trying to coerce to do more than one thing at a time. Every time they successfully force us to do something by threatening to kill the hostage, they can force us to do another thing. If we refuse to comply and start to leave, they have to either decide to cut their losses and kill the hostage, which gives them nothing, or allow us our little success.

"Based on the fact that they kidnapped this hostage from her home in the middle of an enemy country, I think it's very important to them to get their hands on this knight. The kidnapped girl, on the other hand, is not as important to them. Anyone in the household, such as her mother or father, would probably have also worked as a hostage. If we allow them to get their hands on me and her at the same time, they will gladly kill us both; however, they're probably willing to let her go in exchange for the knight they want, which is me as far as they know. The best they will probably have is his description, so until I get close, they won't know the difference."

After about ten minutes of struggling with the medieval-style parchment and ink and eliciting advice from Vennel on the writing implement's proper use, the boys managed to write the note. They left it at the drop point for the Bendel.

"It's too bad," said Ben, "that although the translation stone allows us to write in a different language, it can't help us figure out how to use an ancient quill."

When they finished scouting, the group returned to the inn and slept for what remained of the night.

******

The next morning Jack got up early but did not study his book; instead, he sat quietly thinking about what he would do later that day.

When the others arose, Jack said, "Vennel, you should stay here for this mission. This is a hostage exchange, and our opponents will already be hesitant about me taking two others with me instead of coming alone."

To Jack's surprise, her countenance fell. She looked down at the floor. "Of course."

After breakfast the boys bid Vennel goodbye and departed.

Several hours passed as the boys traveled to a place from which they could overlook the meeting point. A couple of hours before noon, they caught some movement. Several men cautiously moved toward the top of the gorge, but the boys were unable to count them accurately or determine their final positions.

At noon the three boys started walking across the field toward the hill where they were to meet the Bendel.

As they stepped into the wooded area at the hill's base, Jack whispered into the sack on his shoulder, "Garthong, stay here."

A little shadow passed over his shoulder and onto a nearby tree.

Then Jack stepped out in front of the trees and walked a little distance toward the gorge so the Bendel could clearly see him. Jack motioned with his hands for his two companions to stay in the trees.

Within a few seconds a rough-looking man in leather armor stepped out from behind a rock near the gorge and called, "You were supposed to come alone."

"Indeed," replied Jack, "but had I done so, I would have had no ability to guarantee the safety of your hostage after I surrendered myself. My two friends back there will remain standing at the base of the hill, but they will be safe from your archers behind these trees. I alone will go into the gorge."

The man hesitated as if uncertain how to proceed. Then he turned and ran into the gorge. After a moment he returned. "They cannot come any closer, or we will kill the girl."

"Agreed," Jack replied.

The man approached Jack. "I have to search you to ensure that you're not carrying any gemstones, and I'll take your swords."

"No." Jack crossed his arms. "You may search me for gemstones, but I will keep my swords until I've officially turned myself over to ensure that you don't kill the girl as soon as I give up my weapons."

The man searched him then retreated into the gorge's recesses. He reemerged after a few moments. "Fine, you can keep your swords, but come surrender yourself."

Jack shook his head. "No, I will come halfway, and you will send the girl halfway. Then I will go the rest of the way as she approaches the base of the hill. My friends will meet her and escort her home."

"That's ridiculous," yelled another voice deep in the gorge. "Just get over here, or we'll kill her."

"Well, if that's how you're going to play it"—Jack raised his hands in an exaggerated shrug—"I'll be on my way. Farewell." Jack turned and started walking away.

He heard the voice from the gorge shriek, "You insolent knight! What will you tell the family that you work for when they find out that you let their daughter die?"

Jack yelled over his shoulder, "I'll simply tell them that the Bendel lied. You had already killed the girl, and I was able to deduce this before turning myself over to you."

"You're not a knight; you're just a coward!" called the voice.

"A live coward is good enough for me." Jack did not slow his pace.

Jack had just reached the trees at the hill's base when the man in the gorge finally yelled, "Stop! It's a deal! We will send the girl halfway at the same time you are walking. Then she can make it to your friends and get away. Come back."

Jack smiled to himself. He could almost detect a pleading tone in the man's voice, begging him to return. As Jack turned, he thought, *I wonder whether this man would live if he failed to carry out his mission.* The Bendel cartel seemed like the kind of organization that would kill its own people for failure.

"Wait, where are your friends?" the voice called. "My archers say they have not seen them for several minutes."

Jack glanced at the trees. "Hey, guys, show yourselves."

Ben's and Charles's heads emerged from behind the trees.

A girl was roughly pushed out of the hill's rocky opening, and she made her way toward Jack.

Jack walked to the center of the area between the trees and the gorge.

The young woman stood just a few feet away from Jack. She examined him for a moment and frowned. "You're not Sir Meekah."

She was trim with tangled brown hair and dark circles under her eyes. Her clothing, once a fashionable green gown, was smudged with dirt and hung limply from her shoulders.

Jack smiled confidently. "No, I'm not."

The girl's brow furrowed, and her eyes filled with disappointment and suspicion. "What do you want with me?"

"Don't worry," said Jack, "just wait at the base of the hill, and don't let on that you don't know me."

Jack glanced up the hill and contemplated whether the archers would fire upon him before he reached the gorge. He was fairly confident, however, that they would wait until he was within the gorge so that they could execute all aspects of their trap simultaneously.

Jack continued walking until he reached and entered the gap cut into the hill.

A dozen well-armed men stood clustered tightly together in the constricted gorge. Behind them stood another man, who Jack guessed was their leader. The leader's narrow face, small eyes, and long nose reminded Jack of a weasel, and the rest of his body was thin and lanky as well. Jack slowed his pace a little, giving the girl more time to reach the hill's base.

"Now where did your friends go?" asked the leader. "My archers say they can't see their heads sticking out from behind those trees anymore."

Jack twisted his head and saw the girl duck behind one of the trees. "They've probably already begun escorting the girl back to her home."

"No matter," the lanky man said, "there's no way two men could make it up the sides of this hill in less than five minutes, so they wouldn't be able to help you. Now, give us your swords."

Jack returned his steady gaze. "I had something else in mind. I think you should surrender to me."

The leader narrowed his eyes, clearly irritated. "Your little rebellious attitude is at an end. Men, take him."

Jack glanced up. He saw six archers on each side above him. Then directly ahead of him, behind and above the men in the gorge, two figures stepped out from behind rocks at the top of the crevice and looked down into the chasm.

As the Bendel slavers approached, Jack looked back at the leader with a smile. "You had your chance."

The two figures at the top of the gorge raised their hands, and two large fireballs hurtled downward and landed in the middle of the clustered Bendel footmen.

In an instant almost all of the Bendel men were either incinerated or burning.

Jack whipped out both of his swords and cut down the two or three soldiers left standing.

The bandit leader paused. He cast furtive glances around him as if he did not understand what had happened. Then he yelled, "Archers, fire!"

Jack heard the twang of bow strings, but he lifted his right hand and swung it in an arc above his head. Immediately, a thick wall of ice filled the expanse over Jack and attached to both gorge walls. He heard little tapping noises as the arrows struck the ice.

The Bendel leader rushed at Jack with his sword and shield ready. "How did you do all of this?"

Their swords rang as they collided in midair.

Jack gave three quick strikes at the man's face, forcing him to raise his shield and obscure his own vision. Then Jack moved in close and stepped on his opponent's foot while pushing on the man's shield with his shoulder.

The man tried to step back, but because Jack was on his foot, the lanky man lost his balance, fell, and dropped his shield. He struggled to his feet. "You can't be Sir Meekah. He wasn't supposed to be nearly this good. This was supposed to be an easy assignment."

"Well," replied Jack, "I guess you're just unlucky because instead of him, you got me."

The man rushed at Jack, swinging wildly.

Jack flicked his opponent's sword to the side and took off his head with one blow.

Jack heard a loud thud above his head, and the ice ceiling cracked. Evidently, Ben or Charles had sent one of the archers careening off the edge into the gorge while dispatching them. Jack jumped out from under the ceiling he had created as it collapsed.

Jack searched the Bendel leader in the gorge for useful items and money.

Garthong, meanwhile, swooped down next to the leader's corpse and hissed at the body. He bit one of the dead man's fingers. When the man did not move, Garthong appeared satisfied and dived back into his sack.

Jack smiled when he discovered that the Bendel leader had a translation stone. *That is a stroke of luck,* he thought as he headed out of the gorge.

Ben and Charles joined him after a few minutes.

Charles lightly punched Jack's shoulder with his fist. "I have to say, that was a good plan. You managed to delay them for about ten minutes before you actually went into the gorge. We had plenty of time to sneak around the base of the hill and come up the other side."

Ben added, "And I liked the way you used your illusion stone to make it look like our heads were sticking out from behind those trees."

Jack chuckled. "It did work rather well. The illusion stone made it so they were completely unsuspicious of you both. If I had used my lightning in the gorge, I probably would have produced very little damage, if any, since they were all hiding behind their shields. But they were completely open to an attack from behind and above. I thought it was funny when the man searched me and pronounced that I had no gemstones. Sometimes being a blood mage really has its advantages. I found something else that will make you two rather happy." He produced the translation stone.

Both of his friends smiled broadly.

Ben picked up the small green stone, flicked it into the air, and caught it. "What are the chances of that?"

"Translation stones are supposed to be the most common type of gemstone," said Jack, "and unlike the other stones it doesn't do you any good to have more than one. There's a good chance we will find more as we travel in this world."

Charles glanced up at the sky and frowned. "We should move on. The wind is picking up, and it feels like a cold front is blowing in from the north."

Jack nodded. "Besides, we don't want to keep the Celshens' daughter waiting."

They arrived at the hill's base, but the young woman they had rescued was nowhere to be found.

Ben scratched his chin. "You don't think there were more slavers, do you?"

"No, I don't," said Jack. "I think she just didn't trust us and took off on her own. She didn't recognize me, so she may have thought that we actually had some ill intent, and this wasn't really a rescue. It's also possible that she expected us to die and the slavers to come after her again. Let's see if we can track her down."

The boys headed off to re-rescue the person they had just rescued. The young woman was apparently lost because her tracks led in the wrong direction across the field. They ran across the field until the terrain became rocky. They had some difficulty tracking her since none of them were particularly experienced in tracking, but she seemed to be in a hurry and making no effort to cover her tracks.

Garthong searched from the sky but did not see her.

The boys continued their pursuit. The terrain changed again, this time into a forest.

"We're really tracking her slowly," said Jack. "She's probably just walking and still staying ahead of us. We should catch up when she stops for the night, though."

"Look." Charles pointed at a smudge of blood on the ground. "She's cut herself; that rock has blood on it. From the placement of her tracks, it looks like her behavior is becoming extremely erratic." He vigorously rubbed his left arm with his opposite hand. "The temperature is also dropping, especially in the shade. I hope we catch up with her soon. We don't know how well the slavers fed and cared for her while she was in captivity, and I suspect she's becoming hypothermic and exhausted."

Darkness began to fall, which made tracking even more difficult, but the fact that she was bleeding made it possible to stay on her trail. Before much longer they caught up to her. She lay flat on her face as if she had been walking and simply fallen straight forward.

"Hello?" Jack called as they approached.

She did not even twitch. Blood stained the trees and rocks immediately around her.

They turned her over. Her arms, hands, and face were covered in scratches and cuts.

Jack said, "Charles was right. She's probably in the early stages of hypothermia, and in her exhausted state, she became unaware of her surroundings. For the last half hour, she probably went around in circles, running into everything here."

The girl was mostly dry, except for a little sweat, so they wrapped her in Charles's cloak.

Ben said, "Jack, why don't you stay with her while Charles and I search for firewood?"

Jack glanced around. "Actually, we shouldn't be in any imminent danger from enemies since we killed all the slavers, and she needs a fire as soon as possible. It will take a while for us to build a fire in the traditional sense. Charles, could you carry her over there? Ben, stand clear."

Jack turned to a dead tree directly behind him and lifted his hand. Focused lighting erupted from his palm and struck the tree's base. The tree fell over, and Jack said, "Okay, Ben, light it up."

Ben smiled. "With pleasure."

After Ben set the tree on fire, Charles carried the girl back over and gently laid her down by the fire.

"Now we do need to gather some more firewood to keep this fire burning," said Jack. "If you two want to work on that, I'll see what we can do about supper and make sure that she doesn't warm up too quickly."

A little while later, Ben and Charles brought back more wood.

The young men ate some supper and lay down for the night.

Ben took first watch.

When Ben woke Jack up for his shift, Jack noted that Ben had kept the fire burning strong.

Jack added some more wood to the fire and looked down at the girl. *It's funny,* he thought, *we came out here to rescue her, and we don't even know her name.* They had interacted with so many people since they had arrived in this world, but they knew the names of so few of them. Jack glanced down again at the girl, wrapped in Charles's brown cloak. She was slim and a little shorter than Jack with strait, brown hair down to her shoulders. He guessed that she was about sixteen. Her smooth skin reflected someone born of wealth even though it currently appeared that she had taken a beating. She had a small nose and thin lips that fit her face perfectly. Her soft features made her look kind and at peace.

Jack looked over at Ben and saw that he had fallen asleep almost instantly. Somehow Ben had the uncanny ability to sleep just about any time and place. Jack was a light sleeper and often tossed and turned at night. Charles's sleeping habits were somewhere between Ben's and Jack's.

After staring into the fire for some time, Jack turned his gaze out between the dark trees and wondered how much life resided in the forest. Just then, he realized that he did not hear anything—not even crickets or frogs. It was spring, so any recess in the ground that could hold water should have been surrounded by frogs and toads giving their mating calls. *Maybe it's still too cold,* he thought. He tried to remember whether he had heard frogs earlier that night.

He bumped Garthong's sack and whispered, "Garthong, do you smell anything?"

A sleepy, scaly head emerged from the sack and looked around drowsily. Suddenly, Garthong became very excited, scurried up his master, and ran back and forth on Jack's shoulders.

Jack bumped Ben and Charles and whispered, "Get up. Something's not right."

His friends rolled over, and Charles muttered, "What's the matter?"

"Quiet." Jack held up his hand. "Something is watching us."

"Isn't that a little paranoid?" Ben asked quietly. "What could be out there?"

Jack grabbed a burning stick from the fire, lifted it above his head, and threw it into the woods. He did not see anything, but the bushes rustled all around them

"Creepy," muttered Ben. "Either of you see anything?"

"It's not people," said Jack in a low voice. "Humans would have already attacked us as soon as they deduced that we were aware of their presence."

A faint rustling came from behind them, and a voice asked, "What's going on?"

The boys turned to see the girl sitting up.

Recognition dawned on her face when she saw Jack in the firelight. "You! What do you want?"

"Quiet," whispered Jack. "We tracked you down after killing the slavers. You were exhausted and hypothermic. We saved your life twice today, so just trust us for now."

The girl looked confused. "What's hypothermic?"

"Never mind, just stay quiet." Jack patted the air with his open palms down to emphasize the need for quiet. "We're surrounded by some kind of animal. Whatever these creatures are, they don't seem interested in leaving."

"We still have several hours until sunrise," observed Charles. "Whatever they are, they probably haven't attacked because of the roaring fire, but we don't have enough wood to keep it going like this all night."

"It's been a few hours since we all used our stones," said Jack, "so if we use them now, they'll be cooled off in time for us to use them again when the fire starts to die."

"Sounds like a plan to me." Ben took aim between two trees. "Burn!" he yelled, hurling a fireball just outside the ring of firelight.

Movement erupted in the bushes, and several yips came from the darkness.

Ben smiled. "I got at least one."

"They yip like dogs, so they must be wolves," Jack reasoned. "But why would wolves attack people? Wolves usually give humans a wide berth."

"It's probably the girl's blood," said Charles. "They think we're wounded."

Ben said, "Well, give them what for, Charles."

Charles hurled his fireball into the darkness as well, and again, the wolves fled.

"Sounds like you got at least one too, Charles," commented Ben.

As soon as the brush that was burning from Charles's fireball went out, however, they heard a faint rustling of twigs and leaves again.

Jack walked toward the edge of the firelight.

Charles whispered, "What are you doing?"

"I'm trying to get them to gather in front of me," said Jack. "The farther I get from our firelight, the closer they will come to me."

Jack stood completely quiet and still, listening intently with his eyes closed. He could hear rustling on the firelight's edges. Jack opened his eyes and moved his hand in an arc in front of him. Ice leapt from his hand, coating the area in front of him.

Several yips came from the bushes, and the underbrush crackled. Several wolves evidently had legs or other parts of their bodies frozen in the mass.

Jack finished the three that were trapped in his ice block with one of his swords and returned to the firelight.

"I think there are a lot of them out there," said Jack, "and I'm not sure if the blood from the ones we killed will draw more of them or not."

Jack's attention shifted to the girl. Her eyes were wide, and she glanced around nervously.

Jack flicked his open hand forward in an unconcerned manner. "Don't worry. We'll get out of this."

The girl looked up at him. "Not a chance. The Great Northern Wolves hunt in extremely large packs. They don't usually target people, but when they do, they always get there kill. As it gets closer to dawn, they will get bolder until they finally disregard the fire altogether."

"Well, in case you haven't noticed," said Jack, "we are not like most people, and we are not dying in the woods because we got attacked by a pack of ravenous wolves." Jack heard a noise behind him and spun around, a mighty flash of light leaping from his hand accompanied by a resounding crack. "Well, there's one more dead. Let's throw the last of the wood on the fire. Maybe we can get to one of those big trees on the edge of the firelight and climb it. If they're going to become bolder, then we won't be able to maintain our current position even if we could keep the fire going."

They drew their weapons and inched toward a large tree.

Garthong flew to one of the tree branches.

Charles said, "The only problem is we can't carry our weapons in our hands while we climb the tree. We'll have to either leave them at the bottom or put them away."

"Let's climb one at a time," said Jack. "I'll stay until the rest of you are up. Then you can reach down and pull me up, Charles. Girl, you go up first, then Ben. Charles, give her a hand."

Things seemed to be progressing well at first, but as Charles climbed, the wolves became bolder and moved closer.

With the fire behind and tree directly in front of him, Jack only had to worry about his left and right sides. He saw the first wolf coming from the left.

It leaped into the air with its teeth bared and eyes shining yellow in the firelight.

Jack involuntarily took a step backward as he thought, *They're huge! What are these, Alaskan Wolves?* He brought his sword down to bear on the creature's head, killing it instantly.

The wolf's body, however, still possessed a great deal of momentum, and it slammed into Jack, knocking him backward toward the fire. Jack barely caught sight of another coming from the right. This time he jumped sideways, and bringing his sword down in a sweeping arc, he caught the beast somewhere around the middle of the spine. It hit the ground, flopping violently.

Several more wolves closed in rapidly. Jack thrust his sword at one's face, but it dodged sideways. He wanted to give it a follow-up attack, but another wolf sprang in from the other side. Jack swung his other sword in that direction and looked up just in time to see another wolf dive at him. Jack whipped one sword that direction and threw himself sideways toward the safety of the fire, stabbing his other sword into the ground and using it to give his leap extra height as he rolled his body over it. He successfully evaded the attack, and landed closer to the fire.

The wolves seemed less timid now since they faced a single opponent, and they continued to slink closer to the fire. Jack saw one coming from his left, and he attacked with a sideways swing, missing its head by an inch as it slipped backward. Jack turned and thrust his sword toward another furry form. He caught that wolf just above the ear, splitting the skin. Jack backed up closer to the fire, and the wolves retreated slightly.

"Jack, are you okay?" Charles yelled, preparing to jump down from the tree.

"Yeah, I'm okay," replied Jack. "Just stay where you are. I'm going try to make it back to the tree. Be ready to pull me up when I get there." Jack tried to move back to the tree's base, but the wolves cut him off. Jack drew back toward the fire. "On second thought, unless they get even bolder, let's just wait them out. We probably have a little over two hours before our fire dies down, and we'll be able to use our gemstones again."

The wolves seemed to get closer every minute as the firelight waned. But time passing was on Jack's side.

Jack stood completely still next to the fire. He knew the key was to remain calm. The minutes seemed to tick by excruciatingly slowly.

Finally, Ben called from the tree, "I think we're ready whenever you are."

"All right," said Jack. "You two, blast fireballs about six feet on either side of the tree. That should scare them so I can make it to the tree."

They hurled their fireballs and burned several wolves.

By the light of their fires, Jack could see dozens of wolves. *I'm glad we didn't pick a shorter tree,* thought Jack. *Wolves this large could probably reach the branches on a shorter tree.*

Jack rushed toward the wolves between him and the tree, but another wolf slipped in behind Jack and rapidly darted toward him. *I'm going to have to use two spells at once,* Jack thought. He stretched his right hand in front of him and shot forth ice, encasing the wolves there. At the same time, he cast lightning with his left hand directly behind him, obliterating the wolf on his tail. Jack leapt onto the ice block he had created, dropped the sword in his right hand, and jumped for the tree.

Even after jumping off his ice block, Jack could not reach the first branch, but Charles caught his extended arm and pulled Jack into the tree's safety.

The pack gathered around the tree's base as Jack and Charles climbed higher. Then the wolves began to howl mournfully.

"All right, everyone, still alive?" Jack looked around to see his two friends and the young woman all holding tightly to their branches. "Now we just have to wait till morning. Thankfully, it doesn't look like we have to worry about going to sleep and falling out of the tree because those stupid wolves show no sign of stopping that infernal howling."

Jack's friends laughed with him.

The girl, however, squared her shoulders and sniffed indignantly. "How can you laugh at a time like this?" she demanded. "Our lives are in mortal peril."

Ben shrugged. "Our lives have pretty much been in mortal peril for the last several months. Yet here we are, safe and sound, although I must admit, it's a bit uncomfortable."

"He's right," added Jack. "We've had a pretty good track record so far. Besides, being unhappy about danger or death does no good, so we might as well be happy about the fact that we're still alive."

After a few moments of silence, the girl asked, "What do you plan to do with me?"

Jack adjusted his position on his branch. "We're taking you back to your parents."

The girl cast Jack a sideways look as though she still distrusted them. "Why? What do you get out of this?"

"With any luck we'll earn your father's blessing and recommendation that we become Knights of Celel. It actually worked out for our benefit that those stupid slavers kidnapped you. From information I gathered, it seems that most of the prominent families need very little and would be difficult to impress."

The girl looked downcast. "I suppose it makes sense then."

Charles leaned over to Jack and whispered, "Nice going, Mr. Sensitive."

I guess Charles is right, thought Jack. *The girl does look pretty sad now, but she's not crying, so that's a good sign, I think.* "So what's your name?" asked Jack.

"What does it matter?" The girl stared at the ground.

"Hey, perhaps I was a little insensitive before," Jack said quickly. "Just because we found a selfish reason to rescue you doesn't mean you don't have value. When it comes right down to it, it isn't your wealth, power, influence, or strength that establishes your value. You have value simply because you're a person. That means that it was our pleasure to save you from those scumbags just so we could have a hand in making the world a little better place.

"I know being held captive must have been difficult for you. I'm not really sure what I could say to make it better because sometimes bad things happen, and I can't change that. You should know, though, that if anything else bad happens to you and we find out about it, we'll come back as soon as we can to help you." Jack mentally kicked himself for rambling. He just wasn't sure what to say.

The girl raised her head to look at him, and he noticed a sparkle on her cheek where the moonlight reflected off a tear.

She smiled slightly. "My name is Zannel, and you had better mean what you just said."

Jack grinned. "I do. See how good of a job we've done rescuing you already?" He gestured at the huge wolves surrounding their tree.

For a second she wrinkled her brow in confusion. Then she began to giggle.

"There you go," said Jack. "See, all the wolves down there are still howling at us, but there's something funny and wonderful about being safely tucked away in a tree with all of them below us. Besides, when you're working to make things better, it's easier to be content because as long as good people fight for what's right, evil people will eventually lose power."

Jack then introduced himself as did his friends.

Garthong screeched in Jack's ear, drawing his attention to the small lizard. The gother then jumped down to one of the lower branches and squawked repeatedly at the wolves below. The reptile accompanied his triumphant screeching with bold prancing back and forth on the limb.

They all laughed at the little creature's audacity.

Zannel asked, "How did you get that lizard?"

Jack replied, "The adults are a plague outside the city of Hathra in Kliptun, so we hunted them. We found this little guy in the nest, and I didn't have the heart to kill him. Now he pretty much just travels with us."

A clanking noise came from below followed by a ripping sound.

"What was that?" Zannel asked.

Charles replied, "They probably smelled the food in our backpacks and decided to help themselves."

Several of the wolves continued to howl, and Jack's group continued to hear scuffling below as their gear was strewn about their abandoned campsite.

In a few more hours, the sun started to rise, and the wolves finally retreated into the darkness from whence they came.

Garthong stretched his neck and leaped into the air, his wings catching the current of the early morning breeze.

The group stretched to work out the stiffness in their muscles and climbed down from the tree. They picked up the backpacks and started gathering the inedible supplies scattered around what had been their camp.

Ben rubbed his belly. "It seems like I've missed breakfast a lot since our adventure began."

Garthong jumped out of a bush holding a large bone with meat dangling from it in his mouth.

Ben jerked his head toward the gother. "That bone is from one of the wolves we killed last night." His face broke into a broad smile. "That little guy's not scared of anything."

"We're still lost," said Charles, "because Zannel was lost, and we were following her."

"Not a problem," Jack replied. "Garthong," he called, "see if you can spot any groups of people, and fly in that direction."

Within a few minutes of circling, the little gother took off in one direction just above the trees.

The group followed him on foot. By noon they could see buildings in the distance, and they headed for the village.

A Destiny Among Worlds

Chapter 13

ONCE THE GROUP REACHED the village, they had no difficulty obtaining directions back to Juma. To Jack the trip back seemed to go by relatively quickly. Zannel then led the way to her home.

The Celshen family manor house resided outside the city on a large plot of land that resembled a plantation.

Zannel quickened her pace and spoke excitedly as they neared the house. "How did you convince my father to let you come after me?"

Jack paused, a little uncertain how to respond, and smiled innocently. "*Convinced* is a strong word. We didn't technically convince him."

"Well, whatever you did, it worked." She giggled.

Ben leaned toward Jack and asked in a hushed voice, "Jack, did anyone other than the governor and Vennel actually know that we were going to rescue her?"

Jack looked down and shook his head. "No,"

A scream came from just inside the house, and they heard a woman's voice yell, "Zannel is back! She's alive!"

Jack heard the sound of running feet and excited talking inside the house as Zannel bounded up the porch stairs and burst into the building.

Jack slowed his pace. "Let's just wait on the front porch for a little while until things calm down in there."

An orchard grew to the house's left, and a low fence separated it from the yard. The fields in front of and to the house's right looked like wheat fields. A short stone wall enclosed the fields.

After a few minutes Zannel opened the door. "What are you doing out on the porch? Come in so everyone can see you."

They entered the house. Inside stood a well-dressed, middle-aged couple, who Jack assumed were Zannel's parents. Behind them a maid and a bald man, whose dirt smudges over his knees, grubby fingernails, and dark tan suggested that he was a groundskeeper, watched with interest and excitement.

As Jack surveyed Zannel's father, he noted that the man stood with the excellent posture and commanding, authoritative presence of a leader, yet he had a twinkle in his eye when he smiled, suggesting a lighthearted nature. He had short dark-brown hair flecked with gray accompanied by a slightly lighter colored and well-trimmed beard. Despite his signs of aging, he looked strong and capable.

"I am Sir Aldric Celshen," Zannel's father respectfully tipped his head and grasped each of the boy's hands in turn. "This is my wife, Zemara. Our daughter says you three are the ones who rescued her."

"That's correct," replied Jack.

"You have no idea what this means to us, to have our daughter back," Zemara said sincerely.

Zemara had the perfect complexion of one living in luxury. Zannel clearly inherited her petite nose and mouth from her mother; however, Zemara's hair was a lighter brown than that of her daughter. Although naturally attractive, Zemara obviously dedicated a great deal of time and effort toward her appearance with each hair hanging obediently in place and not a wrinkle anywhere in her expensive-looking blue gown. She stood and walked with grace, and Jack suspected that her manners were impeccable.

Sir Aldric added, "It seems odd to me that three young men would go off to rescue some girl they don't know when no one in the family knows who they are."

"It would seem a little strange," said Jack, "but I approached the governor of Juma and asked him if there were any important tasks that needed to be done. He assigned us this one."

"What kind of connection do you have to the governor?" asked Sir Aldric.

"None really. I only met him that one day. The three of us are attempting to become Knights of Celel, and we needed support from one of the prominent families."

Sir Aldric's smile disappeared, and his expression suddenly became serious. "I see. So you want me to back you in the coming tournament?"

Jack exchanged glances with Charles. "What tournament?"

"The one taking place in the next few days," explained Sir Aldric. "Young men aspiring to become knights compete in a variety of challenges to display their skills. Current knights may choose one individual from among the contestants to accompany them on a mission. How well the recruits do on that undertaking with the knight determines whether they are allowed to participate in other missions with the knight and eventually receive his recommendation."

"Then we would like to hear more about this tournament," said Jack, "and yes, if you would be willing to back us, it would be our honor."

Sir Aldric frowned. "You want me to back all three of you?"

Jack replied, "That ... would be ideal ... because all three of us wish to become knights."

"Normally, I would never consider backing you. My family doesn't have enough influence to recommend one of you. Backing three of you is even crazier. I would probably get laughed out of the registration room." Sir Aldric sighed. "However, you saved my daughter's life and saved what little reputation I have left in the process, so I'll back you. Be aware, though, you will not get a second chance from my family. If you perform poorly, my family will lose all credibility, and I will probably be unable to recommend anyone ever again."

Jack asked, "How many of these recruits have actually fought in battle?"

"Almost none of them. Celel hasn't had a serious war in thirty years, not since crowning King Tanner."

"I think we will be all right then," said Jack. "We have been in our share of life-and-death encounters recently, and I think we will prove ourselves."

Sir Aldric commented abruptly, "Then we should continue with these pleasantries later after the tournament. It begins in three days, and we must register and prepare you before then. Come, we will go out to the tournament grounds, and I will explain the rules and the different trials."

Zannel grabbed her father's arm. "Can't that wait? I just got home, and there's so much I want to tell you."

"Don't worry, my dear, you can stay with your mother. She's been worried sick, and it will be good for her to hear the entire tale. But I owe a debt to these three and have to repay it if I can."

Zannel glanced at the three young men before casting her gaze downward in disappointment.

Sir Aldric reached for the doorknob and opened the door. "You boys can stay here at the estate until after the tournament. The level of success you have in the competition will determine what happens next."

Jack inquired, "I have another companion. Would it be possible for her to also stay here at the house while we train for the tournament?"

Zemara smiled. "Of course. An inn is no place for a highborn woman. Besides, Zannel and I always enjoy company. We will send a servant to the inn immediately to bring her here."

Sir Aldric led the way as he and the three young men exited the house and headed toward the tournament grounds.

The tournament grounds were about three miles north of the manor house on land owned by the king. Sets of wooden seats and stairs arranged like bleachers surrounded the grounds.

Sir Aldric gestured with his hand toward a field. "Here is the accuracy range. Small moving targets will hang from trees, and the objective is simply to hit your target with any gemstone. The target will be a wooden disk the size of a typical shield. Some gemstones, such as lightning, are better for precision accuracy and have an advantage in this division."

They walked a little farther, and Sir Aldric pointed to another area. "Destructive powers are tested here by casting gemstones at a reinforced wooden wagon wheel attached to a cart like the ones actually used in war. Fireballs usually carry the top score in this section. One of these tests will be performed at the very beginning and one at the end in case the participants only have one gemstone. An archery test will take place between these tests to determine the contestants' skill with a bow."

Ben cringed a little. "How are we going to pass this test?" he whispered to Jack.

Jack shook his head. "I'm not sure, but we'll definitely have to practice more with the bow. We haven't practiced much since we hunted the gothers, and we weren't particularly good then."

Sir Aldric continued, "By far the most important part of the competition is the one-on-one fights, which are performed here." He pointed at an open section of ground in the tournament area's center. "The other tests are important, but whoever wins first place in the melee competition will bring great honor to whomever he represents, and the victory will almost certainly guarantee the contestant top place overall. The rules for the melee competition are fairly lenient since it mimics a real fight, so using taunts or a punch to gain an advantage would be acceptable. What skills do you boys think you need to work on the most?"

Jack replied, "I think all three of us will need to work on our archery the most, and Ben and Charles will need to work on their pinpoint accuracy. I will need to work on my destructive power. Since I don't have fire, I will be at a disadvantage there."

Sir Aldric taped his chin thoughtfully with his finger. "I know a man who has good bow skills; he can teach you a few things and help you practice. As far as using your gemstones goes, you'll have to practice that on your own. Come back to the house, and we'll set up very similar testing ground for you to use as a practice range. On the way let's stop by the governor's office and register you all."

They went immediately to the governor's office in Juma. The governor apparently did not require retired knights to make appointments because the maid ushered them in immediately.

The governor looked up from the parchments on his desk as the four entered. When he saw Jack, the governor's eyes widened slightly, and his eyebrows lifted, but he quickly regained his composure. "Sir Aldric, such a pleasure to see you. What are you doing here?" Although his words were cordial, the governor's voice did not hold a great deal of warmth.

Sir Aldric confidently approached the desk. "I'm here to register these three boys in my family's name for the rookie tournament in a few days."

"You want to register three?" responded the governor. "Are you sure? If this goes poorly—"

"I know, I know," cut in Sir Aldric, "but my mind is set. Please register all three of them."

The governor pulled out some parchment from behind his desk. "Sign these, and show up on the specified day."

"Thank you, Governor," Jack replied.

The three friends signed their names and exited the office with Sir Aldric.

"I hope you boys do really well in this tournament," Sir Aldric said as they left. "That smug man has been trying to weaken my influence in the city ever since he became governor. Even the assignment he gave you boys was meant to fail. Unfortunately for him, he underestimated you. Let's hope that he underestimated you a lot."

Jack smiled grimly but did not reply. He thought, *So far, many people have underestimated us. We'll find out in this tournament what we're really made of.*

******

Vennel was a little confused. She had sat patiently in her room at the inn since the young men had left her in order to accomplish their mission for the governor of Juma. She had begun to worry when they did not come back that night. Now she followed after a messenger who had sought her out at the inn. The man had said that he was the groundskeeper at the Celshen estate, and he had orders from the lady of the house to retrieve her.

The man seemed very excited and talked very quickly about a recent rescue as they walked.

Vennel tried to focus on the story, but the man kept interrupting himself and retelling parts of the tale as though he really did not know the story very well.

Vennel thought, *They were going to rescue the daughter of the Celshen family. They must have succeeded.*

Their success was not really a surprise to her because they often left to fight somewhere, and they always came back. She had not had an opportunity yet to really see them fight much, but when the three of them practiced, they seemed very serious. She smiled to herself. *In fact, sometimes,* she thought, *the only time they're serious is when they're practicing.*

Vennel's thoughts were interrupted as the groundskeeper pointed ahead and said, "That's the Celshen estate."

Vennel felt very shy as she looked toward the house. The estate was a beautiful sight to behold. She noticed flowers growing on the outside of the stone walls lining the path to the house. Vennel slowed her pace as she approached the building. She thought, *The people who live here must be of noble birth. I don't belong here. I'm just a peasant turned slave.*

Vennel stopped just before stepping up onto the manor house's front porch.

The bald man in front of her turned and gestured for her to come forward as he opened the front door.

Vennel slowly stepped inside. From the doorway several rooms were visible, but Vennel dipped her head downward, focusing only at the floor in front of her. She deliberated on a host of possibilities. What if this groundskeeper had made a mistake and was supposed to bring someone else? Perhaps these people did not have anything to do with Charles and his friends. She cringed slightly as she reminded herself of her place.

A middle-aged woman in a lovely blue gown approached her and stammered, "Hello there. I'm sorry. I was expecting a person of … higher standing. That is to say … when Jack said he had another companion, I just assumed … ." She trailed off as if searching for words.

Trying to save the woman from any additional embarrassment, Vennel politely explained, "I'm Jack's slave."

The woman quickly regained her regal bearing, reached over, and lifted Vennel's chin slightly with her hand so that she could look into her face. "My name is Zemara. This is the country of Celel. There are no slaves here. Don't worry, Celel is a good place. You're welcome to stay here and chat with my daughter and me for a while." Zemara gestured toward a younger woman who resembled herself. "In fact, when Jack said he had a companion coming, we hoped you would be willing to tell us more about the three young men who rescued Zannel."

Zannel sat down in one of several chairs in the room. The chairs were arranged around a large oval table. Large windows draped in rich, purple velvet curtains provided a view of the house's front yard and allowed a gentle breeze to blow inside. A tablecloth matching the curtains covered the table, and a painting of a herd of charging horses with snow-capped mountains behind them hung on the wall over the head of the table.

The lady of the house gestured Vennel toward one of the chairs with her hand as she also gracefully took a seat.

Vennel was relieved that they were conducting their interview in the dining room rather than in the doubtlessly extravagant and intimidating parlor. She took several steps over to the indicated chair and sat down facing the other two women.

The bald man sauntered over and leaned against one of the chairs on Vennel's right as if he also wanted to listen.

Vennel paused to think before saying, "Jack is driven and determined. Even when he's just training, you can see ferocity in his eyes. When he's training, it's like he's in the battle, as though he sees it all around him. It's not anger or hatred that drives his ferocity—it's more like compassion. He's different from most people; they're all a bit different.

"Charles doesn't hide his compassion nearly as well as Jack, and you can see the sadness in his eyes when he looks at those in pain around him. Charles has a warm and tender side that makes him more approachable." Vennel added silently, *And a smile or glance from him is enough to warm the coldest day. He never has a reason to glance at me, but he does it anyway.*

Vennel bit her bottom lip to bring herself back to the present. "Ben is a bit crazy. When he's walking down the road, if he's not telling jokes and trying to be funny, he'll probably pull out his sword and fiddle with it in his hands. The only things he seems serious about are his two friends—even fighting is more like a game than anything else to him. I wouldn't mind seeing them fight more often, but I'm usually tucked off to the side somewhere nearby. They don't want me to get close when they're doing something dangerous."

Vennel had warmed up to her topic, and her voice carried a passion that held her audience. "When we arrived in this country, and they decided to become Knights of Celel, I thought it fit them perfectly. The three of them fit the legends of brave Knights of Celel wandering the wilderness doing good deeds. When they first rescued me, I followed them because it was the law, and I was Jack's slave. Now it's different. Now I feel as though anything I do to help them lets me make a difference in my own small way."

Zannel leaned forward with her elbows resting on the table. "Have the three of them traveled all the way to Celel to become knights?"

Vennel shook her head. "They're trying to go somewhere far away, but I don't know where." She decided not to elaborate on this point since she knew so little about it, and the boys seemed purposely vague on the topic with strangers.

Zannel leaned back in her chair as if processing what Vennel had said. Finally, she said, "I wonder where else there is to go."

The front door opened, and a young woman entered.

Zemara smiled. "This is our maid, Lilen. You can stay with her in the servants' quarters next door.

"Thank you," Vennel stood.

The maid smiled and stepped outside. "Follow me."

As Vennel followed, she thought, *What a strange place this country is that such highborn people would bring me into their home in a social manner.* She smiled a sad smile as she remembered, *But despite how nice they seemed, they didn't even ask me for my name.*

******

When Sir Aldric and the three young men returned to the Celshen estate, Sir Aldric showed them to the guest quarters in the manor house.

Jack looked forward to some rest.

"You can stay here, at least until after the tournament," he told them.

As the three young men looked over their room, Charles asked, "Where is Vennel?"

Zemara, who had come to stand beside her husband, responded, "I had our maid set her up comfortably in the servants' quarters."

Charles glanced at Jack as though hoping for some support. "Was there not enough room here in the guest quarters?"

Zemara squinted one of her eyes and tilted her head. "Of course there was, but doesn't the girl belong to him?" She gestured toward Jack. "It wouldn't be appropriate to put someone of her standing here in the manor house."

Sir Aldric put his hand on his wife's shoulder and nodded once in agreement as if the point were now explained adequately.

Jack turned toward them and said politely, "I purchased her in order to save her from a worse fate; however, there are no slaves in Celel, and she is a member of our party like any other. Is there any way you could reconsider?"

Sir Aldric smiled patiently. "We are one of the prominent families of Celel." He paused as if allowing this statement to sink in before continuing, "Surely you understand that we must make some distinction between peasants and royalty."

Jack shook his head. "Shouldn't it be the other way around? It's natural for people to have different levels of wealth. There's nothing wrong with that. But it creates problems when distinctions are made between people *because* of their wealth. Do you believe that money is what makes a person great?"

Sir Aldric exchanged glances with his wife. "No," he said slowly, "money is not what makes someone great. It's a man's deeds that set him apart."

Jack slowly shook his head. "Apparently not here." He smiled in an effort keep the conversation cordial. "You don't know anything about what Vennel has accomplished or what she's been through."

Despite Jack's respectful tone, he could tell that Sir Aldric and Zemara were not interested in discussing the issue any further. Zemara appeared to be suppressing the offended rage of a hostess whose diligent efforts have gone unappreciated.

Sensing the tension in the room, Jack dipped his head. "Fine, let's make a wager. If one of us three wins the tournament, she can stay in the manor house in the room next to ours."

Zemara replied curtly, "Fine, but if you lose, you all stay in the servants' quarters, assuming we let you stay on our estate at all."

Sir Aldric chuckled. "If one of you wins the tournament, you can do whatever you want."

Jack grinned and tipped his head again. "Thank you again for the opportunity to compete in the tournament. We are all in your debt."

The retired knight nodded slightly and put his arm around his wife's waist, pulling her slowly out of the doorway.

As the door closed, Ben said, "So Charles, do you think you could have found a more controversial topic?"

Charles just grunted in reply.

Jack said, "Don't worry. You heard Sir Aldric; all he cares about is reclaiming his family's position. If we do well in the tournament, they'll be happy to do whatever we request."

Garthong seemed very happy to come out of his sack and explore the room. As the boys unpacked their few belongings, the gother rooted his nose around in Jack's backpack.

Jack pulled a dry piece of meat out of his bag and tossed it to his little friend.

Garthong swallowed the treat in one gulp and looked up expectantly for more.

Jack shook his head and wagged his pointer finger back and forth. "If you want something else to eat, you'll have to catch it yourself."

The gother jumped up on the windowsill, spread his wings, and disappeared into the fading sunlight.

******

In the morning they met their archery instructor and started practicing. The time until the tournament seemed to pass slowly to Jack, and essentially the only person with whom they interacted was their archery instructor. The archery targets for the tournament were actually rather large, but they were positioned at a great distance.

The instructor explained, "Each competitor fires three arrows. The closer you are to your target, the better, even if you miss. Few people actually hit the target more than once during the match."

The three young men also practiced with their gemstones, Jack trying to maximize the destructive power of his ice and Ben and Charles working on their fireballs' precision.

On the second morning, Jack noticed Zannel watching from a window of the manor house. He had not thought about it previously, but he realized that the decline in her family's influence must have placed a lot of strain on her as well as her parents. The entire family relied on them to do well in the tournament.

Jack turned back to the target. He relaxed, pulled back on the string, and aimed. He *had* to hit that target. He released the arrow and watched as it soared through the air. The arrow struck the wooden backstop just to the target's left and landed on the ground about a foot away from the target.

Jack could feel himself becoming frustrated. According to their instructor, they were not really all that bad—they just were not really all that good either. He stared at the target intently, wondering what he could do to improve his aim by even an inch. *I just wish I could hit that target,* thought Jack.

Just then, Garthong swooped out of the sky, and grasping a new arrow out of Jack's quiver, flew to the target and unsuccessfully tried to stab the arrow into it.

Jack could not help himself. He began laughing as did his friends next to him. "Come on, Garthong," Jack called. "Come back to me."

The little creature turned and flew straight to Jack, landing on his shoulder.

Interesting, thought Jack, *he felt my intense emotion and reacted to it. I had suspected that was possible, but this is the first time I clearly saw it.*

******

While the boys practiced, Vennel walked through the town of Juma. It was midafternoon, and the tournament was the next day. She really wanted to go and watch the fights, but she had not gotten up the nerve to ask Jack if she could go. Jack never really stopped her from doing anything or told her that she could not. Really, she was just too shy to ask for permission. Jack had told her that she did not have to ask for his permission when she wanted to do something. It did not really matter, though. What if this time she did something of her own volition and made Jack unhappy? She feared that he might send her away. She did not want to go anywhere. After all, she did not have anywhere to go. Although she was often quiet, she enjoyed the conversations that she had with Charles when they traveled, and she knew that he was sensitive to her safety and welfare.

Someone grabbed Vennel's arm and said, "Hey, let's look over in that shop."

Vennel looked at her friend. Lilen, the maid at the Celshen estate, was a nice girl. She wore a white dress with a pale blue sash tied around her waist. Her curly, blond hair fell just past her chin, and she often shook her head, sending her locks flying everywhere.

Lilen pulled Vennel into a dress shop and pointed at one dress in particular. "Look there! That dress is as fine as any dress I've ever seen. I think it's even prettier than Zannel's dresses."

Vennel gazed at the dress. It *was* the most beautiful dress she had ever seen. The dress was composed of a white, floor-length, linen gown and periwinkle blue, velvet surcoat. The surcoat laced over the bodice and had long flowing sleeves that draped from the elbow almost to the ground. The whole garment was edged in white lace, which Vennel could tell was imported. The contrast in colors and quality of workmanship dazzled her.

A saleswoman, who had been sitting behind the desk in the little shop, walked over and said in a weary tone, "All right, you two looked. Now move on."

Vennel turned her gaze from the dress to the saleswoman. "How much is the dress?"

The woman looked at Vennel and pursed her lips. "Come on, it's not like a peasant girl could ever afford this dress. I don't want to be rude, but you clearly don't have enough money to shop for anything in here, so I will ask you to please move along."

Vennel started to back toward the door, but Lilen said, "Come on, she just asked how much it was. At least tell us, please." Lilen tilted her head and smiled sweetly.

The woman rolled her eyes. "One hundred fifty coin."

Vennel turned and stepped out of the store. She wanted to hide somewhere. She looked like someone who lived on the street, like a peasant. She did not belong in this city or even in this country. Everyone here had so much more than she did. Even if these people did not call her 'slave,' she knew she still was one. At least in the countries from which she had come, she did not stand out as particularly poor. Most people dressed like her in the central countries. Here, almost everyone, even the peasants and servants, looked better.

Lilen caught up with Vennel and put her hand on Vennel's shoulder. "It's okay." She giggled. "They can't stop us from looking."

"That's easy for you to say. You don't stand out in shops like that." Vennel thought it would be so wonderful to own a dress like that. *If I did,* she thought, *maybe people would stop looking at me like I'm a nuisance.* Every shop owner seemed to frown when she walked by. They were not usually rude, but she could tell that she was unwelcome.

"Hey, I've got an idea." Lilen skipped around in front of Vennel and walked backward before her. "We just need to find a place that sells things that are a bit less fancy. The guys you work for have money, don't they? You could convince them to buy you a little bit nicer clothes. Tell them that you need something for the tournament tomorrow. Everyone will be wearing their best, and you'll need to at least blend in with the crowd. Even the servants wear their best so they don't bring shame to their employers."

Vennel's eyes widened. "I could ask, right?"

Lilen nodded excitedly as she fell back in step beside her friend.

While the two walked quickly back toward the estate, Vennel rehearsed what she would say in her head. *I don't need that much money,* she reasoned, *just enough to get something maybe like what Lilen is wearing.* As she drew closer to the estate, she could feel the tension inside her building. She thought, *What if he says 'no' or just completely ignores me? What if he's angry?*

Finally, she looked up and saw the manor house in front of her. She could hear Jack, Ben, and Charles talking somewhere on the other side of house, and she knew that they were probably still practicing.

She stopped and shook her head. "I can't interrupt their practice."

Lilen craned her neck to hear them. "Oh, I doubt they will mind very much. You should just go up and ask."

Vennel walked around to the back of the manor house and saw her three companions practicing their archery. Vennel walked up behind them, but she could not get up the nerve to ask her question.

Ben took aim with an arrow and let it fly, striking the target's edge.

Charles glanced at Vennel and smiled as he congratulated Ben on his shot.

Jack commented, "We're all getting much better at this. We just need to keep clear heads for the tournament."

Charles also fired an arrow, just missing the target.

Jack turned and looked at Vennel.

She just looked back. She wanted to ask, but she just could not form the words.

Jack seemed to deduce that she wanted something, so he gestured at one of the targets. "You want to give it a try?"

Vennel shook her head, but she did not stop looking at him.

Jack bumped Ben on the shoulder. "Go ahead and take another shot." He then stepped toward her. "You look like you need something. What is it?"

Vennel asked timidly, "Am I ... Am I going to the tournament tomorrow?"

Jack shrugged and said with genuine ignorance, "I don't know. You haven't told me."

Vennel grabbed her left hand with her right and squeezed it nervously, looking at her feet.

"What do you need?" Jack asked.

She raised her eyes and met his gaze. Her lower lip quivered. Tears filled her eyes and started to run down her cheeks.

Jack stared at her blankly for a moment. Finally, he repeated slowly, "What's wrong? What do you need?"

Embarrassed, she brushed the tears from her face. Digging a hollow in the dirt with the toe of her shoe, she said in a small voice, "I want to go ... but I don't have anything suitable to wear."

Jack let out his breath, and his shoulders relaxed. He gestured toward the house. "There's a pouch of coin on the table in our room. Take that. You should have enough to get whatever's necessary. Get a nice dress and maybe some other clothes just for everyday use. Either way, feel free to spend it all. You're not a slave anymore. You need to make your own choices."

Jack turned and stepped up next to the line with his friends.

"Thank you." Vennel was uncertain what else to say. After a pause she added, "It isn't really true, though. After all, I am only free in Celel."

Jack pulled an arrow from his quiver and looked over his shoulder. "You are as free as you allow yourself to be. If you need to claim me outside of Celel, you can, but in my mind you were never my slave."

Charles, overhearing this part of the conversation, smiled at her and nodded encouragingly.

Vennel turned to leave. She felt as if she walked on a cloud. She had always known that what Jack had just said was true, but she realized that she was still a slave in her own mind.

She walked immediately to Jack's room, and sure enough, a pouch sat on the table. She opened it as she picked it up and walked back out toward the front yard.

As Vennel stepped out the front door, Lilen asked excitedly, "How did it go?"

"I'm not sure. I'm counting it now." Vennel pushed the coins from one side of her hand to the other as she counted them. Then she looked at her friend with wide eyes. "It's four hundred coin!"

Lilen rolled her eyes. "Oh come on, don't tease me like that."

Vennel laughed. "I'm not teasing; that's really how much is in the pouch."

Lilen pursed her lips as if still not fully convinced. "Well, if there's that much, we should keep it out of sight until we get to town."

Vennel closed the pouch and slipped it into one of her pockets.

Lilen shook her head as they walked. "You must be really convincing. If I ask someone for money, I never get more than a few coin." She gave Vennel a sideways smile. "What do we want to buy?"

"We're going back to that dress shop. I want to see the look on that woman's face when I buy that dress."

They walked through the streets of Juma until they approached the tailor shop that they had visited earlier that day.

Vennel felt a little angry as she boldly pushed open the door and entered the shop.

Vennel noted recognition in the saleswoman's eyes when she saw Vennel and Lilen, but the woman did not interrupt her conversation with her current customer to acknowledge them. Vennel waited patiently next to the dress on display.

The shopkeeper finished with her customer and approached the two girls. She placed her hands on her hips. "Peasants are not good for business. Just leave."

Vennel pointed at the dress. "I'm here to buy that dress."

The saleswoman shook her head and spoke softly as if to herself, "Why is it that peasants just can't leave me in peace?"

Vennel pulled the pouch of money out of her pocket, counted out one hundred fifty coin, and set the money on the dress's stand.

The woman's eyes grew wide, and she let out a gasp.

As the saleswoman stared at the money, Vennel slowly pulled the dress off its hanger.

Suddenly, the shopkeeper smiled and clasped her hands together in front of her. "Is there anything else I can get for you today, my lady?"

Vennel smiled and nodded.

Lilen said, "You need new shoes, just for a start."

As the shopkeeper packed the dress, she asked Lilen, "Can I get you anything, dear?"

Lilen shook her head. "I'm just helping my friend shop today."

The two girls continued shopping until they had purchased everything necessary for the tournament.

As they left the shop, Lilen asked, "Do you want to shop for anything else today?"

Vennel shook her head. "No, I'll get some everyday clothes some other time. Right now, I'm more concerned about getting ready for the tournament."

The girls traveled through town and stepped out onto the road leading to the Celshen estate.

Vennel was so excited that she could barely contain herself as they walked. She thought, *I can't wait for everyone to see me in this dress tomorrow.*

******

The door to the servants' quarters swung open, and Vennel looked up to see Lilen step inside. It was the day of the tournament, and Vennel was almost prepared.

Lilen's eyes widened when she saw Vennel in her dress. Then she giggled and curtseyed. "My lady."

Vennel, startled for a moment, replied, "Come on, don't tease me. I've got to get ready."

Lilen rolled her eyes. "Well, so do I. I'm going with some of my friends later. I just finished helping Zannel with her dress; it's really lovely." Lilen stepped into the second room of the servants' quarters. "If you're not going with your companions to the tournament, you can always go with my friends and me."

Vennel carefully tied a white ribbon in her hair. She scrutinized her reflection critically in the mirror for a moment. "Thanks, but I'll go with my traveling companions."

Lilen stepped out of her room in her own dress and started fiddling with her hair. Then she turned to Vennel with a sly smile. "Is there someone in particular you want to see you in that dress?"

Vennel blushed and replied a little defensively, "Of course not."

Lilen giggled. "Really, because it sounds to me like you have a crush on one of those young knights-in-training."

Vennel responded, "That's ridiculous; I'm just a slave."

Lilen smiled and shook her head, sending her blond curls flying. "Not here in Celel. Besides, who gives their slave four hundred coin for a shopping trip?"

Vennel reached for the door handle. "It's just not that simple."

As she walked toward the manor house, Vennel saw Sir Aldric and Zannel step out onto the porch to wait for Zemara.

******

Jack secured both of his swords on his belt. He glanced over at Garthong, who lay on Jack's bed. "Garthong, you're not going to be able to stay with me during the tournament, so you should probably find some way to entertain yourself here."

Garthong lifted his head and snorted. He jumped to his feet, rushed over to the edge of the bed, and pranced around in an irritated manner.

Jack shook his head and chuckled. "Fine, you can come, but you have to watch from the air."

With that, his little friend jumped onto the windowsill, spread his wings, and took flight.

Jack glanced over at his two friends, who also looked ready. They all wore simple brown pants and gray woolen shirts. This specific garb was required for tournament participants in order to distinguish between competitors and onlookers and keep everyone on an equal playing field. The three friends walked through the house and stepped onto the front porch to wait.

Everyone was definitely dressed in their finest clothes. Sir Aldric wore an expensive red tunic, black pants, and tall boots. He also wore a green cloak fastened by a brooch that bore the family crest, which consisted of a hawk perched on a branch. To Jack's surprise, Sir Aldric did not wear a sword.

Jack turned his attention to the two young women. Zannel's dress was a deep purple with white embroidered vines forming curving patterns over its entirety. The dress had a square neckline and a lace-up bodice that accentuated her feminine features. The sleeves were fitted to the elbow, where they widened to a bell shape. In addition to her dress, she wore a crushed velvet caplet in the same deep purple hue. Her hair was tied loosely behind her head with a delicate purple ribbon. Jack thought she looked beautiful. He wondered if she had dressed up for someone. *Then again,* he reminded himself, *this is supposed to be a big social event, so I would expect her to look her best.*

Jack looked over at Vennel and smiled. He realized, *I don't think I've ever seen her wear any color except brown.* Noticing how attractive she was, Jack glanced at Charles to see his reaction.

Charles seemed to be taken aback for a moment at Vennel's transformation. He shifted his weight while flushing slightly. "Vennel, you look very nice." He smiled a little awkwardly.

Vennel smiled broadly. Then she bit her lower lip, and her cheeks tinted a little as she looked at the ground. "Thank you."

Sir Aldric was telling them a story about his family crest, but Jack paid more attention to his friends' subtle reactions. Jack thought, *This could be good for both of them, but what happens if we find a way to return home?*

Ben was already off the porch. He looked impatient and maybe just a little apprehensive. He did not seem able to stand still.

Zemara came out of the house to join the group, wearing a floor length red velour dress with long fitted sleeves, a wide delicate neckline, and a broad gold belt in the height of fashion.

Everyone walked to the waiting carriage to travel to the tournament.

When they arrived at the tournament, Jack was surprised by the number of people present. He had heard that this was a major event for the surrounding area, but he had still not anticipated this large of a crowd.

Sir Aldric pointed toward some men in the crowd. "There, with the governor of Juma, that man is the governor of Dettall, another prominent city in Celel. The other man with him is a knight named Sir Alter. Sir Alter is very famous as a master of the sword and gemstones. I must go speak with them. You all have a good time and enjoy yourselves."

Jack examined the man Sir Aldric had identified as Sir Alter. He appeared solemn and stern with his mouth pulled into a tight line. The knight had an unkempt beard and mustache, and his dark brown hair hung down over his eyebrows. His clothes seemed less expensive than the two men near him, and his boots appeared to be designed for fighting rather than for show. The knight carried a shield on his back in addition to his sword. Jack glanced around and noticed that many of the noblemen carried swords, but most of them did not have shields. This knight was ready for battle even here in a safe environment.

Zemara and Zannel exchanged worried looks as Sir Aldric departed, and Zemara placed her left hand over her mouth.

Concerned by their reaction, Jack turned and whispered, "Charles, keep an eye on him, will you? See if you can find out anything about those two guys with the governor, Sir what's-his-name—the knight guy—and the other governor."

Charles nodded and sauntered off.

"I'm going to mingle with some of the other contestants," Ben announced. "Do you want to come?"

"No," Jack replied, "I think I'll wander around the grounds a little bit to see what I can learn."

Jack recognized the captain of the Juma barracks in the crowd watching a few men fight, so he walked over to discern what the men were doing since the tournament had not yet begun.

"Hello, Captain," said Jack. "How are you doing?"

The captain glanced at him. "Ah, you're the foreigner. Good to see you again, but hang on a minute. I'm trying to watch these fighters' forms."

Jack studied the men. Three pairs were engaged in one-on-one combat with shields and blunted swords. The men had no armor or helmets, and all wore the plain brown uniforms of the town guard. A group of onlookers had gathered around to watch the fighters. Several of the spectators wore the apparel of the actual competitors in the tournament like Jack, and some of these men had a brightly colored piece of cloth tied around one arm.

Jack asked, "What do the cloths tied around the contestants' arms mean?"

The captain did not look away from the fights. "If a man has a woman in the crowd watching him, and he's fighting for the honor of her household, he may tie a colored band of cloth belonging to her around his arm. The cloth is a symbol that he will protect her and her honor from whatever danger may come. If a man is married, he wears his wife's colors as tradition. Among young, unmarried people, however, the cloth doesn't necessarily have anything to do with a romantic relationship. The cloths can also be given out as a gesture of luck by girls who are not members of prominent families as a way of flirting. Occasionally, the colors belong to a contestant's representing family."

Jack asked, "How serious are those fights taking place now?"

"This is pretty much just our normal sword practice," the captain replied. "We're putting on a show for the crowd before the tournament starts. The blunted weapons are the same kind that will be used in the tournament, as is standard. After all, no one is actually supposed to be seriously hurt today, not physically at least."

"What do you mean 'physically'?"

"Well, people's honor and influence may obviously be hurt, but no one is supposed to die for it. This is only training after all."

Jack asked, "What do you know about the other contestants?"

"Other contestants?" replied the captain. "Oh, you are competing today. Congratulations." The captain shook his head. "If I had been paying attention to your garb, I would've noticed earlier that you were a contestant. Most of these older men grew up with some training and became squires, men who served knights, but a drastic change took place around thirty years ago when the new king rose to power. Now anyone, including the lowest peasant and even foreigners like you, is allowed to become a knight and even gain important positions such as governorship. Merit, honor, and wisdom are the governing traits that decide where someone can go nowadays. Of course, many people still cling to the old ways and try to prevent foreigners or peasants from attaining power, but the king is not one of them. Wealth is obviously still a deciding factor, and people like the governor of Juma still believe in bloodlines as well.

"About the other contestants, though. You'll need to watch out for several in the melee competition." The captain pointed at various people as he spoke. "That tall guy right there is Fanter. He's quite skilled. He has spent his lifetime practicing and has been a squire to a knight for two years. Kelder is another one. He may be small, but he's incredibly fast and strong for his size. He has also been a squire since he was young.

"The one you have to watch out for the most is the big guy right there. He is called Gurtven. He has already claimed the top swordsmanship position in a previous tournament under one of the other governors. He has also gone on several missions with knights. The only reason he isn't already a knight is because he's trying to get a better deal by not claiming to be represented by a prominent family, even though several have offered."

"So prominent families can give wealth or land to individuals they recommend?" Jack deduced.

"Yes, he's basically letting the prominent families engage in a bidding war, and he will join whichever family offers him the most. He's here because winning a second championship will significantly boost his future revenue."

"How many contestants are here?"

"Oh, maybe fifty people. Contestants come from a great distance," the captain explained.

After watching for a few more minutes, Jack thanked the captain and left to explore more of the tournament grounds.

He saw Ben engaged in a conversation with some young people but did not stop. He was confident that Ben would obtain any important information that could be gleaned from these individuals. Jack wondered how many prominent families were present—it seemed like dozens. He also discovered that shops of all types were set up here just for the day of the tournament. Items sold varied from scented candles to battle axes. Since this event provided entertainment for the entire family, shops sold items that appealed to everyone.

Jack meandered through the crowd until he spotted Zemara. She was leaving a group of very lavishly dressed women, who Jack guessed were members of prominent families. Her cheeks were flushed, and she dabbed at her face with a frilly cloth. She ducked behind one of the tents.

Jack almost continued on but decided that he should check on her. He walked around the tent's corner.

Zemara wept into her handkerchief and did not notice him.

"Are you okay?" Jack whispered.

She whipped around and tried to dry her tears. "Everything is okay. There's nothing to worry about."

"Pardon me for questioning you," replied Jack, "but it doesn't look that way. What did they say to you?"

She began crying again and muttered through the tears, "That miserable woman from the Setell family was mocking me about my daughter. Zannel is engaged to one of their sons, a wretched boy named Vanzantel."

"Zannel is engaged? Isn't she a bit young for that?"

"In arranged marriages it doesn't matter how old the children are when the parents establish the engagement. Arranged marriages have been frowned upon in this country since the new king came to power. The king has severely discouraged the practice unless the two young people agree to the arrangement. But desperate families like ours sometimes still arrange marriages to increase the family name's influence and honor."

This concept seemed terribly selfish to Jack, but he held his tongue. This culture was different from the one with which he was familiar, and anything other than listening would do no good at the moment.

Zemara continued, "The boy wasn't so bad when he was younger, but his whole family has become obsessed with power, and now they only care about themselves. Vanzantel seems to enjoy tormenting my daughter about their future, and the rest of the family does the same to me. I'm terribly afraid that instead of marrying upward into a better family, our daughter will be miserable for the rest of her life. I just don't know what to do to fix it." She regained her composure with an effort. "I'm sorry. I shouldn't break down like this in a public place; it isn't befitting of a noblewoman. Thank you for listening. It actually helped." She turned and walked back toward the tent full of women.

Jack thought, *Her family must be more desperate than I thought if they arranged a marriage several years ago to increase their influence.* Jack turned his gaze in the direction that he had last seen Charles and wondered what kind of information his friend was gathering.

******

As Charles followed Sir Aldric, he thought, *I guess I'll just follow at a little distance and eavesdrop on his conversations.* He wondered why Jack asked *him* to follow them. *This is really more Ben's thing.* Ben was definitely better at going unnoticed, and he did not mind eavesdropping on conversations either. Jack was right, though. These three men were probably the most important people at the tournament, and it would be good to know what they were thinking.

Sir Aldric joined the two governors and Sir Alter. "Hello, gentlemen. How good to see you all on this fine day."

They responded with a similar greeting.

Sir Alter commented, "I understand that you have some contestants in the tournament today."

"Yes I do," replied Sir Aldric, "three young men, who should prove themselves quite capable."

At this, the two governors excused themselves from the conversation and continued toward their seats near the melee ring.

Sir Alter said, "You've made quite a bold move by putting three young men forward at the same time. They must all do extremely well today, or you will look like a fool."

"Yes, that is one of the things I want to talk to you about." Sir Aldric rubbed his hands together nervously. "All three of them are quite skilled, and I would like to request that you take the best one on a mission, if he's worthy, and eventually recommend one or all of them for knighthood."

"We are old friends," replied Sir Alter in a cautious tone, "but they must meet the minimum standard if I'm going to take them on a mission. And potentially recommending three at the same time is out of the question. If they're all skilled, I'll take them on missions and recommend them one at a time. The two governors seem to have a very low opinion of the three young men and claim that all three are foreigners."

Sir Aldric nodded and glanced toward the governors. "They are all foreigners, and I know little of their past, but I believe they are sincere in their desire to become Knights of Celel. In truth, I know little about their skill level because so far, I've never seen any of them fight. Even my daughter did not see them fight the Bendel men who captured her but is only aware that they defeated the slavers. I would be grateful for your help. Most of my old friends have died as you know. My wife and I are a little older than we look, and fighting was fierce back in the days before the new king."

Sir Alter replied, "Fighting is still fierce, but the general populous doesn't see it because of us knights. A great war brews to the south, and I fear that all the countries in the world could be swallowed up by it. But if these young men meet the standard, I will take one of them. I will soon undertake a very dangerous mission, and I cannot settle for a poor student."

"I understand. Thank you, my old friend," Sir Aldric said as they parted company with a friendly gesture.

Sir Aldric walked in pursuit of the two governors, and Charles followed.

Even from a distance Charles could see the governors become stiff and exchange quiet comments when they saw Sir Aldric approaching.

As Charles attempted to move closer, he bumped into a large young man with short brown hair and arms as big around as the average person's legs.

"Excuse me." Charles tried to squeeze through the crowd around the man.

The big man, however, grabbed Charles's arm and turned him around.

Charles drew back his right arm, prepared to deliver a straight punch into the stranger's gut, but just before he punched, he saw the man's face. The young man appeared very close to his own age and wore a broad smile that caused Charles to rethink his course of action.

"Hi," said big young man. "I'm Kxull. You must also be in the tournament."

The young man's friendly attitude surprised Charles. He noticed that the fellow also wore the required garb for the tournament. Charles introduced himself and added, "Yes, I am in the tournament."

Kxull said, "I like your shield. Where did you get it?"

Charles glanced over his shoulder at his shield. Although he had obtained his first shield from one of the Caishan slavers, his most recent upgrade had come from Warlord Abgot's armory, where Charles had selected a larger shield before the battle in Kliptun. "I picked it up from a warlord in the central lands."

Kxull replied, "That's amazing! Can I look at it?"

Charles shrugged. "Okay."

The young man examined the shield critically for a moment. "It's a nice one, and I can tell it's been used in battle because of all the nicks. I'll tell you what, if I do better than you in the tournament, you have to give me your shield, and if you do better than me, I have to give you my battle axe." The young man held up a large one-handed battle axe.

Charles was amazed. The axe was beautiful, and even to his untrained eye, it clearly possessed very intricate craftsmanship. "Where did you get that?"

"My father is a smith, and he taught me the trade. We forged this together. It's the finest axe he's ever made, but in truth, we actually made two identical axes at the same time. That's the best part about my bet. If I lose, I still have my axe; you'll just have one too."

Charles smiled. This big guy's happiness was rubbing off on him. "All right, it's a deal," Charles said. "I'll see you after the tournament, and we will settle up."

Charles moved closer to the two governors and Sir Aldric, but now his mind swam with visions of himself wielding a battle axe against his opponents. *This sword always was way too small and light,* he thought. *I need something bigger.* Even in the boys' fencing classes back home, Charles never felt totally comfortable with the weak, light swords. *If I don't win this bet, I should definitely look into buying a one-handed battle axe. It would suit my size and strength a lot better ... and it would look totally awesome.*

He caught the very end of the conversation on which he was supposed to have eavesdropped. The governor of Juma said, "I won't support you in any way. Your time is passed. This is my city now, and your ridiculous little foreign kids can go back to wherever they came from. I'm just glad that after today you'll be finished. You fool, backing three young men all at the same time when you have so little influence left already. I'll be very satisfied when you marry your daughter into the Setell family because after today you will have so little influence that even if you married a dozen children into higher families, it still wouldn't help you."

Sir Aldric inhaled sharply and flared his nostrils. "How dare you insult my daughter!" He pulled his fist back as if preparing to strike the governor, but a hand grabbed his arm and stopped him.

Sir Alter suddenly stood behind Sir Aldric, holding his arm. He whispered something into Sir Aldric's ear before releasing him.

Sir Aldric turned and started walking away. Then he noticed Charles.

Charles felt uncomfortable, not knowing if Sir Aldric would be upset.

The old knight, however, came over to Charles and placed a hand on Charles's shoulder. "I'm sorry you had to witness that. A knight should never give in to anger."

Charles replied, "Don't worry. After today things are going to change."

The old knight looked at Charles grimly. "Let's just get on with the day." Sir Aldric then turned and departed.

Charles meandered through the crowds, looking for his two friends. He found Ben in the middle of a group of young men and women chatting about the tournament.

"Hey, Ben," called Charles, "let's find Jack and get ready for the tournament."

"All right." Ben stood and walked toward Charles.

Charles saw that Ben had a light purple cloth tied around his right arm and a bright yellow cloth around his left arm. "What are those for?"

"I have no idea," replied Ben. "Some of the girls from town tied them on my arms. Both of the girls were kind of cute, so I didn't stop them. Come to think of it, the girls really didn't seem to like each other, but I didn't pay attention as to the reason."

Chapter 14

JACK BEGAN SEARCHING FOR his comrades since the tournament would begin soon. On the edge of the tournament grounds, Jack noticed a group of eight or nine young men in a circle. He decided to wander over to see why they were gathered. As he approached, he noticed more young men and a large group of young women watching from a short distance.

Zannel stood among the group of women. She looked pale and wrung her hands while unchecked tears rolled down her cheeks.

As Jack drew near, he saw a boy, probably thirteen or fourteen years old, inside the circle being beaten by a young man Jack's age. The injustice angered Jack. It seemed as though no matter where he went, even here in Celel, some kind of evil was always at work. Jack immediately grabbed two of the young men forming the circle by their collars and yanked them backward to clear a space on the ring's edge.

"What's going on?" he demanded.

The young man Jack's age inside the circle looked up, anger written all over his long, narrow face. "Why are you interfering? Do you want me to beat you up too?"

The young man's well-manicured facial hair seemed to bristle as he glanced from side to side at his comrades to ensure that they were with him. He had blood on his right hand, and another smudge stained his bright red tunic. The young man ran his left hand through his short brown hair as if putting it back in its proper place. Then he stepped toward Jack, wrinkling the soft, plush leather of his tall boots and fingering the hilt of his sword.

Jack ignored the man's threat and crossed his arms. "What could this kid have possibly done to deserve such a beating?"

"He bumped into my fiancée, so I'm teaching him a little lesson."

Jack narrowed his eyes and stepped into the circle. "Well, you've taught your lesson. You're done."

The circle started to close in again around Jack, but when Jack reached for his swords, the young man paused and held up his hand. "All right, I'm done. Come on, guys. We'll let the little kid go."

The boy glanced at Jack and took off running.

Jack bumped into two of the watching young men on his way out of the circle, clearing a path with his shoulders.

"Hey, don't think this is over," called the young man in the ring.

Zannel ran over to the young man and pleaded, "Please, Vanzantel, just let it go."

Upon hearing the name, Jack turned and looked back at the young man. "You are Zannel's fiancé?"

Vanzantel replied, "Yes, I am. You speak as though you know her."

Jack glanced at Zannel. "Only a little. Her father is the one recommending me in the tournament."

Vanzantel produced a handkerchief from his tunic and wiped the blood off of his hand. "Well then, I'll have to bet big money that you lose. Get out of here; I don't want you talking to my fiancée."

Jack did not know why, but this young man offended him even more than the slavers or the priests of the demon god. "Really?" Jack clinched his fists. "You beat up small kids, go around with a big group of guys, and think you are really something. Are you even in the tournament?"

Zannel's eyes were wide and she clung to Vanzantel's arm.

Vanzantel sneered and gritted his teeth. "That does it. I'm going to teach you a lesson like I taught that little kid."

Jack looked him in the eye. "I have a better idea." He turned to Zannel. "Give me your colored ribbon to wear in the tournament. If I do well in the tournament, this little pest will be humiliated. If I lose, I'll be humiliated.

Vanzantel held his free arm in front of Zannel as if protecting her from this menace. "Not a chance."

"What? Are you afraid?" countered Jack.

Vanzantel, seething with rage, responded, "The bet is on. Zannel, give him your ribbon."

Zannel took the purple ribbon out of her hair, stepped next to Jack, and tied it around his right arm.

"I'll see you after the tournament," Jack said coldly to Vanzantel as Jack turned and walked toward the contestant staging area.

Jack paused as he neared the ring and leaned against a pole. He was still irritated, but he looked around for his friends. He did not see them. He knew he was a little foolish to interfere with a group of young men who were probably all members of prominent families when he was alone, lacking noble standing, and a foreigner. *I could probably get kicked out of the whole country for riling up that bunch*, he thought.

Jack heard a faint sound and turned. Zannel stood in front of him with red cheeks and swollen eyes. He was not sure, but her appearance suggested that she had been crying. Then he remembered that she *had* been crying just a few minutes ago when the little boy was being beaten. *I can't believe I accidentally wrapped her up in this*, thought Jack. *It was just between me and that stupid Vanzantel guy. Why did I have to bring her into it by making that bet?*

Zannel shifted her weight indecisively. She drew in her bottom lip as if she were nervous, but he could detect determination in her eyes. "Thank you for helping the boy." She started to turn away.

Jack felt as though he should say something. He placed his hand on her shoulder and gently turned her back toward him. "Remember what I told you before. Just trust me."

As she left, Jack thought, *'Remember what I told you.' Yeah, that's real comforting. Way to go, Jack. Now she's probably trying to figure out what it was that I told her.* To Jack, however, it seemed rather obvious at the time. *I said I would protect her from whatever danger came, and I meant it. Her family represents us now, so it's actually my duty to protect everyone in her family.*

Charles interrupted Jack's thoughts, saying, "Hey there, Ben and I have been looking for you." He glanced over his shoulder at Ben, who was talking to one of the nearby merchants, and added, "But Ben keeps getting distracted by the food."

Jack noticed Ben's two colored cloths on his arms, smiled, and thought, *I don't know what the story is behind that, but whatever it is, it could only happen to Ben.*

Vennel and Lilen joined them. Vennel's new dress made her blue eyes shine.

Jack watched Charles's gaze pass over Vennel and settle on the white ribbon in her hair.

Vennel followed his stare, and her eyes shifted upward. She asked self-consciously, "Is there something wrong with my hair?"

Lilen, looking back and forth between the two of them, giggled. "No, he's just too shy to ask you for your ribbon, so you should just give it to him."

Charles and Vennel both looked embarrassed as they glanced at each other.

Vennel turned toward Jack.

Jack just shrugged. "You don't need my permission."

Vennel timidly removed the ribbon from her hair, letting her long golden locks cascade onto her shoulders.

As she tied the ribbon around Charles's sword arm, Ben joined them and said, "Come on guys, we have a tournament to win."

A horn blew, and Vennel said, "Good luck, and be careful," before turning and heading for the wooden seats with Lilen.

Contestants could sign one of four different rosters for the melee tournament. A battle for each would take place simultaneously, and the best contestants from all four would fight next. Then the two best contestants would compete.

"Let's all sign a different roster," said Jack. "That way we won't have to fight each other until the end."

Ben grinned. "Someone sure is confident. I like it."

Jack thought, *No, not so confident, just determined. This has become more than just a stepping stone toward knighthood, and it's even more than eventually making it home. I've made commitments to people here, and now it's my duty.*

The horn sounded again.

The governor of Juma stood and informed everyone that he would make the announcements for the day and that the judges would be himself, the governor of Dettall, and Sir Alter. "The first test will be the test of precision," he announced.

The contestants lined up along the field's edge. Several competitors stood in line before the three friends.

A ringside worker pulled back a weighted wooden disk hanging from a tree branch by a rope and let it swing at waist height.

Jack watched the first young man hurl a rock at the small moving target. Jack guessed that the contestant must have an earth stone. Jack had not previously seen anyone use an earth stone. *Fascinating,* he mused, *the defensive prospects are excellent, and the offensive properties are moderate.*

Several more people cast spells with varying degrees of success. Then a big fellow stepped up and shot a lightning bolt that split the target just to the left of its center. This man stood out to Jack because Charles seemed interested in his performance.

Ben hurled his fireball next. Even though he missed the wooden disk by a small distance, he recognized his error in time to cause his fireball to explode as it passed the target, destroying the hanging disk.

Jack stepped up next. This would be the easiest test for him, so he was not particularly nervous. He focused, stretched out his hand, and cast a lightning bolt. The target split dead center.

Charles's fireball clipped the bottom of the wooden disk and earned a fine score in comparison to many of the other contestants. Unlike Jack and his friends, it seemed that many of the competitors were relatively inexperienced with their gemstones.

The archery competition came next, and Jack was relieved to discover that many of the contestants could not hit the target with any of their three arrows. Ben's archery had clearly improved exponentially. His second arrow actually hit the target's top left corner.

When Jack's turn came, he took a deep breath and grasped the bow. He steadily pulled back on the string, aimed his arrow, adjusted his aim slightly for the wind, and let go. The arrow hit the dirt right at the target's base and skittered along the ground under the target. *Well, I'm doing a lot better than some of these people,* thought Jack as he pulled back the string a second time. His second arrow hit almost the exact same place as his first arrow, and he prepared his third. *I just have to hit the target.* He angled his bow up more to account for the drop of the first two arrows. The third arrow whizzed through the air, chipped the target's bottom edge, and fell to the ground. Jack sighed, *At least I scored reasonably well; I'll have to win this thing in the melee competition anyway.*

Charles's arrows came close, but he missed the target with all three.

After all of the contestants shot their arrows, Jack did some mental figuring and realized that in the archery competition he had scored in the top thirty percent. Ben had made the top twenty percent, and Charles was ranked just under Jack.

The governor of Juma stood and announced that they would begin the elimination rounds for the melee competition then hold the last fights after the destruction test.

Jack proceeded to his arena, and a ringside worker came to each ring to line up the participants so that everyone would know the fight order. The tournament organization dictated that pairs of contestants would fight, and the winner of each pair would compete against the winner of another pair. Contestants would receive a brief rest between fights. Four fights would take place simultaneously until the final few rounds, which would take place one at a time.

Weapon racks filled with a variety of blunted weapons stood next to the rings. Jack chose two long swords that resembled his own and returned to his place in line.

The governor of Juma stood and commanded, "Let the fighting begin."

Jack's first opponent was rather large and apparently decided to use his weight and shield to charge Jack. Jack easily stepped out of the way and swept his sword in an arc across his opponent's back.

His next two matches were a little more difficult but still fairly easy. He turned and noticed that Ben and Charles were also moving up the ladder. Jack noted that it was largely the martial arts training the three friends had received in high school that gave them the edge in many of their fights.

Jack's next opponent was about his size and carried a small, round shield, which proved to be very maneuverable.

Jack tested him by doing a couple quick jabs with his left sword while keeping his right back for defense.

His opponent matched him, parrying Jack's sword with his shield and stabbing with his own sword. As they continued, the other young man stepped back briefly and brought his hands together behind his shield.

Jack was not sure for a moment what the young man was doing, but when his opponent separated his hands again and dived at Jack, he had switched his sword and shield hands for a surprise angle of attack. He rushed at Jack's right side, coming at him with a swift left-handed attack while punching with his shield.

As Jack deflected the shield to the side, the other man swung his sword, forcing Jack to retreat. He pushed Jack back again with a similar move on Jack's left side.

This strategy was very new to Jack. He had previously fought soldiers who attacked with their shields, but most of them used large shields, and they did not have the speed and aggressive technique that this man possessed.

Jack changed tactics and went all-out offensive himself. He unleashed a flurry of strikes, and while his opponent deflected them, Jack closed the distance between them and kicked the inside of the man's left leg.

His opponent's foot came off the ground and landed farther back, giving him a very wide stance.

Jack took advantage of the man's instability to fake a downward strike with his left sword. When his opponent tried to block the swing, Jack shoved with the sword's hilt, pushing his foe and knocking him to the ground. Jack aggressively attacked his challenger while he lay on the ground and ended the match.

One more match remained to determine who would win out of each of the four rings. The governor announced that the last four matches for the preliminary rounds would take place one at a time for the spectators' enjoyment.

Jack noticed that Ben faced Gurtven, the big guy who had already won the previous tournament. Charles's fight was against another big fellow called Kxull, and Jack's opponent was Fanter, another of the more skilled fighters.

Charles's match took place first, and Jack was interested to note that Charles's large opponent carried a blunted battle axe.

When the match began, Kxull moved in without hesitation. With surprising speed he swung his battle axe.

Charles blocked it with his shield, but Jack could tell that the axe's momentum rattled Charles. None of them had faced an adversary with this heavyweight style of fighting.

Kxull swung the axe again, this time straight down.

Charles jumped to the side and tried to swing his sword in sideways, but Kxull deflected it easily with his shield. Most people the three friends had fought used both their sword and shield somewhat offensively and defensively, but this man only used his axe offensively and used his shield for both attack and defense. Charles tried to break his rival's defenses with a series of strong sword swings.

Kxull seemed completely unaffected and counterattacked with the large axe.

Charles blocked again, this time countering with a strong thrust.

Kxull, however, diverted the point of the sword with his shield almost effortlessly.

******

Vennel, watching from the bleachers, leaned forward. She clenched her fists and bit her lower lip. She thought, *That man with the battle axe is really good. I hope Charles can beat him.* Charles's opponent was a large fellow, but Charles's had plenty of size and muscle of his own.

The ends of Vennel's white ribbon flapped in the breeze whenever Charles swung his sword or dodged a blow. She found herself staring at the ribbon. Had he really wanted her ribbon? Was it possible that Lilen had misinterpreted Charles's expression, and he only agreed to accept her colored cloth to avoid embarrassing her? Did she, a previous slave, really have a skilled fighter standing behind her honor? *A previous slave,* she repeated to herself. Vennel fingered her gown's soft cloth and glanced next to her at Zannel, who had invited Vennel to sit with her and her friends.

Vennel involuntarily flinched as Charles skillfully averted a deadly-looking strike. She craned her neck to see Charles's face as he jabbed and sidestepped. Sweat dripped from both men. She knew that the competitors carried blunted weapons, but the fight's intensity made it seem like a true life-or-death struggle.

******

No matter what Charles tried, he could not break through his adversary's defense. Jack could see Charles growing frustrated and desperate until he finally charged his opponent with his shield.

Unfortunately, Kxull just held up his own shield, and the two collided. A loud clang rang out as the two shields impacted, and both young men stumbled back without any clear sign of advantage on either side.

Kxull raised his axe, but Charles rushed in, swung his sword upward, and caught the axe high in the air before it could gain momentum. Charles swung his shield into his foe's shield, knocking it sideways, and slammed his own body into his opponent.

Both of them fell to the ground and dropped their shields.

Charles threw his sword to the side and grabbed his opponent's axe. He wrenched the weapon from Kxull's hand and swung it in a downward arc. Kxull could not roll out of the way in time, and Charles won his preliminary fight.

Ben's fight came next, and Jack could read the look of determination on his countenance as the two rivals slowly circled in the ring.

The governor yelled, "Fight."

Gurtven closed in incredibly fast with a series of strikes.

Ben was not nearly as clumsy with his shield as he had been that day in the Caishan caves, and he successfully deflected the strikes. He then charged his larger opponent with his shield and simultaneously twisted his sword in his hand so that the sword pointed downward.

Gurtven, focused on the charge, missed what Ben planned with his sword. The big man easily launched Ben backward by striking his own shield against Ben's, but as he did, Ben stabbed his sword into his challenger's ankle.

Although blunted, the sword still punctured the skin and made Gurtven stumble.

Ben rushed in again and swung his sword down, trying to take advantage of his antagonist's momentary weakness, but this time Gurtven saw through his ploy.

Gurtven deflected the sword to Ben's left side, giving him an opening to shove Ben's right shoulder with his sword hilt.

Off balance, Ben stumbled toward the ring's edge, but he stabbed his sword into the ground to absorb the momentum and right himself.

Gurtven, however, had gained the advantage and came in with a series of unrelenting strikes.

Ben deflected the first one with his sword and absorbed the second with his shield, but the third slipped past his defenses, and the match was over.

Ben would not go on to the final round.

Jack's turn came next, and he stepped into the ring opposite Fanter.

The call came, and the fight began.

Fanter leapt to Jack's left and thrust his sword forward.

Jack flicked the weapon aside and thought, *If you think my left side is exposed just because I don't have a shield, you are gravely mistaken.* Jack moved in aggressively with a series of strikes. He could tell that he had caught Fanter by surprise by the difficulty the young man seemed to have deflecting Jack's attacks. He could see in Fanter's eyes that he was trying to think of a way to overcome Jack's defenses, but Jack did not let up with his attacks to give him time to plan.

Fanter became almost completely overwhelmed, but he finally began counterattacking, forcing Jack to decrease his strike frequency.

Finally, the two backed away from each other, and Jack reflected, *This guy is good; he managed to deflect all of my attacks then re-stabilize the match by counterattacking.*

Fanter rushed in again, still on Jack's left side, and tried to swing his shield to prevent Jack from blocking his sword with Jack's own sword. Fanter then swung his sword in a downward arc.

Jack sidestepped the entire attack by moving farther to his left and shoving Fanter's shield, knocking his foe off balance. Jack moved in for a quick finish.

Fanter, however, recovered quickly and managed to turn around and reposition his shield defensively before Jack could land a strike.

The two backed away from each other and started testing each other again.

Jack then moved in quickly, swinging one sword from the right and one from left.

Fanter blocked both attacks and tried to front kick Jack to keep him away from his exposed midsection.

Jack, however, had already closed the distance too tightly, and Fanter was too close to Jack to finish his kick. The two now stood just inches away from each other.

Jack executed a crescent kick with his left leg, swinging it up from the right in an arc and clipping the side of Fanter's face. Jack brought the kick down on his own left side, wrapped his leg around Fanter's sword arm, and freed his own left sword.

When Jack brought his left sword to his challenger's throat, the judges called the match.

Jack climbed out of the ring as the last match of the preliminary round commenced. Kelder won that match, making him Jack's first opponent for the final round.

All the contestants then made their way to the destruction test.

Gurtven performed first and hurled a very hot fireball downrange, engulfing the wagon wheel target.

Ben, obviously frustrated, had stepped in line right behind him. He took a deep breath and hurled an extremely hot fireball that easily rivaled one of Sumbvi's. His wheel was engulfed in flames and continued to burn in a fierce inferno.

Jack thought back to the black-cloaked man they had encountered on the way there. *I still want to know who that guy was*, he thought.

Charles also scored well with his fireball, and Jack found that it was his turn next.

This was not going to be easy.

Jack stepped up to the line, concentrated with all his might, and hurled a solid block of ice into the target with as much force as he could muster. The ice wrenched the wheel from its axle, and wood shards flew in all directions.

Jack glanced at the judges' faces and saw Sir Alter smile slightly. Jack smiled too. Being able to cause so much destruction with a water stone was a rare skill. He knew he had not beaten either of his friends' scores, but he had performed well.

The governor of Juma stood and announced that Jack was the winner of the precision event. The winner of the archery competition was a guy named Hither, and Ben had won the destruction test. The governor raised his hands to quiet the crowd. "Now we must see which of these warriors will win the melee tournament. The first two contestants will be Gurtven versus Charles followed by Kelder versus Jack."

Jack could sense that Charles was nervous. "Come on man," Jack said, "you've got to win this so we can fight each other in the last bout."

Charles smiled grimly. "We'll see." He stepped into the arena.

Gurtven sauntered confidently toward Charles, but he apparently decided to feel Charles out before making a direct assault because he repeatedly moved in and out, poking with his sword.

Charles tried to move in and pin down his opponent, but every time he assaulted his foe, Gurtven just danced away.

Finally, Gurtven rushed directly at Charles, and a fierce fight ensued, neither of them giving ground or losing it.

Charles swung his shield sideways, trying to catch Gurtven under the arm.

Gurtven moved his shield to cover his right side and caught the edge of Charles's shield with his own. Gurtven swung his sword sideways at Charles.

Despite Charles's awkward shield position, he managed to bring it back up again and catch the strike. Charles swung three times with his sword then shoved his shield forward, knocking Gurtven back a step.

Gurtven moved to Charles's right side and swung his sword low at Charles's leg.

Charles twisted his own sword in his hand and caught the blow. For the moment Charles had the advantage. He swung his shield into his enemy, knocking him back another step. Charles tried to press his advantage with a follow-up strike. He swung his sword in an upward arc.

Gurtven stepped in and struck Charles's sword arm, causing Charles to drop his weapon. Gurtven pressed in with a series of strikes.

Charles deflected the blows with his shield, but each time he tried to maneuver toward his sword, Gurtven cut him off again.

Finally, Gurtven made it through Charles's defenses and struck Charles in the chest with a sword thrust, ending the match.

Great, thought Jack, *that means if I beat this guy, I have to fight Gurtven next.*

Jack stepped into the ring opposite Kelder.

Kelder glared at him "I see that thing tied on your arm. That's a personal insult to me because the Setell family is the one that recommended me. I'm going to make you pay for humiliating their son by wearing that cloth."

Jack smiled. "Wow, it's going be so much more fun to kick your butt now than it would've been a few minutes ago, just saying."

"How dare you!" Kelder whispered through gritted teeth.

Whatever else he was going to say was interrupted by the governor ordering them to begin.

Kelder immediately charged at Jack.

Jack saw the anger in Kelder's eyes, and Jack used his enemy's narrow field of vision to step to the left and side kick his rib cage under his arm. Jack had watched Kelder fight on his way to the finals and knew that Kelder's anger caused him to fight worse than normal.

Jack was careful to avoid the majority of his opponent's attacks rather than block them. The extra strength from Kelder's anger might be enough to throw Jack off balance, but Jack continually redirected his foe's momentum. Jack focused on making insignificant but annoying strikes to irritate his rival and shrink his field of vision even more.

Although it seemed like such a long time ago, Jack could easily replay the often-repeated warning from his martial arts instructor: "Remember, a skilled combatant who lets his emotions control him is a relatively poor fighter, but a warrior in complete control displays and feels whatever emotion he wishes."

Kelder rushed at Jack again, raising his sword above his head.

This time Jack squatted slightly while holding his left sword above his head.

Just as Jack had suspected, Kelder swung downward.

Jack diverted the blow with his left sword, deflecting his opponent's weapon to Jack's left side.

Kelder's momentum forced him to follow his sword forward.

Jack reversed his grip on his right sword so that it was pointed downward along his own forearm. Throwing his left sword to the side, he grabbed Kelder's right wrist with his left hand. In one fluid movement he brought his right shoulder under his opponent's exposed upper sword arm while rotating his back toward Kelder and flipping his opponent over his own right shoulder.

Kelder fell to the ground hard, and Jack quickly stabbed his right sword downward into the man's chest.

As he stepped out of the ring, Jack mused that this had been easier than his previous fight. Jack glanced up and saw the governor of Juma's facial expression. His frown and deeply furrowed brow suggested that the governor was not happy. Apparently, the governor had not expected Jack or his friends to perform half as well as they had.

The governor stood and announced that a healer was prepared to care for any of the minor injuries that the two final contestants might have sustained before they fought the final round.

Jack had not been injured, but he recalled that Ben had stabbed Gurtven in the leg. Jack wondered, *Is the governor actively trying to prevent me from winning?* Did someone usually heal the last two contestants before the last bout? Apparently, there was a way to quickly heal injuries in this world. *I must go see this healer.*

Jack followed Gurtven to the healer's tent and waited outside as Gurtven's wound was tended.

In a few minutes Gurtven emerged and headed toward the ring.

Jack entered the tent and found a woman sitting on the ground in front of him. She looked like she was in her thirties with shoulder-length, dark brown hair and green eyes.

She asked Jack, "Are you injured?"

"No," he replied. "I just wanted to meet you. I've never met a healer. How do you do it?"

The woman smiled at what must have seemed to her like a dumb question. "I have several heal stones, but I'm also well versed in non-magical healing, as you can see." She gestured toward a neat row of pouches and vials beside her. "After all, heal stones aren't the only way to cure people."

"What is all of that?" Jack surveyed her supplies.

She replied, "I have a variety of healing herbs. I learned many of my skills from my employer, the famous 'garden mage' in the city of Sellta. He grows the most potent herbs in the country—maybe the world—by creating the optimal soil for his plants using his earth stones." She smiled again. "You'd better get back to your tournament. You don't want them to come looking for you."

Jack nodded and made his way back toward the ring.

It's amazing, he contemplated, *I must get my hands on a heal stone. It also sounds like earth stones can be more versatile than I imagined.* He hoped that he would reach the section in his book that covered these stones soon. He had not studied the book as much since he had discovered his fifth gemstone. He had also been occupied recently with the tournament and trying to become a knight. He decided that he should become more proficient in the tongue of angels and devote more time to study. *Oh well, I need to focus right now,* Jack thought, bringing his attention back to the present.

As Jack entered the ring, he looked up at Gurtven.

Gurtven grinned, apparently believing that his victory was near.

Jack smiled back, and clenching his teeth, thought of all the people who counted on him. *I can't lose,* he thought, *because I can't afford to lose.*

At the governor's command, the two began.

Gurtven did not hesitate but moved in swiftly.

Jack matched him step for step and reflected his aggressive posture. As Gurtven swung his shield at Jack, Jack moved to the side and launched a flurry of strikes with both swords.

Gurtven backed off briefly before moving in again. He lifted his sword above his head and swung it in a circular motion to increase its momentum before bringing it down on Jack.

Jack, instead of absorbing the blow directly, slanted his sword so that his opponent's sword struck his and continued downward. Jack stabbed with his right sword, but Gurtven placed his shield in its path. Undaunted, Jack stepped in and kicked him in the shin.

Gurtven hopped back for a few seconds.

Jack aimed several fast sideways strikes at the man's legs then stabbed at one of his feet.

Gurtven seemed a little disconcerted by Jack's odd form of attack, but he managed to deflect the strikes. Gurtven paused for a moment then pressed in aggressively. After several strikes he lifted his shield into the air and tried to bring it down on Jack's head.

Jack dodged out of the way but realized too late that the shield was just a ploy.

Gurtven had already stepped in so that he was close to Jack, and he kicked Jack in the stomach.

Jack bent over for a moment and barely managed to dodge out of the way as Gurtven closed the distance between them again.

Gurtven pursued Jack around the ring for a few moments as Jack regained his breath. Jack's opponent was growing more and more aggressive as he became more confident, and the ease with which he deflected Jack's swords seemed to increase.

Jack defended himself from another flurry of strikes, keeping his distance from his enemy as well as he could. Then Jack got an idea. He rushed in, swinging both swords toward his adversary's head.

When Gurtven blocked, he exposed his chest. Jack could see the recognition in Gurtven's eyes as he realized what Jack was doing. Gurtven leapt back to avoid a front kick, but Jack did not front kick.

Instead, Jack jumped as high as he could into the air and launched himself sideways, executing a flying sidekick directly into Gurtven's face.

Gurtven stumbled backward but did not fall. Dazed, the big man brought his sword and shield in front of him to protect his torso.

With his right sword Jack struck his opponent's sword, knocking it to Gurtven's left side and trapping his sword and shield together. Dropping his right sword, Jack grabbed his opponent's right wrist before he could regain his footing and pulled him forward. Jack then brought his left elbow down on the back of his adversary's right shoulder, knocking him to the ground.

Jack held his sword to his opponent's throat and looked up expectantly at the judges.

The governor of Juma's face was a large red mass, but the other two judges looked very impressed.

Sir Alter glanced to his side to see why the governor of Juma had not yet spoken. Seeing his anger, Sir Alter stood and announced, "Let it be known before all present that the contestant, Jack, has indisputably won the melee contest, and based on his fine scores in the rest of the tournament, he easily carries the victory for overall champion."

As the crowd began to cheer, Jack raised his swords above his head and roared, "For Celel!"

The crowd grew even louder.

Jack looked around and saw a group of extremely angry-looking people, who he guessed were members of the Setell family. Jack smiled and waved at them. *I guess that will get them all fired up,* he thought.

He stepped out of the ring and joined his two friends.

"Congratulations," they both said in unison.

Ben added, "You beat that big fellow that got both of us."

"We all did very well," said Jack.

Jack looked over and saw another big fellow—the one Charles had fought in the preliminary match—coming toward them.

Charles explained, "This is Kxull." He introduced Jack and Ben to his new, large friend.

Kxull smiled. "You all fought very well. I have no shame from losing to Charles." He then presented Charles with a beautiful one-handed battle axe.

Jack looked at Charles and raised an eyebrow.

Charles explained, "This good fellow and I made a bet before the match. If you two don't mind, and if Kxull is willing, I want to hang out with him for a while. Maybe he can show me how to use this axe."

Kxull smiled and nodded. "Oh, definitely."

Jack and Ben nodded and began meandering through the crowd.

Within a minute two girls popped out of the crowd and approached Ben. They expressed how amazing he was and how much honor he brought them by wearing their colors. Before Ben could say a word, the two girls began viciously arguing.

For a moment Ben watched them fight. Then he shrugged and followed Jack. "You know, sometimes I think all women are crazy," Ben commented.

Jack smiled to himself as he deliberated whether he should explain the girls' behavior to his friend. Finally, he replied, "You do know that the colored cloth is a form of flirting among the lower class? By wearing both of their colors, you've kind of put them at odds."

"How was I supposed to know? I was just minding my own business chatting with some of the other contestants, and they both came up and tied them on me at the same time. I guess I did kind of make them fight, but oh well."

"Well, with any luck you will have heard the last of them after today. Maybe next time you won't wear anyone's colors."

Ben gave him a sly grin. "Oh yeah, this coming from the dude with a ribbon on his own arm."

"It served an important purpose." Jack fingered the purple ribbon. "I humiliated a family that I quite dislike. Still, it was a little spontaneous of me. I think I made some unnecessary enemies, but on the other hand, I would probably have them as enemies anyway for winning the tournament."

As Ben headed off to find something fun to do, Jack sat down on a wooden bench. *I wonder how Ben has so much energy,* he thought.

He saw several contestants surrounded by those he assumed were their relatives or representing families. Jack absently watched some of the merchants pack away their wares. He was impressed with how quickly the grounds were shutting down.

Zannel approached Jack. In contrast to the puffy eyes he had seen earlier in the day, her face looked radiant. "Congratulations on your victory. Thank you for winning. My family needed this."

Jack replied, "It was a win for all of us." He paused for a moment and untied the ribbon from his arm. "I suppose you need this back. Sorry about putting you in an awkward position with your fiancé."

"No, he needed that." She smiled again.

Zannel tied the ribbon back in her hair. "We should head back to the estate. I'm sure my father has some kind of celebration planned." She turned and walked toward a small crowd that had gathered nearby.

Jack knew that Sir Aldric was somewhere in the center of the crowd, no doubt telling a grand tale about how he discovered these three young warriors. Jack was happy for him. For the moment all the other high families discussed the Celshen family. Jack had repaid the Celshen family for investing in him, and that was all he was required to do, but he still caught himself glancing back at where Zannel had stood a moment before. *I just have to get knighted,* he reminded himself, *and get us all home. I don't need anything else from this world.*

Sir Alter walked up to him. "You're quite impressive. I must say, when Sir Aldric asked me if I would take you on a mission, I was very hesitant, but I must apologize, for your skill has already progressed well beyond that of this tournament. Your friends are skilled as well. They have excelled with their firestones, and you are quite proficient with ice. I have a mission on which I will take you if you're willing to prove yourself like you did today, and I may someday recommend you for knighthood."

"That's great," said Jack. "I'll tell my friends, and we'll be ready to leave whenever you want."

"I will come by Sir Aldric's house tomorrow to explain the details. Be ready to leave immediately," Sir Alter instructed.

Jack watched Sir Alter walk away, wondering what was in store for them next. He then rose and went in search of his friends.

Chapter 15

THAT EVENING AFTER THE tournament, the three young men and Vennel traveled back to the Celshen estate with their host family.

The Celshen family's groundskeeper picked them up with the carriage and made the mistake of asking, "So how did the tournament go?"

Sir Aldric laughed and slapped him on the back. "The tournament was a huge success. I have never seen the governor of Juma look so angry and humiliated. He looked like he came out on the wrong end of a huge gamble. You boys may not have noticed it, but Sir Alter was also very impressed. I am telling you that he doesn't impress easily." Sir Aldric spoke even faster has he warmed up to his topic. "Everyone said that after today my family would no longer be treated like peasants with a collection of victorious memories. It seems as though I've got a little bit left in me after all." Sir Aldric laughed again. "You boys remind me of myself back when I was young." He smiled as his eyes acquired a faraway gaze. "I remember the day that I received my family crest."

As Sir Aldric told his story, Zemara leaned over near the two girls and whispered, "I think he could tell that story two or three times a day and never get tired of it."

Zannel smiled and nodded in agreement.

Zemara added, "Vennel, I will have Lilen prepare a room in the manor house for you. I'm sorry that I misjudged your position when you first came to us. I can see now that your standing is higher than it had appeared."

Vennel bit her lower lip and swallowed nervously. "Thank you."

Sir Aldric said loudly, "And that is how I won my first glorious victory in front of the king and earned my family crest."

Charles leaned near Vennel and whispered, "What did you do during the tournament?"

She smiled. "Zannel introduced me to some of her friends just before the tournament. The five of us watched the tournament together."

Charles raised an eyebrow. "What do you think of Zannel?"

Vennel shrugged her shoulders and leaned close to him so as not to be overheard. "She's nice to me, but she's kind of hard to read. Sometimes she's very outspoken and bold, but other times she's quiet and reserved."

When the group arrived at the Celshen estate, Sir Aldric announced, "Tonight is a night of celebration."

Jack smiled as Garthong swooped down and landed on his shoulder. His little gother had been flying high in the sky during the entire tournament, and now he appeared tired.

Jack looked at his little friend. "Yeah, I'm tired too. It's been a long day." Jack added silently, *We'll all leave on another mission tomorrow. Not much time for rest, I suppose.*

******

In the morning Sir Alter was already downstairs waiting when Jack and his friends descended the stairs.

After they all sat down around the dining room table, the knight began in a serious tone, "This is a particularly secret mission, so I won't be able to tell you where we are going or what we're doing until we get there. Regrettably, I can also only take one of you, and I have decided to take you, Jack."

Jack held up his hand. "With all due respect, we're all trying to be recommended for knighthood, and we work well together."

"I know," replied the knight, "but my policy is to only take one knight-in-training on missions because there are already too few knights to help everyone in need. Spreading everyone out is better because more missions can be completed. In addition, how can I adequately judge whether you deserve to be a Knight of Celel when you always travel and fight in a group? It is essential that knights be capable of fighting alone and carrying out missions alone. I promise that I will take them both on missions when we return. We may be gone for a week or two, so pack supplies and whatever you'll need."

"I still don't like this," Jack said.

"Jack, you should go." Ben said quickly. "We'll be fine here, and we'll get our missions when you come back."

Jack looked at Charles, who nodded.

"All right, I'll pack my stuff." Jack rose to his feet.

Sir Alter also stood. "Fine. I will return with the horses." The knight spun on his heel and strode out the door.

Jack and his friends looked at each other.

Ben finally voiced their thoughts. "None of us know how to ride horses. Do you think that's going to be a problem?"

"Well," Jack replied, "I suppose there's no time like the present to learn."

"Well," said Ben, "You'd better start packing. Charles and I are going to go to town."

Charles looked up at Ben. "We are?"

"Yes, we are," said Ben. "Come on, we have things of our own to do."

The two headed for the door and were gone.

Jack looked at Garthong on his shoulder. "I wonder why Ben is in such a hurry and what he has planned. I suppose I'll find out when I get back."

Jack finished packing. He wanted to take the book that he had received from Hal but decided to leave it so Ben and Charles could study. *They probably won't have much else to do,* he reasoned, *so it will be a good opportunity for them.* Jack hurriedly gathered some food and clothing and strapped on his weapons.

Sir Alter returned and called to Jack from outside the house.

Jack picked up his supplies and rushed out the door.

He stowed his belongings in the saddlebags and tried to mount the horse, but the horse shied away, causing Jack to stumble. He tried again, but the sword on his right hip nearest the saddle became entangled with his leg, and he faltered again.

Sir Alter watched silently as Jack attempted to mount the horse several more times. Finally, the knight grabbed the reins to steady the horse while Jack mounted. Then he tossed the reins back to Jack.

Once Jack had settled into the saddle, Sir Alter asked, "Have you ever ridden a horse before?"

"No," Jack admitted, "this is my first time."

The two rode westward toward the country of Burnadad.

Jack could hear Sir Alter muttering to himself, "A knight who can't ride a horse? I've never heard of such a thing!"

Riding with Sir Alter was an extremely boring experience. The knight hardly ever spoke, and when he did, his topic was almost always mission related. Jack missed his friends' conversations and wished that they were nearby. *Maybe I should've put up a stronger fight about taking them along,* he thought. Ben's and Charles's absence made Jack a little uneasy. Ben was not one to back down when events grew dangerous, and Charles's steady personality provided Jack with a sense of stability. Jack thought, *I'm going to have to be more careful without them here to back me up.* He resolved to complete this mission quickly and return soon.

The only company Jack had was Garthong, but even he did not seem to enjoy the silence, and he spent most of the day flying above them.

They stopped at an inn that night, and Jack was dismayed to find that Sir Alter was just as silent during meals as he was when riding.

After they settled into their room, Sir Alter casually commented, "I have never seen anyone with a pet gother; in fact, I didn't know it was possible to tame one."

"He hatched while I was vanquishing a nest of them," Jack explained, "and he bonded to me, so I'm kind of stuck with him."

The knight smiled slightly and said no more.

******

In the morning Sir Alter woke Jack early. "Let's get going."

Jack felt slightly annoyed that he was not the first one awake like normal. He had not really felt homesick in a while, but as they traveled in silence, thoughts of home seemed to flood his mind.

Garthong circled in the sky, but he was hard to see because the sun had not quite risen yet.

Sir Alter commented, "Your little companion is fairly self-sufficient in his hunting."

Jack looked up. "Yes, he's actually quite bold and capable."

"Well, perhaps he could catch us a rabbit or something small that we could eat."

Garthong dropped his altitude near Jack and begin circling right above them.

Jack adjusted his position in his saddle. The second day of riding was much less fun than the first day. "Sure, he can actually catch things bigger than that. I've seen him hunt a lot, and as he's gotten bigger, he's become bolder." Jack looked up at his gother. "Garthong, find us something good to eat."

As Garthong circled higher in search of prey, Jack replayed his own words in his head and wondered what the gother might consider 'good to eat.'

Garthong circled for a while then dived straight for a tree.

Sir Alter noticed the movement and squinted to see what kind of animal was in the tree.

Whatever it was, the gother struck it at full force, knocking it off the branch. The moment the creature hit the ground, Garthong landed on top of it and started pulling it up into the air.

The creature's back legs clung to the earth while its front legs flailed harmlessly in the air.

Jack could now see that the creature was a large raccoon.

The gother kept all four of his feet dug into his prey's back while he slashed with his teeth at the front and sides of its neck.

A moment later the creature stopped struggling and went limp.

Garthong tried to fly off with his kill, but the raccoon was too heavy for him. As a result he was forced to drag his prize toward Jack and Sir Alter.

The knight looked a bit surprised by the spectacle he had just witnessed. "How big do these creatures get?"

Jack smiled. "About as big as a person."

Sir Alter commented, "Well, that's reassuring."

Jack praised Garthong on his victory and attached Garthong's prize to his own saddlebags.

******

Jack and Sir Alter traveled for three more days uneventfully. On the fifth day they came upon a fork in the road.

"We'll take this one." Sir Alter pointed to the left fork. "The other way weaves through a gorge, and we are more likely to meet an ambush there."

A pine forest stood on both sides of the trail. Jack noted that pine and cedar forests seemed more common in the northern areas of this world.

"There is a spring farther down the trail." Sir Alter glanced up at the sky. "We'll stop there for the night."

Within a few hours they reached the spring, which filled a pool and overflowed into a small creek.

They both dismounted.

The knight knelt and drank deeply from the pool.

The sight of the water made Jack thirsty, but his legs ached so miserably that he just sat on the ground. *It must be from riding that stupid horse for five days straight,* he thought.

Sir Alter brought Jack some water and smiled slightly as he handed it to Jack.

Great, thought Jack as he took a drink. *The guy that I'm supposed impress and need to recommend me for knighthood knows that I can't ride a horse, and I'm probably too sore to fight with any kind of decent proficiency. I'll have to inform Ben and Charles that they need to start riding horses before they get a mission.*

Jack suddenly felt extremely exhausted and sleepy, which seemed odd since the sun was only just beginning to set. *I must be more tired than I thought from riding,* he reasoned.

Garthong came over to drink from Jack's flask but froze as he lowered his nose toward it to take a sip. He suddenly ran around frantically then flew into the sky.

That's weird, Jack observed. *He probably hasn't had anything to drink today. Of course, it's pretty normal for him to get hyper.*

Jack looked over at Sir Alter, expecting to see him unpacking his saddlebags, but the knight lay sprawled out on the ground. Jack could not seem to think clearly or reach a conclusion about what had happened to the knight.

He tried to stand and move toward Sir Alter, but the entire world seemed to close in around him. Then everything went black.

******

Jack woke up, but he could not see anything. His legs were still sore, and his head throbbed. He could not seem to remember what had happened or where he was. He tried to move but could not. He thought, *What on earth?*

Then he realized that chains tethered his wrists and ankles to the wall. He stood to his feet and leaned back against the wall, allowing the chains to go slack. His bonds held his wrists at waist height such that he could sit down completely with his arms elevated. The chain arrangement provided just enough slack to allow prisoners to feed themselves if they backed all the way against the wall and crouched with their heads at waist height.

Jack tried to think. *Let's see ... I was traveling with Sir Alter. We were going on a mission, and we stopped at a spring.* But that was all he could remember.

He stood in silence for what seemed like an eternity before he heard a groan near him.

"Is someone there?" Jack whispered.

"Oh, you're awake," said a voice off to his right.

"Yes. What's happening?"

"It seems to me that you've gotten yourselves captured," replied the voice.

"We? Is Sir Alter here also? I can't see. It's so dark."

"Yes, he's to my right. I am between the two of you."

"Who are you?" Jack asked.

"I am Warlord, or I should say, *was* Warlord Juima. The Caishan slave cartel captured me about two weeks ago. In an attempt to boost my relations with Celel, I placed restrictions on slavery within my borders, and the Caishan apparently didn't approve. I suppose I will live out the rest of my days in slavery—if they don't kill me outright."

Jack wondered if their mission had been to rescue this man, an ally of Celel. That would make sense. *How are we going to get out of here?* Jack asked himself. He had been in some tight scrapes since coming to this world, but he had always had his two friends with him. Jack had to admit that this was probably the worst situation yet.

"Where is your country?" asked Jack.

"We are probably still in it," replied Warlord Juima. "It's Burnadad, west of Celel. They didn't transport me very far when they captured me, so this hidden base is apparently somewhere within my land or on the border of it."

Jack's eyes were adjusting to the darkness, but he could still see very little. "What do you think they plan to do with us?"

"I already told you what will probably happen to me. You two will probably be executed in a few hours or tomorrow. I expect that the Caishan who captured you wants to show you two to his superiors alive to bolster his reputation."

Well, that was a mistake, thought Jack. As a blood mage, he knew that they could not completely disarm him. *I just have to wait until someone with the key gets close enough to me that I can reach it after I attack them.*

A wooden door in the stone wall opened, and several men entered with torches.

"Greetings, prisoners," said a fat, bald man. "I'm here to torture you for information."

One of the bald man's minions walked over to Sir Alter. "This one's still sleeping, boss."

The bald man approached Sir Alter and threw some water into his face.

Sir Alter, coughing and sputtering, looked around, obviously disoriented.

"Well, Sir Knight," said the bald man, "this was not much of a rescue." The man laughed at his own joke. "I want you to describe for me the floor plan of the king's palace in Celel. It seems the king is very particular about whom he allows in the top few stories of the palace, and you are one of the few people who have been there. Apparently, someone down south is willing to pay a great deal of money for any information regarding the palace's upper floors. We knew that our political maneuvering here would attract Celel's attention. We figured the king would dispatch you on this mission to rescue the warlord, so we carefully planned all along to capture you when you arrived."

Sir Alter looked at him with one eye and grimaced. He slowly opened his other eye. "How did you capture us?"

The bald man laughed again. "It was easy. We knew what route you would take and how far away you were, so we drugged the spring. We figured you would stop there. The two of you went to sleep, and we caught you without even a fight. I have to say, though, you're really scraping the bottom of the barrel with the kid you brought. I thought all Celel knights-in-training were required to carry at least one gemstone. My master was quite pleased to receive your gemstones; seven is quite a few, I must say. You used to be a powerful mage, but now you're nothing."

Jack watched keenly, trying to discern which of the bald man's lackeys had the key to their chains. Then he saw the ring of keys poking out from under the blond-haired assistant's cloak on a short leather lanyard. The other lackey was taller and had brown hair.

Jack asked, "Who are you guys?"

The bald man turned to him. "Normally, I wouldn't bother telling a pipsqueak like you anything, but if I'm going to boast, then sadly, I must only boast to those who are about to die. I am the torturer for Keljerk the Cruel. He's in charge of the Caishan assassin squad. You should feel honored that such a powerful group captured you." The bald man continued rambling for a while about how wonderful his job was and how few people could do it as well as he could.

Jack could not seem to formulate a plan. *Even if I killed these guys and got the keys, none of us have any idea where we are or how to get out of here,* he considered. *If we're in some sort of dungeon like it appears, then we would have to get to the surface and probably escape from some sort of fort or city.*

The bald man debated with himself about which type of torture would be most appropriate for the prisoners. "I'm kind of leaning toward flogging them," he mused, "but every time I think about getting into it, I want to burn them."

Jack further contemplated, *If that fool tries to poke me with some burning piece of metal, I don't think I'll be able to resist killing him.*

The torturer selected a cane from one of his assistants. "Oh, I like this one. You see, this stick will hurt a great deal, but it won't leave any permanent marks, so when the boss's right hand comes down, it won't look like I tortured you."

"Did the boss not order you to torture us?" asked Jack.

"No, she would much prefer to do it herself. That's what I hate about her; she's always getting in my way when I'm doing my job."

"She?" inquired Sir Alter. "I thought your boss was Keljerk the Cruel."

"Yes, but the assassins outrank us torturers … and everyone else in the assassin squad." The bald man rolled his eyes. "Selfren likes to torture people, so she usually comes down, kicks me out, and does the torturing herself. She's Keljerk's right hand—and a very annoying one too I might add. So I have to get some in before she gets here."

The bald man began counting as he caned Sir Alter repeatedly.

Sir Alter gritted his teeth but did not cry out.

The process was interrupted when the door opened again, and in walked a tall, slender woman with pale skin and straight, black hair. She wore a black cloak that had a green tint to it. Jack guessed the cloak was some sort of camouflage.

"How dare you start the torturing without me, you little worm!" she roared.

The bald man ducked his head as though he thought she was about to strike him. "Please forgive me, Selfren. I was only preparing them for you."

"How kind of you," she said, her words dripping with sarcasm. "But if you 'prepare' them anymore, I will torture you alongside them. Get out, you dog."

The bald man all but crawled to the door and exited.

His lackeys began to follow him, but the woman stopped them by raising her hand.

"You two are not to leave this room under any circumstances," she commanded. "You are supposed to guard these men. Stand against that wall."

The two men stood obediently as Selfren pulled out a knife from the bald man's supplies and came toward Jack. "I think I'll start with the young one," she said. "The young ones usually squeal more." She moved the knife slowly in front of Jack's face, rubbing it on his skin. "Aren't you afraid, boy?"

Jack inadvertently allowed the corners of his mouth to twitch slightly as he imagined frying the woman with a bolt of lightning.

Selfren apparently noticed the hint of a smile because she jerked the knife down and created a small cut on Jack's chest through his cloak. Jack could feel several drops of blood rolling down his chest.

"Smile like that again, and I may carve you up so quickly that I don't enjoy myself," she whispered savagely.

The door opened again, and a man entered and announced, "Selfren, your presence is requested in the barracks upstairs."

She frowned. "Can't you see I'm busy?"

"Yes, ma'am," the man stammered, "but Keljerk is the one requesting you. Apparently, the governor is displeased about something."

"We're not done yet." Selfren bore into Jack with her eyes for a moment before leaving the room.

"The governor," said Jack aloud. "That means we're in a city."

The two guards glanced at each other, and the brown-haired one said, "Quiet."

Warlord Juima looked at Jack in the torchlight. "We must be in the city of Jukul, but that is within my kingdom."

"It would seem the governor has betrayed you," said Sir Alter. "Not surprising really. He's your brother, isn't he? So if you are killed, he would become warlord."

"Quiet," repeated the brown-haired guard more loudly.

Warlord Juima let his head drop so that his chin rested against his chest and did not reply.

"Does that mean that you have been in this dungeon before?" asked Jack.

"Yes," replied Warlord Juima quietly. "I was born in this city."

"So if we got out of the cell, you could guide us to the surface," Jack pressed.

"How were you planning on getting out of the cell?" Sir Alter's chains clanked as he turned to look at Jack.

"I said quiet," the brown-haired guard yelled, turning toward the corner to select one of the torturing canes.

323

"Those two"—Jack nodded his head in the guards' direction—"are about to die."

The two guards grabbed their sword hilts.

The blond-haired guard demanded, "What are you talking about?"

Jack said, "Oh sorry, sometimes I can look into people's eyes and see the day that they're going to die, and you two are going to die today."

"That's crazy," said the brown-haired guard. "How are we going to die?"

Jack peered at them. "I can't really see from this distance. But if you came over here, I might be able to predict better."

"Oh, please." The blond guard swatted his hand incredulously in Jack's direction. "There's no possible way you could know such a thing."

Jack inconspicuously opened his right hand. "Look! It is becoming clearer. Even you should be able to see it now."

The two guards looked in the middle of the room.

Sure enough, two shadowy figures resembling themselves stood by a door. Then the door in the image opened, and a woman in a black cloak entered and stabbed them both in the back.

As the images faded, the two guards drew their weapons.

The brown-haired man picked up one of the canes and wedged it against the door.

The blond guard's face paled, and his breathing became more rapid. "What on earth was that?"

"It looked just like us dying, and it looked like Selfren killing us," replied his counterpart.

Jack glanced to the side and saw Sir Alter staring at him with a most bizarre expression on his face. He obviously could not believe what he had just seen either. The knight raised an eyebrow at Jack but did not make a sound.

Jack had never been so glad to have an illusion stone.

"Quickly, you two," called Jack in an urgent tone, "come over near me. Let me look into your eyes, and I will tell you the exact time this will take place."

The blond guard rushed over to Jack.

Jack knew that he still could not quite reach the keys. Jack gazed deeply into the man's eyes for a long moment then shook his head. "Because this affects both of you, I can't see it unless you're both here."

"This is some sort of trick," muttered the brown-haired guard, but he took a step closer to Jack anyway. "How do I know you're telling the truth about us dying today?" He stood a couple feet behind his friend as his friend inched closer to Jack.

Jack stared intently at the men's faces and said in a hypnotic voice, "Look into my eyes, and know the truth."

Jack suddenly grasped the key ring firmly with his right hand and opened his left hand.

The surprised guard in front grabbed the other end of the lanyard.

The guard in back grabbed his friend to pull him away.

Both guards looked up, met Jack's gaze, and tried to scream as the color in his eyes turned to a deep, dark purple. The screams, however, never escaped their throats because a loud crack and bright flash filled the room. The guards slumped to the floor.

Dragging the dead blond guard closer by the lanyard on the key ring, Jack created enough slack to unlock the chains holding him to the wall. He then freed the other two prisoners.

Sir Alter rubbed his wrists where his shackles had been. "What just happened? How did you do that?"

Jack replied, "I'm a blood mage. That's why they didn't find any stones on me when they captured us."

Sir Alter lifted both eyebrows. "The images of them dying at the woman's hand .... That was .... You used an illusion stone. You must have a lightning stone as well. How on earth did you survive putting two stones in your body? And, wait, you used ice at the tournament. So that makes three stones."

"I actually have five in my bloodstream," said Jack, "one being a translation stone. I'm not really sure how I survived. Someone did it to me a few months ago, but I never got to see who did it. But enough about me." Jack removed the cane wedged against the door. "Let's get out of here. First, we need to get up to the barracks, find out what they did with your gemstones, and get them back. Then, we need to get out of this city. The warlord should be able to show us the way around the city."

"Let's take their swords with us." Sir Alter picked up the blond guard's weapon. "We should be able to find more in the barracks up top."

Jack took the other guard's sword.

"Fine, I'll lead the way," said Warlord Juima.

The three escapees rushed out into the hall and ran down a narrow corridor. Unlike the door to their own cell, the doors on the right and left possessed bars, allowing them to see inside the cells. There did not seem to be any other prisoners in the dungeon.

They turned a sharp corner and entered a small room with a table and a few chairs. Two Caishan guards looked up in surprise as they entered, but Sir Alter and Jack ran them through before they could draw their swords.

Jack and Warlord Juima each took one of their swords.

Warlord Juima pointed at a small wooden door on the other side of the room. "I think that will lead up to the barracks."

Sir Alter opened the door and started running up the steps with Jack close on his heels.

When Sir Alter opened the door at the top of the stairway, the bright daylight streaming through the barracks' windows momentarily blinded them.

Sir Alter quickly selected a shield from the barracks wall. "We need to find Keljerk. I expect him to have my gemstones."

Warlord Juima also grabbed a shield. "Let's get going. It's only a matter of time before someone checks on us."

"We need to be careful." Jack held up a hand. "If we rush out into the city, the city guards and the Caishan can spot us."

"You forget, this is my town," said Warlord Juima. "The soldiers will obey my commands. I am warlord here." With that he boldly stepped out of the barracks.

Jack and Sir Alter rushed after him, but the moment they left the barracks, Jack knew it was a mistake.

Standing in front of them, in a small cluster looking very surprised, were an imposing man Jack presumed to be Keljerk, Selfren, and another man adorned in very expensive-looking clothing.

Approximately two dozen soldiers, some city guards and some slavers, stood nearby.

The soldiers immediately drew their weapons and stepped in front of their commanders.

"Just great," said Jack. He glanced at Sir Alter with a sideways smile and quipped, "At least we found the guy who's carrying your gemstones."

For just a moment Jack thought the hard lines on the knight's face softened a little, and a slight smile appeared for an instant.

Well, thought Jack, *I guess this is how it ends. There's no way the three of us can take down twenty-five armed men ... but we sure are going to try.*

Selfren pushed her way through the guards to the front and asked casually, "Keljerk, would you like for me to kill one in particular first, or may I start with the kid?"

Keljerk crossed his arms calmly. "Kill them in whatever order you like."

Selfren stepped forward and drew two thin swords from her cloak. The blades had a faint greenish sheen like her clothing. She looked at Jack through narrowed eyes. "You know, it can be very difficult to inflict a fatal wound with one blow from a sword when facing a skilled opponent, but my swords are special. Like most assassins' swords, they're dipped in a special toxin that poisons my target even if I only inflict a scratch."

Jack met the woman's gaze and glared. Something about this woman really made him angry. Maybe it was the apparent enjoyment that she derived from the suffering of others.

Selfren laughed and pointed her right sword's tip at Jack. "Oh my, if looks could kill, my boy, then you might have a chance. Sadly for you, though, it's over. Nothing can stand against my hatred."

As she ran toward him, Jack braced himself. *I can't let her touch me with either of those blades,* he thought.

While Selfren was still in midstride, something struck her on the back of the neck from behind. She pitched forward onto the ground, screaming in pain and flailing wildly, but it was to no avail.

Jack looked at the bloody, writhing mass and exclaimed, "Garthong!"

The soldiers all stood still for a moment, staring blankly at the scene, as the small lizard ripped into Selfren's neck with his sharp teeth.

Garthong finally released her neck and fluttered onto Jack's shoulder. A drop of blood fell from the gother's jaws onto Jack's left arm as Garthong's victim still squirmed and bled in the dirt at Jack's feet, an artery in her neck gushing blood.

Wow, thought Jack, *where did he come from anyway? Has he just been flying around all this time?* Jack gripped his weapons harder as the soldiers started to slowly move to surround the three of them. Jack thought, *Maybe I should've looked deeper. Perhaps there was an easier way to see the king than becoming a knight. If I had found another way, maybe I could have gotten us all home. Now Ben and Charles will have to find their own way back.*

Chapter 16

CHARLES STUMBLED A LITTLE as Ben almost pulled him out of the house.

"What are we doing, Ben?" Charles protested. "Maybe we should go back and argue with Jack about him going on this mission alone after all. Why are you so determined to get out of the house right now? Jack is supposed to leave soon; we should at least show him some support before he goes."

Ben shook his head. "It would be worthless to argue with Jack. It's not Jack's choice whether we come; it's up to Sir Alter. This is just a hunch, but I don't think Sir Alter changes his mind very often. But, Charles, you're missing the point. Jack hasn't told us that he doesn't want us to come, so we're going to do the most natural thing humanly possible, which is to pretend that we don't care and then go anyway."

"What?" Charles exclaimed. "You mean we're going to sneak around after Jack on his mission without telling him? Besides, Jack did say that he was sorry we couldn't come, so that means we're not invited." Charles hardly noticed the gentle breeze and tranquil, blue sky as he increased his pace to fall in step with his friend.

"Well, of course Jack would be sorry that we couldn't come. That's why we're going anyway. It'll be a wonderful surprise for them both."

"Why are we heading toward town?" asked Charles.

"Because Sir Alter said he was bringing horses. That means we have to rent or buy horses of our own. Unless, of course, you think that the two of us can keep up with their horses by walking, which to me just sounds very unpleasant."

"What about our supplies?"

Ben glanced over his shoulder as if to ensure himself that no one followed them. "No problem. I already told Zemara that we're going out for a week or two to explore the wilderness, and she's having Lilen pack us some food and water."

"You mean you lied to the family that is sponsoring us to be knighted? Isn't there something terribly wrong with that?" asked Charles.

"I didn't lie." Ben dismissed his friend's argument with an exaggerated swat of his hand. "We *are* going out to explore the wilderness. We've presumably never been where Jack is going, which means that we're exploring, and unless he spends the entire time in a city, we'll be exploring wilderness."

"Sometimes it's frightening to me how your brain works, Ben. What about Vennel? Won't she be worried about us if we just disappear?"

"Of course not," replied Ben. "I told her the same thing that I told Zemara. I also told her that you were just too embarrassed to invite her along, so she would have to stay."

"You told her what!"

Ben took off running toward town and upon arrival made a beeline for the stables.

I can't believe he would tell her that, Charles thought, following him. *Wait, what if he didn't actually tell her that?* The comment could have just been a ploy to make Charles chase him so they could get to town faster. Charles shook his head. *This is so annoying. If he did tell her that, what will I say to her when we get back from the mission?*

Charles caught up to Ben, who was haggling for horses with the stable master. Ben bought a tall, flashy, dapple gray horse for himself and a stout bay for Charles. He also purchased all the necessary tack for the horses, including two pairs of saddlebags.

The stable master saddled and bridled the horses for them.

As they led their horses toward the Celshen estate, Ben turned off the road to the left and started walking through a field.

"Where are you going?" asked Charles.

"Well, we can't walk straight back up to the house. If Jack sees us with these horses, it's game over. We'll have to sneak around back, pick up our supplies, and leave just after they do."

Charles thought for a moment and said, "Ben, we don't know how to ride these horses. When did you plan to acquire that skill?"

Ben snapped his fingers. "Good idea. Let's practice now." He turned, placed his foot in the stirrup, and struggled onto his horse.

The horse took off at a brisk trot, bouncing Ben up and down on its back.

Ben yelled over his shoulder, "Yeah, this is awesome," as the horse carried him across the field.

Great, thought Charles. *Now I have to try. I hope Ben bought horses that are already broke. Surely the stable master wouldn't sell riding horses that weren't broke.* Charles stepped toward the horse's side, placed his foot in the stirrup, slowly lifted himself up, and settled into the saddle.

The horse just stood there; nothing exciting or unusual happened.

Oh good, Charles thought, letting out his held breath, *at least, they've been broken.*

Charles tried bumping the horse with his heels and relaxing his grip on the reigns. They always did it that way in the movies.

The horse stood there for a few more seconds. Then it turned and started walking lazily back toward the stable in town.

Over the next ten or fifteen minutes, Charles finally convinced his horse to turn around and plod slowly toward the Celshen estate. *This is ridiculous,* he thought. *If I had walked, I could have already been there by now.*

When he finally arrived behind the Celshen family's house, he found Ben, covered in mud, standing next to his horse.

"What happened?" Charles asked.

"Well, we disagreed about which direction to go a couple of times." Ben rubbed his muddy left shoulder. "And it seemed like every time we did, I went one way and he went the other. I think I finally understand him now, so we shouldn't have too much more of that. I'm kind of glad that I didn't go for the cheaper horses that weren't broke yet; if we had been short on cash, I probably would have. Let's get our supplies and get going after Jack. He just left about fifteen minutes ago."

Charles packed his saddlebags and thought, *Why are we even doing this? Jack can take care of himself. On the other hand, having some backup couldn't hurt.*

The two friends struggled onto their horses again and followed after Jack.

"See, isn't this awesome?" said Ben. "We're off on another adventure instead of sitting around at the Celshen estate."

Charles threw him a sideways look. "I think I could've enjoyed sitting around at the estate."

That night they had to make camp outside the village in which Jack and Sir Alter stayed.

Charles rubbed one of his arms to warm it. "This is really cold. Following people without being seen is really unpleasant in this kind of weather."

"Don't worry about it." Ben pulled his cloak tighter around himself. "We'll be up first thing in the morning and hot on their trail again."

They tied their horses to a nearby tree with some tall grass around it, bundled up as well as they could, and went to sleep.

*****

In the morning Charles awoke with the sun shining on his face. He cracked an eye open and surveyed his surroundings. The wind was chilly, but the sun felt warm, and everything looked bright and alive.

Charles woke up Ben, and they ate a quick breakfast. When they entered the village, however, they found that Jack and Sir Alter had already left hours previously.

"I can't believe those two," Ben exclaimed. "What kind of weird people would get up at the break of dawn and start traveling? They didn't get to enjoy any of their morning."

Charles and Ben had to work hard tracking the other two riders. They finally caught up that night, but in the morning Jack and Sir Alter were already gone again when Charles and Ben woke up.

This pattern continued for several more days.

By the fifth day the two followers were better at waking up early, and their tracking skills had improved substantially. When they came to a fork in the trail, they were able to quickly identify which direction Jack and Sir Alter had taken.

They rode for a while, chatting about what they thought Jack's mission would be.

Suddenly, Garthong landed on Charles's shoulder.

The impact felt light, but the quick movement startled Charles, and he reined in his horse. Charles looked with annoyance at the little critter, who had attached himself to Charles's shoulder, and said, "Garthong, you are going to ruin the whole thing. Quickly, go back to Jack."

Garthong looked up in the sky and screeched loudly.

"What is he doing?" asked Ben.

"He looks kind of agitated," Charles observed.

Ben and Charles turned simultaneously and looked at each other. Then they kicked their horses into a canter.

Charles thought, *If Garthong abandoned Jack, there must be a good reason. Something must've happened to Jack.*

Before long they reached a clear area on the side of the trail with a spring. The ground all around looked heavily trampled as though many people and horses had walked on it recently.

"I don't see any blood," Ben observed, "so there must not have been a fight."

"Regardless," replied Charles, "something is obviously wrong. Jack talks to Garthong, and he seems to obey Jack. I think we should see if he can find Jack."

"Good idea."

Charles looked at the lizard and said slowly, "Find Jack. Show us where he is."

Garthong leapt into the air and flew westward.

The two boys followed as fast as they could on their horses deep into the night. The moon was high in the sky when a city finally emerged in front of them.

"It's going to take some time to search a city." Charles sighed. "I think we should sleep for the rest of the night."

Ben grimaced in frustration but nodded. "I agree. If they haven't killed Jack yet, there's no reason to assume that they will in the next few hours. Hopefully, they want him alive for something."

******

The two slept as well as they could and waited for morning. They woke up early and ate a quick breakfast.

"We're going to have to go into the city and appear like normal travelers." Charles stretched his sore legs as he mentally prepared himself for another period of time in the saddle.

They mounted and headed for the city.

In the daylight Charles could see the city clearly. Its layout looked as though someone had built a small village on the top of the hill, and the village had grown bigger and bigger until the houses spilled off the top of the hill and down the sides. Walls completely encircled the city at the hill's base.

"Man, it must be such a pain to haul supplies to the top of that hill," said Ben.

Charles smiled and thought, *Leave it to Ben to joke around at a time when I'm so tense and stressed.* But Charles could tell by the expression on Ben's face that he also felt nervous.

Charles pointed toward the hill's apex. "Let's start up there and work our way down as we search."

As they passed through the gates, they could tell that something significant was occurring. Many guards wandered the streets, and very few townspeople traveled about the city.

"Let's leave our horses here near the gates," said Charles. "If we have to fight, we don't want to do it on horseback."

"Yeah, that seems like a good idea," replied Ben. "If our horses were injured, they would be worthless for escaping. Besides, if the gate is shut, it won't do us any good to be on our horses. We would have to dismount to take the gatehouse anyway."

After tying their horses to a hitching post, the two started walking up the hill. As they neared the top, they noticed many men bearing the all too familiar Caishan seal on their clothing and armor.

"This doesn't look good," observed Ben. "I would guess that the slavers in the city have something to do with Jack's disappearance."

Charles nodded and set his jaw. "If they're holding Jack somewhere, we probably won't be able to find him just by walking the streets."

"Well, we're pretty sure he's here." Ben glanced up at the sky even though they had not seen Garthong for a while. "With Garthong up there if he shows up anywhere outside of a building, we should know about it quickly. They probably don't know that Jack is a blood mage because we didn't see any evidence of a fight when the two of them were captured."

Charles rubbed his chin. "So you think Jack will be able to conjure up his own escape, and we just need to be ready to back him up when he does?"

"That's what I'm thinking," replied Ben. "Let's head back to the gatehouse and secure it. Then we'll come back up the hill. All of the important buildings seem to be at the top of the hill, so Jack is probably in one of those buildings, but we're going to need a clear escape route for him to leave the city when he gets out."

At the hill's base, Ben and Charles loitered for a few minutes, trying to look inconspicuous while waiting for an opportunity to climb the gatehouse steps without attracting attention.

The guards on the street did not seem particularly interested in the two strangers or their business. Charles decided that something abnormal must have already happened because the guards all talked amongst themselves, some excitedly and some angrily.

The boys' opportunity finally came, and they started ascending the gatehouse steps.

Charles glanced at Ben. "Let's try not to kill the guys inside because we're not sure yet if the city guards are involved."

Ben nodded as they quietly drew their weapons and sneaked into the dark gatehouse.

Inside, two guards sat at a wooden table playing a card game with their backs to the boys.

Two more guards walked out the opposite door onto the wall as the boys crept inside.

Ben and Charles leapt toward the guards at the table. Before the guards could react, Ben and Charles smacked them over their heads with the flat sides of their weapons.

At the sound the other two guards rushed back in from the wall with their weapons drawn.

Charles turned his intimidating frame to face the men. "We're here to get our friends back. If you don't want to die, I suggest you give up."

The two guards stood still and exchanged looks as if trying to decide what to do.

Finally, one of them asked, "Why are you trying to take this gatehouse?"

Charles raised his eyebrows. Neither of the guards seemed poised to attack, so he answered, "Caishan slavers kidnapped two of our friends and brought them to this town. We need the gatehouse so we can escape once we find and rescue them."

Silence fell for a moment.

Then one of the guards asked, "Who are you?"

Before Charles could answer, Ben boldly stated, "We are Knights of Celel."

Charles thought, *I hope that lie doesn't come back to haunt us sometime in the future.*

The guards both sheathed their swords, and one of them said, "Strong rumors say that these Caishan slavers have kidnapped our warlord as well. A few days ago the slavers showed up and just moved into the city in force. The governor seems to be supporting them even though Warlord Juima has clearly demonstrated that he's against the slave organizations. If your mission is to rescue our warlord, then we will hold the gate for you."

Charles looked at Ben and shrugged. "That sounds good to me."

"What if they're lying?" replied Ben.

"We can't kill them," insisted Charles. "They claim to be on our side, so if we killed them, and we were wrong, we would have murdered them. Trusting them seems like the best move, and their reason makes sense."

"What about the two we just knocked out?" asked Ben.

Charles glanced down at the first two guards' crumpled forms. "Well, since we didn't kill them, it won't matter whose side they're on, and these two can keep an eye on them."

The second two guards nodded.

"Be careful," one of the guards cautioned. "Many guards in the city would support a new warlord if he promises wealth, but others may help you if they discover your purpose."

Charles asked, "If the warlord is in this city, where do you think they would keep him?"

"There is a prison under the barracks at the top of the hill," one of the guards answered.

Charles looked at Ben. "Let's head back up the hill. If they have this Warlord Juima guy, they hopefully have him imprisoned near Jack."

The two young men began walking back up the hill. To avoid attracting unwanted attention, they circled the barracks rather than approaching it directly or remaining in one place too long. As they circled the hill's summit a second time, they noticed a crowd gathering in front of the barracks.

"That man looks like a governor," said Charles in a hushed tone, "and that other guy must be the head of the Caishan."

Ben nodded. "It looks like they're conducting some sort of deal. I suspect they don't fully trust each other since they both have soldiers with them. The governor must be making a move to gain power by allying himself with the Caishan."

"That would line up with what the gatehouse guards told us about the warlord being kidnapped." Charles pressed himself against the side of a building for better concealment. "Let's watch and see what happens."

Garthong reappeared and landed on Charles's shoulder to rest.

A few more minutes passed. Suddenly, the barracks' door burst open, and three men ran outside.

"Hey, that's Jack," Ben whispered.

"Yes, and Sir Alter."

Ben gripped his sword hilt. "Can you hear what they're saying?"

"No, but they're talking either to or about Jack."

"Look," Ben said, "that creepy lady is stepping toward Jack. Let's attack."

"Not yet." Charles grabbed Ben's arm. "Jack can take care of himself against one opponent. Let's stay hidden until we're ready to hit the entire group. We'll use our fireballs to make a clear path through the soldiers. We have to assume that Jack has already used all his magic to escape and that Sir Alter doesn't have any gemstones because the Caishan would've taken them."

The woman suddenly started running toward Jack.

Garthong immediately flew off Charles's shoulder and dived toward the woman.

Although accustomed to violence, Charles just stared at the little lizard's savage attack.

"Wow," Ben observed, "that little guy is really going at her. All of a sudden I don't think Jack is so crazy for keeping that thing around."

As the enemy soldiers surrounded the three escapees, Charles and Ben both raised their hands. Fire leapt from their palms and struck the enemy formation from behind, sending burning soldiers flying in all directions.

With a roar Charles charged toward the slavers' backs, wielding his massive battle axe. The first three did not even have time to turn around, and the others tried to dodge away from his vicious attack.

Jack did not take advantage of the opportunity to run. Instead, he assaulted the group of slavers from the other side, cutting down the first one in a single stroke. He kicked another in the abdomen and jumped on top of him when the man bent over. He then shoved his hand forward, hurling ice over the soldiers' shields below him.

Sir Alter ran straight behind Jack, slicing through the frozen soldiers and striking down the last one standing in front of the Caishan leader.

Ben sprinted through the throng to the governor and stabbed him from behind.

As their leader fell, the governor's guards looked uncertain and began retreating.

The other man who had run out of the barracks with Jack rebuked the town guards and called, "I am your warlord! Attack the slavers, and kill them all!"

At first the guards seemed hesitant, but with their leader dead at Ben's feet, they had no reason to stand against their current ruler. They advanced against the slavers.

Sir Alter swung his sword in a sideways arc at his enemy. "Keljerk the Cruel, I pass judgment on you!"

Keljerk blocked the sideways swing with his own shield and thrust his sword at the knight.

Sir Alter deflected the blow and recommenced his attack.

Charles did not see more of that fight because a slaver came at him from the front while another charged toward his rear.

Ben killed the slaver behind Charles and joined his friend. The two fought side by side, and after Jack sliced his way through another enemy, the three were united in battle.

Charles's axe whistled through the air.

The slaver in front of him foolishly tried to block the weapon with his sword.

The axe hit the Caishan so hard that it smashed him to the earth.

Another slaver tried to stab Charles in the side.

Charles deflected the blow with his shield, and lifting his axe into the air, swung it downward from left to right.

The enemy raised his shield in time to stop the blow, but the momentum knocked him backward into several other slavers.

Two more slavers circled around behind Charles.

Before Charles could fully turn, Ben stepped behind him and sliced one soldier's knee, dropping him to the ground, then deflected the other soldier's sword. In one swift motion, Ben brought his sword from the ground in an upward arc, slicing the second man's arm, before turning and finishing the first one, who still lay on the ground.

Charles glanced to his other side, where Jack's flurry of attacks completely overwhelmed two more slavers. As Jack's speed broke through their defenses, he gave two more quick thrusts and ran them both through.

The city's guard now rushed to their aid, preventing them from becoming surrounded. More Caishan slavers joined the battle, but with the city guard on their side, it became an even fight.

"I won't lose!" Keljerk yelled over the din of the battle.

Charles looked up to see Keljerk still in a brutal conflict with Sir Alter.

"I didn't know how to awaken all of your stones," the Caishan leader said," but I got some of them." He raised his hand and shot a fireball directly toward the knight.

Sir Alter raised his shield in time, but the fireball flung him backward several feet and threw him to the ground.

Sir Alter turned his head to look at Jack and yelled, "Jack, use your lightning stone!"

Running to the knight's defense, Jack yelled back, "I can't! I already used it, remember?"

Sir Alter stood. "You can use it again; just trust me!"

Keljerk turned toward Jack. "So you *do* have some power. Let's see it." He raised his hand and shot a lightning bolt at Jack.

Jack lifted both of his swords, placing them directly in the lightning bolt's path. It struck his swords and launched him backward, sending sparks of electricity flying everywhere.

Charles watched as Sir Alter rushed toward Keljerk, but before the knight could swing his sword, Keljerk turned and hurled another fireball that sent Sir Alter flying backward again.

This time Keljerk charged toward the knight as he lay on the ground and swung his sword in a swift downward arc. Just before his sword made contact, however, a massive charge of electricity struck him in the side. His body split into several pieces as Charles looked on in amazement.

How did Jack shoot his lightning when he said he had already used it? Charles wondered.

Without a leader, the slavers began retreating.

The warlord issued commands to sound the alarm and close the gates. He then made his way to the governor's mansion to regain control over the city.

Jack approached the recovering knight. "How was I able to use my lightning a second time?"

Sir Alter swung his shield over his back. "For a blood mage you sure don't know much about your own power, do you? Blood mages are different from normal mages. When normal mages use gemstones, the stones heat up and will shatter if used again before they cool. Any type of blood mage, though, dissolves the stone in blood, which prevents the stone from shattering. Theoretically, as long as blood mages had enough fresh blood, they could continue to cast their stones as many times as they wanted. Iconic blood mages, however, have a limited amount of blood in their bodies, and if they heat it up too much, they will die. That limits the number of spells they can cast.

"The important thing is not how many stones you have in your body but rather how long it takes to heat up your blood. *You* can safely cast about five times. If you were about 350 pounds, you could probably cast six times. At your weight if you did try to cast six times, you would probably be successful, but your blood may boil and either kill you or cause permanent damage. An advantage you have as an iconic blood mage is that you have four combat stones in your body, and you can cast five spells before your blood boils. You can cast all four of your stones one time then cast one of them again. You could also cast one of your stones five times or one of them three times and one of them two times."

"I see," said Jack. "This information could help me a great deal in the future because it gives me more options in battle."

"That's right," replied the knight.

"I should have figured this out on my own," Jack said to Charles as he joined Jack. "I actually already used that ability when we hunted the gothers and didn't even know it. When the wind started to die, I tried to produce more until my blood started to warm."

Charles nodded. "Yeah, you cast the same stone three or four times in a row without even realizing it."

Sir Alter picked through Keljerk's remains and retrieved his stones. "It seems I will have to reawaken most of my gemstones now, but three of these stones don't belong to me. It would seem he already had them. Traditionally, the one who kills the enemy mage decides who keeps the stones, so these three are for you, Jack."

Jack inspected the gemstones. "This is a translation stone, but these two are odd stones. I've never seen any like them."

Sir Alter said, "This pure white one is a light stone, but I'm unfamiliar with the pitch black stone."

"We'll have to look up the black stone in the book," Jack said, passing the gemstones on to Charles for examination.

Charles looked more closely at the black stone. For some reason it was almost difficult to see the stone. Shadows seemed to envelop the stone, but no objects were nearby to cast shadows.

Jack also searched Selfren's corpse and found two more stones.

Charles did not recognize these stones either. The first stone's appearance was a combination of yellow and orange swirled together. The second stone was almost entirely black with a small line of swirling yellow and orange encircling the stone.

Sir Alter commented, "The yellow and orange stone is a sound stone; I've seen another knight carry one. But this dark stone, like the other one, is not familiar to me."

Jack examined both dark stones together. "I suspect that both can be used for stealth in some way because this was an assassin squad."

"Sounds like I want at least two of these stones," chimed in Ben with a smile. Ben stepped forward toward Sir Alter. "Well, Sir Knight, did we do well enough for you to recommend us for knighthood?"

Sir Alter paused for a moment as if considering his words. He finally replied sternly, "It's almost humorous that the two knights-in-training whom I explicitly forbade from coming on this mission would disobey my command and then actually ask me to recommend them for knighthood."

"That's not exactly fair," Charles said, rather startled.

The knight let out a small chuckle. "I can't be too unhappy with you; your timely arrival is what saved our lives. Despite the skills of all three of you, however, I think I want you to go on more missions before becoming knights." As they began to protest, the knight raised his hand. "But you are certainly the heroes of the day, and I think you two should keep the gemstones that we obtained."

"Fair enough," replied Ben, "but I think the slavers may have something else that we could use." Ben searched both of the Caishan assassins and commandeered a small knife and a few bottles of unknown liquid. "This may come in very handy if I can figure out what's inside these bottles."

Charles commented, "I wouldn't advise tasting them to determine their contents."

Ben chuckled. "Man, I'll never know what's inside if I can't taste it."

The boys all grinned and continued to crack jokes as their group prepared to leave the city.

As the young men and Sir Alter neared the city gate, men approached with Jack's and Sir Alter's stolen horses and equipment.

Warlord Juima also joined them. "I'm sure it's not anywhere close to what you deserve, but I have a payment for your group to thank you for rescuing me."

"Actually"—Sir Alter held up his hand—"Knights of Celel do not accept payments for their missions, but we humbly thank you anyway."

Ben grimaced and whispered to Charles and Jack, "We might need to find a different career—maybe one that pays better."

Charles smiled as they all mounted their horses and began riding out of the city.

The journey back to the Celshen estate was relatively uneventful. Sir Alter gave them some pointers on their horseback riding, and in a few days they saw familiar fields and the grand manor house before them.

Ben bumped Charles and whispered, "Hey, don't make a fool out of yourself. I told Vennel the truth about where we were going before we left."

Charles smiled and relaxed. "Well, that's good. At least you were honest with one person." Charles thought, *It does seem as though the two of us have gotten closer. ... She's pretty, thoughtful, and all around a really nice girl. But I'm leaving this world, so I should be careful not to get too close to her.* Charles could not take her back to his world, nor could he stay in her world and leave his whole family back home. Then he told himself, *It's not a big deal. I just need to make sure that I stay just friends with her. After all, we started as friends, so we can stay just friends. That way I won't hurt her when I leave.*

A Destiny Among Worlds

Chapter 17

WITH NEW GEMSTONES AVAILABLE, Ben found himself studying their book a great deal more. He had specifically requested both of the black stones.

"Whatever these are," he had said to Jack, "I'm sure they'll help me sneak around, which could be a great deal of fun on or off the battlefield. After all, if assassins carried these, they probably used the stones to help them approach and dispatch their targets silently."

It took him about a day to determine which section of the book mentioned black stones. The book had only one paragraph about them, but he had to work for several more days before he could read the entry.

Ben was excited when he finally read about his two new stones. *Interesting*, he concluded silently, *the stones are a corrupt light stone and a corrupt sound stone.* He was not really sure how they became corrupted, but the awakening was apparently the same as for a normal light stone and sound stone.

Charles also studied the book as much as possible to awaken his light stone and sound stone. Charles, however, became distracted soon after awakening his two stones.

The city's watermill for grinding grain malfunctioned, and no one knew how to repair it. The town issued an official request to prominent families to see if any of them had any ideas, and Charles had volunteered to attempt to fix the mill.

Charles had assured Ben, "It's just a watermill. If I can understand the inner workings of a hydroelectric dam, I should be able to figure out a watermill."

Ben managed to awaken his stones, and he tested his corrupt light stone as soon as he awakened it. He held it in his hand and focused. Total darkness suddenly enveloped him. No light reached him from the window or oil lamp.

"Wow," he said aloud, stepping out of the darkness.

He surveyed his handiwork. He had created a sphere of darkness approximately ten feet in diameter. The dark sphere lasted about six seconds before the room returned to normal.

Over the next couple of tries, he discovered that he could change the sphere into different shapes and throw the dark sphere in any direction. *This is so cool,* he thought. *At night I could go virtually anywhere. If I activate the stone, it would be completely dark, and no one would notice me.* Unfortunately, it did not seem to have as much use during the day. *Everyone would notice a big black spot walking through the field. They may not see me, but they would be able to tell that something was there.*

He also tried using his corrupt sound stone and discovered that he consumed all sound. He tried singing and beating on the walls after activating it. Then he went downstairs and discovered that the servants had heard nothing.

After a few hours Jack walked up to the room. "Ben, how's your progress?"

Ben showed Jack the progress he had made and went on to say, "The duration for both stones seems to be about six seconds, but I'm hoping that with practice I can stretch it out to ten."

"Excellent. Keep up the good work." Jack sat on his bed. "I'm studying the other book. You remember the book we got from the temple written in the tongue of angels? I'm hoping there's some information in it that may be able to help us. The book is fascinating. I haven't figured it all out yet, but it seems to tell this world's creation story with an explanation of the gemstones' origins.

"Interestingly enough, the information seems to have almost nothing to do with the religion that we encountered in Xin. Most of that religion's followers probably have no idea what is actually written in the book. It's sort of like how in our world's ancient past, it seems several religions also had many followers who were ignorant of their own doctrine. Only after someone translated the holy books into the common tongue did the people understand their own religions."

This discussion did not particularly interest Ben, but history and geography always seemed to fascinate Jack.

Of course, Charles had to ask Jack to tell them the story when he returned from his day with the watermill.

Jack began reading but kept pausing as he translated. Finally, he said, "Instead of giving you a word-for-word translation, let me see if I can just give you the ideas. I'll try to put this in my own words. The Creator began to make this world, and it bore many similarities to other worlds that the Creator had made. Let's see, according to this the Creator decided to put the angels in charge of finishing the world. Some sort of war or falling out took place among the angels. Because this world was devoid of life and incomplete, the angels who still worked for the Creator decided to fight the largest of all the battles here. Apparently, the angels who worked for the Creator won the war or, at least, part of it.

"I'm not actually sure how many years this word here translates to, but I get the impression that even though the war was over, conflict still existed for a long time. According to this, the fallen angels actually came to this world for some purpose later, but the other angels who still worked for the Creator returned and drove them off again. At some point an angel, though I'm not sure if it was a good one or bad one, returned to this world. It says he 'used the earth' to summon people here, but the word 'earth' in this instance also feels like it could mean 'stone' or 'rock,' so there might be a type of gemstone that allows a gateway to open between worlds. Maybe the king of Celel has such a stone or would be familiar with this concept."

Charles leaned forward. "That's really interesting. What happened next?"

Jack sighed. "I'm not sure. That's all I've translated so far because the translation stone doesn't give me a word-for-word translation. It seems very difficult, but I've never really translated anything before coming to this world, so maybe translating is always this difficult."

Ben thought, *Well, I suppose that was a little interesting, but I'm glad that I got the five-minute CliffsNotes version, and I'm not the one translating the book.*

Ben's thoughts were interrupted by Lilen calling them downstairs for the evening meal.

The three boys went downstairs and sat with Sir Aldric and Zemara.

Lilen started bringing food in from the kitchen and putting it on the table.

Zannel and Vennel came in together through the back door and made their way to the table.

Sir Aldric was always eager to talk about political affairs with anyone willing to listen. No matter what took place in the world, Sir Aldric always seemed to know all about it and be thrilled to share the information. Tonight Sir Aldric wanted to talk about a controversial mission that rumors said the king had suggested at court. "I don't know anything about the mission, but I do know that the Setell family and the governor of Juma both stood in strong opposition when King Tanner presented the mission."

At the mention of the Setell family, Ben noticed that Zannel looked uncomfortable. Zemara also seemed troubled, and Vennel reached over and put her hand on Zannel's shoulder. Ben had noticed the two girls becoming closer friends, and Vennel seem to know what was bothering the family. Ben thought, *If I had paid more attention, maybe it wouldn't be such a mystery, but whatever. If someone wanted me to do something, then they should have asked for my help.*

Ben was pretty sure he could also read a change on Jack's face when Sir Aldric mentioned the Setell family. With Jack one was always dealing with micro expressions. Ben thought, *Maybe he likes Zannel.* Then Ben shook his head. Jack was way too smart to get hung up on a girl he would never see again once he got home. Now, Charles, he was a real softy, and Ben did not know what he would do with Vennel. *Jack must feel sorry for Zannel, or Zemara, or someone, for some reason, probably because of whatever is making everyone upset.*

******

As the days passed, Jack mentioned that he and Ben needed higher-quality swords. Although Ben liked the feel of his familiar sword, he certainly had no objection to an upgrade. Charles recommended that they hire Kxull and his father to forge new weapons for them. As skilled blacksmiths these craftsmen also added an aggregate to the sap with which they coated their weapons' handles. This material provided durable insulation for protection against lightning bolts while simultaneously enhancing the grip. Charles also requested that they forge mage bands like the one he had purchased from Vennel to allow more efficient gemstone carrying.

The boys also continued to practice their archery and horseback riding. Sir Alter came once a week to give them lessons on mounted combat. According to Sir Alter, the possibility of a major conflict down south was becoming more likely, and he was frequently needed at the capital for discussions.

It seemed to Ben that way too much discussing took place and not enough action. It had been three weeks, and they still had not received a new mission.

Ben also decided to test his gemstones on Charles. He waited quietly until Charles came up to their room. It seemed to take forever, but Charles had to show up eventually. Finally, Ben heard Charles coming up the stairs. Ben concentrated and activated both of his new stones at the same time. The light in the room vanished, and Ben tried to circle around behind Charles. When the light returned, however, he discovered that Charles had walked forward, and Ben was not standing directly behind his friend as he had intended.

Charles turned and looked at Ben. He shook his head and smiled. "I should have known."

"Wasn't that awesome?" Ben exalted happily.

"Yes, I just wanted to stumble through the dark in my own room today. It was my personal mission when I woke up this morning. I couldn't hear you or even myself walking. Did you use both of your stones at the same time?"

Ben nodded. "At night I can be completely invisible and silent like a ninja."

"Yeah, like a blind ninja," replied Charles, "for all of six seconds."

Ben frowned. "I just have to become better at moving silently all the time and use my stones just at the right moment."

"Well, if you try to encircle me in darkness again, I'll use my light stone, and we'll see what happens when I shine as much light as possible into your little dark sphere."

"That actually sounds cool," said Ben. "We should totally try that."

Charles rolled his eyes but could not hide his smile as he collected a few items and left.

Ben thought, *I have to find someone else to test this out on.* Ben started considering on whom it would be the most fun to test his gemstones. He thought, *I probably shouldn't use it on anyone belonging to the Celshen household ... but that would be super fun. Yeah, I could use it on one of them when they're completely not expecting anything.* Then Ben reconsidered, *This is probably one of those moments when I should dismiss this thought, but I never really liked doing that. It's not nearly as much fun.*

Ben casually asked Vennel later that afternoon, "What are the three family members' plans tonight?"

Vennel lifted her eyes to the ceiling as she recalled the information. "Sir Aldric is staying home tonight. Zemara is going to a party for high-society ladies. Zannel and I are going to a party at the same place but on a different section of the property."

Ben contemplated his options. Sir Aldric was going to stay home that night, and he would not be any fun anyway. If he did find Ben, he would want to talk for the next two hours. The old knight seemed to be running on an emotional high ever since the three of them excelled at the tournament. Ben could not really blame him. His life had been sinking, but now he could walk around town with his head held high.

Zemara also seemed very pleased except for brief periods when a shadow appeared to cross over her face. She was going out to visit some of her friends that night. According to the servants, it was very unusual for her to be so social. It seemed to make sense. Previously, she probably wanted to hide from her friends because she was ashamed, but now she could brag to them. *It would be fun to follow and scare her and all her friends, but highborn ladies aren't the kind who would take a joke very well,* he decided.

350

That left Zannel and Vennel. Although Vennel now seemed almost as comfortable with high-society girls as with Lilen, her hard past had taught Vennel to monitor her surroundings, so she might not be easy to trick or scare.

He pictured the possible outcomes of playing jokes on Zannel and her friends. *I might get into trouble if I follow any of the Celshen family around*, he thought, *so I can't follow Zannel or her mother. I know, I'll follow the servant who goes with them and see what the servants do while the prominent families all hang out. That's perfect because if I freak out all the servants and get caught, I can just tell them to get over it because I outrank the servants.*

With a plan settled in his mind, Ben packed a snack and dressed all in black. Then he waited by the window until he saw the ladies, the groundskeeper, and another servant leave the house around dusk.

He sneaked out the window and trailed them as they headed toward town in the carriage driven by the groundskeeper. Ben thought, *Good thing the groundskeeper is never in a hurry.* Following them was not as much fun as he had hoped, but it was certainly better than anything Ben had done since their last mission.

The group traveled down the stone road that wound through the property then turned out onto the dirt road that led to the town's main road. After a little distance the group turned again and headed toward the estate of another prominent family.

As the groundskeeper dropped them off at the estate, Zemara gave him instructions about when to return.

A young man met the group and directed the visitors to different areas.

Ben stealthily followed the servant, who entered a small building full of other servants. Several of the occupants stood to welcome the newcomer.

Ben presumed that most of the servants were already acquainted. Although the night was a little chilly, the crowded room was no doubt stuffy, and several of the window shutters were thrown open for ventilation. Several tables held card games, puzzles, and other interesting activities, but after ten minutes or so, Ben became bored. None of the servants discussed anything particularly interesting. Then a thought occurred to Ben. *A bunch of young women from the prominent families are gathered here. That means somewhere on the premises, the prominent families' young men are also probably gathered. That's the group I should find.*

Ben had to avoid a few servants wandering the grounds and the gardener, but for the most part security remained minor. Before long he discovered two large buildings connected by a stone path. Well-manicured bushes lined both sides of the walkway. Both buildings were constructed from stone and had cedar shakes on their roofs. Flowers and bushes grew around the buildings' perimeters, which made it easy for Ben to hide in the darkness.

Ben peeked in an open window and observed the young men in different groups. Many of the young men sat at tables drinking and engaging in many of the same activities as the servants. The possible war in the south seemed to be a popular topic in this room.

Ben felt excited as he leaned closer to better hear a conversation. *This exciting feeling must be what it's like to be a thief,* he thought. *I never really liked people who stole things, but there is something exciting about sneaking around and not getting caught. Jack would probably kill me if he found out I spied on our host family.*

He crept close to a different window where he could hear more. Ben overheard a conversation taking place among a few of the young men a little older than himself. They discussed the promising young recruits who might be knighted in the near future.

"Apparently," one young man said, "Sir Alter took three of them on one mission and gave a dazzling report of them at the capital. Now all the lords and ladies there want to meet them, but Sir Alter says he wants them to go on more missions before he recommends them. If he does recommend them after only a couple more missions, those three will be the first applicants he's ever recommended who haven't completed at least five missions."

Suddenly, Ben felt guilty about snooping around and spying. Sir Alter would be very disappointed. Ben had just made up his mind to leave when he thought he heard someone in the building at the stone path's other end say the name Jack.

Ben quietly crossed over and listened at the window. The prominent families' young women were holding their party in this building. A girl inside was talking about the tournament, and one of the others said she would love to meet some of the high-ranking young men.

Ben smiled to himself and thought, *It's kind of nice to have a fan, even if they haven't met me.*

A different girl laughed and said, "But Jack, the guy who won the tournament, is already spoken for."

The girls giggled.

Then Ben heard a voice he recognized. *That's Zannel,* he thought.

Zannel said, "He's not spoken for, or have you all forgotten that I am engaged? Even if I liked him, I couldn't do anything about it."

"That's so sad," said one of the other girls. "That Vanzantel guy is such a creep. I think he likes being mean and insulting to just about anyone."

"You should ask your father to cancel the arrangement," said the first girl. "After all, your family doesn't need to boost its influence by marrying you into that family anymore."

Zannel replied, "It's true, we don't, but it would still hurt our family's reputation a great deal if my father canceled the engagement without a good reason."

Another voice that Ben did not recognize said, "Maybe Vanzantel will get caught for some of the crimes he commits, and your father will have a good reason to cancel the whole thing."

This is interesting, contemplated Ben. *I wonder if Jack and Charles knew that she's engaged.*

"What kinds of crimes does he commit?" asked Zannel a little defensively.

"According to my servants, his servants talk about valuable things that he steals from other prominent families. His family's wealth and influence always keep him and his friends from getting in trouble, and he's good at not getting caught."

"Sadly," replied Zannel, "I don't think he'll ever be caught. It seems to be my fate to marry him, so unless I have a guardian angel watching over me, it's all over."

A guardian angel, considered Ben. *I didn't know anyone in this land knew what an angel is. I suppose the ancient language is called the 'tongue of angels,' and people worship that demon god, so there must be some sort of legends about both in this world like Jack's book said.* Suddenly, Ben smiled. *She needs a guardian angel, and I need something interesting to do. To top it off, if she likes Jack, she should have the opportunity to try thawing out that cold heart of his. This is going to* be awesome fun. *All I have to do is confirm that Vanzantel is a thief and get him caught in the act.*

Ben sneaked back toward the Celshen estate to work on his plan. As he traveled down the road, he thought, *If I can't get enough information from outside the house, I'll have to sneak inside to see if I can find some of the stolen items. The hardest part is going to be keeping this hidden from Jack and Charles because neither of them would go for this. They're way too good. They would both think that this could backfire and negatively affect the Celshen family. That's why I'm the perfect guy for this job—because I'm a good guy, just not too good. Jack is all black and white—this is right and that's wrong—and that's just the way he thinks. I know better.* After all, he reasoned, *there are shades of gray, and it's just important to stay mostly in light-colored gray, or better said, sometimes you just have to get your hands dirty.*

Ben decided that he would find out where Vanzantel lived the next day and eavesdrop on his servants to learn what he usually stole and where he hid his loot. *Then I have to find something valuable that belongs to a family wealthier and more powerful than Vanzantel's family. That way, despite his family's wealth, they won't be able to bury the truth.*

That night Ben could barely sleep because of his excitement. In the morning he casually mentioned to Jack and Charles that he planned to explore the land around the town.

Charles looked unconvinced. "That's what you were so excited about last night?"

"Of course," Ben replied casually.

"Try not to get into too much trouble, all right?" said Jack. He turned and went upstairs to translate more in his book.

Ben departed at his first opportunity. As he ran out the door, he thought, *At least I'm doing something kind of important and good. Those two are just goofing off. Well, Jack is sort of goofing off since he's reading his book. Charles is definitely goofing off because he's working on a watermill, which is fun to him for some reason.*

The Setell family estate was larger and obviously wealthier, or at least more concerned about *looking* wealthier, than the Celshen family estate. The house was divided into three major sections with two sections on the ground floor and a third area in a partial second floor above the second section. A great deal of shrubbery grew around the manor house's perimeter. The bushes on the home's right side had just begun blooming with purple and blue flowers. The bushes on the left side looked more shaded and had not yet started to open. Ben suspected from the buds that these bushes would have pink or red flowers. Cornfields surrounded the estate's yard.

The house had received some sort of paint to make it green like the surrounding plants. The house's first section on the ground floor looked like guest quarters, and the family lived in the adjacent second section. Ben did not yet understand the purpose of the third portion built above the family's living quarters. Two other buildings, which Ben discovered were the servants' quarters and a storage building, stood at a little distance from the house.

Ben loitered in a stealthy manner at the estate all day, trying to overhear conversations, but he failed to gather any useful information. *This is so frustrating,* he thought, *but it's easier to sneak around at night anyway.* He waited until darkness fell. His stomach started to growl since he had not eaten since breakfast, so he snacked on some food he had packed.

Ben was careful to stay under the cover of darkness while he sneaked up and listened outside the servants' quarters. Eventually, everyone on the entire estate went to bed, and he was dismayed by his lack of information.

This pattern continued for two more days, but finally, one night outside the servants' quarters, he overheard one of the servants speaking in a concerned voice.

The servant said, "Vanzantel is out late tonight. That means he'll come home with something valuable and put it in his special storage room."

"Special storage room?" the other servant asked.

"Yes, it's one of those two rooms upstairs, where we're never allowed to go." The first servant continued, "I hear he's had his eye on a statue that belongs to the Hukel family."

"What kind of statue?"

"It's a statue of some kind of huge cat rumored to live in the mountainous area down south near the Great Southern Desert."

People in this world are not very creative, thought Ben. *They have the Great Northern Mountains and now the Great Southern Desert. I wonder if they have a Great Island and whether the ocean is called the Great Ocean.*

Armed with this new information, Ben climbed onto the guest section's roof, from which he had easy access to an upper story window. He pressed himself against the roof and waited for Vanzantel to return.

Before long Vanzantel arrived and walked directly to the front door as if nothing were amiss. Two other young men accompanied him. They all wore dark clothing, and Vanzantel carried a sack over his shoulder. They all entered the house and soon arrived in the top story.

Ben crept up to the window and peered through the slit in the closed shutters. He saw them take a metal helmet, which appeared to boast very expensive craftsmanship, out of the sack.

Vanzantel spread his arms and stretched with apparent satisfaction. "Not too bad of a haul tonight. I think I'll sell this piece. I know a merchant who buys stuff and resells it down south, no questions asked."

The three started drinking, and Vanzantel told the other two about the cat statue, which he intended to target next. The three of them planned to scope out the Hukel family estate the next night to decide how to best steal the statue since the family was throwing a party that night.

Vanzantel said, "You two distract any servants who might be around the house, and I'll climb up the side of the house and look in the window to see how difficult it will be to get into the room. It's still pretty cold at night, so no one will be out on the balcony. I'll be able to climb up and down without anyone noticing me. Even if they do see me, they'll just think we're being mischievous like usual. Since nothing will be missing, no one will be the least bit suspicious."

After more drinking and laughing, one of them eventually passed out and the other two made clumsy beds out of some blankets in the corner and went to sleep.

Ben poked a knife blade into the slit between the shutters to push up the inner latch. He opened the shutters, slipped into the room, and explored carefully.

The room contained several tables and chairs and numerous shelves filled with different types of ornaments, jewelry, armor, and sundry other valuable items. Ben also found three trunks full of expensive objects. He shook his head as he thought, *All this stuff must've been stolen. That's why it's all hidden up here. If Vanzantel sells some of the things he steals, that means he must've been at this for years. It also means he's very good at stealing, and his family's influence must be enormous. I won't be able to get him caught in the act of stealing one item and make it stick. He would either slip out completely or blame one of his two friends. If I want to get him caught, I need to bring the guard here into this room so that the evidence is irrefutable.* Ben smiled as he formulated a plan. *Now all I need to do is invite myself to the Hukel family estate tomorrow night.*

******

The next day Ben casually asked Zemara whether the Hukel family included anyone his age. To his delight, he discovered that they had a son a year younger and a daughter a year older than himself. Their names were Don and Felara, respectively.

As dusk fell, Ben arrived at the Hukel estate as though he had been invited and asked the servant to direct him to the party. The servant brought Ben into the manor house, a square, three-story building with a balcony on the second story. Only a small sliver of moon shone that night, and the sky was cloudy, making it very dark.

Ben managed to make it inside and find the party on the second story without arousing suspicion. He stepped outside onto the balcony. He was reasonably confident that the light was sufficient for him to be able to see Vanzantel, but unfortunately, he was not sure whether he would be able to identify him. He quickly adjusted his plan when he went back inside and noticed that torches lined the walls in the party room. *I'll just have to carry one of those with me out onto the balcony,* he decided.

Ben soon bumped into Felara and Don, and to his pleasure, found that Don was also a knight-in-training and shared many of Ben's interests. Felara had watched Ben's tournament fights and apparently developed a small crush on him, so Ben had no trouble keeping the two siblings near him as they socialized.

After a little while Ben quietly stepped out onto the balcony. He saw Vanzantel's two friends below conversing with some servants and Vanzantel climbing up the wall. Ben waited until Vanzantel neared the window on the third story. Then Ben stepped back into the party and found Felara.

"Hey," Ben said, "would you be willing to step out on the balcony with me?"

Felara blushed and placed her hand in front of her mouth. "But it's so cold."

"No problem, this will keep you warm." Ben casually grabbed one of the torches inside the room and stepped out onto the balcony.

Don saw them go outside and came out to join them.

This is just perfect, thought Ben. He looked out the corner of his eye and saw a dark shape trying to remain completely still pressed against the wall.

Felara said something about the stars, but Ben ignored her.

Turning, Ben held up his torch. "Hey, look at that."

Both of the Hukel family members also turned. In the torchlight they could clearly see Vanzantel's face.

"Oh my, what are you doing there?" Felara cried. "Vanzantel, you pest! Stop climbing on our house, or I'll tell my father!"

Vanzantel's upper lip curled in anger. He quickly climbed down and left with his friends.

"What a weird fellow," said Ben. "You don't think he stole anything do you?"

Felara's eyes widened. "No, I don't think so."

Don placed his hands on his hips. "I wouldn't put it past him. He's a creep, and he always picks on me. I'm going tell our father, just in case."

"Well, sorry, that kind of ruined the mood," said Ben. "Maybe you guys can invite me over some other time when you have another party."

Felara cast her gaze downward in disappointment but politely replied, "Okay, I'm going to go back inside now."

Ben quickly hung the torch on the wall inside the party room and stepped back out onto the balcony. He jumped on the balcony rail, climbed up to the window, and slipped through it. The room contained several valuable-looking objects, but only one matched the description of the cat statue for which he searched.

Ben carefully picked up the statue, wrapped it in a cloth, placed it inside a sack he had stowed under his cloak, and returned to the window. He had already attached a string to the sack, and he used it to lower the statue into the bushes at the base of the wall. He then nimbly climbed back down to the balcony.

Ben mingled among the party goers for a few more minutes and watched Don take his father out onto the balcony and point up at the window. Ben could not hear what he said, but he did not need to.

Ben hastily went downstairs and outside. Within a few minutes he heard a commotion inside the house, and Ben guessed that the head of the Hukel family had discovered the theft.

The servants were immediately called into the house for questioning.

Ben took advantage of the opportunity to dart into the bushes. He collected the statue and headed toward the Setell property.

Ben ran the entire way. It began to drizzle, but it still felt warmer than Ben was used to. *We've been in this world for a while,* he thought, *so it must be summer now. I suppose since we continued traveling northward, it's probably rather warm now down south where we came into this world.* Ben ran through a cornfield on the Setell land as a shortcut. Then he hopped over a fence, rushed through the darkness, and climbed up the house's edge. Ben unwrapped the statue and peered through the second floor window.

He saw Vanzantel and his friends talking. He heard Vanzantel say something about how he would now have to wait a few weeks before stealing the statue since someone had seen him.

A table stood behind Vanzantel and his two friends. Although shadows encompassed the table, it still remained within sight of the door.

Ben confirmed that the table was the perfect spot. Then he estimated how many steps it would take to reach the table. Ben closed his eyes and concentrated. Except for a single lantern near the three friends, the room was already fairly dark. After Ben created his dark sphere, he shrank the darkness until it just barely surrounded him. He also used his corrupt sound stone to conceal any noise created as he climbed through the window and walked toward the table. He felt the table's edge and set the statue down on its surface. *Yes,* he thought, *this will be visible from the door, but it's shadowed enough that the three of them probably won't notice it unless they come over here.*

Ben returned to the window and stepped out just as his darkness vanished. He turned and looked back, listening to the young men's conversation. The three thieves gave no indication that they had seen or heard anything out of the ordinary. Ben excitedly bumped his own fists together. He had just walked within eight feet of three people, and none of them had seen or heard him.

Ben waited in the darkness, and before long he saw a few torches bobbing up and down on the road.

Six men approached the house and banged on the door. A servant answered the door, and the men pushed past the servant and entered the house.

Vanzantel and his friends had already begun drinking and paid no attention to the noises downstairs.

Ben could hear angry voices below him. He smiled; his plan was almost complete. The arguing downstairs grew louder. Ben could not understand the exact words, but he suspected that the head of the Setell household said something like, "My son had nothing to do with stealing your statue," and the head of the Hukel family demanded to see Vanzantel anyway.

Within a few minutes Ben heard knocking on the door to the second-story room where Vanzantel and his friends lounged.

Vanzantel called, "What is it? We're busy."

"It's your father," called a voice through the door. "Open this door immediately!"

Vanzantel laughed, and his friends started laughing too. "We're having fun," yelled one of his friends, "so you adults just go away."

For a few minutes Ben heard only silence from the hall outside the door, and he thought that they might have left. Then he heard a key turn in the door lock.

The door flew open and seven men burst into the room. Ben immediately recognized the captain of the guard from Juma, and he had four soldiers with him. Ben also recognized Don and Felara's father and knew that the other man must be Vanzantel's father.

The captain of the guard spoke with an authoritative tone, "Vanzantel, we have witnesses that put you at the Hukel family estate acting in a highly suspicious manner at the same time that a valuable statue was stolen. What do you have to say for yourself?"

Vanzantel casually set down his drink. "I don't have to tell you anything, and I don't care if anyone saw me at the estate or not. It was a party after all; of course my friends and I were there."

One of the soldiers pointed at the statue on the table. "Isn't that the statue we're looking for? A statue of a great cat?"

"That's my statue!" shouted the head of the Hukel family.

Everyone, including Vanzantel and his friends, turned their heads and saw the statue. For a moment no one spoke.

Then Vanzantel and his two friends leapt up and charged toward the window where Ben hid.

Ben jumped away from the window, hurriedly climbed to the ground, and sprinted through the cornfield. *I think I've overstayed my welcome*, Ben realized. *If even one of them makes it out the window, the soldiers will pursue them, and if they accidentally caught me, I would be in big trouble.*

As he ran back toward his room in the manor house, he thought, *I'm sure I'll find out what happened eventually. I'd wager this will be the talk of the town for next few days.* Ben sprinted down the stone path toward the house then ran straight to his room, where Jack and Charles were sleeping. Ben dived into his bed and let out a big sigh of relief. *That was some of the most fun I've had since we came to this world. I can't wait to do something like that again*, he thought as he drifted off to sleep.

******

Ben woke up in the early afternoon the next day and found that the entire household bustled with excitement. Even the servants seemed happy and excited.

Ben walked up to Charles and asked, "What's going on?"

Charles replied, "Apparently, the captain of the guard in Juma arrested that Vanzantel guy, Zannel's fiancé, last night for theft, so Sir Aldric has gone over to the Setell estate to cancel the engagement. They discovered Vanzantel when he stole a statue from the Hukel family, but upon further exploration of his room, they found many other valuable stolen items."

Ben casually smiled and walked out the front door. Everything had turned out exactly as expected, and no one suspected a thing. Then Ben felt a hand on his shoulder, and he whipped around to see Jack.

Jack asked, "So, do you like your new gemstones?"

Ben could feel a drop of sweat rolling down his cheek. He shrugged. "Oh, yeah, they're a lot of fun."

"That's good. It's good for you to get some practice using them." Jack smiled. "Things seem to be a bit excited around here this morning. I'm going to go for a walk somewhere where it's quieter." Jack walked toward the orchard.

Ben stood perfectly still. *Sometimes,* he thought, *I wonder if Jack knows everything that happens, and sometimes I think he just asks suspicious questions at odd times.* Ben shook his head and headed off in search of his next adventure.

Chapter 18

JACK WAS FRUSTRATED BY their lack of progress toward knighthood, and he knew that Ben and Charles shared his annoyance.

They sat alone at the breakfast table after everyone else had dispersed, discussing their predicament.

"It's been more than an entire month since our last mission," Jack moaned, leaning his head back against his chair and staring at the ceiling. "It's summer now, and it's actually nice outside. We certainly need to find something interesting to do. I don't think I've done anything but read this book and practice in that whole time."

"Well," replied Charles, "I fixed the town's watermill, which was actually kind of interesting because it seemed to be technologically superior to almost anything we've seen so far in this world."

"Great." Ben propped up an arm on the table and rested his head on his hand. "But why do we care if these people discovered the watermill before the wheel?"

"Well, technically," replied Charles, "they have discovered the wheel as well. I just found it interesting that the watermill technology seemed so advanced."

"All right." Jack leaned forward. "Sir Alter is coming today for our weekly lesson, but this time when he gets here, we'll force him to give us a mission, got it? We won't let him leave until he gives us a mission because I'm sick of sitting around all day doing nothing. I don't care if there's a war brewing down south; if they're unhappy about it, they should send us to go deal with it."

"I assume by 'they' you're referring to the king and his nobles, who only seem interested in discussing the war? Am I right?" Ben smirked.

"Yes," Jack replied. "I can't stand this tedious and unproductive sitting."

Just then, the door opened, and in came Sir Alter. "All right, boys," he said, "are you ready for your lesson?"

"Actually," replied Jack, "we want a mission."

Sir Alter smiled slightly, "I'm sorry, but there aren't any missions available at the moment for you boys."

Ben's countenance perked up, and he raised his eyebrows. "Interesting. So there are missions—just not for us. That means that full knights do have missions. Why don't you tell us about some of those?"

"That's ridiculous," Sir Alter waived his hand as if dismissing their notions. "Full knights do not have missions either."

Jack shrugged. "You can tell us about missions, or we can go to the capital ourselves and learn some crazy rumors. We want to hear about missions one way or another."

"Fine." The knight sighed heavily. "The king put forward two missions that were dismissed as impossible undertakings. All the nobles agreed that no one could complete them."

"That's fascinating," said Jack. "Please tell us about them. At least we'll get to hear about dangerous missions."

Sir Alter stood still for a moment as if deciding whether he would actually tell them any details, but he finally relaxed his expression. "The first mission was to stop a warlord who rules a kingdom south of Dulla. This warlord is called Gunda, and he is actually encouraging the slave cartels to unite and attack our nation. His actions have something to do with the war brewing down south, but I don't know the details. Reports say that he actually gives citizens of his own cities to the slave cartels in order to obtain the goodwill of all three leagues. Gaining favor with more than one or two of the slave organizations has been extremely difficult for any warlord in the past. Warlord Gunda is basically bribing all three slave cartels by capturing people through any means necessary and handing them over to the cartels. He is also well defended and has several mages under his command.

"The other mission was an attempt to strengthen our country's relations with the country of Dulla. Other than Celel, Dulla and Holdom are the two most powerful countries in the north, and if a massive world war takes place, it will be important to maintain both of these countries as allies. We already have fairly good relations with Dulla, but we're not very friendly with Holdom. For some reason the king is predominantly interested in building relations with Dulla. Holdom does not actually have a king but only a warlord, which is unusual for a country that size. The world's other six greater nations are ruled by kings."

"That sounds interesting." Charles cocked his head. "Could you tell us more about this country?"

Sir Alter took a seat facing the three young men as he gathered his thoughts. "Several hundred years ago, the king of Holdom died with no heir to the throne. Normally when this occurs, either the most powerful warlord takes control or someone no one knew was related to the king is discovered and crowned as the new king. This individual is often an illegitimate child or the descendants of a sibling to the crown from long ago. The most powerful warlord in Holdom at that time, however, remained loyal to the dead king. He continued searching for an heir to the throne, partly because he could not to use the kingdom's crown gemstone. One of Holdom's kings from ages past had somehow bound the stone to his own bloodline through some form of blood magic."

"You're saying," Jack interjected, "that I could potentially bind any additional gemstones I possess to my bloodline or to my friends' bloodlines?"

Sir Alter squinted one eye and tilted his head. "It is possible although the art was lost ages ago. Anyway, according to the story, the greater earth stone that resides within the kingdom can only be used by someone of the king's bloodline. Now it's just a tradition, but one day each year, Holdom's lords hold a holiday and feast and allow anyone who wishes to touch the stone to see if they can use it. Personally, I believe that King Tanner has found an heir to the throne, and this person is already a Knight of Celel. In fact, my suspicious have recently been supported. The king has tried to keep it a secret in the past, but some spies recently discovered the information and released it to everyone in an attempt to breed mistrust between Celel and Holdom."

"It's not a secret anymore, right?" asked Ben.

"That's correct," replied the knight.

"Then what's this man's name?" Ben pressed.

Sir Alter paused for a moment and pursed his lips. Then he shrugged. "According to the rumors and my own previous suspicious on the matter, his name is Sir Sansall. Rumors say that in the fall Sir Sansall will travel to Holdom on the day of the celebration in order to touch the stone and prove his bloodline."

"All right," said Jack. "Cool story. Going back to Dulla, though ... How did the king want to bolster relations with them?"

Sir Alter replied a little impatiently, "The king actually thinks that the two brothers, who despise each other, can be brought together. Basically, if our kingdom had a hand in reconciling the two brothers and making them love instead of hate each other, then logically, the two brothers would be indebted to the kingdom of Celel. Personally, despite the king's profound wisdom, I thought this sounded like a ludicrous idea. Anyone who has ever met those boys knows that they can only be enemies."

"We actually passed through Dulla on our way here," said Ben.

"Yes," added Jack, "and that would make the two brothers the king is talking about Dagder and Daggoth."

Ben shook his head. "Yep, I don't see those two coming together for any reason."

"Enough talk." Sir Alter stood. "We must get on with your practice."

"One more question," said Jack. "You're not actually going to give us a mission for quite a while, are you?"

Sir Alter looked even more serious than usual. "No, all lesser missions are officially on hold, and only a few knights who happen to be on tour or on essential missions are out of the country."

Jack nodded grimly. "Fine, why don't you go ahead and stay in the capital for the next couple of weeks. We'd like to travel around the country and become familiar with Celel. If we're going to be knights here one day, we need to know our way around."

"That actually sounds like an excellent idea," responded the knight, "because it will give me more time in the capital, which I need at the moment."

Their practice took place as usual before Sir Alter bid them farewell.

In parting the knight said, "You three are becoming fine horsemen, and your archery has only continued to improve. You all deserve a break for a few weeks."

After Sir Alter departed, Ben asked, "We're going to explore the country? I suppose that's better than sitting around here."

Jack laughed and shook his head. "Not a chance. We're taking advantage of the package deal."

Ben and Charles both looked at him, confused.

Charles asked, "What do you mean?"

Jack smiled. "Sir Alter said the king presented those two missions, meaning that he wanted them performed, and everyone else was too afraid to do them. We're going to do them both at the same time."

Charles raised a hand in front of him. "Hang on a second. This sounds very unwise."

Ben jumped up and down in excitement. "No, it sounds awesome! Do you have a plan, or are we just going to wing it?"

"Oh, I've got a plan," said Jack, "and it is going to be awesome. Ben, tell our host family that we'll be traveling, and we need some supplies. Charles, prepare our horses. I'll talk to Vennel to see if she wants to come and whether she'll pick up some stuff in town for us. We'll leave within the next few hours."

Both of his friends nodded and headed in opposite directions.

I couldn't ask for better friends, thought Jack. *They haven't even heard my plan yet, and they're completely on board.*

A little while later Jack found Vennel and Lilen talking in the parlor. As Jack approached, he pulled out a list of traveling supplies. "Vennel, if you don't mind, we would really appreciate it if you would pick up some things in town."

As Vennel stood to receive the list, Jack took her by the elbow and guided her out of the room saying, "We're going to leave on a trip lasting several weeks. If you want to come, then you'll need to be ready in a couple hours." He dropped his voice so that Lilen could not overhear. "I warn you, though, it won't be a leisurely stroll; we'll do a lot of fighting. Sometimes we may ask you to just lie low somewhere for a while."

She asked, "Would I be of any benefit on the mission?"

Jack replied, "We don't have anything specific we need you to do on the mission, so it's up to you if you want to go or stay."

She glanced through the supply list. "I'll pick up the supplies from town right away, but I think it would be best if I just stayed here for this mission."

Jack thanked her as he turned back toward his room to pack. He noted with pleasure Vennel's more confident manner and her willingness to make her own decision regarding her participation in the mission.

******

The three friends used the trip to Dulla to plan what Jack called "phase one" of their mission.

"The first thing," explained Jack, "is the two brothers. If we're going to reconcile them, we'll need to solve the problem between them and give them a common enemy. By taking them with us on our mission to stop Warlord Gunda, we secure the additional help that we need to complete the mission and provide the two brothers with their common enemy. Warlord Gunda has made clear his desire to overthrow the northern kingdoms, so in all likelihood, the two brothers have already heard of him as an enemy."

Ben said, "The only problem I see is getting the two brothers to go on a mission with us."

Jack nodded. "That is the sticky part. We're going to have to kidnap both of them. Even if we could convince them both to go on a mission with us, which I doubt we could do, there's still no way the two of them would willingly go together. I need to return to the library in Dulla. I read some interesting things when I was there before about their father, and I need to review the details. It will take a few days anyway to figure out the brothers' schedules and come up with good kidnapping locations."

Charles asked, "What if, by capturing the two brothers, we accidentally give them *us* as a common enemy?"

"That's a possibility," replied Jack, "but I'm already friends with Daggoth, and I'm pretty sure that he already would like to soothe the tension between himself and his younger brother if he could. This plan should appeal to him. As for Dagder, once we give him what he wants most, I think he'll come around to our side."

"What does he want most?" asked Charles.

"No one in his kingdom is allowed to give Dagder a gemstone, which prevents him from excelling. In fact, it forces him to come in behind virtually every mage in the kingdom as a warrior because he's not allowed to do his best. He wants to measure up to his older brother, and although he would never admit it, he wants to impress his father and older brother more than anyone else. He thinks that he cannot impress anyone unless he becomes a mage. Again, even though he doesn't realize it, his older brother is already impressed with him as a warrior. If we can just get them to complete the mission with us, by the time it's done, their problems should be resolved."

Days passed, and they finally arrived in Dulla.

Jack, as he had planned, returned to the library to do additional research on the princes' father.

Ben sought out Dagder and Charles followed Daggoth to gathered information on their current and future whereabouts.

After a few days the three systematically compared notes in their room at the inn.

To Ben's pleasure, he had learned that within the next few days, Dagder would sail on the lake near the city for several days. This meant that the three of them would also get to sail on the lake—the same lake on which Ben had wanted to sail previously.

Charles, however, had not identified a good opportunity to kidnap Daggoth. "Daggoth simply doesn't leave the city," Charles explained. "He spends the majority of his time in the palace or at the special building for mages."

"No problem," said Jack. "After we kidnap his younger brother, we'll just require him to come alone to a designated location outside the city. Of course, he most likely won't come alone, but we can deal with that when the time comes. First, let's get a boat and scout out the lake."

"What a great idea." Ben grinned.

They found a sailboat that also had ores, which they rented from a man who lived on the lake's edge. The boat had a rudder and a place where the oars were stowed, but the primary form of propulsion came from its central sail. Several different pieces of rigging adjusted the sail. After receiving some advice from the owner on controlling the vessel, they spent the better part of a day learning how to sail. In time they successfully scouted around the lake.

"According to his servants," said Ben, "Dagder likes to sleep on his boat, and he can sail for days at a time."

"All we have to do," Jack concluded, "is wait until night when he goes to sleep and sail up alongside him."

Charles said, "The main problem is that if we try to follow him in our boat, he'll notice us for sure."

"You're right," said Jack, "but as small as this lake is, it wouldn't be a problem to sail all the way across it in one night. We can stay along the coast, which will make it appear as though we have nothing to do with him, and wait until it's dark to sail into the lake's interior."

They made their final preparations and waited for the time the servants had said Dagder would set sail. The boys tracked him as they slowly traveled around the lake's perimeter.

Jack pulled the rudder a little to the left. "Ben, how did you get the servants to give you all this information about Dagder?"

Ben stood at the bow and shaded his eyes with his hand. "My method was actually rather complicated. People naturally talk about abnormal events, so what I did was wait until night, approach some of the servants, and ask them a few relatively unimportant questions about Dagder. Then I just walked away and hid. While in hiding I listened to their conversations that night, and one of the servants brought up the weird stranger who had asked questions. This obviously intrigued the other two servants. Once they were talking about me, the conversation easily switched to the topic of my questions, which was Dagder. His future plans, which I hadn't asked about, were paramount in their minds, and they naturally began to discuss them. Before I knew it, I had all the information I needed."

Darkness began to fall, and the group turned their boat's bow out toward Dagder's lone craft on the lake.

The prince's vessel was about twenty feet long with a small cabin on one end that likely housed a cooking and sleeping area.

Jack instructed Garthong to remain out of sight during the kidnappings so he would not give away their identities in case either of the princes remembered the unique reptile from their previous stay in Duthwania.

The three kidnappers all wore dark clothing, and they fastened dark cloths over their faces as they had done when working with the bandits against the Caishan cartel.

As the boys had hoped, Dagder gave no sign of suspicion. He slept on deck since the night was pleasant. The sound of the peaceful waves brushing against his boat's hull had apparently lulled Dagder into a deep sleep.

As the boys' boat bumped the side of Dagder's vessel, he opened his eyes and sat up. Dagder looked in their direction, but he was far too late.

The three had already leapt onto Dagder's vessel with their weapons drawn.

Ben grabbed Dagder's hands and began to tie them while Charles held him face down on his own deck with a knee in his back.

Dagder struggled against Charles's firm hold. "Do you know who I am? I'm the king's son, you filthy pirates or bandits or whatever you are. My father will have you hunted, no matter how far you go, to get me back!"

"Don't worry." Jack sheathed his swords. "Your father isn't the one we want."

Dagder tried to turn his head toward Jack's voice. "So you know who I am?"

Jack replied, "Oh yes, we do."

No one spoke as they headed back to shore.

Once there, the kidnappers wrote a letter that would be delivered to the city. The note stated that if Daggoth wanted to see his younger brother alive again, he would have to come alone to a designated area in the forest a half day's ride outside the city.

Dagder seemed to enjoy complaining, even to his kidnappers. He also commented that they must be functionally illiterate because they struggled to write a simple ransom note.

Jack thought, *It must have appeared that way. None of us can use these weird medieval writing implements very well.*

Dagder also told them that they were fools because his brother probably would not come for him anyway.

The area the kidnappers designated for the meeting with Daggoth was not actually the place where they intended to meet him. The location given to Daggoth was, however, fairly close to the actual meeting location. They hired a peasant to wait at the designated area and direct whoever came there to the actual meeting place. This step would prevent Daggoth from scouting out the actual meeting location in advance.

Jack had specifically chosen the actual meeting location as a small lake with an island in its center. A dense forest surrounded the lake, and a constant fog resided on its surface. Closely packed trees also covered the island.

"Why are we meeting them here?" asked Ben.

Jack replied, "Because, unless I miss my guess, Daggoth will probably bring three to five mages with him, depending how many he thinks he can conceal. This position gives us a unique advantage over the attacking force."

Time passed, and the hour of the meeting came. The boys had constructed two wooden platforms out in the water on the small lake. The structures were just large enough for a person to lie on. Ben and Charles were easily concealed lying on these platforms in the dense fog, and they could slide off of them into the water if they needed to avoid a direct attack.

Jack examined the scene as he heard horses approaching the water. The large trees lining the lake's edge made the entire body of water seem dark and eerie. Many of the trees were actually hardwood trees rather than evergreens even though this fairly northern country possessed many evergreen forests. Most of the creatures around the lake became silent as the sound of hoof beats grew louder.

Jack saw Daggoth arrive at the water's edge and look around.

The peasant directing him pointed across the lake to the island, turned, and left.

Jack climbed up into one of the trees on the island overhanging the water and peered over the fog through the holes in his mask. As he had expected, two more men crept out of the bushes on the lake's bank and silently slipped into the water.

Daggoth also waded into the water and started swimming.

Jack waited until the three approaching men had passed between Ben and Charles and were about twelve feet from the island. The water was still too deep for the men to touch the bottom, but they were close enough to the shore for Jack to easily see. Until this point the three men had made steady, silent progress.

Ben then activated his corrupt sound stone, and Charles shined his light stone over the water directly at the three men.

The men turned, expecting an attack, and looked into the light. Despite being disoriented and half blind, all three raised their hands and shot fireballs in Charles's general direction.

While the three mages were distracted, Jack jumped out of his tree into the shallow water and hurled the end of a rope and a sheet of freezing water toward the three paddling men. The ice descended around them and settled onto the water, trapping them in a single sheet of ice with their heads exposed.

Ben and Charles maintained their positions on the water for a few minutes in case more men, who had not yet shown themselves, were on the opposite shore.

Jack used the rope, which had become frozen in the sheet of ice along with the three men, to pull the entire mass to shore. Jack was pleased with how accurate his shot had been. Remembering how Hucklee had frozen both of Sumbvi's hands closed, Jack had encased all six of the mages' hands in ice. It was a clever idea for an ice user. With the mages' hands unable to open, they could not cast any spells. As Jack's ice had hit his opponents, he had forced their hands shut. The ice also froze their upper torsos together and created a frozen sheet of ice on the lake's surface.

When they were close enough to shore to touch the lake bottom, Jack said, "Now walk out of the water, and don't try anything."

Daggoth peered at him through the fog. "You are a skilled ice user. I wasn't expecting mages."

Jack ignored his comment and ducked under the ice sheet, which hung suspended out of the water. He searched the three men thoroughly, removing their gemstones and other weapons. The ice began to melt due to the warmer air temperature, and the men broke free, but Jack already possessed their gemstones.

"Greetings," Jack said to the three dripping men on shore. "Two of you, I don't need, so we will tie you up and leave you with your gemstones. I'm sure another group of men will be along within the next hour or so to see what happened when you don't return."

Daggoth looked up. "I'm the one you wanted. Am I right?"

Jack answered, "That is correct."

Charles joined Jack and tied up the two accompanying mages.

Jack piled these men's gemstones about ten feet in front of them.

One of the tied mages asked, "Why aren't you taking our gemstones?"

Jack smiled under his mask and simply said, "Perhaps you'll find out one day."

Charles bound Daggoth and escorted him to a small wooden boat they had stowed on the island's opposite side.

Ben already waited in another boat with Dagder.

Jack handed Ben Daggoth's gemstones.

Daggoth frowned; he knew he was too far away from his gemstones in the other boat to be able to use them.

Jack saw the look on his face and said, "We have to make sure we don't get you in proximity to your gemstones until a little later."

Daggoth asked angrily, "What do you want with the two of us? If it's a ransom, I'm sure my father will pay."

Jack dismissed the comment with a wave of his hand. "Oh please. If we wanted a ransom, surely I wouldn't have left your two colleagues' gemstones. The price of their gemstones combined with yours is worth far more gold than anything your father would offer. For now, just stay quiet; all will be explained shortly."

The three boys rowed across the lake and escorted their prisoners through the forest to a small clearing where five horses waited. The group mounted and traveled until darkness fell.

After they set up camp, Jack said, "All right now, sit down, both of you. We have a problem that also happens to be your problem. This problem is called Warlord Gunda, and we need help from you both to bring him to justice."

The princes sat silently for a moment.

Dagder's eyebrows shot up. He worked his mouth a little as if trying to form words.

Daggoth pulled his head backward and glanced around as though checking to make sure everyone else had heard the same thing he had.

Jack crossed his arms. "Our mission is a dangerous one. Extracting a warlord who has surrounded himself with as much security as he has will be extremely difficult. We will also have to deal with several mages under his command. Daggoth, I'll start with you."

Jack guided Daggoth off to the side, where they could speak in private, while Ben watched Dagder.

Once they were alone, Daggoth asked, "Why do you need the two of us to help you with this mission? Surely you could have found or hired a mage and a warrior to assist you."

"Indeed, we could have, but extracting Warlord Gunda is only half of the mission." Daggoth remained silent, so Jack continued, "This mission's primary purpose is to unite you and your brother in friendship. You see, certain interested parties want the two of you to get along in order to strengthen your kingdom, and my mission is to bring the two of you closer together. As important as it is to extract Warlord Gunda, we are primarily using him as a means to provide you and your brother with a common enemy. You do love your younger brother, don't you?"

Daggoth squared his shoulders and huffed. "Of course I do, but I don't see how this mission could change our position toward each other."

Jack held up his index finger. "Leave that to me. You just be ready to do whatever you can to help him. Now, I must also ask that you swear an oath on the lives of your younger brother and father that you will not raise your hand against my friends or me. That way, I can return your gemstones to you."

"Are you so convinced that I would honor my oath?"

"Yes. You act like we haven't met before, but just because you can't see my face doesn't mean you don't know me. I know you, and I know you will honor your oath."

"Who are you?" Daggoth squinted at the small portion of Jack's face visible thought the mask's eyeholes.

"At the proper time, I will show you."

Daggoth asked, "How could you know that Warlord Gunda has been such an emphasized topic in our father's strategic discussions?"

Jack ignored his question. "Does that mean that you will swear the oath?"

Daggoth considered briefly before shrugging. "If you were trying to trick to me, you surely would have chosen a more realistic lie, so I suppose I believe you." He then swore an oath.

"Now," Jack instructed, "please return to the camp. It's your younger brother's turn to speak with me."

Ben brought Dagder over to Jack and returned to the nearby camp with Daggoth.

Dagder was still indignant that he had been kidnapped and upset about the way he had been treated, which according to him was inhumane.

Jack listened for a few minutes then suddenly asked, "Do you want to know why you are here?"

Dagder responded hesitantly, "Yes."

"Good. This mission has two objectives. The second one I already told you, but the first one is to convince you to forgive your brother."

Dagder jerked his head up to look at Jack, almost falling off the log on which he sat. "What?"

"That's right. The kingdom of Dulla is currently unstable, and when your father dies, it will become even more unstable. My purpose is to right the wrongs done to you and, in turn, for you to forgive your brother for the wrongs that, technically, your father committed against you."

Dagder crossed his arms and sneered. "How dare you! Are you all some of my brother's friends? Did he put you up to this dastardly deed? I did notice you are all mages; you must hate what I've done with the mage council. I'll tell my father and have you all locked away forever."

Without saying a word Jack punched Dagder in the face, knocking him backward off the log on which he had sat.

"Feel better now?" asked Jack. "That should lay to rest any ridiculous idea that I work for your brother because, by law, no one in the kingdom is allowed to strike you or your brother. Clearly, I am not of this kingdom."

Dagder sat down again and rubbed his jaw.

Jack added, "I know that you are a brave and skilled warrior, so you can drop the spoiled prince act with me."

Dagder looked uncertain for a moment, but then he hung his head as if embarrassed and ashamed.

Jack leaned forward. "Since I am not of your kingdom, I can also give you what you want most in life, which is the respect of your brother and father and everyone in your kingdom."

Dagder crossed his arms again. "How can you give me respect? Everyone in the kingdom loathes me as my father's unimportant younger son."

"The law in your country clearly states that no one in the country can give you a gemstone, am I correct?"

Dagder clinched his fists and curled his upper lip. "Yes, my father made that law."

Jack smiled. "However, nowhere recorded did your father create a law saying that you cannot possess or use a gemstone."

Dagder replied angrily, "What's the difference?"

"Simply this," said Jack, "I already demonstrated that I am not from your country and not bound by your country's laws. On this mission we will have to fight at least one mage, and I am going to give you your first gemstone, under the condition that you allow your brother to teach you how to use it."

Dagder's eyes grew wide, and he stuttered, "What? You're not serious are you?"

"Of course I am," replied Jack. "When this is over, you and your brother will both be mages. After the mission I will tell you the story of how all this came to be. Then it will be solely your choice whether history repeats itself in your kingdom." Dagder looked slightly confused, but Jack continued without pausing, "Will you swear an oath to me that until this mission is complete, you will not raise your hand against my friends or me?"

Dagder replied, "This is crazy, and it will never work."

"There's always the possibility that the mission will be unsuccessful. I am asking you and your brother to trust me, and I'm telling you that if you do, we can change the world. Besides, what do you have to lose? I've offered you by far the best deal you've ever had."

Dagder peered through the slits in the mask into Jack's eyes. "I don't know why, but when you say that, I'm inclined to believe that you mean it." Dagder stood up and swore an oath.

The two made their way back to the fire and sat down.

Then Jack reached up, pulled the cloth away from his face, and added, "I think since you are both committed to the mission now, I'll show you who I am."

Daggoth stared at Jack and stammered, "But you—" He stopped.

Dagder searched Jack's face. "You do seem a little familiar, but I don't remember who you are."

"That's not surprising," replied Jack. "I came to your kingdom not long ago and learned some mage skills from your brother once I got permission from you."

Daggoth chuckled. "Despite the fact that I said you couldn't be trained in our country, you still found a way. I'm still not sure if I should be mad at you, but I won't make the mistake of saying that another one of your ideas is impossible."

Dagder added, "You've certainly already demonstrated the ability to make and implement creative plans—not just before in Duthwania but also when you captured us both. Besides, you must have great confidence in your plan to capture two princes just to accomplish the task."

Jack replied, "I believe there's always a way."

******

The three friends and the two princes traveled to the kingdom of Gidanna, where Warlord Gunda reigned supreme. The journey to reach the city of Gattel, the capital of Gidanna, lasted almost a week. Finally, the five sat on their horses atop a hill overlooking the castle.

"We will camp here tonight," Jack decided, "and prepare for the coming fight."

The hill was covered in lush green grass and a few fairly short trees, but it was far enough away from the city to avoid any unnecessary suspicion from travelers. The group had also moved farther west off the road so that any travelers on the road would not notice them. They picketed their horses and made the camp ready for a hasty departure.

Jack warned, "We may have to come out of the city in a hurry. If so, we need to ensure that we don't leave any kind of evidence."

Ben leaned his backpack against a tree. "This stuff is all ready to go. Remind me why I will be the only one who has to carry something." Jack replied, "Because, as you'll recall, you won't be going in as deep as the rest of us."

Chapter 19

THE NEXT MORNING JACK looked out over the fortified city below them. Garthong landed on Jack's shoulder, and Jack absently scratched his little friend's chin while he contemplated their situation. Jack could tell that this warlord was focused on an impending war. Gattel possessed a tall wall, perhaps thirty feet high. Unlike many city walls, it did not have towers only at its four corners. Instead, twelve additional towers distributed along the walls increased the defensibility of the traditionally vulnerable areas between the corner towers and the four gatehouses along the outer city wall.

The city itself was also divided into two distinct areas. The peasants lived inside the outer wall, but another wall separated the peasants from the upper class, and Jack suspected that the wealthier merchants also had shops inside the second wall. The interior wall had only two gatehouses, located on opposite sides. Four towers stood at the interior wall's corners. Two smaller towers, located opposite one another, defended the two longest wall sections, which would normally be interrupted by two additional gatehouses.

Obviously, Warlord Gunda did not believe that significant traffic was needed into and out of the interior wall district. A very tall tower, the keep, also stood in the very center of the city's interior portion. Jack guessed that the warlord conducted his daily business and probably lived in this tower. Even from a distance, Jack saw sunlight reflecting off of armor or weapons from soldiers down on the wall. Jack thought, *Getting inside the first tier of walls probably won't be that hard, but I doubt that they let just anyone into that second tier.*

The other four members of Jack's group joined him in overlooking Gidanna's capital.

Daggoth asked, "What's the plan so far?"

"I think this morning I'm going to have you two go ahead and check out the city's first tier." Jack gestured toward Ben and Charles.

They both nodded and headed down the hill.

Jack knelt down and started drawing in the dirt.

The two brothers watched curiously.

Jack pointed toward his drawing of the city. "We're going to take one of the two gatehouses along the interior wall, and Ben will hold it while the rest of us progress through the city toward the keep. We'll decide which gatehouse to capture based on their scouting information."

Daggoth examined the dirt sketch. "How will we prevent the other guards from hearing the noise and sounding the alarm?"

Jack briskly rubbed his hands together to remove the dirt. "Ben has a corrupt sound stone. It will suck all sound away, and nothing will be heard."

Daggoth's eyes widened. "That's how you captured my mages and me so easily. I ordered them both to fire at the shore and not look at the light, but neither they, nor even I, could hear my command."

"Yes, that's correct." Jack nodded. "You two will hold the ground just inside the keep's entrance with Charles, and I will seek out and challenge the warlord. Beware, I'm told that he employs several mages, and it's likely that at least one will come upon you all while you are there."

Dagder asked, "How will we prevent him from sounding the alarm?"

Jack replied, "Charles has a normal sound stone, which he can use to create sound waves that cancel out other sound waves."

The two brothers exchanged glances, and Daggoth said, "You can do that?"

"Yes," Jack replied, "you will have a window of about six seconds to kill the mage. Dagder, you will need to attack the mage and any guards with him head on. I'm told that you are a skilled warrior, so they should be no problem. Daggoth, you will be off to the side. Split your spells between offense, trying to kill the enemy mage, and defense, protecting your brother."

Daggoth stroked his chin. "This sounds like a reasonable plan."

"Yes," replied Jack, "unfortunately we must always be prepared for the unthinkable, such as three mages converging on you simultaneously, so don't get comfortable. Just be ready for anything."

******

That evening Ben and Charles returned and gave their report. They confirmed that anyone could go through the first gates, but the second tier gates remained closed, and only authorized personnel were allowed to pass through them.

"As I expected," said Jack. "We can only assume that security at the keep will be much higher."

"We also figured out which of the two inner gatehouses will be easiest to capture and hold," Ben added.

Jack noticed that Charles seemed somber and asked, "What else happened in the city?"

Charles sighed. "What we heard about this man is true. The warlord is not only giving his own citizens to the cartels but also sending out mounted horsemen to kidnap people in the sparsely populated areas of neighboring countries. Anyone who resists is killed by being burned alive."

Jack put his hand on his friend's shoulder. "Did you actually see a sentence carried out on someone?"

Charles nodded. "The guards accused a family of harboring someone who was supposed to have been handed over to the slave cartel. The soldiers burned the family's older members and handed the younger ones over to the cartels."

Jack looked his friend in the eye. "We will put a stop to this. Either we will capture the warlord and haul him back to Celel or, if we can't capture him, I will challenge him to a fight to the death." Jack then addressed the group with a plan summary.

Ben and Charles, who were already familiar with the group's strategy, willingly agreed based on what they had seen while scouting.

"The biggest weakness with this approach," said Jack, "is that it does not account for any way out of the outer wall. We will be able to get in easily, but if we're detected, we may have to attack one of the four gatehouses along the outer wall to escape the city. My solution is to start many fires inside the innermost wall near the keep. Because we will have conquered one of the gatehouses along the interior wall already, they will have no way of knowing if or when we exit the interior wall. So if we start fires on our way out, they will presume that the attacking force is larger than it actually is, and they may be unable to guess our objective. Even still, this will only make it *easier* to overcome one of the gatehouses on the exterior wall; it will not make it simple. There is also a good chance that all of us will have exhausted our gemstones before this time."

Daggoth declared, "In that case, this mission sounds nearly impossible."

"Maybe it does," agreed Jack. "Basically, it has to go according to plan or things will get sticky, but if this warlord isn't stopped, he may very well unite all the countries of the south and the slave cartels together against the north. If he is successful, all the northern kingdoms would easily be crushed."

Dagder crossed his arms. "I like this plan, no matter how crazy. My father never let me do anything dangerous or that could prove my worth. This is my chance, and I'm going to take it."

Jack replied, "Then let's go. Tonight will be remembered as the night that the north struck its first blow for freedom."

The company traveled to the city, and as expected, walked straight into it through the first gatehouse. They entered in a group of two and a group of three to attract less attention.

As the five walked through the streets toward the interior wall, Jack could not help but notice the shabby, single-room houses in which the peasants lived or the unsavory people walking about on the street at night. Peasants wandered around drunk or homeless, and people seemed to lurk in the shadows. The streets were not straight but instead twisted and turned around buildings.

Two guards stumbled out of a building with bright light and loud music emanating from it. They staggered toward Jack's group, obviously drunk.

Jack and his band crossed the street to avoid traveling in close proximity to the guards, but one of the guards ordered them to halt and came toward them.

"What are you peasants doing out so late?" he asked. "I'm afraid I must demand a tax for breaking curfew."

"How much money is this tax?" inquired Jack.

"Just enough for my buddy and me to get another drink at that there tavern," he slurred.

Both guards wheezed and laughed.

Jack pulled a coin out of his pocket. "Go ahead and have another."

The guard greedily grabbed the coin, and the two hobbled back toward the tavern.

As Jack's group started moving again, Ben said, "We could have easily gotten rid of those two. It would have been simple to just knock them out or something."

"We could have," Jack replied, "but although they were drunk, someone might have found two guards passed out slightly suspicious. We need to remain completely unnoticed if we can."

The group reached the southern gatehouse in the interior wall. Ben and Charles had chosen this gatehouse because a large two-story building stood next to it. This building easily concealed their presence until they were right at the wall's base.

Jack pulled out a rope with knots at regular intervals along its length from Ben's backpack. He found the middle, and holding out the rope's center, said, "Garthong, I need you to loop this over one of those large stone blocks on the wall. Then stay out of sight."

A little shadow crept out of the sack on Jack's back and flew up to the wall, holding the middle of the rope and positioning it as he had been instructed.

Jack secured the two ends of the rope at the wall's base, and the five started climbing quietly.

"Remember," whispered Jack, "when the guards notice us, we have six seconds to kill them, or the sounds of the skirmish will reach the other guards."

The group reached the top and moved toward the gatehouse. Jack peeked through the doorway. Four guards were on duty inside the gatehouse, standing at their watches in the building's four corners.

Jack turned back toward the group and whispered, "We can't sneak up on them, so when Ben gives the signal, we all charge."

Ben raised his hand into the air then brought it down.

The group rushed in with their weapons drawn.

Jack watched as the guard in front of him screamed and withdrew his weapon from its sheath, but no sound emanated from the guard's mouth or anything nearby. The guard drew his sword just in time to block Jack's first swing.

Jack, however, deftly drove his second sword through the guard's abdomen and threw him to the ground. Jack turned. Finding that the other guards had already been dispatched, Jack motioned for the rest of the group to follow him, leaving Ben to stay behind and hold the gatehouse.

The group ran down the gatehouse steps into the street below and began weaving through the buildings' shadows toward the keep. They paused as a patrol of eight guards walked down the street. Then the group pushed forward again. They encountered several more patrols before they reached the keep. The group watched for a few moments and determined that seven people were probably inside the keep's base.

"All right," whispered Jack, "this is your time, guys."

Charles and the two brothers rushed into the keep.

The guards drew their weapons, and one of them grabbed a hammer and struck an alarm bell that hung inside the keep entrance. They were all too slow.

Charles had already raised his hand, and no sound escaped the room.

Jack sliced through one of the guards on his way to the spiral staircase in one of the building's corners and saw no more of the battle.

On the keep's second floor, Jack glanced around and saw a dining room with a line of long tables covered in large red cloths. Rich tapestries adorned the walls, and dozens of chairs stood around the table. The room must have overflowed with beauty and luxury when in use, but now it lay shrouded in shadows since its only illumination came from the few flickering torches in the stairway.

Jack hardly noticed these sights because he was already on his way to the third story. This level had a hallway extending from the staircase. One of the keep's external walls formed the hallway's right side, and three doors stood along the left side. Jack quickly ran down the hall and peeked into each of the three rooms, but he discovered that they were only guestrooms. Each room contained a bed, a table, and a few chairs. The warlord evidently reserved these accommodations for important guests because the furniture looked very ornate and expensive.

Continuing up the stairs again to the fourth story, Jack discovered another living area that lacked the musty smell of the previous rooms and possessed a little more clutter. Jack surmised that the room had experienced more recent use. This floor looked more promising. The area opening off the stairs was wider than the similarly placed hallway on the previous floor and seemed to make a right angle turn to the left at its far end to form an L-shape. This long, narrow room provided luxurious living quarters filled with assorted ornate furniture, and purple curtains adorned the keep windows on Jack's right. An oval table supported two vases filled with various types of flowers.

Jack paused. From the floor plan of the previous story, he knew that there was a room or rooms to his left even though he could not see a door leading there. *The door to that room must be around the corner,* Jack thought.

He quietly crept up to the corner and peeked around it. At the far end of this section of the L-shaped room on the left side, he saw a single door with two guards standing in front of it. He presumed that this door must be the entrance to the warlord's bedchamber. The area in which Jack crouched was dark since the only lit torch hung on the wall next to the guards.

The guards had not yet noticed him.

Jack crept as close as he could to their right side and charged.

Both guards drew their swords.

Jack easily ran the first guard through before he could make another move.

The other guard swung his sword toward Jack.

Jack easily deflected the strike, and jerking his second sword out of the first guard, he executed three more strikes, finishing the second guard.

A Destiny Among Worlds

Jack opened the door and charged into the room.

The warlord sat up in bed, awakened by the clanging of swords. Warlord Gunda screamed, "Help!" and grabbed a sword from the table by the bed.

Jack stood still for a moment.

The warlord hesitated. "Perhaps I don't need this sword. You must be a knight rather than an assassin, so you can't kill me if I'm unarmed."

Jack took a step closer. "That's pretty much true, but I can take you into custody and haul you back to my king."

The warlord frowned. "I will not be going back with you. Any moment now, my backup will arrive, and every second that we wait is better for me."

Jack stepped over to the bed, grabbed Warlord Gunda by the arm, and hauled him toward the door.

As Jack rounded the corner of the L-shaped room and began to move back out toward the stairs, four men ran out of the stairway. They all carried swords and shields. Jack could tell that three of the men were just guards, but the fourth man's appearance indicated that he was different. This man wore a green cloak with a dark purple strip around the collar. A long piece of light gray cloth tied tightly around his waist served as a belt and draped down over his clothing.

Jack shoved Warlord Gunda to the ground and charged forward at full speed.

The man in green raised his hand, and Jack felt a tingling sensation. *Wait a second,* Jack thought, *this feels just like when I was a kid and rubbed balloons in my hair to build up static electricity.* Jack halted and formed a sheet of water in front of him, extending the liquid to touch the keep's wall.

A lightning bolt struck the water and blew a large hole in the keep's wall.

The enemy mage frowned and raised his hand again; this time a fireball leaped from his palm.

Jack swung his left hand up and created a massive air current in front of him, rocketing the fireball backward into the guards' shields.

Their shields absorbed the fire, but the shockwave effect sent the three guards and the mage flying backward. The enemy mage and one of the guards fell through the doorway into the stairwell, and Jack quickly finished the other two guards who were still in the room.

Jack heard the sound of the warlord's footfall behind him just in time. Jack jumped to the side, barely catching a glint of torchlight reflecting off a knife in the warlord's hand.

The ruler dived at Jack, but in the poor light, the warlord's foot struck one of his own table legs. Warlord Gunda pitched forward, his momentum carrying him through the hole in the keep wall. He fell, screaming.

Jack thought, *Well, so much for taking him back in custody. Unfortunately, this means that we won't discover who else was involved in the warlord's plan.* Jack turned his attention back to his remaining enemies.

Jack battled the third guard, using the stairway's narrow space to his advantage to prevent the enemy mage behind the guard from getting a shot off without hitting his own man.

Finally, the mage sneered. "I'll get you no matter what." He placed his hand directly in the center of his own guard's back. The mage shot lightning directly through the unsuspecting guard toward Jack.

Jack was surprised by his enemy's actions, but he felt the tingling sensation just in time. As the guard collapsed, Jack raised both of his swords, crossed them over each other in front of him, and blocked the strike. In the process Jack jumped backward into the room between the stairwell and the warlord's bed chamber. Jack's foot slipped on the threshold. He hit the ground hard and rolled.

Jack stood just as his adversary swung his sword at him from the right. Jack deflected the blow and stabbed with his other sword.

Jack's opponent maneuvered his shield in the weapon's path and knocked Jack's sword aside. The enemy mage pushed his shield forward, pinning down Jack's right sword arm, and repeatedly struck with his own sword.

Jack deflected the first three blows, but the fourth he only partially deflected, and his opponent's sword glanced off Jack's left shoulder. Jack grimaced with pain as he felt blood run down his arm and chest. Jack dropped to one knee, sinking below his rival's shield, and stabbed with the arm that had been pinned. He sliced the mage's left leg.

The man screamed and tried to bring his shield down on Jack's head.

Jack avoided the shield and stood up close to his foe's body. Jack placed his hand right over his adversary's heart and whispered, "Goodbye."

For a split second the enemy mage's eyes widened. Then he began convulsing and collapsed on the ground as an electric serge passed through his body and out the hole in the keep.

Jack surveyed his fallen opponent. He had never before used his lightning stone at point-blank range, but it had worked rather well. Jack searched the corpse and collected three gemstones.

Jack heard a little screech behind him as Garthong flew in through the hole in the keep's wall.

The creature attached himself to Jack's shoulder while flapping his wings excitedly.

Jack thought about sending him away again, but he was in too much of a hurry. Jack rushed down the stairs to rejoin Charles and the two brothers.

******

Charles raised his hand as he watched the guard strike the bell. *Not fair*, he thought. *Creating sound waves to block other sound waves is way harder and takes a lot more concentration than other types of magic. Ben's corrupt sound stone just automatically absorbs all sound.* Charles watched Dagder block one of the guards' attacks with his sword then bash him over the head with his shield, catching the man completely by surprise.

As the guard dropped to the floor, Dagder turned his attention to a second guard, who was running toward him.

Daggoth swung his sword at the guard ringing the bell.

The guard tried to dodge out of the way, but Daggoth's sword sliced the edge of the man's wrist.

The guard stumbled backward and tried to swing his shield at Daggoth.

Daggoth slammed his own shield against his opponent's shield and brought his sword down on the guard's head, finishing him off.

Charles assaulted the guard nearest him, swinging his battle axe down in a right to left arc.

Overtaken by Destiny

The guard jumped back out of the way then sprang forward, thrusting with his own sword.

Charles deflected the blow, grabbed the guard's shoulder with his shield hand, and shoved the man off to his right.

The guard managed to bring his hands up in time to avoid slamming into the wall, but as he turned, Charles's axe came down and severed one of his arms from his body.

Charles swung again, this time splitting the guard in half.

Charles looked around and saw that Dagder had already finished his second guard, and Daggoth had one pinned against the wall. The last guard tried to run out of the keep, but Charles made it in front of the door first and swung his axe sideways as hard as he could.

The guard brought his shield up into its path, but when Charles's axe struck the shield, it lifted the guard off the ground, hurled him through the air, and slammed him against the floor.

After Daggoth finished off his opponent, the three men fell back to the rear of the room with Dagder in front to wait for Jack's return. Several minutes passed, although to Charles it felt like several hours. They heard a loud explosion above them in the keep.

Daggoth whispered, "Get ready. That explosion will draw more enemies quickly." He stepped off to the right side of their little group.

Four guards rushed to the keep and stepped inside before they realized that the keep's base had been taken.

Dagder immediately charged toward all four.

Charles quickly followed.

Two of the guards ran back out the door while the other two tried to stand their ground.

Dagder, with surprising speed, thrust his sword forward past his opponent's shield and flicked it outward. He immediately stabbed again, running the guard through.

Charles brought his massive axe down on the other guard, smashing him into the ground. Two more direct strikes ended that fight.

Charles looked at the other two guards standing just outside the keep's entrance.

They yelled, "The keep is overrun! Sound the alarm!"

Charles rushed outside and smote one of them over the head with his axe.

Dagder slew the other.

The two rushed back into the keep.

Where is Jack? Charles thought.

Eight more guards poured in through the door followed by a man wearing gold-colored armor.

Just before Charles charged toward these new guards, the man in gold armor raised his hand.

Charles watched as a massive rock formed directly in front of the man's hand and came hurtling toward him. Charles barely managed to bring his shield up in time to place it between himself and the projectile, but he was thrown against the wall and collapsed to the floor, dazed.

Daggoth hurled a fireball at the enemy mage, but a shield of water emerged from the man's hand and absorbed the fire.

One of the guards rushed to Charles and stabbed his sword into Charles's left shoulder while he lay on the ground.

Charles grabbed the man's right leg with his other arm and hurled him against the wall while screaming in pain. Charles grabbed one of the chairs that had been around the table in the room's center and hurled it at the other guards, who deflected it with their shields.

This is bad, thought Charles. He felt blood spilling over his back. *But I've been injured before, and I know now that I can take it.* He picked up his shield and tried to hold it close to his body so that his shoulder hurt less. He moved forward toward the guards.

Dagder had slain the first guard he encountered, but four more had converged upon him and pushed him all the way back against the opposite wall.

Daggoth attempted to fend off two guards while still monitoring the enemy mage's movements.

Charles changed direction and ran straight toward the enemy mage. He knew that the man in the gold armor saw him because he raised his hand, but Charles raised his hand as well. A blinding light shone forth from Charles's hand, forcing the enemy mage to retreat.

Charles then turned and cast his fireball into the two soldiers attacking Daggoth.

Daggoth hurled a wall of ice at the man in the gold armor.

The enemy mage lifted his shield and caught most of it. He then turned and struck Charles with another boulder, hurling him into the table.

Charles lifted his head to see Daggoth cast another sheet of ice and encase three soldiers attacking his brother.

Dagder quickly finished off the last soldier and charged toward the man in the gold armor.

At that moment another guard patrol arrived, and four additional solders ran into the keep.

These new guards intercepted Dagder, leaving Daggoth to deal with the enemy mage alone.

Charles pulled his legs under himself and slowly stood, using his axe to prop himself up.

Daggoth shot a lightning bolt, hurled a sheet of ice immediately behind the lightning, and rushed toward his opponent, prepared to attack with his sword if his enemy survived.

The enemy mage created a sheet of rock in front of himself. The lightning split the stone into two parts, forcing the mage to use his shield to block the ice.

Daggoth swung his sword in a sideways arc.

The enemy mage retreated into the room's interior, exposing his back to Charles.

Charles hobbled toward the gold-armored fellow then realized what the man's plan was. Only four guards had come in with that last patrol, but there were typically eight guards to a patrol. This meant that he was holding some men outside in reserve.

Charles yelled, "Daggoth, look out behind you," but he was too late.

Four guards ran inside, and the one in the lead stabbed his sword at Daggoth's back.

Charles's warning, however, had not gone completely unheeded, and Daggoth tried to jump to the side. Despite Daggoth's dodge, the guard's sword sliced his right arm.

The mage in the gold armor raised his sword to finish off Daggoth.

Meanwhile, Dagder broke free from the guards he was fighting by jumping on top of the table. He ran across the table and leapt toward the man in the gold armor. Dagder hurled himself into the man just before the enemy mage dealt Daggoth the final blow.

The man in the gold armor turned toward Dagder as he and the enemy mage both stood to their feet. The mage raised his hand, launching a boulder into Dagder's raised shield.

Charles finally reached the enemy mage. Charles was not even carrying his shield now, just his axe. He swung the axe down while roaring as loudly as he could. The axe struck the enemy's right shoulder, splitting a generous chunk off.

Drained by the effort, Charles dropped to one knee. He looked up.

Eight functional guards remained, who were about to finish off all of them. Three of the guards raised their swords over Charles.

He closed his eyes, waiting for the last strike.

A few seconds passed.

Charles opened his eyes to see the three guards still standing before him with raised swords, but they were not moving. In fact, it was hard to see with the blood running down his forehead into his eyes, but he thought they were encased in ice. *Jack must've arrived,* he thought. He tried to focus, and sure enough, he saw Jack slicing through the last few enemies.

Jack quickly came over to where Charles knelt and looked down at him. "You're an awfully big fellow to take a break at a time like this. Come on, let's get out of here."

Jack grabbed Charles, and Dagder lifted his brother.

Jack asked, "Charles, which guy had the gemstones? Quick, we don't have much time."

Charles could not answer. His head throbbed.

Dagder pointed at the enemy mage's corpse. "There. He has them."

Jack leaned Charles against the wall and rushed over to the man. Jack quickly stood, hurried back, and grabbed Charles.

They all began to move toward the door.

"Did you get the gemstones?" asked Dagder.

"No," replied Jack. "He had them fused into his armor. It would probably take ten minutes to pry them out, and we don't have time. I did get a few from a mage upstairs, though."

Charles thought he heard alarm bells sounding from somewhere in the city. *That's not good,* he reflected, his mind feeling hazy, *the last thing we need is fifty patrols bearing down on us.*

******

For a few moments Ben watched as his friends headed toward the keep. They walked through an empty street below him between some sort of produce stand and what appeared to be a blacksmith shop. He thought, *How did I get stuck babysitting the gatehouse while everyone else gets to fight?*

Ben dragged the gatehouse guards' corpses into one of the dark corners. Then he retreated to the shadows in one of the other dark corners himself, impatiently waiting for his comrades to return. *I should've gone with Charles,* he thought. *I could have been more useful in that group.* He knew, however, that if soldiers came across their fellow guards' bodies in the gatehouse, an ambush would be waiting for Jack and his team when they returned.

Ben looked out into the night. He saw a few scattered guards patrolling on the wall, but they all stayed in their assigned areas, so none of them came near the gatehouse. Ben imagined creating a large void of light and simply throwing it along the top of the wall. He pictured the expressions on the guards' faces as they became surrounded by darkness for a few moments. *Unfortunately,* he reminded himself, *I can't waste my gemstones just for fun.* He would have to entertain himself some other way.

He pulled out the small poison-coated knife that he had found on the slaver assassin after their previous mission. Ben thought, *I need to figure out what kind of poison this is and what kind of poison is in those three bottles that I got at the same time. We'll probably go up against the slave cartels again, and it would be very helpful to know what kind of poison they might use.*

He fiddled with the knife, contemplating how he could use it with a shield. *The main problem is that with my sword in one hand and my shield in the other, I don't have a good way to use this thing. If I could come up with a way to attach the knife to the back of the shield where only I could see it, maybe I could perfect some sort of attack. Having this knife coated in poison is actually somewhat inconvenient.* He didn't like the idea of pulling it out of a sheath because he could accidently cut himself or someone else. *Without carrying an antidote to the poison, it's actually too dangerous to use.* He contemplated these ideas for some time. *Charles could probably come up with an effective way to attach the knife so that I could quickly and easily detach it from the back of the shield.*

Ben's thoughts were interrupted by the sound of a child screaming, "Let me go! Let me go! I haven't done anything wrong."

Ben stood and poked his head out of one of the gatehouse slits. Inside the second wall, three guards were clustered together. One of them dragged a boy, who looked like he was about fourteen.

One of the guards said, "Should we just throw him out where the rest of the peasants are supposed to be or kill him?"

The boy said, "Kill me? Aren't we being a little extreme here? I just wanted to see what it looked like on this side of the wall, so I sneaked in here."

A different guard crossed his arms. "I say we just kill him. I have no patience for brats like him. They just irritate me and make our job take longer."

Ben deliberated with himself, *If Jack was here, he'd probably jump down there and save that boy. But I'm not as caring as Jack. I can't jeopardize the mission just because the guards are going to kill some random kid.*

Ben sat down again. He heard the guards striking the boy repeatedly. Ben reminded himself, *I have to stick to the mission. Helping that kid could endanger the entire mission.*

About twenty seconds later Ben frowned. *Who am I kidding? Even someone as uncaring and insensitive as I am can't just let this happen.*

Ben stood and pulled his shield off his back. He gripped his sword and slipped out the side of the gatehouse. At the stairs' base, he hid behind the produce shop and peeked around its edge. The boy lay on the ground curled into a little ball, trying to keep his arms over his head. The three guards were taking turns kicking him. Ben thought, *I have to pull this off without making a sound or attracting any attention.* He emerged from behind the wall, surrounded himself in darkness, and stepped forward. *Let's see, four steps till the first guy. One, two ....* The guards became surrounded in darkness as well, and Ben could hear their confusion.

"What's happening?" asked one.

"No idea," said another. "Did something happen to the stars?"

Three and four. Ben thrust forward with his sword and felt it pierce through flesh.

The first guard let out a gurgling noise, and Ben pictured the other two looking that direction.

Ben thought, *Now one step to the right*. He swung his sword, but the guard must have moved because Ben did not hit anything. Either that, or he had miscounted the steps.

Ben heard one of the guards off to his left say, "This must be a trick by the boy to escape."

Ben stepped in that direction and swung his sword. The sword made contact with something, but Ben was not sure what.

Something hit the ground near Ben, and he heard a weak voice from below say, "This is some kind of attack. It must be magic."

Ben turned his head when he heard footsteps moving in the opposite direction. He started after the sound as the darkness lifted. Sure enough, the last guard stood right in front of him.

The guard turned his head to look over his shoulder and saw Ben. The man drew his sword and spun around.

Ben rammed his shoulder into the man's chest, knocking the guard to the ground. Ben kicked the man's flailing sword away and shoved his own sword through the man's chest. Ben then turned toward the boy on the ground. He walked over and tapped the teenager with his foot.

"You all right?" he whispered.

The boy moved his arms away from his face. "Yeah, those guards only thought they were tough; they didn't bother me a bit." As the boy stood, Ben saw a flash of pain cross his face. The boy started to reach for his side then seemed to change his mind as he forced a smile.

Ben looked up when he heard an explosion come from the keep. *Well, I guess the secrecy is all over*, he thought. He saw part of the tower wall blowing away. Ben knew that he needed to return quickly to the gatehouse. "Sorry, kid, but I've got a job to do. I suggest you make yourself scarce. This whole place is going to be crawling with soldiers in the next twenty minutes, and they'll probably want to kill just about anyone they find."

"Who are you?" asked the lad.

"It doesn't matter. All you need to know is that we are enemies of the warlord."

"So am I." The boy proudly squared his shoulders. "I'm on a scouting mission to investigate the interior of the second wall. I'm part of a group that hates the warlord's tyranny and wants freedom."

"That's great," replied Ben hurriedly. "Now, I suggest you get out of here because, like I said before, it's going to get really nasty."

Ben turned and ran up the stairs to the gatehouse, but as he turned his head, he noticed that the teen had followed him.

The boy said, "My name is Wilt."

Ben looked at him and thought, *Does this kid just not get it?*

Wilt smiled. "I don't suppose you'd mind if I go through the gate with you as my exit strategy for getting out of the interior wall. That wasn't supposed to happen until tomorrow morning, so I don't actually have another way out right now."

Ben sighed. "Fine. Just stay in the dark, don't move, and be quiet."

They heard another commotion coming from the keep. An alarm bell sounded from the same direction with other bells soon relaying the signal from various locations within the city. Ben remained perfectly silent and still. Even over the peal of the bells he thought he could detect a few soft footsteps.

Then he heard a voice call, "Hey, you in the gatehouse, double-check the gate to make sure it's secure."

For a second Ben was not sure what to do. Then he answered, "All right. I'll check."

Two men strolled into the gatehouse from the voice's direction. Ben rushed at them, ramming his sword through the first guard's throat before he even turned his head. Then Ben pulled his sword up and swung at the other guard, killing him as well.

Ben heard the boy behind him yell, "Look out!"

Ben turned to see two men standing in the opposite entrance pointing crossbows at him. Ben had not seen crossbows in this world yet, but he knew what they looked like from movies back home.

Both guards fired their crossbows.

Ben dropped his sword and shoved his right hand toward the archers. A fireball erupted from his palm. It swallowed the arrows, which collided with it as it traveled toward the men, and consumed both surprised archers.

Well, thought Ben, *there's no sense in hiding now. Anyone from anywhere near here saw that fireball. I might as well get this gate open and stop pretending.* He retrieved his sword, rushed over to the crank, and turned it to open the doors below him. As soon as they were open, Ben jammed a sword from one of the fallen guards into the crank and looked at Wilt. "Come on."

The two rushed down the gatehouse stairs, and Ben saw Jack and his team coming down the street toward him.

"Well, there you are," Ben called as they approached. "Nice to see that you kept quiet the entire mission just as you hoped."

"It couldn't be helped," Jack replied. "I ran into a mage in the warlord's chambers."

Ben asked, "Did you get the fires started here in the interior wall section?"

Jack nodded. "I did, but with the wounds that our group sustained, I didn't have much time to spread the fire around, so there's really just one fire."

Wilt's eyes opened wide. "You were in the warlord's chambers? Does that mean you killed Warlord Gunda?"

Jack looked at the teen and stated flatly, "He's dead. Who are you?"

The boy told Jack his name and began expounding upon his magnificent scouting mission.

"I don't mean to cut you short," said Jack, "but I really don't have time to listen to your tale right now. Let's just keep going."

The group exited the interior wall and headed for the nearest gatehouse in the exterior wall. "We just have to get outside that gate," said Jack, "and we're home free.

A Destiny Among Worlds

Chapter 20

THE GROUP CONTINUED TOWARD the outer wall, dodging through alleyways in an attempt to avoid the patrols. Jack glanced at his bedraggled companions. *We just have to keep going a little farther*, he thought.

Jack peered around a building's corner into a dark, empty street. "This is really odd."

"What?" asked Ben.

Jack leaned back against the building. "The guards here .... The patrols don't seem to have increased at all, but the alarm bells are sounding. In fact, it's remarkably easy to avoid the patrols. It's as if they were not actually searching for us."

Ben looked confused. "But why wouldn't they search for us?"

"I'm not sure," replied Jack.

They hid behind another group of houses, and Jack said, "I'm going to press forward just a little and take a look at the gate."

Ben put his hand on Jack's arm. "You're wounded. Let me go."

Jack nodded in consent, and Ben slid silently into the darkness.

Jack turned and looked at the two princes.

Dagder held his brother and almost constantly spoke to or gently shook him in an attempt to keep him awake.

Daggoth and Charles had both lost a great deal of blood, but Charles could hobble on his own.

A minute later Ben returned with a grim expression on his face. He looked at Jack seriously. "We're not getting out of that gatehouse, and I kind of doubt whether we're getting out of any of the gatehouses. There were at least a hundred guards. Some were in the actual gatehouse, and the rest were either on the wall or grouped on the ground nearby."

Jack shook his head. "Not a bad strategy. Rather than searching for us directly, they immediately secure the perimeter. Then they have time to sweep the city over the next few days. We're in no condition for fighting right now. At the very least we need to wait two hours for our gemstones to recover, but in reality we also need to patch up our wounds." Jack turned, looked at the boy, who remained with them, and said, "Wilt, wasn't it?"

The boy looked up at him and nodded.

Jack placed a hand on Wilt's shoulder. "You mentioned something about a scouting mission. Does that mean you're part of a group?"

The boy again nodded excitedly and pulled himself to his full height. "We are the underground resistance."

"Do you think the underground would be willing to hide a few people until tomorrow night?"

The boy nodded vigorously. "Of course. It would be our honor to hide mages who fight against our enemy. Come, I will show you the nearest hideout." The boy turned and rushed down another alley with Jack's group trying to keep up with him.

Jack reached out to steady Charles and winced as pain shot down his arm due to his own wound.

As they traveled, Jack saw torchlight moving along the various streets around them. He whispered, "This isn't good. Warlord Gunda may have been the target, but someone else here is giving the orders now. In fact, they may have been the brains behind the whole thing all along. These guards are searching in grid patterns, which frankly, is a more advanced tactic than I would've expected from most of the people we've fought so far. Whoever is here must be a strategist from one of the cartels or one of the stronger nations in the south. They must have been using this warlord as a way to secretly spread their influence. The king must have suspected that the warlord was just a puppet, but neither the king of Celel nor I expected the puppet master to be here in the city."

For a moment Jack contemplated staying and hunting the real commander, but he knew that they were in no state to carry out such a mission. *I'll try to gather some information from the underground on who might actually be pulling the strings around here,* he thought.

A few minutes later they came to a cottage that resembled every other house they had seen in the city's lower-class section. Stone columns supported the house's four corners. Wood planks formed the walls, and it had a thatched roof.

"Here." Wilt abruptly halted and slipped inside the house.

Jack and his friends entered behind him.

Jack was a little surprised to find that the house appeared abandoned. He noticed fire damage along one wall. The only furniture that remained in the house was a fire-scorched table in the middle of the room and a broken chair in one corner.

Wilt walked over to and moved the table before stomping three times on the floor.

Jack heard a scraping noise followed by the sound of something heavy moving, and a trap door opened into the floor.

Wilt skillfully lowered himself inside and whispered, "Come on," as he disappeared.

Jack helped Dagder lower his brother through the hole, and Ben and Jack lowered Charles after him.

Jack went next. When he reached the bottom, Jack realized that he stood in an underground tunnel.

Several men crowded around them with weapons drawn and pointed at them.

"Who are these strangers you brought into our tunnels?" one of the men asked, directing a cold stare toward Wilt.

The speaker, who stood immediately in front of Jack, was a bald, heavyset man, and he carried a one-handed battle axe with his shield like Charles. The bald man had a thick beard and a short, thick nose that sat above a bushy mustache. The other two men behind him were of average height and build and seemed a little anxious about having visitors. The first man appeared angrier than he was anxious. He grabbed Wilt by the collar and repeated his question.

"Please, pardon our intrusion." Jack held his open hands loosely in front of him to show that they held no weapons. "We are from the powerful northern kingdoms, and we came here to carry out a mission. Rest assured, we are on your side in resisting the corrupt rulers here."

For a moment the bald man seemed unsatisfied. Finally, he relaxed. "I am Waldun, Wilt's father. Apparently, he told you that we are the underground and showed you where our hideout is. I'm not sure what you did to earn his trust, but even I can tell that you made a huge ruckus up on the surface. What exactly was your mission?"

Jack replied, "Warlord Gunda has been conspiring to unite the slave cartels and the three mighty southern nations together against the three powerful northern nations. Our mission was to stop Warlord Gunda, which has been done. Unfortunately, he died in the process, which means that we won't know if he worked alone or not. It now appears to me that another individual actually controlled the warlord."

Waldun raised an eyebrow. "Well, if you killed the warlord, at the very least it should improve things for a little while around here." He rested his chin on his hand. "Some strange people did arrive a few months back. They seemed to move into the interior wall section almost immediately upon arrival. We haven't seen or heard about any of these people since that day, but they certainly didn't leave by normal means, or we would have spotted them."

"I see," replied Jack. "I fear that our mission may have only delayed the inevitable. As long as the man pulling the strings exists, they will find another puppet to whom they can attach their strings."

"Regardless," Waldun said, "it looks like you and your friends need your wounds tended. We have a healer who can assist. Follow me please."

The group walked along the hallway as one of Waldun's men reached out of the tunnel entrance to reposition the table before closing the trapdoor. Jack observed that most of the passageway was dark with torches placed only at certain intervals. Jack and Waldun carried torches to help light the way. The ceiling was high enough for Jack to stand to his full height in most places. As they continued, the passageway opened up into an underground room. The room was large enough for probably five of the cottages that they had seen on the surface to fit inside it. Jack was surprised to find that the room contained approximately thirty people.

Waldun called a young man over to him. "Go get your grandfather; tell him I need his healing skills."

The boy dipped his head and ran into a side passage.

As Waldun gave a few more instructions to other underground members, Jack cast his gaze around the room. The ceiling was smooth and rounded as though the room had been dug out of the earth. *Interesting,* Jack thought, *this place was created by humans at some point.* Along the walls the rock had been cut away in several places, leaving flat stone slabs that served as seats. A solid stone table also rested in the room's center.

Waldun gestured toward one of the flat rock slabs along the wall. "Please sit, and if you're not bound by too much secrecy, tell me more about your mission."

Jack recounted their scouting trip and plan and explained how it had gone awry when the mage in green found him in the warlord's quarters.

Before Jack could finish his story, Wilt spoke up and added the part about how Ben had heroically saved him.

Waldun nodded his head in gratitude toward Ben before turning back to Jack. "The mages you described encountering are more powerful than any I have heard of existing in this kingdom. I suspect that they came with the true leader you mentioned."

An old man appeared, accompanied by the boy Waldun had sent to fetch him and a young woman. These three began tending to the group's wounds.

"Thank you for hiding us," Jack said to Waldun. "By tomorrow night we should be able to fight our way out of the city if all goes well."

"Good," Waldun replied. "I've already made preparations to leave evidence that you stayed in a particular building on the surface, so you should start from that point and make your escape from there."

Jack smiled. "I see. So you keep them from discovering your underground tunnels by leaving false evidence in different locations whenever they search for you."

"Yes. It's actually very convenient. No matter how thoroughly they search, they fail to find us. Then we leave evidence of whatever they're searching for in a random place. Whichever guards were in charge of searching that area are usually punished for not having found us. For the most part we lie very low, so they rarely search for anyone. This strategy has worked well so far."

A Destiny Among Worlds

"It's a good plan," said Jack, "but be careful. Whoever is pulling the strings now is far smarter than Warlord Gunda."

Waldun nodded gravely and excused himself to attend to some other important matters.

Dagder approached Jack a little hesitantly. "You said that you did get a couple of gemstones from the mage in the upper tower, is that right?"

"Yes, I did, and it would be beneficial for us to awaken these stones now so we can use them in our escape." Jack extended his hand with the three gemstones resting in his palm. "I have two lightning stones and a fire stone. Choose one of them."

Dagder reached out his hand, but just before he touched the gemstones, he paused.

Seeing his hesitation, Daggoth weakly placed his hand on his younger brother's shoulder. "Go ahead. Technically, this doesn't even break the law our father made, because he's not a member of our country. Besides, this needed to happen a long time ago. I don't know why Father made the choices he did, but I don't want them to separate us anymore."

Dagder grabbed the red fire stone. "I think I'll use this one. Fire is popular in our kingdom."

"Good. Also, take this." Jack extended his other hand. "It's a translation stone. You'll need it to awaken your fire stone." He handed Dagder the green stone that he had obtained from Keljerk the Cruel.

"Now, sit back, both of you," Jack continued, "I need to tell you a story. Please double-check the story when you return home. It should be easy; I found it in the library the first time I visited your kingdom.

"Long ago when your grandfather ruled Dulla, he had three sons, and he was proud of them all. Dulla was not as powerful then, partly because your father had not yet conquered much of the land around it and partly because the kingdom of Celel was a small territory at that time. All three of the sons fought in many battles and were accomplished swordsman. They all became powerful mages as well. When your grandfather died, your father, as the oldest, became the new king.

"On the day that he was crowned, two armies appeared inside the capital city of Duthwania. The two younger brothers were afraid that they would lose their power when their older brother became king, and they had secretly brought their armies inside the city walls. When your father was crowned king, they attacked. When the battle began, both younger brothers attacked your father, accusing him of attempting to remove them from their governorships. That day your father slew both of his brothers by his own hand. Once they were dead, the fire for rebellion fizzled out."

Dagder whispered, "Father had to kill his own brothers himself?"

"Unfortunately," Jack continued, "I could not find anything in the historical records that expressed your father's opinion about what happened. However, the fact that he did not give you, Dagder, any gemstones but gave you a political position at the capital instead of governorship over a powerful city inside Dulla, suggests that your father was very concerned about a similar struggle happening between you two.

"I personally disagree with his choice because it's a father's duty to believe in his sons and teach them to make the right choices. I suspect that he never wanted you, Daggoth, to have to go through what he went through that day, and he wanted you, Dagder, to live in peace and have the long life that his brothers never could. I'm sorry, but I have no more to tell you. If you wish to know more, you'll have to ask your father."

After a long silence Dagder said, "I can't believe I've never heard any mention of this story. I didn't even know that I had two uncles. To think that all this happened before I was even born."

Daggoth added, "The pain he must have gone through that day when he had to slay his own brothers is unthinkable."

Dagder turned to his brother and said, "Daggoth, I'm sorry for treating you like an enemy instead of as a brother. Maybe Father was right to take steps to prevent me from turning out like my uncles; perhaps he saw how much I envied you."

Daggoth shook his head. "No, Brother, you were always the better swordsman. It was always I who envied you. That's why I was so proud when I became a mage, and you didn't. I'm sorry for being happy about your misfortune. I'll teach you how to use your gemstone. Together we will grow stronger and protect our kingdom, for we were both born of a king's bloodline."

Jack commented, "It may take you a few weeks to master the tongue of angels well enough to awaken that stone, but I wish you all the speed I can. I'm glad that in some small way I was able to contribute to bringing the two of you together."

They both thanked Jack, and Dagder helped his brother over to a mat, where he could lie down and his wound could receive additional attention.

When the old man and his assistants finished treating their wounds, the group went to sleep to recuperate before their escape on the morrow.

******

The next afternoon Jack awoke to a shrill scream. He immediately bolted up, drew his swords, and looked around him. A few people were scattered around the room, and all of them stared at him. Jack looked to his right and saw a girl of about fourteen standing with her hands over her mouth and eyes wide with fear. *That's weird*, thought Jack. *She's looking at me.* Then he felt several soft feet upon his shoulder.

Jack rolled his eyes and sheathed his swords. "I see that you've met Garthong. He won't hurt you. Is there anything I can do for you?"

Garthong slipped back into his sack and poked out his head.

"I'm sorry," she said, regaining her composure. "Waldun sent me to wake your party and inform you that now is the time to prepare for your escape."

Ben rolled over. "He apparently picked the right person; you woke us all up almost instantly with that scream."

"If you'll please follow me, I will take you to Waldun," she said, ignoring Ben's comment.

The group rose and followed the girl through a tunnel, which eventually opened into another well-lit room. Waldun and several other men huddled around a table in the room's center with serious expressions on their faces. Jack noticed maps spread out on the table and walked over to join the group.

"None of you look particularly thrilled," Jack observed.

"No," replied Waldun. "The number of soldiers at the gates is astronomical. I didn't even know that there were this many guards in the city."

"Indeed," Jack replied thoughtfully. "This city has received reinforcements for their garrison from somewhere, but we'll have to devise a way to escape despite the numbers. Even though our gemstones have recovered, many of us, including myself, are still wounded and will not perform at our best as swordsman. A full head-on fight is out of the question."

Waldun searched Jack's face. "What are you suggesting then?"

Jack smiled. "Where I come from, there is an old book that mentions a man escaping from a walled city by being lowered down the side of the wall in a basket. I believe it would be much easier to take a section of wall between two towers than a gatehouse. We could potentially even clear the towers on both sides. I doubt there will be more than ten guards in either tower and probably about four on the wall."

Waldun looked at the map. "Indeed, that is not a bad plan if we can find ropes for each of you. We will need to lower all five of you at the same time in order to achieve maximum speed. Once it's done, we can simply disappear back into the city, and you can escape."

"Perfect," said Jack. "I presume you can have the necessary materials by tonight?"

"Yes, that shouldn't be a problem. I'll gather enough people to quickly and safely lower you all simultaneously."

Jack and his friends returned to the main room in which they had slept, and Ben and Charles began awakening their lightning stones.

Jack watched his friends for a moment. "Please tell me that you have both studied the book well enough to have those awakened by tonight."

Charles grinned. "I've actually spent a good bit of time reading about the stones that all of us possess, so I think I've got this."

Ben added, "Yeah, I think so too."

Jack surveyed the room taking in Ben and Charles still working hard on their gemstones and the two brothers talking happily. *This is actually great*, thought Jack. *Very little has really gone as planned, but assuming we get out of the city, both missions will still be successful.* Jack glanced to his left and saw Wilt coming toward him.

The boy halted in front of Jack and looked up at him. "Do you think we will ever become free?"

"Maybe. In my experience as long as people have strong hearts and hope, many things are possible." Jack thought for a moment and added, "But why ask me?"

"I don't know." Wilt shrugged and a thoughtful look passed over his young face. "Maybe I'm just searching for hope. We have been in the underground for as long as I can remember and, according to the men here, much longer than that. In all that time we've never struck a serious blow against the warlord. We hid here in our tunnels and longed for the day when we would have a chance to change things. But then you came, and you changed so much in just one day."

Jack replied sadly, "I doubt that I've changed very much at all. The oppression from a new warlord will probably continue after I'm gone, but perhaps one day I will return, and if I do, maybe I can change things for the better. From what I've seen, much of this whole world is full of evil, and I long for the opportunity to change it."

Wilt asked seriously, "Will you promise to return one day, and free everyone in the city?"

"You think a great deal of me." Jack allowed himself a small smile. "All I am is just one person with a couple of friends. I don't even know if I can make a difference here, but what I will promise you is that if I can make a difference, I will."

The boy smiled and wandered off.

Jack added silently, *I will make a difference if it takes my dying breath.*

Time passed until nightfall arrived, and the group set out for the section of the wall that they had selected as their target.

******

General Dulcapa, atop a black horse, slowly moved in front of the ranks stationed at Gattel's east gatehouse, performing his troop inspection. *These troops,* he thought, *are barely worthy of an inspection. My hardcore soldiers fight like real men, but these city guards are weak and unskilled. It's no wonder some enemy was able to fight right through to the keep and kill Gunda. The whole city of Gattel is a joke. The only reason I chose the country of Gidanna was because it is directly above Jofna.* His reflections continued, *I'm still amazed that they killed the warlord here. Whoever these people were, they must be from Celel. Even still, my spies gave no warning that a mission was underway, and I can't imagine the lords of King Tanner's court approving such a risky mission or any of the knights being willing to accept it.* Dulcapa contemplated still further, *And the plan used was very ingenious. I don't usually think of Knights of Celel specializing in covert missions; they're usually very flashy and certainly not stealthy.* He waved his hand to signal that the troops in front of him had passed inspection.

General Dulcapa was a towering man bearing a powerful presence that intimidated everyone around him. He typically wore a cruel expression on his face with his thin lips pressed together in a tight line on his clean-shaven face and his piercing, brown eyes shifting suspiciously around him. The pale moonlight reflected off of his polished, silver-colored armor. His commanding attitude combined with his height made him an imposing figure in the darkness.

Four mage guards, also astride black horses, traveled behind him as the general moved on toward the northern gatehouse.

General Dulcapa thought, *The northern gatehouse is the one that I would expect a normal Knight of Celel to attack because it's the most convenient one if they're heading back to their own country, but the cunning man in charge of this mission probably won't attack this gatehouse for the exact same reason. He knows that it will probably be the strongest.*

General Dulcapa arrived at the northern gatehouse and began surveying the troops. Again, he walked his horse in front of the soldiers, but his mind remained on his opponent. *I have this nagging feeling that, whoever this person is, he's smarter than anyone I have faced in a long time, and he will probably try something unexpected.*

******

When Jack and his friends reached the shadows at the wall's base, Waldun said, "My men will secure the ropes and lower you. If you're going to clear the towers, I suggest you do it now."

Jack looked over at Ben. "How long can you hold your sphere of darkness?"

"I've been working on it pretty hard, and I think I can pull about eight seconds." Ben rubbed his hands together in anticipation. "Why? What were you thinking?"

"I don't think we need to clear the towers." Jack pointed at the sky. "Look, the moon is small, and it's cloudy. If we take out the guards on the wall, I think that will be good enough, and it would be much safer."

Jack relayed his new plan to Waldun, and Jack and his friends stealthily made their way up the stairs leading to the top of the wall.

Once there, Jack glanced out toward the open fields beyond the wall and saw a dark mass in the distance, which he recognized as a forest. He glanced over his shoulder toward the town and noted the dark little buildings laid out below him and the small bobbing lights from the guard patrols in the street. Each gatehouse held so many torches that they looked like beacons.

Jack and his friends crept along the top of the wall and moved near the guards stationed upon it. There were actually six guards, which was more than Jack had expected. It did not really matter, though.

Ben activated his corrupt sound stone, and they crept up behind the guards.

Just as Jack and his friends were about to pounce, the guards all exchanged confused looks.

Jack realized that they had been having a conversation. *That's right*, he thought. *Ben's corrupt sound stone sucks in all sound, which means they can't hear each other talking.*

The guards suddenly noticed Jack and his friends. They tried to draw their swords, but Jack leapt forward and ran the first one through so quickly that he did not even free his sword from its scabbard.

The attackers quickly dealt with the rest of the guards.

Jack and his friends crouched quietly for a moment.

Jack said, "That took longer than I expected. Ben, did your stone continue working that entire time? I didn't hear any sound escape."

Ben replied, "It quit working before we were done. It took us about twelve seconds in all."

"Don't worry, guys," said Charles. "I figured out what happened and activated my sound stone as soon as I heard the first noise. I prevented all the unwanted noises from escaping toward the towers."

"Good thinking," Jack said, waving his hand to signal that they were ready.

Wilt stepped out of the darkness on the wall and handed them their ropes.

"All right," whispered Jack. "Everybody ready?"

They all nodded, and the five of them began their decent down the wall as Waldun's crew steadily lowered them from the opposite side. Even with their wounds closed, Daggoth and Charles were still too weak to hold the rope reliably, so they sat in rope slings while being lowered.

The moonlight reflected off the pale wall, but Ben activated his corrupt light stone to conceal them from the guards on the towers

******

General Dulcapa glanced over his shoulder at his mage guards. "None of you found any other possible way out of the city other than the gatehouses, correct?"

"That's right," replied one of the mages. "According to all of our information, there were fewer than a dozen assassins, and any other way out of the city would require more than that."

Dulcapa, annoyed by the man's confidence, said, "Go ahead and reinforce the walls and towers with a few extra guards, and have someone check on the guards along the interior wall and in the interior gatehouses. If those men are not vigilant, our adversaries may attempt a second attack to distract us and facilitate an escape."

Two of the mages immediately wheeled their horses and trotted off into the darkness to carry out his orders.

******

Ben's stone ran out of time just as they reached the bottom of the wall. They let go of the ropes and jumped the rest of the way. They crept stealthily across the field, but Jack heard one of the men in the tower on their left shout and knew that they had been seen. The five fugitives started running as quickly as they could across the field toward the hill on the tree line, where they had left their horses.

******

General Dulcapa heard a shout, and the alarm began to sound. He looked in the direction of the shout and thought, *That's coming from one of the walls. How could these men escape over the wall? Regardless, they'll be heading north.*

He immediately ordered a portion of the soldiers to form up and ordered the north gate to be opened. The soldiers filed out quickly, and the general followed with his guards.

******

For a few minutes the archers tried to shoot Jack and his friends with arrows through the darkness, but they never came anywhere close, and the escapees safely reached the hill, where they had left their supplies. They stopped to breathe for a moment.

Jack said, "The danger in being seen isn't really for us; it's for the men inside the city who lowered us. I hope the guards were so obsessed with us on the outside that they didn't look inside."

Jack looked down at the gatehouse as the others quickly saddled the horses. He could see a dark mass emerging from the gate with a few spots of light mixed in here and there. "They seem to be pursuing us," Jack observed.

******

As they exited the gatehouse, the general thought, *At this point I doubt we're going to catch them. They doubtless have some kind of escape plan already worked out, and we don't have enough mounted men to pursue them immediately, but I want to get a look at these men.* He reached out his hand, and light spilled forth. The fields lit up, and seeing a hill in front of him on the tree line past the range of accurate bow shot, the general cast light toward it.

******

Jack watched as a bright light suddenly shone from the soldiers marching out of the gate, and Jack could see them all as clearly as if the sun had risen. Jack guessed that the mage creating the light must have a greater light stone since the entire area was bathed in light. Jack identified the point from which the light originated, and at that location he saw a man looking back in his direction. Because of the distance it was difficult to clearly distinguish the man's features, but he wore shining silver armor and sat atop a black horse. Jack could not shake the eerie feeling produced by that man's bearing. He thought, *Somehow I just know that this man is the mastermind behind this whole thing.*

******

As the light splashed over the hill, General Dulcapa saw several figures saddling and mounting horses with one individual standing stationary on the ground looking back at him. *That would be my rival,* thought Dulcapa, *the one who wants to get a look at me just as badly as I want to get a look at him.*

The general saw the figure spring lightly onto his horse, and the entire group rode into the trees. *How interesting. From the way he moves, I would guess that he's young. We will meet again,* the general declared silently. *There is a war coming, boy, and you're going to learn how nasty it can be when inexperienced boys fight wars with men.*

A messenger arrived and reported, "Sir, it appears as though the assassins were lowered down the wall with ropes."

"So they *did* have help." The general coldly eyed the mage guard nearest him. "Very well. I doubt it will take me more than a few months to place another puppet warlord over the city. When I do, my plan will resume exactly as though it had never been interrupted. After I get my plan back up and running, I think I will have to hunt down some of those annoying peasants who helped my enemies escape and make an example of them. It's not really that big of a deal," he added in a sarcastic tone with a little shrug. "I was going to hunt them down anyway. They've just annoyed me a little more than normal today."

The general began barking orders, and soldiers ran in all directions, trying to accommodate his wishes. The general pulled out some parchment and wrote a letter describing the delay. He called a messenger to him. "Take this down south; just follow this map, and it will take you to the man to whom you are to deliver this."

The messenger nodded, jumped onto a horse, and rode into the darkness.

The general smiled to himself and thought, *I guess I'll have to deal with at least one somewhat formidable opponent in this war after all, but it's not as if the overall outcome will change. Plans are already in motion that will make it impossible for the north to win this war.* The general wheeled his horse and rode toward the keep.

One of his mage guards called, "My lord, don't you want to pursue the escaping men?"

The general replied without turning, "Not really. There's no way we would catch them by tracking their horses through a forest in the middle of the night."

His guards nodded and turned their horses to follow their master.

Chapter 21

JACK AND HIS FRIENDS rode their horses as fast as they dared back to Dulla's border. Once they reached the border, they eased their pace. Jack felt confident that the enemy would not risk pursuing them into one of the three great northern nations.

After the two princes parted company with Jack and his two friends and headed toward their own capital, Charles turned to Jack. "So what's bothering you?"

"What do you mean?" Jack replied.

Charles stroked his tired mount's neck. "You've been really quiet ever since we left Gidanna. Both of our missions were successful, so what are you so unhappy about?"

"I'm unhappy about the *way* the mission was accomplished," said Jack.

"Why?" Charles pressed.

"Until now we've always saved and helped people, but we didn't stop the mastermind. We only stopped a puppet, which will only delay our enemies' overall plans. Those people in the underground will most likely be discovered because of what they did to help us. We may have helped people across the world by delaying this war, but we didn't help people in that city. In fact, they will probably be even worse off than they were before we came."

"You're right," replied Charles. "I hadn't thought of it that way."

"From a strategic or intellectual point of view," Jack continued, "this mission was incredibly important, but I can't stop thinking about the people we left in that town. Besides, we didn't even capture the puppet since he died, so we don't have any details on the mastermind's plans."

Ben countered, "But it's possible that without the puppet the mastermind may choose a different city, or he may leave for a time. We also don't actually know that the underground people will be discovered."

"You're right." Jack sighed. "Many possible things could come out of what we did, but we didn't go to Gattel specifically to help people, and we didn't actually help people there. I feel sorry for the people in that city, and it grieves me that we couldn't do anything to help them. Isn't that what we decided to do when we came into this world? We didn't just decide that we would get home; we also decided to try to make a difference. I feel as though I may have let my own personal ambition take precedence on this mission. This was more about impressing the king so that we could get home than it was about helping people, and I didn't realize it until now. After all, the point of life is to be able to make a difference. Isn't that why we are helping everyone that we can in this world?"

His two friends nodded, and they continued on in silence for a while.

Ben finally broke the silence by saying, "Well, we made a difference for those two brothers, and even if we didn't directly help the underground in Gattel, we gave them strength, courage, and a chance to fight for what they believe in. That being said, maybe we'll get a chance to help them even more sometime in the future, and until we return, it's their job to stay alive."

Jack smiled. "I'm sorry. I didn't mean to be all gloomy, guys."

Ben changed the subject saying, "We need to come up with a good cover story for what we've been doing to tell Sir Alter." He paused for a moment to think then snapped his fingers. "We could tell him that we were gambling, and it took us a while to get our money back after we lost it all."

Charles turned to Ben wide-eyed and open-mouthed. He replied indignantly, "What on earth would we be doing gambling? That story implies that we were so irresponsible that we lost all of our money."

Jack grinned. "I think we'll go with a different cover story, Ben."

Ben shifted his weight in his saddle. "I think we should say that we traveled around Celel's southern border and found a good place to practice using our gemstones, so we stayed there for a while. Then we met a few friends and decided to hang out with them as well."

Charles glanced at Jack. "I suppose we did travel south, and we did meet some friends, and we did practice with our gemstones. I guess that is truthful in a vague fashion."

Jack thought for a moment. "I wonder how much trouble we would get into for telling him the truth."

"I don't know," replied Charles. "He didn't tell us *not* to go on the missions. Technically, the king wanted someone to go, and no one said that we *couldn't*, so it might be worth a shot."

Jack stated, "Well, it may be a little hard to hide the fact that we were wounded. Besides, he would probably hear about what happened and figure it out eventually."

Charles nodded in agreement.

"Fine," replied Ben, "but you guys take the fun out of everything. Imagine the incredibly cool story we could've come up with."

Jack smiled again. "Do you really think we could've come up with a story more unbelievable than the truth in this instance?"

All three of them thought about it and shook their heads.

They periodically practiced using their gemstones on their more leisurely trip back to the Celshen estate since they felt safer after crossing the border into Dulla and then Celel.

After one practice session Charles observed, "I discovered a fascinating thing about lightning. It's the only spell that we can't seem to control after we cast it. I think that's because the lightning travels so fast that we can't mentally affect it. Since electricity naturally goes to ground, however, we can actually manipulate it somewhat *before* we cast it. I've noticed that when I cast my lightning bolt, I mentally pick a target and a path for the lightning to take before I even fire the lightning. If something unexpectedly interrupts the path I've chosen, like a shield, then the lightning immediately takes the shortest path to ground.

"When a mage picks you as a target, electricity that the mage is accumulating near his hand must become either negatively or positively charged, and the target—in this case, you—becomes oppositely charged. The mage creates a mental conduit between the two locations for the electrical charge to travel along. That must be why you feel the tingling sensation when someone is about to strike you with a lightning bolt. That sensation is also the only way you can successfully block the lightning because you have a moment of realization before the lightning actually starts to travel."

Jack thought for a moment. "That means we can become much more skilled with our lightning because, with practice, we can pick a target and make it charged but at the last second choose a path that doesn't necessarily have to be straight."

"That's kind of cool," Ben interjected. "That means if I get skilled enough with my lightning, I could almost use it like a heat-seeking missile."

Charles laughed. "The analogy is a good one, but the physics are completely different."

"I know," said Ben, "but it sounds way better."

Charles added, "Lightning is an ideal weapon for accuracy and precision, and we haven't even scratched the surface of its potential."

Jack nodded thoughtfully. "I think that's actually the case with all of our gemstones. We should try to think of other creative ideas to experiment with."

The remainder of the trip back to the Celshen estate was relatively uneventful.

When they arrived, Sir Aldric stated enthusiastically, "You're back!"

"Yes." Jack casually adjusted Garthong's backpack on his shoulders. "How have things been around here?"

The old knight replied, "Things were fairly calm at first, but several very important international incidents have surprised many people in the country. Apparently, someone killed Warlord Gunda, and even more importantly, someone kidnapped both of the princes of Dulla."

Before the old knight could continue his long description of all that had taken place, there was a knock at the door.

Lilen answered it, and Sir Alter entered.

Jack noted that the knight looked as serious and stern as ever. Jack asked, "So did you have someone watching the estate waiting for us to return?"

"Of course I did," snapped Sir Alter. "I wanted to make sure I was here the moment you returned."

Jack mumbled, "I was being sarcastic."

"What do you think you crazy kids were doing kidnapping foreign princes and killing enemy warlords?" Sir Alter demanded.

Jack thought, *Good thing we decided to go with the truth since he already knows.* "Well," he said aloud, "the king did request that those two missions be performed, and since no one else wanted to go, we decided to take the initiative. In our defense, the warlord died accidentally; we didn't actually kill him."

The knight placed his hands on his hips and let his eyes bore into Jack. "Are you crazy? Kidnapping foreign princes was never part of the plan. The entire capital is in a frenzy. Half of them want your heads on pikes, and the other half want to knight you immediately."

Jack shrugged. "We don't really care what the people in the capital want. Just tell us what the king thinks about our actions."

Sir Alter narrowed his eyes. "King Tanner has given no comment at all so far. Apparently, he is considering the matter."

"That's disappointing," said Jack. "I knew everybody else would split down the middle, but I expected the king to be rather thrilled that someone fulfilled his desire to carry out these missions."

Sir Alter sighed. "Well, we need to try to rectify the situation immediately. I've already spoken to several important individuals, and some of them may be willing to change their minds about you in exchange for a few favors."

Ben grinned. "That does sound like some honest politics."

Jack added, "Indeed, I'm not sure we want to do favors in exchange for support in this matter."

Sir Alter laid his hand against his face, closed his eyes, and shook his head. "The governor of Juma has graciously offered to support you in this matter if we take care of a problem he's having in the Great Northern Mountains. I cannot stress how important it is to win his support since your representing family is from his province."

Jack replied, "We're foreigners, and that creep has despised us since the moment we arrived in this country."

The knight countered in a measured tone, "Which is all the more reason to gain his support now while you have the chance. If you can change his mind about you, it could be extremely beneficial later."

Ben shrugged.

Charles nodded.

Jack sighed. "That makes sense, and if we can make him a friend instead of an enemy, it would be better. Fine, what's his favor?"

Sir Alter said, "There was supposedly a very powerful gemstone-studded sword that was carried by a mage in ages past. The governor wants us to find the sword in the legend. The mage is said to have died deep in the Great Northern Mountains, and many people have searched for the sword, but all have failed to find it. The governor claims to have discovered a map that leads to the mage's last camp.

"Because it will soon be the end of summer, this is the perfect time to search. You see, the Great Northern Mountains are always covered in snow, and the rivers that flow there are always covered in ice, but in the winter journeying into the mountains is far too treacherous. In the summer the ice on the rivers will be thick enough that we can walk across it but thin enough that we can easily puncture through it to access water. There will also be game that we can hunt during the summer. This will be a several week long trip through the cold, but if we find this sword, you will receive not only the governor's support but also great fame for accomplishing what so many have failed to do."

Jack asked, "Are you coming with us on this mission?"

Sir Alter nodded. "The four of us will go together since the king does not currently need me. We leave in three days. I will be back then with the map and a guide provided by the governor to take us through the mountains."

"That sounds good," said Jack. "We'll be ready."

After Sir Alter left, Sir Aldric continued telling the boys about all of the important events that had taken place in their absence. Jack paid little attention, however, to the old knight's report on all of the political problems supposedly occurring at the capital.

Vennel walked through the front door in the middle of one of Sir Aldric's stories. She seemed pleased that they had all returned safely, but Jack thought her eyes sparkled a little when she saw Charles. She silently greeted the group and listened attentively.

Garthong climbed out of his sack and lay on Jack's shoulder to sleep.

The group eventually dispersed, leaving Jack and the old knight alone.

Sir Aldric's monotonous discourse continued. Apparently, the governor of Juma had recently denounced some knight Jack had never heard of as a traitor, and everyone in the capital debated whether the evidence the governor had produced was substantial enough to warrant an execution. Jack's eyelids grew heavy as Sir Aldric continued the narrative. The knight was apparently convicted in his own province, but he had appealed his case all the way up to the palace. Rumors said that if he were found guilty again, the king might hear his case personally because the king had nominated this particular person for knighthood himself several years ago. If the accused knight were found guilty, it would be very embarrassing for the crown.

A knock at the door interrupted the retired knight's droning.

As Lilen opened the door, Jack curiously glanced over his shoulder to see who stood outside. Jack did not recognize the young man, but he was a tall, handsome fellow with brown hair and a flashy smile.

The old knight stood. "Ah, Elfond. It is good to see you. Zannel is out back with her mother."

The young man nodded in respect and continued through the room toward the back door.

Jack inquired, "Who was that?"

Sir Aldric explained, "Well, I had to cancel Zannel's engagement to Vanzantel, so I invited Elfond of the Entell family to begin calling at my house in an attempt to win my fair daughter's heart."

Jack asked, "What do you know about this guy?"

The old knight thought for a moment. "His family is very powerful and influential, and the young man is a knight-in-training like you. His father is in charge of army provisions, which makes him very important during wartime. Because Celel has not had a major war for a long time, it's now more of a ceremonial position that conveys the king's confidence in him. If I ever want to get back into the king's conference room, I will need something very big to help me get there."

Jack thought, *The last guy you picked for your daughter purely for political reasons turned out to be a thief. Perhaps you should let her choose a suitor for herself or pick someone for nonpolitical reasons.* Then he reminded himself sadly, *It's not my job to fix my representing family's problems unless they ask me to help.*

Sir Aldric suddenly changed the subject, "By the way, there's an elderly man staying in town who claims to be an old friend of yours. He hoped that you would stop by when you returned."

Jack thought, *An old friend?* Then he remembered Elton. Jack asked, "Was his name Elton?"

The retired knight crinkled one eye closed and turned his gaze toward the ceiling. "I think it was."

Jack respectfully asked to be excused and rushed to town. When he arrived, he found Elton with his merchant caravan.

The old man smiled as Jack approached. "Well, have you gotten into any trouble lately?"

Jack nodded and grinned. "I've been doing my best." Jack gave the old man a hug. For some reason Jack had missed the elderly man a lot more than he had expected. "It's good to see you again. You must stay at the Celshen estate with us for the next two days. We have another mission after that, so we'll be gone for a while, but we would love to have a chance to catch up with you until then."

The old man nodded in consent. "I would be thrilled, but you must tell me of your adventures."

Jack replied, "First, I have a question for you. I want to ask you now since it's just the two of us. We met a girl named Vennel on our travels, and she didn't have anywhere else to go, so she came to Celel with us. Charles has also developed a fondness for this girl."

Elton nodded. "I see, but if I recall correctly, you boys are trying to get home."

Jack sighed. "Yes, we are."

Elton inquired, "Is your home someplace to which you could take this girl when you leave?"

Jack shook his head sadly. "I don't know. Our home is very different, and it would be extremely hard for someone to adapt. On the other hand, she doesn't have anyone in this world. None of us actually told her that we are from another world, but I think she knows that we plan to leave. She just doesn't know that she isn't coming with us. We would also like for her to be cared for if something happened to us here before we leave." Jack settled comfortably on the edge of Elton's cart. "She's an ex-slave like you, and she has experience buying and selling goods. I thought maybe you could offer her a job in your caravan. I would be happy to provide the collateral needed to expand your business in order for you to support an employee."

Elton scratched his chin thoughtfully. "It sounds like Charles needs to decide how he feels before you leave. If he truly cares about this girl, he could stay in this world or take her back with him."

Jack nodded. "Charles also needs to find out how she feels, although I kind of suspect that she shares his affection."

"If the two of them decide that it would be better for her to stay in this world alone," Elton said, "I'm sure I could use a hand in the business. You need not worry about her if you leave. She has a place here."

Jack was relieved and expressed his sincere gratitude to Elton for his willingness to care for Vennel. "I felt a little hesitant asking you to take on such a responsibility," he added, "but I thought you would understand, being an ex-slave yourself."

The two walked back to the Celshen estate, and Sir Aldric gladly agreed to let Elton stay for a couple of days.

Jack and Elton found Jack's three traveling companions and Zannel lounging behind the house.

Upon seeing their old friend, Ben and Charles stood and greeted him warmly.

Jack introduced Elton to the two young women and explained how the three of them met the old man.

******

As time passed, Elton entertained them all with stories from his travels.

Elton's merchant caravan seemed to carry Vennel back to her past. She had loved the adventures that she shared with Dunnel as they traveled from city to city. Although the central realms were often in turmoil, she had felt fairly safe under Dunnel's watchful eye. She realized that she felt even more secure in Celel, and she relished the freedom that she experienced here. She realized, however, that she felt most stable and protected with Charles, Jack, and Ben.

She tried to focus on Elton's amusing accounts, but she found herself casting covert glances in Charles's direction. Once, out of the corner of her eye, she thought she saw him watching her.

As Elton ended one of his stories, Lilen opened the door and announced, "It's time to eat."

Zannel and the three young men stood and walked inside.

Before Vennel could follow them, Elton said, "Vennel, I know that you are a former slave just as I am, and I can remember how limited my options were as far as a career went. I've heard that you are a hard worker and that you have experience as a merchant. If you're interested in a job, I could use a hand selling goods." He smiled at her look of uncertainty. "You don't have to decide now. I will be here several weeks before I move on to another city in Celel. If you ever have need of a job later, my offer will still stand."

Vennel tried to conceal her surprise. *Why would a stranger be so generous?* She glanced at Jack's retreating back. *They've been talking about me,* she decided. "Thank you," she said as she and Elton started toward the house. Since Elton seemed satisfied, she said no more, but her mind churned. Although she appreciated Elton's kindness, she found the thought of abandoning the three young men unsettling.

*****

Charles sat down at the table and waited for everyone else to be seated. He glanced at Vennel on the other side of the table.

Charles was distracted by Sir Aldric declaring a toast, "To your healthy return." Sir Aldric raised his drink and added, "And to two more successful missions that no one, even the crown, knew about."

They all chuckled.

Sir Aldric laughed heartily at his own joke. "At this rate you'll be knighted or hanged within a month."

As everyone chuckled again, Charles thought, *With successes like these, we really could be knighted soon, talk to the king about his knowledge of other worlds, and then return home.*

Sir Aldric turned toward Elton and stated loudly, "The boldness of these young men reminds me of the time I impressed the king and earned my family crest ...."

Charles shut his eyes and shook his head slightly, thinking, *Not this story again.* As Sir Aldric reiterated his tale, Charles found himself becoming lost in his own thoughts. *I hadn't realized we were so close to possibly going home. Our journey here really is coming to an end soon.* Charles glanced across the table at Vennel. *What am I going to tell her? I don't think she could adapt to our world, and I can't leave my whole family back home and never see them again. I don't want to hurt her, but I need to tell her that she can't come where we're going.*

Vennel looked across the table at him and smiled shyly before her gaze danced away.

Charles thought, *I'm a fool. Even though I never told her that I like her, I know I've let it show. I feel like I've led her on. I somehow let our relationship grow too serious, and now I need to end it before I leave for home. I'll have to tell her the truth about us leaving without her and let the matter rest.* Charles looked down and realized that he had hardly touched his food. He did not feel hungry.

Sir Aldric finished his story, and Elton laughed loudly saying, "That is a good tale." Elton then told a story of his own.

Everyone finished eating, and as the servants cleared away the dishes, Sir Aldric suggested that they retire to the parlor, where they could talk more comfortably.

Sir Aldric's family, Jack, Ben, and Elton all migrated into the next room.

Charles intentionally hung back, and to his surprise, Vennel did the same.

She leaned against the doorframe listening to everyone in the room talk, but she did not enter.

Charles waited a few minutes until the servants finished clearing everything away and it was just the two of them left in the room. He then slowly walked over to the doorframe opposite Vennel and leaned against the wall that adjoined the parlor. He heard the muffled sounds of everyone inside talking. He dreaded this conversation. He was not sure how to begin. Finally, he straightened and turned toward Vennel.

She looked back at him expectantly.

Charles spoke solemnly, "Vennel, you know that the three of us are going to go home after we are knighted, don't you?"

Now she seemed confused. She nodded. "Yes."

Charles started to continue but then paused. He took a deep breath and said, "Our home is very far from here. We're not even from the same world. We came to this place by some kind of mistake, and we all have families back home that we need to find." Charles stopped again and thought for a moment before continuing, "When we first met you, you were just another stranger that we rescued. We were going to get you to a safe place, and well, I'm not really sure we had much of a plan for you after that. The time that the two of us spent together and how we became friends—it wasn't really supposed to happen like that. I'm leaving, and I won't be coming back."

Charles had not realized that he had been looking down as he spoke. He raised his head and looked into Vennel's eyes.

She looked stunned and had tears streaming down her cheeks.

Charles said, "I'm sorry."

She turned and walked slowly toward the stairs to her room, looking dazed as if she were in a dream.

Charles called softly, "Vennel, wait. I'm sorry."

She picked up her pace. In a moment she disappeared up the steps.

Charles did not rejoin everyone in the neighboring room; instead, he walked to the back of the house and stepped outside. He took a deep breath of fresh air, and although he had a tear rolling down his own cheek, he said, "I know I did the right thing."

******

To Jack the days of catching up with Elton passed pleasantly until the morning of the third day when the elderly gentleman took his leave. After saying their goodbyes, the three young men began packing supplies for the cold, snowy journey.

Ben knelt next to Jack, packing his own supplies and grumbling about how they had to go where it was cold and how summer should to be warm.

The boys said their farewells to the Celshen family, and Jack noticed that Vennel was absent.

Sir Alter arrived and showed them the map.

Jack saw a line of tall foothills that formed the southern border of the mountain range. He saw a valley on the other side of these foothills across which they would have to travel, and there were taller mountains after that. A river flowed along the northern edge of the valley before turning south. Farther north the mountains finally ended at the coast, and only water lay beyond that.

Sir Alter gestured toward a short, stubby-looking man with brown hair that seemed to be graying prematurely. "This man will lead us to our destination."

Jack noticed that the man had weathered lines on his face that creased into a scowl, and his beard and mustache were unkempt, giving him the appearance of a hardened woodsman.

The stubby man waved his hand. "I don't like strangers, and I don't like for them to know me, so just call me Guide."

The group departed for their long journey on horseback; however, at the foothills' base, they planned to leave their mounts at a stable and continue on foot.

Two days passed before they reached the range's foothills, left their horses, and began their ascent. That night their guide showed them how to dig a hollow in the snow to create a barrier from the wind. They huddled close together trying to stay warm, and Garthong burrowed deep within Jack's clothing, refusing to budge. Sleeping on his stomach all night made Jack uncomfortable, but with his lizard firmly attached to his back, Jack could not roll over without hurting his cold-blooded friend.

At breakfast the next morning, their guide laid down a layer of sticks on top of the snow to form a raised base for the fire. This allowed the moisture from the melting snow to drain away without extinguishing the coals. Jack observed their guide murmuring constantly to himself while going through these arduous preparations and finally kindling a fire. Despite complaining to himself almost constantly, the man seemed to prefer his own company and conversation to that of the group.

Having experienced a restless night, Jack had spent a great deal of time devising a method to keep Garthong warm without him staying in Jack's clothing. His solution was to warm several fist-size stones in the fire at each meal, wrap them in a blanket, and tuck the bundle into Garthong's sack.

Garthong gave a disgruntled squawk when Jack called him out of his clothing, but when Jack tucked the lizard into the warm backpack, he accepted it with a contented, high-pitched hum.

They reached the valley the next day. The snow remained deep on the valley's edges, but patches of exposed ground were present in the middle. To Jack's surprise, a small community of about twenty people lived down in the valley. After a little more inquiry, Jack discovered that these individuals were trappers and miners. They lived in the valley during the summer months, harvesting what they could, and brought their wares out to sell before winter.

The travelers stayed that night in a small empty building in the valley. It was a little warmer in the building, but despite the more comfortable surroundings, Jack felt uneasy.

The stubby man serving as their guide kept looking around suspiciously and fidgeting nervously.

The next day they headed toward the river, and to their dismay, it began snowing. The closer they came to the river, the deeper the snow became.

The guide stated simply, "It's a good thing there is deep snow here; it means the ice on the river will be thick enough to cross safely."

The ground again turned upward into a steep incline. They reached the river and began to cross it. Near the middle they stopped and took turns using a pickaxe that the guide carried to hack a large hole in the ice to fill their water jugs.

"Remember this place," said the guide. "It will be easier to break the ice in this same place on the way back."

After several more hours of walking, Charles paused. "Look, you can see the valley so much more clearly from here."

Jack looked down and surveyed the valley. It looked like a small green spot in the middle of a sea of white and gray. A few small clusters of evergreen trees stood scattered around it.

Jack said, "It is rather beautiful here. If it wasn't so cold, it would actually be nice."

They continued up the mountain on what the guide claimed was a trail, although Jack saw no evidence of a path. They finally reached a small flat area.

The guide pointed at a large clump of snow. "Here."

Jack and the rest of the group exchanged confused looks before realizing that he was digging. They all pitched in, and after about fifteen minutes, they broke through approximately a foot of ice and found a cave on the other side. The group lay down for the night inside the cave.

Jack took first watch. Then he woke up Charles for his watch.

******

Charles examined his sleeping companions, all bundled up as tightly as possible. *I wish I had some effective way of telling time at night,* he thought. *There's probably some way to do it using the moon and stars, but even if I was skilled in astronomy on earth, it wouldn't do me any good here.* Then it occurred to him that this planet did have a moon, but it could not be the same as Earth's moon. The star constellations were all different, but at first glance one would not necessarily be able to tell the difference between the two planets' night skies.

Charles walked over to the entrance hole they had dug in the ice and looked outside. He immediately regretted his decision because of the bite of the cold wind on his face. He pulled his head back, but as he did, he thought he saw something outside move. Charles thought, *What on earth could that be? There must be animals around here because trappers live in the valley, but I wouldn't expect to actually see one.*

Charles stuck his head out of the hole again and surveyed the land before him. The moon reflected off of the snow, making the landscape almost seem bright except for the dark patches where rocks protruded from the snow. Then Charles was sure he saw something move, and with closer inspection some of the dark blotches on the snow seemed to be slowly nearing the cave. Charles pulled his head back inside and thought, *What could possibly be coming? Are they animals? Wolves maybe?*

Charles rushed over to Jack and Ben, kicking them both.

Jack shot up like a rocket and drew both of his swords. "What's going on?"

As Charles explained about the strange figures approaching in the darkness, Ben rolled over and groaned.

Charles kicked Ben again.

Ben muttered something about how he was going to fight the enemy only if they came right up to him. He pulled his sword and laid it across his chest.

Sir Alter woke up due to the noise Jack and Charles made and drew near. "What is it?" he asked.

Ben finally stood up when Jack started explaining what Charles had seen.

The knight awoke the guide and asked if there were any types of animals that traveled in large groups at night in the mountains.

The guide began rambling about several different types of animals that it could be. "But don't worry," he assured them, "there are not any animals in these mountains that are vicious toward humans."

Charles looked at Jack. "I think I should use my light stone to light up this hillside and see what we have down there."

Jack nodded.

The two went back to the cave entrance and poked their heads out of the hole in the ice.

Charles stretched out his hand, and the entire hillside lit up like a football stadium.

Jack called urgently to the others inside the cave, "Men are approaching—dozens of them." He spoke in a loud, commanding voice, "Grab your stuff. We're getting out of here now."

Charles watched Jack turn back toward the cave's opening.

While Jack's back was turned, the guide drew a knife and dived straight at Jack.

Charles did not have time to draw his axe, but out of the corner of his eye, he saw Ben reach out his hand. Lightning shot fourth; it traveled straight into the guide, rocketing his dead corpse against the wall.

Charles exclaimed, "This whole thing is a trap! We have to get as far away from here as possible."

Sir Alter scrambled through the hole in the ice. Once outside the cave, he called, "Come, we must make it back to the valley."

The three boys also exited the cave, leaving most of their supplies behind, and the group rushed down the mountainside.

Charles could barely hear his friends over the whistling of the wind and shouts of the men all around them.

A group of five men hunkered behind a wall of shields in front of them.

Ben put one hand on Charles's shoulder and another on Jack's, launched himself into the air, and hurled a large fireball directly at the soldiers' feet.

The fire dissipated rapidly, but it liquefied the snow under the soldiers, and they all fell forward into a puddle of melted snow.

Charles and his friends leaped over them and continued down the slope.

Charles noticed a group of men off to the right and yelled, "Archers!"

The whistling of the wind changed slightly as the projectiles streaked through the darkness, but just then, a new gust of wind appeared and carried the arrows off to the side. Charles realized that Jack had just waved his hand to create the wind with his air stone. Charles decided to follow up by unleashing a lightning bolt at the archers. He hit one, and the rest scattered. Charles looked over his shoulder and saw dozens of men scurrying down the mountainside after them.

Sir Alter glanced at his comrades. "I hope you boys are ready to move quickly." The knight turned around and raised both hands. Two bolts of lightning shot up past their pursuers and struck the snow and rocks behind them.

An avalanche? Oh man, thought Charles, *this is just like a movie ... except in a movie the main character usually gets skis or a snowboard or something.*

Snow and rocks split apart and tumbled down the mountainside.

"Quickly," said the knight, "we have to make it to that huge rock there and take cover behind it."

"What happens if we get buried?" countered Charles.

Sir Alter replied, "This is summer, so the amount of snow and rock coming down shouldn't be so much that we can't dig our way out. In actuality, it probably won't kill very many of our pursuers either. I'm just using it to shake them off our tail so that we can make it to the valley."

They reached the rock and pressed their bodies up against it as well as they could. About five seconds later snow and rocks began spilling over the rock's edge above them.

Charles held his arms over his head in case a stone dropped straight down, and a few seconds later the roar ended. Charles brushed the snow off his head and shoulders. He had snow piled up to his waist.

"All right," said Sir Alter as they recommenced their descent, "let's go."

"Look there," said Jack. "The river is just up ahead."

"It sure was easier to get down this mountain than it was to climb up the stupid thing," Ben commented. "Perhaps next time we can try to fight *before* we climb the huge, snowcapped mountain."

As they approached the river, eight more soldiers emerged from the snow.

Charles could not tell whether they were purposely covered and waiting to ambush them or had been buried by the avalanche.

Charles yelled over the whistling of the wind, "Whoever laid this trap seems to have expected us to survive the early stages."

Jack yelled back, "You're right. Everyone, watch out for more soldiers at the river."

Sir Alter raised his hands and hurled a fireball at each of the two soldiers directly in front of him.

The impact lifted both soldiers off their feet and sent them rolling down the mountain.

Jack leapt toward two others while launching a stream of water at their legs. The water seeped into the snow, melting it slightly. Jack then froze the water that he had created. Within moments the slightly thawed snow also returned to ice, and both soldiers became frozen in place up to their thighs.

Jack was now slightly in front of the rest of the group, and Charles saw two enemy soldiers charge toward him. Jack deflected the first soldier's sword, grabbed his opponent's shield, and pulled the soldier toward him. He then shoved the man backward into the second soldier. Both enemies fell to the snow, and Jack dropped a layer of ice over them.

Ben cut down one of the other soldiers with his sword.

Charles struck a man with his axe, hurling him to the side.

As they reached the riverbank, six more soldiers emerged from the snow, confirming Charles's hypothesis that they had been purposely buried and were waiting for them.

Charles swung his axe sideways at the first soldier he reached. As his opponent blocked the weapon with his shield, Charles rammed his own shield into the soldier, sending him flying backward onto the ice-covered river.

Charles glanced over his shoulder to see Jack and Sir Alter finish off three enemies together and then turn to help Ben, who fended off two more.

Charles jumped out onto the ice to finish off the soldier there, who was still trying to regain his footing. Charles slipped a little as he landed on the icy surface but made it to his opponent and dropped his axe onto his enemy's torso. Charles's companions were right behind him.

Sir Alter yelled, "Come on. The valley is just up ahead. Going downhill, we should be able to make it to the settlement in no time."

They began to hurriedly traverse the frozen river in the same location that they had crossed on the way up the mountain. They avoided the hole that they had created to gather water during their previous passage since it had only a thin layer of ice covering it.

Just then, several rows of soldiers stood to their feet on the opposite bank. There were at least two dozen men, and standing in front of them was none other than the governor of Juma.

Sir Alter yelled, "What is the meaning of this?"

The governor replied with a smile, "It's quite simple really. I work for the Caishan slave cartel as a spy in exchange for large sums of money. Because you boys stopped that stupid Warlord Gunda, the Caishan have been placed at a disadvantage in comparison to the other two slave cartels, so they put a bounty on you in retaliation. Normally, I don't get involved in such things, but killing the three of you will strengthen my position as governor. Thanks to your meddling, my authority has become somewhat precarious. Many people in the capital think that my position should be returned to the Celshen family like it used to be."

Charles thought, *I knew Sir Aldric used to have more influence, but he never told us he used to be a governor.*

Jack whispered to his friends, "We don't need to hear his explanation, guys. He's just trying to stall for time while the soldiers behind us catch up."

"Oh, you're far too late," replied the governor, overhearing his warning. "You must have already used most of your gemstones to get down the mountain. Look behind you; my men are already nearby."

Charles turned and saw another two dozen men behind them, closing in quickly and stepping onto the frozen river. Charles took the left arm off of the first one to reach him.

The second one rammed his shield into Charles's shield.

Because Charles was on the ice, he slid backward and only avoided falling by propping himself up with his axe.

Jack sliced up two guards and deflected a hard strike from another, but he had to give up ground in the effort.

As Ben and Sir Alter carried on their battles, the soldiers also pushed them back.

Charles realized that they all now stood clustered together in the middle of the wide river. He noticed a soldier slip his sword past Sir Alter's guard and inflict a minor chest wound. Charles smote the soldier over the head, but as he did, another enemy came in from behind. Charles swung out his shield just in time to avoid a sword slash across his back. As Charles moved, another sword slipped in and punctured his right shoulder. Charles dropped his axe and launched a fireball, scorching two soldiers and sending another two flying backward.

This isn't going well, thought Charles. At least last time he had been injured in the left shoulder such that he could still swing his axe normally. He glanced at the river's shore, where the governor and his other two dozen men were slowly walking forward onto the ice. Charles thought, *I can't believe it—we're only fighting half of the enemy's attacking force. I can't believe it's going to end like this.*

His thoughts drifted to his parents as he picked up his axe and slammed it into another soldier's chest. Pain shot through his shoulder, but he ignored it. Then he thought of Vennel. *I want to see her again. I didn't even say goodbye.*

A shield struck Charles. He fell face forward onto the ice and slid several feet. He rolled over and saw Sir Alter and Ben both lying flat on the ice as well.

Ben reached for his sword, which rested just a few inches in front of him, but a soldier stepped on his hand.

Jack was the only one still standing, and he only had one of his swords. The soldiers had pressed Jack dangerously close to the edge of the hole that the group had made in the ice to gather water on the way up the mountain.

The governor lifted his hand.

Some of the soldiers circled around Jack while the rest held their weapons toward Charles and the others lying on the ice.

Jack, panting, turned to face the governor.

The governor addressed Jack, "As you can see, it's over. I still have three dozen soldiers alive, and you don't even have both of your swords. I offer you a deal. Come work for me. I'll fake your death and those of your friends and make you all wealthy. Outside of Sir Alter and the members of the Celshen family, no one in Celel really knows who you are, so I can even give you prominent positions after the untimely demise of these people. So if you want money, fame, or power, all you have to do is just say the word. I'll spare your two friends and give you all you could ever ask for. That's option one. Option two is for you all to die here by my hand, and there is no option three."

Jack inquired, "How will you explain our deaths? Since this was a trap, I assume you didn't tell anyone that we were on a mission?"

"That's an easy question." The governor waived his hand dismissively. "You were all spies, and you persuaded Sir Alter to come all the way out here so that you could kill him because he had become suspicious. Thankfully, Sir Alter informed me of his departure, and I, in turn, became suspicious. I followed Sir Alter and arrived in time to kill you but, sadly, not before you had already slain the noble knight."

Charles wondered what Jack would do. *He always does the right thing. There's no way he'll take this deal.* Charles, however, could not think of any other way for any of them to survive. *Jack will go down fighting,* Charles

437

decided, *and as soon as he makes his move, I'll do everything I can to grab my axe and kill this one guy before I die.*

He thought again about Vennel. *Maybe going home wasn't the most important thing after all.* He couldn't stand the idea of never seeing her again. *I love her. How could I have pushed her away? If I can't take her with me back to my world, I will have to stay here.* Then he looked around in despair as he thought, *It's too late now.*

Jack commanded quietly, "Garthong, fly."

The little lizard rocketed out of his backpack into the air and screeched in annoyance at the cold.

Jack cracked a smile that Charles did not understand and steadily met the governor's gaze. "Well, I guess we'll find out if you are correct. I'm going to explore the ridiculous possibility that there is an option three."

Jack quickly lifted his sword with the point down and thrust it into the thin layer of ice next to him. The ice split, and Jack dropped into the frigid water.

The governor shook his head. "Strange fool. He was right. There was an option three: to die by freezing to death underwater instead of by my sword. Even to the end he defied me and wouldn't even let me kill him." He laughed and sneered. "Well, at least he's dead."

Charles felt a tear rolling down his cheek. Jack was actually gone. He had just watched one of his closest friends drop into the depths, and it was over for them all.

Suddenly, he heard a loud cracking noise, and the ice began to shake. Charles looked around and realized that the ice on the river's surface was breaking, but strangely, it was not fractured near the weak place through which Jack had fallen. It was cracking along both riverbanks.

Charles saw the soldiers and governor desperately scramble toward the banks then turn as the ice gave way. Then they rushed upriver and downriver, ignoring Charles and his friends in their urgency. Fissures, however, formed before them upriver and downriver as well.

A huge slab of ice remained in the river's center on which everyone was trapped, but for some reason that Charles did not understand, this ice slab did not float downstream. Charles looked around, confused. Then the ice slab itself started cracking, and large splits erupted from all over, spitting icy water into the air.

The governor screamed in a shrill, high-pitched tone, "What's happening?"

Charles could tell by the confused expressions on their faces that Ben and Sir Alter had no idea what was occurring either.

Then Charles became aware that the soldiers were flailing and screaming. He stared at the scene, and to his amazement, ice flowed like water up out of the cracks in the ice as if the substance itself were alive. The ice latched onto the governor's and soldiers' feet and crawled up their legs. They continued to scream, but their legs were now fixed to the river's surface.

Charles was not sure if he should get up and do something or not. He was also unsure whether the ice under him would give way due to all the cracks in its surface. He glanced back at the soldiers. The ice squirmed its way up their bodies on the inside and outside of their clothing until it reached their heads and completely encased them.

The governor was the only one remaining whose head was not completely encased. His head bobbed up and down frantically, accompanied by a constant flow of cries and curses, as if this last little bit of movement might delay the process.

The ice around them then re-formed, connecting the ice slab on the river's surface back to the bank nearest the valley. The governor was frozen facing downriver, and he looked hopefully at this new path to land as if thinking of breaking free and running toward the valley.

Suddenly, another split in the ice appeared, and a hole formed in front of the governor.

Charles stood and looked down into the opening.

To his amazement, steps constructed out of ice formed underwater, and Jack walked up the steps. As soon as Jack's head poked up out of the water, he began gasping for breath. Steam billowed from Jack's entire body.

Jack stepped out of the water completely and smiled at the governor. "Well, all things considered, option three seems to have worked out well." Jack turned back to his friends. "Good thing I can hold my breath for at least a minute and thirty seconds."

The governor's senseless rambling was dampened as the ice slowly encased his mouth.

Jack glanced at the group. "Do you think he'll survive like that until we get down into the valley? I left his nose open for him to breathe, but he might freeze to death."

"Then again, we all might freeze to death," Ben muttered under his breath.

"What just happened?" Charles asked, grabbing Jack and giving him a crushing hug despite the pain in his own shoulder. Charles marveled that although Jack was wet, his whole body felt warm to the touch. Charles released his friend and turned to help up Ben and Sir Alter.

Jack responded, "Well, I had this crazy idea. I'm an iconic blood mage, so it's my core body temperature that regulates my spell casting. If I could find a powerful enough coolant system, I could, theoretically, cast my spells an unlimited number of times. Just like a car engine uses antifreeze in its coolant system, I used the cold water as mine. What I did was, admittedly, insanely risky and stupid. Since I cooled my body at such a dangerously high rate, I was forced to use even more spells than necessary in order to avoid freezing to death. That's actually why I created the underwater stairway. It wasn't just to look cool, as Ben may think. I needed to continue casting to keep warm."

They all walked over to the riverbank nearest the valley.

Jack turned and hurled another sheet of ice out over the river.

Charles asked, "What was that for?"

"I'm still soaking wet," Jack explained, "and as the wind blows, it cools me down rapidly, so I needed to cast another spell to warm up. It's kind of cool actually. Apparently, I can't freeze to death unless I'm unconscious or sleeping."

"Well, I'm *so* happy that one of us is warm," Ben grumbled, "but I want to go back to the valley, where it's not quite as miserable."

Jack smiled as Ben walked past him.

Sir Alter shook his head. "I never imagined that much power, even in an extreme circumstance like this. What are we going to tell the king?"

Jack smiled again. "The same thing we always do—the truth. I'm sure some evidence exists somewhere on the governor's property, and I think the governor will help us figure out where in exchange for his life. Besides, having that many soldiers on the payroll isn't something that can be easily hidden."

Garthong landed on Jack's shoulder, making a guttural noise as if chiding Jack for making him go outside. Then he dived back inside the backpack and squirmed unhappily in the damp environment.

Charles asked, "Jack, how did you prevent the ice from flowing downriver when you broke it away from all the edges?"

"It was easy," said Jack. "I created an underwater pillar of ice to hold it in place, and I used ice to crack the original ice. It would have been easier to manipulate the existing water and ice, but because I couldn't do that, I had to use only the ice I created. I actually did something new today that I hadn't tried except in practice. We've all experimented with controlling our spells' temperatures as we cast elements. In this case I actually created water underwater and floated my water up through the cracks in the ice. Then I froze the water solid as it climbed up the soldiers. In the past I cast ice or changed the water into ice almost immediately after casting it. This was the first time that I guided the water throughout the duration of my control over it and changed the temperature at different times as it reached the soldiers.

"I actually just figured out that this was possible as we ran down the hill. I sprayed water at those soldiers' feet and froze the water that I'd created after letting it soak into the snow. I discovered that we can alter the temperature of an element at any point after we cast it during the six or eight second window that we control it. Today, of course, freezing the water was particularly easy since the temperature is below freezing anyway. I suspect this would be a much more difficult task in warmer surroundings. Sadly, it will probably take a lot more practice before I can actually use this as a battle tactic."

They bound the governor and forced him to walk in front of them through the snow. As the group traveled toward the settlement in the valley, the sun started to rise. Day came, and the group reached the place in the valley where they had stayed previously. They patched up their wounds and slept there for a few hours. They gagged their prisoner, and when they searched the governor's pockets, they were pleased to discover a book detailing his financial payments to several different groups.

Jack tapped their prisoner on the shoulder. "Thank you, Governor, for detailing your crimes in this book so we can prove them to the king."

The governor mumbled something through his gag.

Jack ignored him, saying, "It really is convenient that you brought this. I suppose it makes sense, though. You couldn't trust anyone else with this book, so you must have always kept it with you."

After a quick meal the group recommenced their return journey to Celel. They crossed the border at the base of the last mountain and reached the stable where they had left their horses.

Jack asked Sir Alter, "Where are we going next?"

The knight replied, "I must return to the capital. You all may rest at the Celshen estate some if you like, but be at the capital by the end of five days. I'm going to personally recommend to the king that he knight you. I will also send a formal notification to the Celshen family."

Surprised, Jack looked at the knight. "That would be fantastic."

"The three of you certainly deserve it," Sir Alter replied. "You've accomplished more daring and dangerous missions than many full-fledged knights. I must also add that you all never wavered on making the right choice. You all are truly knights of the highest level, and I have nothing more to teach you. Indeed, in these last few months, you have blown past me. I suspect that if you wish it, you could even become governors one day."

Without another word the knight mounted his horse and set off at a fast walk toward the capital with the soon-to-be ex-governor trailing behind on foot, led by a rope tied to Sir Alter's saddle.

The young men turned their horses toward the Celshen estate.

As they traveled, Ben asked, "Do you think there might actually be awesome legendary weapons that we could find?"

Jack scratched his chin. "It's possible, but I suspect that buried treasure is kind of rare here just like in our world. It is true, though, that people in this land don't have the machinery and equipment to search as diligently as people can in our world, so perhaps some legendary weapons still exist. We still haven't read many of the awakenings in the book, so there must be some amazing things left in this world that we have not discovered."

Charles added, "I prefer to focus on things that are more likely to happen." He looked at Jack. "That knight Sir Aldric mentioned to you—the one the governor accused of being a traitor ... What do you think will happen to him?"

Jack shrugged. "I'm sure his case will be reexamined, and there's a good chance he'll go free. He's probably innocent, so it's a good thing that we exposed the governor."

Ben changed the subject by saying, "Hey, if we have to go to the capital, why not go there now and explore for a bit? It seems like we've barely traveled anywhere in this country so far."

Charles thought for a moment. "That seems like a good idea. I'll go tell our representing family that we are going to be knighted and meet you guys in the capital. There's something I need to take care of there."

Jack surveyed his friend as if understanding more than Charles had said and nodded. "Vennel should also be there to see us knighted."

Charles said softly, "Guys, I think when you two go home, I'll stay here. I've thought about it a lot, and I want to stay."

Jack remained quiet as though he had seen this coming.

Ben exclaimed, "What? That's ridiculous! Why would you stay—"

"Go to her, Charles," Jack interrupted. "Remember, if you don't find her at the estate, look for her with Elton. We'll see you at the capital."

Ben rolled his eyes and sighed.

As Jack and Ben turned their horses toward the capital, Ben asked, "Do you know what the capital is called?"

Jack answered, "I believe it's called Sellta. Let's take our time getting there and explore a little along the way."

Ben nodded, and with a nudge to their horses, they were on their way.

Charles traveled alone back toward the Celshen estate. He thought, *I've risked my life many times in this world, and I almost died on the ice. If I was willing to die in this world, why was I unwilling to stay?* At least now he had a second chance. He hoped Vennel was still back at the Celshen estate. *What if she left with Elton?* He nudged his horse and picked up his pace. Now he felt a new sense of urgency. Charles wished he could remember how long Elton had said he would stay in the country. *If she isn't at the estate, I have to find her before the knighting ceremony.*

Chapter 22

VENNEL WALKED IN THE garden behind the Celshen family's house. She looked over her shoulder and saw the morning sun casting its gentle hues over the world. Only a few wispy clouds hung in the blue sky, but the garden seemed dreary and sad. A little over a week ago, everything seemed to be going well, but now she felt as though she had nothing left. She reached down and lightly stroked a yellow flower petal. She thought of Charles again, and she looked north to the mountains since that was where their mission had taken them. This might be their last mission.

She felt a hand on her shoulder, and she turned to see Lilen standing behind her.

Lilen asked, "What's the matter?"

"They're leaving," Vennel replied.

Lilen wrinkled her brow. "You mean the three young knights-in-training? Where are they going?"

Vennel stared at her feet. "Somewhere far away where I can't follow. Now I'm not sure what I'm going to do. Maybe I'll take Elton's job offer and become a merchant."

Lilen smiled sadly. "You love Charles, don't you?"

Vennel burst into tears as she nodded in assent.

Lilen shook her head. "Then what are you doing here? If he's going somewhere, then follow him."

A Destiny Among Worlds

Vennel replied between sobs, "I ... can't."

Lilen crossed her arms. "You're telling me that you are one hundred percent certain that it's impossible for you to follow him? Did you talk to him about this? Did he say it was impossible?"

Vennel's sobs abated as recognition passed over her face. She began slowly, "I'm not a hundred percent certain ... ." She continued with more conviction, "But I don't know what the people are like where they're going or what kinds of things go on there."

"They are *people* in both places," Lilen countered. "Just how different could it be? You traveled quite a bit when you were a merchant. You know that people are mostly the same the world over."

Vennel set her jaw. "Yes, you're right. I have to talk to him again. He didn't say that I couldn't go. He assumed that I wouldn't."

They heard the sound of a horse's hooves approaching the house.

Lilen said, "It sounds like the family has company. I'd better go see who it is."

Vennel watched her friend walk briskly toward the house. Then Vennel turned and stared absently down at the flowers around her feet. Small purple and pink flowers grew in neat circles around larger flower bushes. She thought, *I don't know how it will work out, but at least now I have hope.*

She heard footsteps behind her. Expecting Lilen to be rejoining her, she turned and started when she saw Charles standing before her. She tried to say something but could not find the words.

While she recovered from her surprise, Charles said, "I'm so glad you're still here. The whole ride back I was afraid that you would've joined the merchants. I'm sorry for what I said before, and I changed my mind. I'm not going to leave with the others."

Vennel tried to say something, but Charles held up his hand, saying, "Let me finish. On the mission we all almost died, and you were the only thing I could think about. I guess what I'm trying to say is, I want to stay with you."

Vennel blushed and replied quietly, "That's how I feel." Then she shook her head. "But you can't stay. You have a family in your world. I've been thinking about it, and I decided that I want to go with you. I don't have any ties anywhere except you."

Charles grasped both of her hands in his. "It doesn't matter right now. We'll decide later. The only thing that matters is that we'll be together. I have other news. The three of us are being recommended for knighthood, so pack your things; we're going to the capital."

She smiled. "Everyone will be thrilled to hear the news about your success. I can just imagine the look on Sir Aldric's face when he learns that he has three new knights to his family's name."

******

Two days passed before Jack and Ben reached the capital, and they were surprised to find themselves looking out over the ocean. The two young men sat on their horses on a hill overlooking the city of Sellta. Jack saw two sets of walls surrounding the city, a tall exterior wall and a smaller interior wall. Many towers and gatehouses stood along both walls. The entire city looked bright and cheerful in the sunlight.

The city's external wall was different from any other they had seen because the city was built on the coast. Instead of the wall surrounding the entire city, it traveled from the ocean shore, around the city, and to the shore on the other side. Towers rose along the beach, overlooking large docks. Jack was not sure if the shoreline had been straight at one time or not, but whether or not it occurred naturally or was dug out by humans, a recess in the land allowed the ocean to flow into the city's interior. The city provided an excellent harbor because of the way the land surrounded the sliver of ocean that flowed into its center. Several ships lay moored at the docks, and more could be seen out at sea.

Rather than just a keep inside the interior wall, there was an entire castle, which consisted of multiple fortified stone structures surrounding the keep and a small courtyard in the complex's center. One of these fortified buildings was also encircled by a smaller wall, perhaps half again the height of a man, with only one gatehouse. The surround structure was six stories tall with magnificent arched windows. Jack guessed that this building was the palace. *With the way the palace is surrounded by its own wall,* Jack realized, *the city technically has three sets of walls associated with it.* The palace and the market district were positioned side by side in the city's center, but another market district stood by the docks with goods that came and went by sea.

Ben commented, "This is truly a glorious sight. I can't wait to explore the city." He pointed toward several objects in the city. "What do you think those bowl-shaped things are for?"

Jack followed his gaze and saw six tall towers that rose above the town just outside the innermost wall around the palace. The towers had no windows and did not appear to serve any type of defensive purpose. Each of the towers had a large half sphere on top of it.

Jack leaned forward in his saddle. "I wonder ... They look like they're designed to catch rainwater. The water seems to flow by gravity from the towers to a large reservoir outside the palace. That looks like an aqueduct connecting the six towers to the reservoir, and see how the reservoir is elevated above the ground? That means that gravity could potentially feed the water into the palace buildings. The technology of this city is amazing. Theoretically, the palace, and perhaps other important buildings, could have running water."

Jack shook his head in wonder. "This level of technology seems far superior to anything we've seen in any other country in this world. I suppose that's natural, though. This is supposed to be one of the wealthiest and most powerful countries in the north, so they would have resources to devote to research."

Jack and Ben rode through the first gatehouse and headed toward the palace. They found a three-story inn just outside the castle and were pleased to discover that it had running water.

Tables filled the inn's ground floor, and the two travelers sat down to eat their evening meal. As they ate, the number of other diners increased significantly, and Jack guessed by their appearance that they were predominantly merchants.

Ben finished his meal quickly, pushed back his chair, and stood. "I'm going to head out and look around."

Jack watched him saunter outside.

Garthong slipped out of his sack and settled on Jack's lap.

As Jack ate, he slipped chunks of meat under the table, where the gother hungrily devoured them.

The tables in the establishment quickly filled, and one of the workers approached Jack and asked if he would mind others sitting at the table with him.

Jack was a little surprised but nodded his acceptance.

Four men, who appeared to be merchants, joined Jack at the table.

One of the merchants courteously dipped his head and thanked Jack for allowing them to join him.

The merchants immediately began talking about the state of trade in Sellta, giving Jack an idea.

He wondered if he could gain some useful information about the prominent countries in the north and south from these men, who obviously traveled a great deal. He thought, *It would be interesting to learn about the cultures of this world even if we are on the verge of leaving.*

During a lull in the conversation, Jack asked, "Have any of you done any trading in Holdom or Dulla?"

One of the merchants, a middle-aged man with bushy eyebrows and a mustache, piped up, "Yes, I trade in Holdom quite frequently."

Jack turned to the man and asked, "The people who live there, what are they like?"

The merchant smiled and swallowed a mouthful of meat. "Well, the country is a bit different from Celel. The people of Celel are very financially successful in comparison, and the people from right here in Sellta are seafarers by nature. In Holdom the people look down on sailors because even though some of the country touches the coast, it has no major coastal cities. Most of the sea trade in Holdom comes by land. You see, there is a smaller country near Holdom called Wuskl, which is little more than a large peninsula that juts out into the sea. Almost all of the towns and cities in Wuskl are located on the coast, and the country relies on fishing and trade to survive because the soil is poor. The people in Holdom look down on the poor fishermen living in Wuskl and dislike the fact that Holdom is required to trade with them in order to acquire many goods that come in by sea.

"The smaller, weaker nation of Wuskl was on the verge of being conquered by Holdom several hundred years ago, but a wealthy merchant in Wuskl founded the Caishan slave cartel and gained wealth and power. The people of Holdom usually don't like to get involved in anything on an international level unless it directly involves them, which is why they were slow to react to a new cartel being born near their country. Now the descendants of the man who started the cartel rule the puppet government in Wuskl and intimidate Holdom's residents."

The merchant narrating the story took a long drink. "The people of Holdom put a great deal of stock in honor, and honorable people can be found even among the nobility." The group snickered as he continued, "If a person from Holdom breaks an oath, it's considered extremely dishonorable. Holdom is also filled with sadness because it was once the crown jewel of the north, but now it's the weakest of the three main northern kingdoms. The country's people, even the nobility, constantly long and hope for a king to rise up, unite the country, and return it to what it once was. Whenever there is even a rumor that someone of the king's bloodline might exist, however, the Caishan hunt them down and kill them. If the country of Holdom became strong again, it would, of course, put the Caishan cartel's base of operations in jeopardy."

"Why wouldn't the Caishan just relocate?" Jack asked.

The merchant thought for a moment and sliced off another piece of meat. "A slave cartel needs great access to the sea in order to efficiently transport large numbers of people anywhere in the world. In fact, the Caishan cartel is the only cartel not located on an island. There are, however, several smaller islands just off the peninsula's coast, and I believe that the Caishan use some of those islands on occasion."

Jack was surprised for a moment and asked, "Where are the other two slave cartels located?"

The merchant wiped his mouth. "The most powerful of the cartels is the Bendel, and it's located on an island south of Malldan. The Zangan slave cartel is located on an island just east of this country."

Jack inquired, "Where is the country of Malldan?"

The businessman's bushy eyebrows shot up as if surprised by Jack's ignorance. "It's one of the three great southern nations. It's located on the southeast most tip of the world. I don't trade down that far, so I know little about them, but I've heard that these are terrifying countries in which to trade unless you have the blessing of the kings and warlords." General nods and murmurs of agreement went around the table as the merchant continued, "I don't have any connections down south, so I don't trade down that way. The merchants who do trade there have the rulers' blessings. Those merchants are very wealthy and powerful, and they're good at removing anyone else who tries to trade there. In the north free trade is encouraged, even by the smaller countries, although it didn't used to be this way."

Now Jack was even more curious. "What changed?" he asked. "And why?"

The merchant took another drink and leaned back in his chair as if warming up for a long narrative. "The stories that I heard when I was a boy portray the north as being just like the south. The north was full of evil rulers, who took advantage of their people in order to gain more wealth and power for themselves, and the concept of justice was virtually unheard of throughout the world. At that time the kingdom of Celel was less than half of its current size, and the ruler was one of the weakest warlords in the entire north.

"The warlord was an old man, but he ran across a very young man who seemed wiser than any individual in the entire world. Yet, as the story goes, the young man was incredibly ignorant of history, geography, proper etiquette, and many other things that normal people know. This young man created great works that increased the productivity of his warlord's kingdom. He built watermills and altered the way that the people grew crops. The small country's wealth and power grew, and the young man was promoted within two years to the warlord's right-hand man. Once this was done, the young man created a type of justice system far more complicated than any that the world had seen before.

"The warlord became ill and was near death due to a terrible sickness that wracked his body with coughing, burned him with fever, and prevented him from breathing well. He summoned all the healers he knew but to no avail. Even those with heal stones proved to be ineffective. The young man, however, devised a way to treat the disease and heal the warlord. He called the treatment 'antibiotics.' After recovering, the warlord adopted the young man as his own son and handed him the reins of power.

"The young man encouraged free trade and did previously unthinkable things such as hiring peasants for positions of power. He brought an end to any form of corruption he could find, and people all around saw the wealth and power of his kingdom expand. One of the two neighboring warlords attacked this city, which was rather small at that time. The young man defeated him then marched out and conquered that warlord's lands. The other neighboring territories actually requested to be annexed and incorporated into the country of Celel, and the young ruler of Celel appointed each warlord as governor over what had been his kingdom. The more the country grew, the more powerful and wealthy it became, but the young man, who was now a king, was not satisfied with his improvements. He trained his soldiers well and required excellence from them. It wasn't long before he created the concept of knighthood. The Knights of Celel traveled throughout the north dealing out justice and protecting the innocent.

"The king of the neighboring country of Dulla died during the young man's rise to power, and after a brief civil war, his oldest son became king. The two new young kings of Dulla and Celel formed an alliance. Since that time, the entire north has changed. The slave cartels have little power in the north in comparison to what they once possessed, and the smaller warlords who surround the countries of Celel and Dulla have almost all become better rulers. It's even rumored that good warlords rule in some of the central kingdoms due to the changes here in the north. The young man, of course, is our own King Tanner. He is now an old man, but a good king he still remains." The merchant placed his hands behind his head and stretched as if proud of the entertaining way he had woven together his narrative.

Jack thought, *It's clear now that the king of Celel is from our world. The technological advancements that he made were ways of implementing things he already knew rather than new technological discoveries. No wonder this king is rumored to know about other worlds.* What remained unclear to Jack was whether the king was unable to ever go home or simply decided not to go home. *I understand why he might stay. After all, all I ever wanted to do in life was make a difference. Maybe he feels the same way, and he discovered that he could make a difference in this world.* Jack further contemplated, *Maybe I don't really want to go home either. I've done so much here—I've made a difference and protected people. If I could make as great of a difference as the king of this country, I would have no regrets.*

One of the other merchants at the table, a short, heavyset man with round cheeks and cheery eyes, interrupted Jack's thoughts by saying,

"I can't believe you've never heard that story. Young people nowadays have no idea about the way things used to be. You probably don't know anything about what's going on down south either, and that's some important stuff."

"What do you mean?" Jack asked.

"Everyone's worried about the prince of Malldan," the jovial-looking merchant explained. "The king is old and has little interest in doing anything other than enjoying his last years, but his son is ambitious. When the king dies, many believe that the southern nation of Malldan will march to war under the son's command. According to rumors, the prince has already been trying to unite the other two powerful southern nations, Imtad and Klantiff, with his own in an alliance against the world. All three kings of the great southern nations are old, but they all have aspiring sons. Many northern nobles believe that the prince of Malldan will be able to convince the other two princes to work with him."

"Please," Jack requested, "tell me about these nations' cultures."

The merchants all looked at each other, and some scratched their heads.

Finally, a different merchant, an elderly man with weathered features at the far end of the table, said, "Few people know very much about Klantiff. It's located to the west of Malldan and is one of the powerful southern nations. The Great Southern Desert also lies beyond its southern border, so it has no coastal territory. Because of this isolation, very little trade passes through the nation, and I don't think I've ever met anyone who claimed to be from that country.

"Malldan, however, is a different story. It has a long history of battle, and its warriors believe that victory by any means is success. The soldiers of that country would gladly burn an entire village just to kill one enemy. It's said that an influential general from this country, who was banished for treason long ago, sailed to the island south of the country and started the first slave cartel. The Bendel slave cartel claims to be the oldest. I'm not really sure if that's true or not, but it's definitely the most brutal and vicious.

"The first men to join the Bendel slave cartel were the pirates inhabiting the island. The Bendel cartel is considered to have the most powerful fleet of ships in the entire world, and they have highly trained archers who specialize in ship-to-ship combat. The Caishan cartel, which used to be the weakest of the slave cartels, has long envied the Bendel cartel's awesome power. With the changes in the north, the Zangan cartel has lost a great deal of power due to the fact that it's off the coast of Celel. I'm afraid I don't know much else about the slave cartels or the southern nations. I mostly just hear stories."

Jack inquired, "You didn't mention much about Dulla. Do any of you know much about that country?"

The first merchant with the bushy eyebrows said, "The people there are very proud people. Like Holdom, Dulla has been around for many years, and it has perhaps the proudest history of any of the northern kingdoms. Some even say that it used to control land all the way to the eastern coast. The people of that country are also rather hotheaded; it can be difficult to calm them down once they're angry about something. Insulting one of them in a formal setting would be liable to start a war. I understand that the nobility don't necessarily act this way, but it is the general mindset of the people themselves. As a result of this attitude, the country carries a great deal of respect in international affairs."

The merchants, having finished their meals, thanked Jack for his table, stood, and departed to prepare their wares for the next day.

Jack leaned back in his chair. He now had much more than just supper to digest. *It sounds like the war everyone's concerned about may actually be a few years off,* he thought, *but I still can't shake the feeling that there's more to this. When we went down to stop Warlord Gunda, someone else there was really in control. It seems as though there are powerful forces at work that, for the time being, have remained invisible.*

Jack retired upstairs to his room, contemplating the potential ramifications of what he had heard. This was a more enjoyable topic to consider than that of leaving this world without Charles. What would Jack tell Charles's parents? He pushed the thought from his mind again. He then wrote a letter to Sir Alter to inform him of their whereabouts within the capital and found a messenger to deliver it.

Ben returned later that night after exploring much of the city. When he returned, Ben said, "I hope the king summons us soon because I've already seen the city, and there's not much else to do."

******

Two days passed. The early morning sun shone through the inn window.

Hearing a heavy footfall outside, Jack rolled over and looked at the door.

Garthong squawked in an irritated manner as Jack's change in position forced him to move.

Jack answered the door after the first knock and was pleased to find Charles.

Jack smiled. "You're back; how did it go?"

Charles wore a broad grin as he stepped into the room. He said, "I brought the Celshen family and Vennel with me. They've all come to watch our ceremony. We arrived last night. They're staying in rooms at the palace. I left early this morning to find you guys."

Ben sat up in bed, rubbed his eyes, and yawned. "Well, we haven't heard exactly when the ceremony is yet. Hopefully, we'll hear sometime today."

The three went downstairs and began eating breakfast. A messenger arrived from the palace to inform them that their ceremony would take place that afternoon, and they would receive more specific information later.

Charles finished his breakfast quickly and rose to his feet. "If we've got a few hours, I'm going to take Vennel out so we can see the city together."

Ben rolled his eyes. "First, you say you're not coming home. Now you're subjecting us to hearing about your dates?"

Charles paused with his hands on the back of his chair. "Well, that's not actually decided yet. The two of us haven't decided if she's coming home with me, or I am staying here."

Ben's mood lightened immediately, and he said, "Well, have fun."

Jack added, "If we get any more information about the ceremony, I'll let you know."

******

Charles left his friends to run some errands before his rendezvous with Vennel.

Later, the two of them visited the marketplace by the docks then walked toward the city gates. After exiting the city they hiked along the coast until they stood on a rocky bluff overlooking the sea. The waves crashed against and battered the rocks below them, sending drops of water cascading back into the sea. The sun was high in the sky, and a faint breeze blew, making the tall, sparse grass on top of the bluff shimmer and wave.

Charles turned toward Vennel and watched the wind gently toss her long blond hair from one side of her face to the other as she gazed out over the water.

Charles wiped his sweaty palms on his pants and cleared his throat.

Vennel turned toward him, her blue eyes shining in the pleasure of the moment.

Charles licked his lips. "I don't know many customs of this world, but in my world if a man is going to propose marriage, he has to kneel and asked the girl if she'll marry him. Then he has to present her with a ring as a symbol of their engagement." As Charles spoke, he covertly pulled out a ring, which he had picked out earlier that morning, and held it by his side. "I know we agreed that we would both be willing to change worlds in order to stay with the other, but I wanted to make a more pronounced commitment, a promise to remain together as long as we live."

Vennel stood perfectly still with her lips slightly agape as if she did not know what to do.

Charles knelt down. "Vennel, will you marry me?"

A small gasp escaped Vennel's throat. She covered her mouth with her hand.

Charles raised his right hand to reveal a ring crafted from gold and studded with diamonds. One large diamond glimmered in the center, and the band had small diamonds set into it at regular intervals, sparkling in the sunlight.

Vennel tried to speak then paused. She finally inhaled sharply and replied, "Yes, of course."

As Charles stood, he noticed the sunlight reflect off the tears on Vennel's cheeks.

Vennel giggled as he slid the ring onto her finger.

Charles explained, "This is the finger that it's traditionally worn on in my country." He laughed as he pulled her close. As he held her, he said, "I never dreamed that being brought into this world could bring me so much joy. At first I seemed to be tossed this way and that with no control over what happened next and no way to get home. But now, whatever we face, it will be together."

******

Soon after Charles returned, Sir Alter found them. When he saw them, he mumbled something about how they never did as they were told.

Jack smiled. Technically, the knight had not ordered them *not* to come to the capital immediately.

Sir Alter said, "The king may ask all of you about the incident with the governor, but he should do it after the proceedings and probably separately. Just be honest, and everything should go well."

"Oh, because we planned to lie to the king—potentially our only ticket home." Ben said under his breath, earning him an elbow in the ribs from Charles.

Jack would have been lying if he had said he was not nervous, and he knew his friends probably were too. It was at least possible that they might go home soon. *Besides,* thought Jack, *who wouldn't be nervous about meeting a king?*

Sir Alter instructed, "When you hear the town bell ring six times, come to the palace grounds. The ceremony will begin when the bell rings seven times. Now, I must return to the king's side; there are important matters being discussed right now about your next mission."

As the knight left, Jack said, "Our next mission? Hmm, I wonder if the king will be willing to let us go home. What do you guys think?"

"We have been very successful," Charles commented, "so from that standpoint the king would be foolish to want us to go home. But trying to force us to stay here also sounds relatively unproductive for him."

Ben added, "I think there's a good chance no one told the king why we want to be knighted since we didn't really explain it to Sir Alter. He probably just thinks we are promising new recruits. Anyway, who would expect us to go through all the trouble to become Knights of Celel just to leave?"

Jack frowned. "Either way, I don't necessarily see this going well."

The time seemed to pass incredibly slowly until the bell finally rang six times.

Jack and his friends stepped through the gate in the interior wall and onto the palace grounds. The many buildings that they had seen from a distance when they arrived at the city looked even more grand and imposing when directly in front of them. Some of the buildings were six stories tall, and several had relief carvings of battle scenes on their exteriors. A number of the buildings possessed multiple real glass windows.

A clean-shaven man with a dark complexion approached them and gave a little bow. "Greetings, my name is Fada. I am one of the king's servants, and it is my duty to prepare the three of you for the ceremony. Please follow me; I will take you to a place where you can get ready." Fada wore the same crisp white shirt, navy blue pants, and wide red belt that Jack had seen some of the other palace servants wearing.

The three young men followed Fada into a three-story building near the wall. As they entered, they discovered many people bustling about inside.

Jack asked, "What are all these people doing?"

Fada glanced around. "Those servants are bringing in food and taking it to the second story, where others are cooking and making preparations for the feast that will take place after your ceremony."

"There's going to be a feast?" Jack asked. "Is this really that big of a deal?"

"Of course," replied the servant. "The three of you, I'm told, have set a record by becoming knights in under a year."

Ben stretched his neck and cracked his knuckles. "Yeah, we just thought it would be a cool change."

Charles rolled his eyes at Ben before turning back to Fada. "This does sound like a great honor. I only hope that we can live up to our reputation in the future."

The three friends followed the servant into a side room, where he pointed to several sets of clothing laid out on a wooden table.

Fada said, "These garments are the traditional attire. Sir Alter requested that the three of you wear these instead of your current garments. You can change in any of those small rooms." The servant gestured toward several doors at the back of the room. "I'll return in a few minutes to escort you to the Grand Hall."

After the boys changed clothes, they strapped on their weapons and shields over their new clothing and waited for the servant to return.

"This is ridiculous." Ben spread his arms wide and looked down at himself. "Who said that I wanted to wear a red bathrobe draped over this weird red and green garment thing?"

"Cheer up," Charles muttered. "Mine is red and yellow. But Jack gets to wear red and blue; that's way better."

Jack only partially listened to this exchange. Instead, he contemplated how to present his case to the king for the friends to return home.

Fada returned and waved his hand for them to follow.

They exited the preparation building and walked along a narrow stone path that wound through a green, well-manicured lawn until they reached a wider stone road leading to the Grand Hall. The building in which the Grand Hall was located looked huge and majestic from the outside with intricate relief carvings, a slopped roof, and tall spires. Large cat-like stone statues, which served as gargoyles, extended from the roof. Several pillars stretched up from the ground to the roof, reminding Jack of an ancient Greek architecture style.

As they stepped inside, Jack was surprised to find that the interior looked so much like he had imagined. Two rows of large stone pillars traveled almost all the way to the front of the building, and a wide red carpet ran straight down the middle.

People crowded on both sides but stayed behind the line of stone pillars. The crowd stared at the four of them as they walked into the building. Jack knew that the Celshen family and Vennel were somewhere in the crowd.

The building had many holes serving as windows, all about one story off the ground, and a wooden platform traveled around the edge of the room several feet below the openings. Jack thought, *I suppose even if an enemy breached the walls, archers could still fire from inside structures like this one until the buildings themselves were completely conquered.*

Sir Alter joined them with his usual grave expression. The knight wore a similar style garment as that of the young men. His clothing consisted of a red robe draped over a black tunic with red edging. Even in this formal setting, however, Sir Alter wore functional rather than decorative boots and kept his sword and shield within easy reach as he had when Jack had first seen him.

Fada bowed his head respectfully before departing.

The knight surveyed them critically for a moment then nodded approvingly. "Very good. You all look like you are important enough to be here now that you're dressed in royal clothing." The knight turned so that he faced the hall's far end and stood silently with Jack and his friends behind him.

Jack turned his gaze in the same direction and saw a large ornate chair that he reasoned must be King Tanner's throne. Jack thought, *It's interesting that this whole country even follows the same kind of time as our world.* The king must have instituted a timekeeping device in Sellta and instructed a servant to ring the bell every hour. *The bell is being rung seven times, and it's in the evening, so that means he's running the entire city on a normal timescale where it resets every twelve hours.*

Jack leaned toward Sir Alter. "Do you know what the king calls his timekeeping device?"

The knight wrinkled his brow. "I never really paid that much attention. I understand that a strange contraption that works off the sun sits on a platform next to the bell. It is said that when the king first came to power, he was always annoyed by not knowing what time it was. He invented a new contraption to keep track of time and put someone in charge of ringing the bell at specified intervals."

Charles whispered to Jack, "Fascinating, I wonder if he's created some sort of variation on the sundial. Theoretically, it wouldn't be that hard to create one, but I wonder if you would have to adjust it in some way to account for this being a different planet. This planet may not move relative to its sun in exactly the same fashion as ours."

The bell started ringing again, and two doors opened to their right. Seven men entered and walked to the front of the Grand Hall. One of the men sat on the throne, and the others positioned themselves on either side of and behind the royal seat.

Two servants followed the group, carrying a furled cloth on a pole between them. The servants held the cloth high behind the throne before letting the loose end drop.

Jack realized that it was a flag. The standard was dark blue with a bright red star at the top, a white star in the lower left corner, and a black star in the lower right corner. Jack wondered briefly what the flag design symbolized, but his curiosity quickly returned to the king.

The king was tall and thin with an educated air about him. His hair was long and white, and he had a bushy beard with a few brown strands that looked as though they were fighting diligently to exist in the sea of gray. Despite being older the king appeared rather muscular and healthy. Jack guessed that he was in his sixties. The king looked toward the group and lifted his head slightly, signaling them to approach.

Jack and his friends followed Sir Alter forward toward the throne.

When they reached the throne, Sir Alter declared, "My liege, these three have distinguished themselves greatly, carrying out missions that none thought were possible. They have demonstrated a strong desire to help protect the innocent and followed through by risking their own lives to see this goal achieved. I, Sir Alter, Knight of Celel, hereby swear that, in my opinion, these three are ready for knighthood." The knight knelt.

The king said, "Very well, Sir Alter. I accept your recommendation." The king, looking into the crowd, asked, "Which high family do these young men represent?"

Sir Aldric, standing in the crowd's front row near the throne, stepped forward and said in a clear voice, "My liege, I am Sir Aldric of the Celshen family. I testify that these young men represent my family and that I recommend them for knighthood."

King Tanner said, "Very well, Sir Aldric. I also accept your recommendation and will personally bestow the honor of knighthood on these three young men."

One of the men standing behind the king stepped forward, opened a scroll, and handed it to the king.

Sir Alter and Sir Aldric stepped to the side as the three young men approached the throne.

The king instructed, "Repeat after me. As a Knight of Celel, I solemnly swear to pursue justice with vengeance without being devoid of mercy. I swear to fight for the innocent and show compassion. I swear that I will speak in the tongue of angels, and my words will carry the strength to destroy evil and the power to display love. And last, I solemnly swear that I will act with meekness, always controlling my power so that it may never be used for evil."

When the three young men finished swearing the oath, Jack was amazed by how accurately it expressed how he felt. He thought, *A true knight must do more than just destroy evil and seek justice. The true knight must search for opportunities to change that which is evil into good. If I ever lose sight of mercy and compassion, I will become a heartless avenger who punishes evil yet accomplishes little because everyone, including myself, has committed some kind of unjust act sometime in their lives. I must search for people who can change and give them a second chance.*

The king stood and drew his sword. "Now kneel."

The three friends knelt, and the king touched his sword on the right and left shoulder of each of them.

As they stood, the king said, "Knights of Celel, when you speak, it is as though I have spoken. When you act, it is as if I have acted. Take this responsibility and authority, and change the world."

Jack, Ben, and Charles nodded then turned toward the crowd, which began clapping and cheering.

The king announced, "Let the feast begin to honor and celebrate our new knights."

The crowd began cheering even louder.

Ben leaned over and whispered to Jack, "Listen to that crowd. How much do you want to bet that they were all really here just for the food?"

Jack smiled and whispered back, "Isn't that why *you're* here?"

Ben grinned. "Of course, where else could I get an all-you-can-eat buffet completely free? So I had to do a couple of missions and get knighted, but it was well worth it for a feast."

Overtaken by Destiny

Jack surveyed the crowd and saw Vennel clapping and beaming at Charles. Next to her stood Zannel and Zemara, who craned their necks and clapped excitedly. Jack smiled when he noticed Elton standing just behind them. The old man was reserved, but Jack could tell from the sparkle in his eyes that he was pleased.

Sir Aldric rejoined his family and clapped boisterously.

The celebration began, and servants led the boys into the banquet hall. A stage, surrounded on three sides by lines of long tables, occupied one end of the room. Jack and his friends were seated at one end of the king's table next to Sir Alter.

The entertainment style interested Jack.

Five people stepped out onto the stage.

One performer hurled a massive block of ice into the air.

The next entertainer shot the ice with a bolt of lightning, shattering it and sending pieces flying all over the room. The candlelight reflected off the shards of ice as they fell, creating a beautiful chandelier effect.

Before the ice hit the ground, however, the third person stepped forward and created a massive gust of air that swept up all the ice shards, swirled them around the top of the room, and dropped them down to the floor in a pile.

The next performer created a large chunk of earth in the middle of the stage.

The fifth person ran and jumped on the dirt, leaping off of it into the air.

As the acrobat's momentum carried him upward, another person rushed out onto the stage and hurled a gust of air into him, lifting him up two or three times higher than a person could naturally jump.

The performer in the air hurled a ball of fire into the dirt below him before performing a summersault and landing with a graceful bow.

Tongues of fire shot up all around the edges of the stage. Jack realized that there must have been a trap door in the platform's center, and the person with the earth stone had covered the door entrance by making a mass of dirt with a hole in the center. The hole in the stage must have had some type of hollow tubes that stretched out from it and allowed whatever was shot into the central hole to spew out the small holes lining the stage's edge.

Another person emerged, darted up to the earth mound, and stuck his hand into it. Water shot out of the holes, extinguishing the fire and creating a moist, steamy atmosphere all around the stage.

Another person stepped out onto the platform and lifted his hand. Light shone brightly from his palm, creating a beautiful rainbow in the room's center.

Charles bumped Jack with his elbow. "That's really cool. That last person is using a light stone. He's bending the light artificially to allow him to reflect it off the water at the correct angle to produce the rainbow."

More entertainment commenced, but Jack thought that the first show was the best.

As the feast ended, Sir Alter said, "The king has summoned the three of you to the Grand Hall tomorrow, and you will have your chance to ask him whatever questions you please at that time. Shortly after your conversation with the king, several other knights will arrive because a new mission is at hand. So get some sleep, and be ready."

That night the three young men were given quarters in the palace because knights and their families were apparently allowed to stay in the palace if they wished. The three of them slept soundly in their luxurious quarters and waited eagerly for the next day.

Chapter 23

CHARLES AWOKE AS SUN beams streamed through the window in their room. He looked around but did not see Jack anywhere. Ben lay flopped out on his bed with his head buried in the pillows.

Garthong ran about on Jack's bed, periodically gnawing on one of the pillows.

Charles chuckled to himself. The expensive pillows in the palace were stuffed with feathers, and the predatory lizard could probably still smell his quarry somewhere within the fabric's confines. Either that, or he was just bored. Garthong did, after all, have a tendency to get into trouble when Jack was not present.

The door to their room opened, and Jack strolled in with a tray of food.

Jack said, "Hey Charles, you're up. I got us all some food from the kitchen here in the palace. I figure we should go ahead and eat because we don't know how early the king will summon us."

Charles reached over and tapped Ben's shoulder.

Ben rolled over. "What is so important that you have to wake me up on a beautiful morning like this?"

Charles answered nonchalantly, "Oh, it has something to do with the king summoning us to his throne room."

Ben grumbled but sat up and started grabbing food off the tray.

Jack noticed the pillow on his bed and scolded his gother, who began wandering around the bed with his head down as though he were heartbroken by his master's rebuke.

As they ate, Ben asked, "So do we still think there's any chance that the king can and will help us get home?"

Jack shrugged. "Maybe. I'm sure we'll have to complete this mission that he already has planned for us first, but if he's from our world, he should understand our desire to return home."

They continued to debate the topic for the remainder of the meal.

As they finished their meal, there was a knock at the door. Charles arose and answered it.

Vennel entered and asked, "How long are you going to be gone on the mission?"

Charles shrugged. "We don't really know. It would probably be best if you stayed with the Celshen family until we returned. When we get back, we hope to know more about our future plans."

She nodded. She and Charles hugged and said their farewells before she departed.

Charles watched her retreating form as she walked down the hallway. He wished that she could travel with them.

Finally, Fada knocked on their door and informed them that the king was ready to see them in the Grand Hall.

They followed him through several hallways lit with torches and exited the palace. The palace was the central building in the complex. It stood six stories high and had a tower on each of its four corners. Many guards patrolled the palace grounds, and guards were also stationed at various doors. The front door to the Grand Hall was no exception, but the two guards there opened the large wooden doors as they approached.

The three friends walked inside the throne room. Approximately twenty guards adorned with polished, silver-colored armor stood stationed along the wall. Visors covered the guards' faces, and their shields bore the same three stars exhibited on the flag.

As the group entered, the king dismissed everyone near the throne with a wave of his hand and gestured for the three young men to come close.

They all knelt on one knee at the base of the throne.

The king said, "Rise. It is good to see the three of you. This is my first opportunity to talk with my new knights."

The three new knights stood.

Jack said, "I was told we are allowed to ask any question during this audience, is that true?"

King Tanner leaned forward. "Yes, but first, I want to thank you for catching the traitor. The governor of Juma will be tried for treason very soon. You may be asked to give additional testimony at some point, but the evidence appears to be overwhelming. In his book we discovered payments made to several different individuals. These payments were designed to frame a good and loyal Knight of Celel, so I thought you should know that you saved one of your own by catching this dangerous man. I shudder to think how much information he has funneled to the various slave cartels and other kingdoms for sheer profit." The king paused for a moment, and his expression lightened. "But you had some questions, so please ask."

The three fidgeted for a moment, not sure how to begin. Charles could feel his pulse rate quickening.

Finally, Jack asked, "Are you originally from this world?"

The king raised an eyebrow and began to laugh.

The three remained silent, unsure how to proceed.

The king said, "No, I am not. I am from what I believe is the same country from which you come. I'm an American."

Jack asked, "Did you ever find a way to get home?"

"Yes, I did." The king leaned back and gazed into the distance for a moment as if gathering his thoughts. "There are gemstones that will allow you to travel between worlds, and to my knowledge I'm the only one in this world who knows how to use them correctly. When I was first summoned into this world, it took me a long time to understand what happened. Eventually, I discovered that a mage had awakened a teleportation stone but was unable to figure out what the stone did, so he tried to use it in order to find out. Unfortunately for him, due to the natural safeguards in a portal designed to prevent people from becoming trapped, it takes some time to transport a person through it if the user is not skilled enough to draw them properly. The mage had already departed from the area by the time I came through the portal that he had created.

"I suspect this has happened several times throughout the last few thousand years of this world's existence. Ultimately, I was able to discern how the stones worked, and I have several of them. It's actually kind of funny; they are some of the easiest stones to obtain because collectors are usually the only ones interested in them." He turned his piercing gaze upon them. "And your next question is probably whether I would be willing to send you home. Am I right?"

Jack glanced at Ben and Charles. "Yes."

The king replied, "Very well, but this next mission is crucial, and I want you three to be part of the escort. I don't know if anyone has told you this, but there is a powerful country in the north called Holdom. I have found the heir to Holdom's throne, and I am sending him to that country. If all goes well, he will be crowned king, and the three kingdoms of the north will be united for the first time."

Charles thought, *Why do we need to accompany this guy? Surely there are other knights who could handle this.*

The king's gaze turned from Jack to Charles. "Sir Charles, do you have a question for me?"

Charles thought, *Wow, Sir Charles! I guess I'll have to get used to that.* He responded haltingly, "With all due respect, your majesty, is there no one else who could carry out this mission?"

The king smiled. "Yes, there are many, and I'm sending most of them. Approximately twenty knights will go on this mission, not just the three of you. I'm also sending another fifty skilled soldiers. You three are not from this world, and that provides you with a unique perspective on what takes place here. That unique perspective gives you advantages and disadvantages compared to the people born here. This mission's success is absolutely critical. It is so crucial that even the very nature of the mission is being kept secret."

Charles thought, *Not really. Everybody, including us, seems to know that Sir Sansall is the long-lost heir, and it's our aim to help him reach Holdom in time for the fall festival, where they test candidates for the crown.* Aloud he said, "I'm up for this."

Ben nodded. "Yeah, why not?"

Jack responded, "Since we are now your knights, it seems only fair that we should have to carry out at least one mission for you before we return home."

"Only one mission." The king leaned forward again and rested his elbows on his knees. "Be aware, though, when you return home, you may no longer be under my command, but you have sworn oaths as knights, and regardless of the world in which you live, you will still be knights. Nothing can ever take that away from you now except yourselves." King Tanner looked intently at each of his new knights in turn, letting his gaze rest briefly on Ben, Charles, and Jack. "Always let justice burn within your heart." The king straitened. "Now, if you have no more questions, I will summon the rest of the knights and the soldiers and give you all the mission's details."

As the three new knights stepped back, the king waved his hand, signaling the guards to open the doors.

Charles thought that he counted eighteen knights, including Sir Alter, walking through the doors. Then Charles felt a tap on his shoulder. He looked in the direction of the tap and saw Jack staring at one of the knights. Charles followed his gaze, and sure enough, the knight at whom Jack was staring looked very familiar.

Charles whispered, "Who is that?"

Jack whispered back, "Don't you guys remember the man in the dark cloak who was a fire mage? The one we helped on our way to Celel? Apparently, the man in the dark cloak is Sir Sumbvi, Knight of Celel."

Fifty or so soldiers marched in behind the knights and stood in a square formation. Several servants brought in a table with some maps and set it before the king. The king began reiterating the mission's details. The knights gathered around the table and watched as the king drew a line from the capital of Celel to Menchida, the capital of Holdom.

The king said, "This is the path that you will take. This man must be protected." He pointed at one of the knights gathered around the table. "This is Sir Sansall. The soldiers will set up a formation around him, allowing you knights to freely move and engage any attacking enemies without making Sir Sansall vulnerable."

Charles examined the knight and thought, *I don't really know how a king is supposed to look, but he may fit the bill.* Sir Sansall was of medium height and rather stocky. He possessed a strong jaw line, brown eyes, and shaggy blond hair that just covered his ears. He looked older than Charles's parents but younger than King Tanner. His confident posture and the experienced look in his eyes did give him a dignified air.

The king leaned over the table toward his knights and raised his voice. "You knights and soldiers have long fought to protect the north and foster good and justice throughout this world. Now is the most important time. A victory here is crucial. No matter what, take this group to Menchida."

The knights nodded solemnly and loyal murmurs of agreement rippled through the group. Then they turned and followed the marching soldiers out of the palace.

Horses waited in the palace courtyard for the knights and soldiers, and the group quickly mounted. Several other horses pulled carts driven by Fada and a number of other servants. Charles thought, *Those must be our supplies for the journey.*

As the group marched out of Sellta's gates, enthusiasm soared within the ranks, but over the next few days, the excitement simmered down substantially. It took four days for the group to reach the border of Celel. After they crossed the border, they felt a degree of tension for the rest of the day. The soldiers, however, relaxed as they continued to travel without any sign of an enemy.

The group traveled along the northern border of Dulla for another five days without any indication of trouble, and some of the group's members began to think that all the security was unnecessary.

Ben complained more than once about the terrain despite the fact that this was the same type of rough road that they had used to get to Celel the first time. Travel was very slow here in comparison to the higher-quality roads spread all over Celel. The road along which they now passed was not even a real road but just a wide dirt path. The journey became even slower as they left Dulla's border behind them.

Ben asked Jack, "So how much longer do you think this journey will take?"

Jack examined a sketch of the northern countries. "According to the map, we are more than halfway, but considering the way the terrain is changing, we probably still have at least ten days ahead of us. Also, now that we've left Dulla's border, I would expect any attack to happen soon."

"Yeah." Charles adjusted his position in his saddle. "Before, we could've retreated farther into Dulla if we were pressed hard, but now there's nowhere to go but forward."

Jack nodded and whispered into the sack on his shoulders, "Garthong, give this place a look from the sky. See if there are any potential enemies nearby."

With a little screech Garthong rocketed into the air and began flying around, but over the next two days the only thing that he became excited about was an occasional rodent that he could eat.

Hills and sparse trees now surrounded the area through which they traveled. The constant elevation change along the road prevented them from seeing potential enemies until they were very close, which made an ambush a distinct possibility.

The three friends talked a great deal on the journey, but they did not converse very much with anyone else. Charles thought they probably should mingle more, but they did not know anyone except Sir Alter, who did not speak much on missions, and Sir Sumbvi.

Humorously enough to Charles, Sir Sumbvi had not noticed them yet. The man seemed completely oblivious to what was happening around him. It was true that he was bringing up the rear while the three boys rode toward the front, but still, the knight seemed to pay very little attention. Charles remembered that Sir Sumbvi was not a particularly attentive man, but he seemed gloomy and distracted, which made him pay even less attention to his surroundings than normal.

That night Charles suggested to Jack that they go talk to Sir Sumbvi and see what was bothering him.

The three friends walked through camp toward Sir Sumbvi, who sat all alone.

The camp resided inside a loose perimeter of carts with the soldiers and servants sleeping in and around the carts. Most of the knights gathered around the fire in the camp's center. A few knights seemed to know each other and reminisced about old times. Other knights exchanged histories and became acquainted. Still others seemed more reserved and preferred to listen to the others or retire early for the night. Sir Sumbvi stayed a little ways away from the fire. He sat just close enough that the occasional flame would briefly combat the shadows and reveal his face.

The three friends drew near and stopped in front of Sir Sumbvi. Jack said, "It's always nice to meet old friends."

Sir Sumbvi looked up at the young men, but the darkness obscured their features because they faced away from the fire. The knight turned his face away and muttered, "I have no old friends anymore."

Jack smiled, and the moonlight glinted off his teeth as he sat down next to Sir Sumbvi, turning his body so that he faced the fire. "You must forgive me. I'm so young that an old friend to me may simply be someone I haven't met recently."

Someone threw additional wood on the fire, causing the blaze to flare and cast light all around it.

As the light splashed over Jack's face, Sir Sumbvi sprang to his feet. "What are you doing here, Jack? And Ben and Charles?"

"You know," Jack replied with fake indignation, "it's appropriate to refer to a knight by the title sir."

Sir Sumbvi sat back down. "When did all of this happen?"

Jack, Ben, and Charles briefly recounted their adventures since they met him.

Sir Sumbvi shook his head. "I heard that a knighting ceremony took place before I arrived, but I just came back from a mission, so I missed the festivities."

"What's bothering you?" Jack asked.

Sir Sumbvi sighed heavily, and his shoulders slumped. "My brother and I were both Knights of Celel, but he was killed about a month ago, along with an old friend of mine. We never even found their bodies."

"So what are you doing here?" Jack pressed.

"What do you mean? Where else would I be?" Sir Sumbvi kept is gaze trained on the ground at his feet.

Ben said, "Jack's right. You haven't found their bodies, so you don't know that they're dead. You should be out searching for them. If Jack or Charles went missing, I would never stop searching until I knew for sure what had happened."

Sir Sumbvi thought for a moment then said bitterly, "The trail has already gone cold."

Ben spoke again, "Then do whatever you have to do to thaw out the trail. As soon as this mission is over, head off wherever you need to go, and find out what happened."

"I suppose you're right," Sir Sumbvi replied. "I'll never get closure unless I find out how they died."

Seeming to feel better, Sir Sumbvi told them a great deal about what had happened to him since they had last seen him.

******

Jack awoke the next morning to a weird screeching noise. He looked up and saw Garthong flying around overhead as happy as could be. The camp bustled with activity as the soldiers and knights ate breakfast, packed their supplies, and cared for their horses. Then everyone mounted, and the company recommenced its journey.

The morning seemed to pass slowly as the group traveled. Sir Sumbvi brought his horse up near the front and rode with the three boys.

Jack sent Garthong up into the air again. Jack thought, *It's a beautiful day—not too hot and not too cold.* The sun shone brightly, and he could not see a cloud in the sky.

Suddenly, Garthong made a shrill, high-pitched noise that immediately attracted the attention of everyone below him. Garthong flew straight back to Jack and dived into his sack.

Jack spoke quietly but firmly to everyone nearby, "Be on the alert. Pass the word quietly on to the back."

Within a few minutes everyone was alert.

Jack loosened both of his swords in their scabbards and waited as the group slowly moved forward. Jack saw no abnormal movement and heard no unexpected noise. He thought, *It's too quiet, and something spooked Garthong. He doesn't go off like that for no reason.* Jack was becoming better at identifying the different noises that his gother made, and that one was definitely a warning call.

A large hill covered in trees spanned the right side of the road, and a very sharp rise with a few large rocks stretched along the left side, but Jack saw nothing that could serve as a hiding place. Just ahead of them, the road's elevation dipped slightly so that hills would soon completely surround them. Jack thought, *If anything's going to happen, it will probably be right there.*

As the road started to drop, Jack heard a faint whistling in the wind. He looked to his left just as he was knocked off his horse. He hit the ground hard and thought, *What was that?* Then Jack realized that he had been hit with a massive gust of air. The wind was so quiet that he had just barely heard it before it struck him.

He was not the only one either; about six of the other knights had also hit the ground. The knights and soldiers shouted and drew their weapons.

Jack heard several loud cracks from lightning, and the road in front of them burst into flames. Even though Jack had stood to his feet, he had trouble seeing since so many horsemen swarmed around him.

Many of the horses spooked due to the lightning and fire. The mounted knights tried to bring their horses under control while simultaneously searching for enemies.

Jack remembered, *The whole point of this mission is to protect Sir Sansall.* Jack turned and headed toward the soldiers.

The armed guards had dismounted and formed a defensive formation around Sir Sansall. Jack had almost reached the soldiers' line when the soldiers suddenly disappeared, and a large dark void replaced the light. Someone was clearly using a corrupt light stone.

Jack headed straight for the darkness.

Two fireballs hurtled toward the black void from behind trees on the right. Jack heard screaming from soldiers inside the darkness, and the dark field began moving rapidly back toward the trees on the road's right side.

As Jack followed, he glanced to his right and left and realized that many men now attacked from the front and rear, and the clash of swords began to ring loudly.

Jack recognized the symbol on one of the enemy soldiers and whispered, "Caishan."

The darkness in front of Jack disappeared, and several charred corpses of Caishan slavers lay on the ground.

Sir Sansall must have been captured, Jack reasoned, *but he managed to get an attack off before they brought him completely under control.*

Jack remained cautious as he rushed toward the trees, unsure whether the enemy would attack as he approached. He reached the tree line and began running through the vegetation. He discovered that the forest only extended about forty feet, and a field lay on the other side.

Overtaken by Destiny

Jack saw a horse-drawn cart with several men in the back moving quickly across the field.

Two of the men noticed Jack, pulled out their shields, and positioned themselves on the back of the cart with their shields up to prevent spells from striking anyone in the cart.

Jack sprinted through the field, but even as he did, he thought, *This is ridiculous. There's no way I can keep up with a horse.* The Caishan were already too far away for Jack to use ice. *Maybe I could hit one of the wheels with a lightning bolt. From this distance and with how fast it's moving, though, I don't have a good chance.*

Then, remembering the entertainers at the knighting ceremony, Jack had an idea. He stretched out his hand, and a strong wind poured out of his palm. Jack pulled the wind around him so that it encircled him. Then he pushed himself forward using the wind.

Jack felt incredibly light as he rocketed across the field. He thought, *This gives a whole new meaning to the phrase 'running like the wind.'* After approximately eight seconds he ran out of air and cast again. Jack was amazed; he was actually outrunning the horse and cart. With one final cast, he caught up to the cart, jumped into the air, used the wind to push himself over the two guards' shields in the back of the cart, and landed directly behind the guards.

Jack immediately dropped to one knee and slammed his elbows into the two surprised guards' backs, knocking them both out of the cart.

Two more guards crouched in the cart's front section, struggling to deploy their weapons in the cramped quarters. Behind them sat the driver and another man with a mask covering the lower half of his face. Sir Sansall lay between Jack and the remaining Caishan guards with his hands and feet tied to opposite sides of the cart. The Caishan had encased the knight's hands in clay. *That's ingenious,* Jack thought. *I've never seen an earth stone user create clay rather than just rock.* Jack drew one of his swords and cut the ropes holding Sir Sansall.

One of the guards swung his sword at Jack, but instead of deflecting the attack, Jack ducked, grabbed Sir Sansall, and pulled him backward, causing them both to fall out the back of the cart. There was a flash of light and a loud crack, and a bolt of lightning grazed Jack's right side as he fell. The two knights hit the ground, and Jack tried to help Sir Sansall pull the clay off one of his hands.

A yell came from the cart, and the horse pulling it halted.

All four men jumped out of the cart.

Three of them ran toward Jack with their weapons drawn.

The masked man had also drawn his weapons, but he moved slowly toward them, lifting his hand.

Jack thought, *Here it comes*, and he raised his own hand.

Lightning came pouring forth from the masked man's hand, but Jack created a sheet of water that connected to the ground in front of him.

The lightning struck the water and rocketed into the earth, sending dirt, stones, and grass flying in all directions.

Jack leapt toward one of the soldiers in front of him, thrusting the soldier's sword aside while simultaneously kicking the inside of his left leg.

Off balance, the guard fell forward. He stabbed his sword into the ground to keep himself from falling completely.

Jack twisted and slashed his sword across the soldier's back.

As the man dropped to the ground, Jack ran toward the masked man. Jack had no way to know how many gemstones the enemy mage possessed. *It will be harder for him to use them on me without hurting himself if I'm right next to him,* Jack reasoned. *If I can distract him, Sir Sansall can hopefully either escape or recover and help me fight.*

Jack swung the sword in his right hand.

The enemy mage sidestepped and knocked the blade aside.

As Jack's body turned slightly to the right under the force of the block, he used the extra momentum to thrust with his left-handed sword.

The masked man jumped back to avoid the blow.

Jack leapt toward his opponent, swinging down with his left sword while pulling his right sword back for a right-handed thrust.

His opponent sent Jack's first attack glancing to the side and raised his shield to avert the second.

The cart rested just behind the enemy mage, giving Jack an idea. He came at his opponent again with a flurry of quick strikes then thrust with his right sword again, forcing the masked man to bring up his shield. Jack then executed a powerful front kick straight into the shield, knocking the masked man backward into the cart's left rear corner.

His foe struck the cart and fell with a gasp.

Before Jack could close in and finish off his adversary, he heard something behind him. Jack whipped around just in time to block a sword strike from one of the two remaining guards.

The other guard fought Sir Sansall, who had managed to free one of his hands and pick up the sword from the first guard Jack had killed.

Jack swung his sword at his enemy, but it glanced off his opponent's shield. Jack thought, *I'm running out of time. All that masked guy has to do is raise his hand and blast me with something.*

The soldier in front of Jack thrust his sword at Jack's midsection.

Jack twisted to the left so that he was at a ninety degree angle to the guard. He grabbed the guard's arm and pulled the man forward. The man stumbled and quickly regained his footing, but Jack had successfully placed the soldier between himself and the masked mage on the ground.

The guard stepped forward, swinging his sword in a downward arc.

Jack swiftly turned his back to the enemy, crossed his swords, and thrust them above his head, catching his opponent's sword. Then Jack unleashed a back kick straight into his opponent's shield.

The soldier fell backward on top of the masked man, who had just managed to stand.

As the two of them floundered on the ground, Jack quickly turned and raised his hand. Lightning sprang forth and split them both into pieces.

Jack heard another loud crack behind him.

Jack spun and realized that Sir Sansall had fired lightning at the two soldiers who had fallen off the cart and were now running through the field toward him.

Sir Sansall returned to fending off the other guard next to him.

Jack rushed at the guard engaged with the knight and swung his sword in an upward arc, slicing into the soldier's arm and forcing him to drop his sword.

Sir Sansall turned to Jack and jerked his head toward the forest. "Run! Back to the group. Quickly!"

Jack chuckled. "Run? That's ridiculous. I just put that guy out of the fight. There are only two left, and you haven't even used all of your gemstones."

A Destiny Among Worlds

Sir Sansall put his hand on Jack's shoulder. "You don't understand. The Caishan obviously ordered this group to capture me, but the enemy commander is bound to be nearby. Since the prize is right here, this is where he'll come."

Jack replied, "I see. Can you hold those two guys while I grab the gemstones off that masked man?"

"Only if you can get them very quickly."

Jack rushed over to what remained of the masked mage and started searching. Suddenly, he heard Garthong's warning cry right in his ear. Jack looked up and saw a half dozen men on horseback riding toward them. One man wore polished plate armor and rode a powerful gray horse while the others wore leather armor and sat astride smaller mounts. Jack assumed that the man in the plate armor was the enemy commander.

Jack quickly abandoned his search and yelled, "You were right! I think the enemy commander is here!"

Jack and Sir Sansall circled around the two guards in front of them and kept running. Since neither Jack nor Sir Sansall carried a heavy shield, they were easily able to outrun the two guards pursuing them on foot.

The men on horseback, however, were gaining quickly.

Sir Sansall thrust his right arm behind him and let fly a fireball toward the approaching horseman. Before it struck, a wall of water materialized from the Caishan leader's hand and absorbed the fireball.

"They're going to catch up soon." Jack looked forward again at the tree line and saw two horsemen riding out from the direction of the Celel force toward them. Jack thought, *That's Ben and Charles. Oh you two ... you have no idea how happy I am to see you.*

Several of the horsemen behind them fired arrows, and Jack felt one whiz past him.

Jack's side still throbbed where the lightning had grazed it, but he had been fortunate. If he had been touching something conductive, the electricity might have coursed through his body instead of following the trajectory that its master had set.

Several more arrows whistled past them, and one struck Sir Sansall in his right leg. The knight fell and skidded on the ground. Jack turned, brandishing both his swords, and stood between Sir Sansall and the approaching Caishan horsemen.

Sir Sansall whispered, "You fool, run. They won't chase you. They're here for me."

Jack responded calmly, "I am a Knight of Celel. I don't abandon my mission or my friends." He added silently, *I wish I was as confident as my words sound.* Jack could feel the earth shaking as the horses bore down on him.

They were right in front of him.

Then they disappeared, and Jack could not see anything. Jack thought, *What happened?* He heard the sound of a horse whinnying in terror, and he imagined the animal rearing just in front of him. Jack realized that Ben must have been behind him activating his corrupt light stone. Suddenly, Jack could see immediately around him again, but he still could not see the horsemen, and the phenomenon confused his eyes.

He turned and saw Ben and Charles grab Sir Sansall and pull him up so that he was suspended between their horses. Jack saw light pouring from Charles's hand, and after dissipating to create a light sphere, it constrict again and flowed into Ben's hand. The two of them had somehow created light within darkness by using both of their stones together. While light filled the sphere, a layer of darkness remained between their adversaries and themselves, preventing the two opposing forces from seeing one another.

"Hurry," Ben whispered as he gathered his horse's reins. "We only have a few seconds. Remember, just because they can't see us doesn't mean they can't hit us with stuff."

Jack took off running after them, trying to stay within their sphere. He heard the whiz of arrows as the horsemen behind him shot blindly into the black sphere.

Although Jack and his friends could not see them, it sounded as though the enemy horsemen were gaining control over their startled mounts.

A chestnut horse's head entered the realm of light inside the dark sphere.

Ben whispered, "No you don't. You can't block what you can't see." Just as the rider's face was about to cross the threshold of darkness, Ben hurled a fireball that struck the rider.

Jack heard the horsemen behind them reigning in their horses and slowing. Unfortunately, just then, the darkness disappeared.

Charles turned his hand backward at the last second and shined his blinding light toward their pursuers.

As they kept running, Jack commented to Charles between breaths, "Very nice. ... You cast your stone about two seconds after Ben didn't you? That way ... you would be able to blind them right after we lost our cover."

Charles nodded. "Yes, and the best part is that it blinded their horses too, so it should buy us a few extra seconds before they can follow us."

The knights hastened toward the trees while the Caishan men spurred their horses forward.

Jack felt a tingling sensation and leapt sideways just as a bolt of lightning crashed into where he had been running. He hit the ground, rolled, and came back up running. Jack's lungs screamed for more oxygen, but he thought, *I have to keep running.*

Charles shot a lightning bolt behind him, but a wall of dirt sprang out of the enemy commander's hand.

Ben cast his lightning, but another earthen wall appeared in front of it.

The trees were close now.

Charles cast his fireball.

Instead of blocking it the commander altered his course and dodged the fireball.

Charles yelled, "He must be getting low on gemstones. He's probably trying to conserve his last few."

Jack heard a change in the wind and saw arrows flying from the trees toward them. Jack thought, *Did the enemy get in front of us?* Then he realized that the arrows were falling just behind them in their pursuers' path.

The horsemen lifted their shields above their heads and kept riding.

Jack glanced over his shoulder and saw the enemy commander raise both of his hands. Two lightning bolts shot forth, one just behind the other.

Jack dropped onto his face as the two bolts of lightning passed over him, but as he hit the ground, Jack realized that he was not the target. Instead, the lightning headed toward Sir Sansall.

Sensing the lightning strike, Sir Sansall pulled his hand free from Charles, swung toward Ben's horse, and slipped out of the first lightning bolt's path. The knight then shoved his free hand behind him, pouring dirt out from his palm. The knight was just in time. The lightning struck the dirt and plunged into the ground, but as Sir Sansall hung from Ben, who still held his arm, his weight ripped Ben off his horse.

Charles's horse reared due to the close proximity of the first lightning bolt, and the movement threw Charles to the ground.

As they all lay sprawled on the dirt, Jack thought, *Where are all the other knights? We could really use the help right about now.*

Just then, men ran from the trees with their weapons drawn.

The Caishan men wheeled their horses and rode off as quickly as they could.

Several bolts of lightning streaked across the field, picking off two of the horsemen. The archers from the woods also continued to fire arrows.

The enemy commander and his remaining men, however, escaped and headed back toward the cart, probably to collect the masked mage's gemstones.

Sir Sumbvi walked up to Jack as he lay on the ground. "Well, you three were quite the heroes. While everyone else was stuck fighting, you somehow managed to discover and thwart the enemy's plan. You'll be glad to know that the other knights dispatched all the men who attacked the main group. I'd be a bit surprised if the enemy could muster a large enough group to make a second attack before we reach the capital, so we should no longer be in danger."

"That's good," Jack muttered. "I'm going to stay here on the ground for a while longer." Jack still panted heavily. He thought, *I wish I had the ability to use my air stones again. I would do my best to flow it all straight into my lungs.*

After a few minutes Jack pulled himself up off the ground and returned to his horse. He glanced at Ben and Charles. "Good thing you two showed up when you did."

Ben replied, "You better know it. If the two of us didn't pull you out of trouble, who knows where you would end up."

"I just wish I'd gotten my hands on some of those gemstones," Jack lamented. "It could be really handy to have a few extra."

The company placed Sir Sansall in one of the carts because of his wound. He seemed relieved but in a strange way that Jack did not fully understand. When Jack mentioned it to Ben and Charles, they agreed that Sir Sansall seemed to have more energy now than before his injury.

The next few days until they reached Holdom's border passed slowly since they tried to remain vigilant in case of another attack. As Sir Sumbvi had predicted, however, the enemy was either unable or unwilling to marshal another force large enough to make a second attack within the journey's last few days.

As they traveled, Jack found himself paying less attention to his surroundings and thinking, instead, about his most recent fight. He thought, *I was too reckless. I used up all my gemstones early and was completely useless later in the fight.* Even when his friends came to assist him, they were still not strong enough. *If the other knights and soldiers hadn't arrived when they did, that would've been the end of us.*

His thoughts then drifted to his gemstone use. What he had discovered about his air stone was fascinating. *I should be able to apply that information to broaden my understanding of how to use my other gemstones. Exerting more fine-tuned control over my gemstones will allow me to use them in more complicated ways. These mage fights are almost exclusively based on the number of stones that the individuals have and the individuals' skill in using their stones. I need to become even more skilled in my fine-tuned control over the elements after I create them.*

Jack looked at one of the soldiers marching behind him. "Hey, could you throw me a few of those rocks on the road?"

The soldier tossed him three rocks.

Jack gently threw them into the air, stretched out his hand, and created air in front of himself. Before the rocks hit the ground, Jack used the air to catch and lift them. Then he moved them around in a circle until his air stone ran out.

Jack thought, *Some of the stones can last ten seconds, but six or seven seconds seems to be more common. If I can figure out how to keep my stones active longer, it should give me a strong advantage.*

A Destiny Among Worlds

Chapter 24

THE NEXT DAY JACK looked out over the walls of Menchida, the capital of Holdom. From the outside the capital looked old and past its prime, but Jack could tell that at one time it had been a mighty city. He saw that the buildings on the other side of the wall were made almost entirely of stone. He marveled at the construction and wondered, *Where could they have quarried so much stone to build such a city?*

Jack looked at his two friends. "Perhaps with a king the city can return to the glory that it obviously once had."

Ben nodded. "Even the buildings outside the city, like the farmhouses, look old and rundown."

When they reached the city, the soldiers remained outside the gates, and only the knights continued forward. As they entered, they saw brightly colored garlands and streamers hanging everywhere, which bespoke excitement. Townspeople scurried about and exchanged festive greetings. The bustle and enthusiasm of the festival contrasted strongly with the old stone buildings lining the streets.

As Jack examined the stone buildings, he discovered that the walls had no tool marks on them. He looked closer and realized, *Mages, not workers, created this city.* It amazed him to think that enough mages with earth stones could actually create a stone city. *This city must truly have been the gem of the north.*

Jack noticed approximately two dozen horsemen adorned in gray plate armor coming down the street toward them.

As the horsemen approached, one of them addressed Jack's group, demanding, "What business does such a large armed force have here in our city?"

One of the other soldiers commented, "If you don't want to answer, that's okay. We wouldn't mind cutting you down where you stand."

Sir Alter hung his arms loosely at his sides to indicate that he held no weapon. "We are here for the festival. It appears that it has already begun, so we must apologize for being late."

The leader of the horsemen narrowed his eyes. "Who are you, and why are you here for the festival?"

Sir Alter answered, "Our king believes that he has found an heir to your throne, and we are the escort to ensure that this man reaches the palace safely."

The horsemen laughed. One of them said, "You are all fools. It has been hundreds of years since we had a king."

Sir Alter maintained a calm demeanor. "It is customary for anyone who wishes to touch the king's stone to be allowed to do so during the festival. Isn't that correct?"

The leader of the horsemen nodded. "Fine, five of you can come to the palace, but I won't let your entire armed company near our palace."

Sir Alter turned and pointed at several knights. "You will accompany Sir Sansall to the palace."

Sir Sansall lifted his hand. "No, Sir Alter. You and those three young knights"—He gestured toward Jack, Ben, and Charles—"will accompany me."

Sir Alter lifted his eyebrows slightly but made no argument. "As you wish."

The rest of the knights headed back toward the gate where the soldiers waited, and the five of them continued forward.

They were forced to stop as a parade passed through the street in front of them, and cheering townspeople gathered all around their group. The parade consisted of groups of soldiers with their polished weapons and armor and many different types of performers.

Jack's group turned to the side and traveled parallel to the parade for a little while until they found a break to cross the street.

Sir Sansall said, "We must reach the palace before the celebration ends. We need a good crowd so that enough witnesses will be present to confirm the new king. If there are only a few people, they could potentially be bribed or murdered in order to prevent a new king from gaining power."

In front of them, rising above the other buildings, stood the palace. The building was huge, covering far more area than the palace in Sellta. The entire structure rested on a plateau approximately four stories above everything else, making it visible from almost anywhere in the town. Jack noticed that the roof of the primary palace building possessed a flat area, and he asked Sir Alter, "What's that big flat place for?"

Sir Alter replied, "Long ago when this nation had a king, every new king traditionally carved a new statue of himself, a warrior, or an animal—pretty much whatever the king wanted—and placed it on the roof. Many statues have stood on the roof since the building's creation. They traditionally show not just the way that the king rules but also some form of a character trait by which he wants to be remembered."

People filled the stairs around them, and Jack could barely hear the knight's answer to his question over the din of people talking around him.

Several long flights of stairs with landings between them led up to the palace entrance. The initial stairs were about 300 feet wide. These stairs terminated after several flights in a generous landing, and a narrower staircase led the rest of the way to the final large landing at the palace entrance. These narrower stairs were approximately eighty feet wide at their base and twenty feet wide at their termination. The stone staircase achieved the width transition with a graceful, sweeping curve on each side.

Jack's group slowly pushed their way through the crowd until they neared the top of the narrower staircase. Another group of people waited separately from the crowd on the large landing paved with stone between the top of the stairs and the palace.

In front of the palace, soldiers wearing silver-colored armor stood at attention on the landing's front edge. They carried long spears and shields and wore small steel helmets with a black cloth that extended from the base of their helmets and draped over their shoulders.

Sir Sansall turned. "We need to get past these guards and into that group of people. Follow me."

The knight walked up to a man dressed in a red and gold robe. "We are here to test ourselves on the stone."

The man furrowed his brow and looked at them as if they did not belong. Then he shrugged. "Well, anyone is supposed to be able to touch it if they want, so go ahead." He casually waved them through.

Ben looked at Jack. "How many people do you think are actually here to see if they are descended from the king?"

Jack surveyed the group. "It looks like about fifty other than us."

They stood and waited. Apparently, the ceremony was not ready to begin just yet.

Jack gazed around again. The style of the palace's architecture definitely gave the impression that the country at one time possessed a huge amount of resources. The stone blocks comprising the palace walls looked much larger than the blocks used to create the stone buildings in any of the other cities Jack had seen. The building formed a large rectangle, and the roof jutted approximately ten feet past the top of the walls. Several marble pillars braced the roof's overhanging portion. Small spires also shot up from the palace roof and ended in blunt points.

Jack looked under the overhang. Just outside the palace doors stood two stone statues that were about twice the size of a man. The stone statues held huge axes that were crafted out of steel with thick wooden handles.

Gold filigree depicting various images ran along the palace's walls. Pictures of landscapes, battles, and other events definitively confirmed the country's long and glorious history. A thin protective layer of crystal that was as clear as glass covered all the images.

The pillars holding up the roof were all crafted from marble, perfectly smooth and straight. Even the veins within each of the marble pillars matched those of the other pillars.

Jack shook his head in wonder. *Mages created all of this. Remarkable,* he thought, *an earth stone can create any kind of earth element.* He glanced at Charles and saw his eyes wide with wonder as well. These earth mages' skill was incredible. Gold, marble, granite, silver—it was all the same to these artisans of ages past.

Jack whispered, "No wonder this country was so wealthy. They could, in fact, create their own currency. They must have had to dedicate their lives to their art in order to create these different elements and weave them together in such an intricate fashion."

Jack gazed out over the city and saw several other sizable stone buildings scattered around the town. He also noticed a large, flat empty area with no buildings about a quarter mile in front of the palace.

Jack elbowed Charles and pointed at the empty spot in the city. "What do you think that's for?"

"I'm not actually sure," replied Charles. "It's very interesting; it's just a big square."

Sir Alter looked where Jack pointed and explained, "Some very old cities have places like that where the troops could gather quickly to be dispatched to different sections of the walls. To tell you the truth, very few cities actually had large enough populations to make it a common practice, but this city has one because it has been a large city for ages past."

A group of men filed out of the palace doors and took up positions at the head of the stairs, spaced several feet apart from each other. They each lifted a horn and blew into it. The instruments were loud like a trumpet but only produced one shrill note. Several men brought a cart out through the palace doors and positioned it on the landing within easy view of the stairs. A stone pedestal stood in the cart, and the only object on the stand was a small brown gemstone.

Jack almost smiled. He had expected something a little more impressive than a little brown rock. *I suppose I'll figure out what it does when Sir Sansall touches the stone*, he thought.

A procession of what Jack presumed to be noblemen followed after the cart and formed a half circle around it at a little distance. In all, there were six noblemen and a seventh man, who was very tall and broad shouldered with gold-colored armor. This large man seemed to have authority over the rest of the men. A servant brought out a short wooden set of stairs and placed them behind the cart so that the crowd could see the faces of those touching the stone.

The huge man in gold-colored armor pointed at the first man standing in the line of people waiting to touch the stone and commanded, "Come."

Jack watched as the man climbed up the wooden stairs and touched the small stone with his finger.

Nothing happened, and the man in the gold armor waved the person down the crowded stairs and pointed at the next person in line.

It seemed like it would take forever to get to Sir Sansall since they were in the very back. Jack just wanted to finish and head back. After all, their home waited for them after this mission.

Person after person touched the stone until Sir Sansall's turn finally came.

Sir Sansall leaned on Sir Alter because of his injured leg, and the two made their way toward the stone.

Jack and his friends fidgeted a little. They were the only ones left in line other than the two knights walking toward the stone.

Sir Alter reached up and touched the stone, but nothing happened. He helped the other knight up the wooden steps.

Sir Sansall stretched out his hand.

Jack held his breath; it had all come to this moment. Now their whole journey was coming to an end, and they could go home.

Sir Sansall touched the stone.

Nothing happened.

Jack heard both of his friends exhale loudly next to him, and Jack was sure that he must have done the same. *What was the point of this mission?* Jack wondered. *The king must have gotten his information wrong. Sir Sansall is not the heir to the throne after all. It was all for nothing.* Jack could see Sir Alter's face. He looked crushed. Sir Sansall's expression, however, had not changed at all.

The two knights stepped down into the crowd and turned, waiting for the three boys to join them.

The huge man in gold armor called loudly, "Hey you, you're holding up the ceremony. Come!"

Jack looked up and realized that the big man had pointed at him when the two knights had stepped down.

"Sorry," Jack mumbled. He headed toward the little wooden stairs. Jack thought, *I guess the three of us have to touch the dumb rock too before we go home.* Then he thought, *What if the king doesn't let us go home because we failed the mission? ... But it wasn't our fault that we failed.* Jack stepped onto the wooden stairs, casually reached over, and picked up the stone.

The big man scowled at him and made a guttural growing sound. "You're only supposed to touch the stone, not pick it up. Open your hand."

Jack still had his fist extended palm downward. He opened his hand to drop the gemstone, but the stone did not fall out of his palm. Jack thought, *What's wrong with this thing? It's stuck in my hand.* He felt a burning sensation in his palm. He pulled his hand back slightly and turned it palm upward, examining the stone.

The stone started to glow, and it made Jack's skin a little uncomfortable as its temperature increased.

The people in the crowd looked terrified and amazed as they stared at the glowing stone.

The noblemen at the top of the steps turned to look at him and gasped.

Jack gritted his teeth as the pain became more intense.

Then the stone started to change. It seemed to melt, yet it maintained its original shape. The elements within the stone appeared to move, and Jack saw what looked like a drop of blood rise to the surface and swirl gently within the brown background. Jack heard a whisper coming from the stone, but the whisper was so loud that everyone in the crowd could hear the voice. At first Jack did not understand what the voice said; then he realized that it whispered in the tongue of angels, and he began to recognize the words. Jack ignored the crowd and tried to listen. He realized that the whispered words were an awakening for a gemstone.

As Jack stared at the swirling blood in the stone, it seemed to draw him into it. Suddenly, wisps of mist emerged from the stone and coalesced into the form of an elderly man wearing a royal robe and crown. The crowd continued to stare at the glowing stone, so Jack guessed that the people could not see the apparition. Time seemed to slow as Jack watched the man. Jack saw him reach out his hand as if passing it through the ages to place it on Jack's shoulder. Jack heard him speak without an audible voice—as if the essence of this king spoke directly to Jack's own consciousness.

The king said, "My son, I bind this stone to my blood so that it may forever be protected from those who would usurp the kingdom. Every ruler wishes to progress beyond his predecessor. Remember that the best way to prosper a kingdom is to invest in the people you rule. No king builds a kingdom by himself. Prosper the people who follow you, and more people will follow you. Rule with wisdom."

The apparition flickered and disappeared.

Jack shook himself as he again became aware of the crowd, which still stared at the stone. Although the whisper continued, the stone stabilized and returned to its original appearance. Jack could not feel the heat anymore.

Jack could not see Ben and Charles, who were off to his left behind the noblemen, but he looked down at Sir Alter, whose normal stern expression had actually changed to one of utter shock. Then Jack looked at Sir Sansall. *That's weird,* thought Jack. *Sir Sansall is the only one here who doesn't look surprised.*

Suddenly, Jack realized that the king had not made an error. The king knew all along that Sir Sansall was not the heir to the throne. Sir Sansall was just supposed to be the decoy. Jack reasoned, *This stone is reacting to me, and that knight isn't surprised, which means Sir Sansall knew it would react to me, which means the king also knew.* No wonder Sir Sansall had ordered Jack to leave him behind and called Jack a fool for staying to save him. *Sir Sansall wasn't the mission. I was. It's just that only the king and Sir Sansall knew about it. But how can this thing react to me? I can't be of this bloodline. This is some other world.*

The voice stopped whispering, and Jack realized that the awakening was completed.

He looked over at the huge man in gold armor. "Now what?"

The big man stood with his eyes open wide and jaw hanging slack. "Uh, show us the power of the gemstone!"

The crowd yelled, "Show us! Show us!"

Jack lifted his hand and realized, *I don't even know what kind of stone this is. I guess it was brown, so it's probably an earth stone. If I make a big rock right here in front of me, it could roll down those stairs and hurt people.* Jack turned to the open area at the top of the stairs to his right. He spread his fingers. Instantly, earth poured from his hand, and the rock materializing in front of him grew larger and larger. Although the entire event only lasted a few seconds, it seemed to Jack that the rock took forever to reach full size.

Jack looked at the boulder in his hand and whispered, "It's bigger than a van or truck." He gently set the massive round rock on the flat area.

Cheering erupted from the crowd, and people began dancing and singing.

The big man in gold armor stepped up on the cart and yelled, "Let it be known that Holdom has a king again!"

Jack looked over to where his friends stood. Charles looked completely shocked, and Ben cheered with the crowd as loudly as he could. Jack could not hear what Ben said, but he smiled as he thought, *That crazy guy probably thinks that he's going to get a promotion out of this. I actually have no idea what will happen next.*

Jack glanced at the noble lords around him and noted that even though the man in the gold armor and some of the noblemen seemed pleased, a few of the nobles looked rather angry. Jack thought, *Great. I just became king of some country that didn't really want a king—or at least the nobles didn't. Wait a second; am I actually okay with being king? I don't know. For now I should just go with it. I'll think about it later.* Jack waved to the crowd, which seemed to excite the people even more.

Then he looked at the huge man next to him. "What now?"

The man returned his gaze. "I honestly have no idea. It's been many generations .... I have no idea what's supposed to happen next. I suppose we need to crown you king. But first—" He knelt on one knee.

The crowd became silent and also knelt.

Then all the lords standing around the cart turned and knelt.

Jack looked out over the crowd. "Please, everyone stand." But that was as far as Jack got. He could not think of anything else to say. *What am I supposed to tell these people?* he thought. Finally, he stuttered, "Celebrate."

The crowd leaped to their feet and cheered.

Jack thought, *Good, that should distract them for a while. Now I just have to escape back to my friends.* He wanted to find King Tanner. *I know he must've known about this, that sly dog, and if he knew, he must be here somewhere.*

Jack stepped away from the cart and walked over to his two friends.

Charles lightly punched Jack's shoulder with his fist, and Ben less lightly slapped Jack on the back.

They were quickly joined by Sir Alter, who still look shocked, and Sir Sansall.

Jack grabbed Sir Sansall's arm. "I want to talk to the king. Where is he?"

The knight smirked. "Well, talking to yourself isn't a great way to start ruling a kingdom, but I'm sure your loyal followers will make an exception since you are the first king that they have had in so long."

Jack replied, "That's not very funny! I need to talk to King Tanner, now."

Sir Sansall smiled more kindly. "Sure. He's waiting for you in the crowd, but you'll probably have to wait a little while. I doubt that the lords of this country will let you just disappear into the crowd."

Jack turned, and sure enough, all the lords who had been around the cart had gathered behind him.

The man in the gold armor also stepped near and asked, "What do you want us to do, your highness?"

Jack replied, somewhat irritated, "I don't know. I've been a king for all of three seconds, and you expect me to order you all to do something? Fine, I'm going to sit right here outside the palace for the next hour, and I want all of you to go do whatever you want to do, and leave me alone until then."

The gold-armored man bowed at the waist. "What do you want us to do with the huge boulder you created outside the palace?"

Jack sighed as he looked at the large rock. "Just leave it there for now."

The big man turned to the rest of the group. "You heard him, let's go."

After they left, Sir Sansall said, "Very smooth. I'm sure those orders made a lot of sense to them."

Jack glared at the ground. "I don't care. I want to know what's going on before I do anything else. I haven't even decided to stay here, and you want to crown me king. What about my friends? I don't know what they want to do. I need all the information before I can make a decision."

"That seems reasonable," said a voice behind him.

Jack turned toward the unknown voice and saw a knight from their group walking up the stairs to join the five of them. Jack said, "Take off your helmet, King Tanner. I figured you would be in the escort somewhere."

The knight took off his helmet, and sure enough, the king's white hair and gray beard were unmistakable.

"Just as a warning," the king said, "the lords of this kingdom are not loyal to you yet, and giving them an hour to plot against you while you figure out what's going on isn't the best idea."

Jack crossed his arms. "I don't really care. I didn't ask for this kingdom, and if I lost it tomorrow, I wouldn't have lost anything that I had yesterday. I want my questions answered."

The king smiled. "Fair enough. I must tell you a story. This story goes back many years." The king looked at Sir Alter and Sir Sansall and said, "Please excuse the four of us."

The two knights bowed their heads slightly, walked down the stairs out of earshot, and waited.

King Tanner looked back at Jack and said, "At one time I had a good job in America. I had just graduated with my doctorate degree in psychology, and I was excited. I wanted to change the world for the better, but within two weeks some ignorant mage who found a teleportation stone and didn't know how to use it sucked me into this world.

"I used my scientific knowledge to further my own position in this world and even obtain the kingdom of Celel. By the time I gained the ability to return home and traveled back, I discovered that the last of my family members had died while I was in this world. I realized that I didn't have anything back in our world, and I didn't even have the opportunity to change it for the better. I was unnecessary there, so I came back here and tried to change this world.

"After a few years of ruling my kingdom, I discovered that a war would one day be inevitable, and my small kingdom would not be able to win that conflict. I began devising a series of plans so that when this war began, good would conquer evil. This country of Holdom was my best shot at creating a powerful ally. They believe firmly enough in tradition and honor that I knew they would recognize a new king if he actually was part of the bloodline according to their legend.

"I searched this world as well as I could, but despite the fact that there are probably people here in this world with enough similar genes to be crowned king, I had no way to find them. Even if I did find someone, they would need to be skilled in combat, have the wisdom to rule a kingdom, and possess enough knowledge of military tactics to command a battlefield. This individual would also have to be a good person, and there are not too many of those people in this world—even fewer back then.

"Then I got an idea. There is a book that few people in this world can read, although anyone who spends enough time trying and possesses a translation stone will eventually be successful reading it. It tells of the creation of this world."

"I think I have a copy of this book," said Jack.

"Oh, very good." King Tanner continued, "Then you may have noticed that nowhere in that book does it say that humans, or any other forms of life, were created in this world. I thought about it and realized that since angels completed this world's creation, they didn't have the ability to create life for it. They could mold all the aspects of this planet, but they couldn't populate the planet they created. I guessed that since the people in this world were similar to the people in our world, the people in this world may have originally come from our world, although I'm not sure how.

"Armed with my hypothesis, I traveled back to America, where I was pleased to find that they had recently instituted mandatory genetic testing and subsequent storage of that information for all infants born in the United States. The United States provided the perfect opportunity because it's a melting pot of different races. No matter where the original people of this world came from, someone in America would likely have shared DNA with the people of this world.

"I gathered DNA samples from the graves of several kings who ruled this nation long ago and tested the DNA back in our world. Because Holdom's earth stone mages in the past were so skilled, they often created airtight tombs that preserved their dead ancestors' remains for many years. I was able to take samples and reseal the tombs without detection.

"I hired some people to assist me in hacking into the federal database, and I monitored it while I worked to build rapport as a class coordinator and continued to rule Celel. I was pleased to find five matches that I thought would be close enough to the original DNA bloodline of kings here to be able to use their stone.

"I chose you for my plan, and I got a job as the class coordinator at the private school near your home. I put you in all the classes that I knew you would need to prepare you for your journey in this world. I saw that you made two good friends and decided that it would be helpful for you not to be alone here the way I was, so I put them in those classes as well and allowed the three of you to grow together. I taught you all the morality I could and all the important life lessons I knew of and tried to be a mentor to all three of you.

"Unfortunately, the government discovered that I hacked into their database, and they came to arrest me, forcing me to leave our world and destroy all evidence of my plan. When you boys were about to graduate, I realized that you had all the skills necessary to fight in this world, so I decided to bring you here. My kingdom has so many spies from the slave cartels and great southern nations that I decided not to summon you in Celel. I wanted to keep your presence a secret from my enemies. I took some gemstones with me and traveled to a remote area near this continent's center where I thought that I could secretly summon you here and tell you the whole story.

"Regrettably, one of my enemies discovered that I wasn't in Celel and sent people to track me. I'm still not exactly sure who sent the men, but I believe he's a general working for one of the three great southern nations. As I summoned you three here, I realized that I wasn't alone. I quickly stabbed some of the gemstones I had with me into you, Jack, and ended the summoning. I had already discovered that during a summoning process I could place gemstones inside my own or someone else's bloodstream without endangering their life. It has something to do with the conditions inside the portal, and I had already spent a great deal of time researching this phenomenon.

"Anyway, after I inserted some of my gemstones into you, I attempted to use a heal stone to cover the wounds I inflicted so you wouldn't bleed to death. Alas, the mages who had tracked me attacked. When I ended the portal, I thought the three of you would simply return to America with a weird story, but after I fought off the mages, I tried unsuccessfully to summon you to this world again. I conducted some experiments but was unable to discover why I could no longer summon you, so I returned to my country, where I could conduct more extensive testing. I didn't actually discover that you three were training to be knights, or even in my country, until after you uncovered the governor of Juma's treason.

"My original plan was to tell you everything when I brought you into this world, including my future plans, and give you a choice. I must apologize for how I ended up forcing you into this world against your will. You have to believe me that I still care deeply for all three of you, and I sincerely hope that you didn't forget about Dr. Taylor, your old mentor."

When Dr. Taylor finished his story, Jack felt a tear roll down his cheek. He could not decide if he was happy at being reunited with his old mentor and discovering that he was not dead or angry about the way events had played out. Ben and Charles also had tears in their eyes, which Jack suspected were for the same reasons.

Finally, Jack said, "I forgive you. More than anyone else you, Dr. Taylor, turned me into the man that I am today, and you gave me the ability and opportunity to make a difference. That has been my heart's greatest desire since I was a child; I think I got that from you."

Charles nodded. "I think I've lived more in the last few months than in my whole life previously."

Ben said, "Wow, Charles, that was profound. In my opinion this was a great adventure, so I have no complaints."

Dr. Taylor's face grew more serious. "If you all still want to return home and live there, you may; however, I need you here to win this war, and I would ask you to stay."

Jack smiled. "These teleportation stones can be used once every two hours just like any other gemstone, right?"

Dr. Taylor answered, "Yes."

"Good. Then I see no reason why I can't be king here with my right and left hand assisting me and still visit my parents on occasion."

Charles looked surprised. Then he nodded slowly. "Yeah, that's good enough for me. I can't deny that I also want to make a difference."

Ben grinned. "Charles can't leave; he has a girl here." This comment earned him an elbow in the ribs from Charles. Then Ben's face brightened. "This is definitely the right answer for me because I'm not planning to give up the ability to shoot lightning bolts anytime soon."

Jack smiled at Ben's joke and asked Dr. Taylor, "Do the gemstones work in our world?"

Dr. Taylor nodded. "Yes they do. How do you think I blew up my lab when the feds came for me?"

Jack sighed contentedly. "Good because I'm going to need some kind of proof for my parents. I imagine this will be a bit hard for them to swallow." Jack thought for a few moments as he looked out over the city that now belonged to him. "It doesn't look the way I expected it to, but I guess we found our way home after all."

Charles asked Dr. Taylor, "May I inquire as to why a whisper that sounded like an awaking began when Jack picked up the stone?"

Dr. Taylor replied, "The stone was originally a greater earth stone far more powerful than the lesser stones, and it was the crown jewel of this kingdom. Remember, this kingdom is extremely old, and very few people had found any greater stones at that time. Though greater stones are a little more plentiful now, they are still very rare. The king of this land decided that he always wanted one of his descendants to rule, so he tied the greater gemstone to his own bloodline so his descendants could never be overthrown. When someone of the correct bloodline touches the stone, the blood of the first king that still resides in the stone automatically speaks an awakening. That way the new king can instantly prove that he is a descendant.

"The stone cannot be awakened to anyone not of the correct bloodline. It's an art that has been forgotten long ago. If you watched Jack closely, you would also have noticed that his irises turned a different shade of brown as though he were using one of the stones he possesses in his bloodstream because both are types of blood magic. There are three normal types of blood magic, but technically, a stone tied to a particular bloodline is also a variation of being an iconic blood mage. Anyone who uses a gemstone through a form of blood magic that uses their own blood will exhibit the same color change in their eyes as Jack."

"Why did it hurt so much when I held it in my hand?" Jack looked at the earth stone resting in his palm.

Dr. Taylor furrowed his brow. "I'm not sure. I didn't expect that, but it's possible that the gemstone reacted to the other gemstones already in your bloodstream."

"Did anyone else see … a person?" Jack asked hesitantly.

Dr. Taylor narrowed his eyes and looked at Jack with a piercing gaze. "No, what did you see?"

"I think I saw the king who originally bound the stone to the bloodline."

Dr. Taylor shook his head slowly. "Apparently, he somehow bound part of his consciousness to the stone."

Jack asked, "Why did you create such an elaborate plan to conceal who the real heir to the throne was?"

Dr. Taylor replied, "Long ago when I found you, I told the most trusted friend that I had made in this world that this trip would one day take place. Sir Sansall is that old friend. He's seven years younger than me; in fact, he was just old enough to join Celel's army when we met. We both knew it would be impossible to conceal the entire plan from all the spies in my kingdom, so we devised a scheme to let the enemy think that they knew everything. In reality, Sir Sansall didn't think he would survive the journey. I was always slightly more optimistic, and as I had hoped, you found a way to save him even when he didn't want you to try." Dr. Taylor placed his hand on Jack's shoulder for a moment. "On a personal note, I have to thank you for saving his life. You never get over the terrible feeling that you have when your friends volunteer for suicide missions. It's one of the worst things about being a ruler."

Jack squared his shoulders. "Do you have any advice on how to rule a kingdom?"

The doctor replied, "My boy, there are no easy answers in life's greatest adventures."

Jack frowned. "I suppose that's a 'no'?"

Dr. Taylor smiled. "You are free to ask me any specific questions you like, but as far as an overall grand plan goes, you already possess all the knowledge and skills you need."

Jack turned and looked down the stairs and out over the entire city again. "There's just something so weird about this whole thing being my kingdom. I can tell that this adventure hasn't ended. It's only just begun."

Glossary

People:
Abgot: warlord of Kliptun
Acelet: warlord of Vergill
Aldric: retired Knight of Celel; head of Celshen family; husband of
    Zemara; father of Zannel
Alter: Knight of Celel
Dagder: prince of Dulla; younger brother of Daggoth
Daggoth: prince of Dulla; older brother of Dagder; skilled mage
Delger the Cruel: officer in the Caishan cartel
Derek: older brother of Ben
Don: member of Hukel family; younger brother of Felara
Dulcapa: general from a powerful southern nation; exercising control in
    Gattel
Dunnel: merchant; owner of Vennel
Elfond: member of Entell family; suitor of Zannel
Elton: escaped slave; merchant
Fada: servant of King Tanner
Fanter: knight-in-training
Felara: member of Hukel family; older sister of Don
Felter: fire mage hired by Warlord Gaekkin
Fenha: brother of Fenta; owner of orchard near Gredune
Fenta: sister of Fenha; wife of Hrot; lives in Xin
Gaekkin: warlord south of Kliptun antagonistic toward Warlord Abgot
Gunda: warlord of Gidanna
Gurtven: knight-in-training; winner of previous tournament
Hal: governor of Gredune
Hrot: husband of Fenta; lives in Xin
Hucklee: skilled water mage; sworn enemy of Sumbvi
Juima: warlord of Burnadad
Kelder: knight-in-training; recommended by Setell family

Keljerk the Cruel: officer in the Caishan cartel
Keyvin: captain of the guard in Hathra; bodyguard of Warlord Abgot
Kxull: knight-in-training; blacksmith
Lilen: maid of Celshen family
Meekah: Knight of Celel; recommended by Celshen family
Ogol: captain of the guard in Gredune
Sansall: Knight of Celel
Sarah: younger sister of Charles
Selfren: member of Caishan assassin squad
Sumbvi: skilled fire mage; Knight of Celel
Tanner: king of Celel
Taylor, Isaac: Doctor of Psychology; coarse coordinator at Eagleton Private Academy
Thompson, Keith: retired police officer; martial arts instructor at Eagleton Private Academy
Vanzantel: member of Setell family; fiancé of Zannel
Vennel: slave purchased and freed by Jack
Waldun: member of resistance in Gattel; father of Wilt
Wilt: member of resistance in Gattel; son of Waldun
Zannel: member of Celshen family; daughter of Sir Aldric and Zemara
Zemara: member of Celshen family; wife of Sir Aldric; mother of Zannel

Cities:
Dettall: city in Celel
Duthwania: capital of Dulla
Gattel: capital of Gidanna
Gredune: city in Vergill
Hathra: capital of Kliptun
Jukul: city in Burnadad
Juma: city in Celel
Menchida: capital of Holdom
Quilvich: city in Splintell
Sargosa: capital of Vergill
Sellta: capital of Celel
Xin: city in Kliptun

Countries:
Burnadad: one of the northern nations; located west of Celel
Celel: one of the three powerful northern kingdoms; located on east coast
Dulla: one of the three powerful northern kingdoms; located south of Celel

Gidanna: one of the central nations; located north of Jofna; ruled by Warlord Gunda
Holdom: one of the three powerful northern kingdoms; located on west coast; searching for rightful heir
Imtad: one of the three powerful southern kingdoms; located on west coast
Jofna: most powerful kingdom in the central lands; located on east coast
Klantiff: one of the three powerful southern nations; located north of the Great Southern Desert
Kliptun: one of the central nations; located east of Vergill; ruled by Warlord Abgot
Malldan: one of the three powerful southern kingdoms; located on southeast coast
Splintell: one of the central nations; located southwest of Dulla; in civil war
Vergill: one of the central nations; located west of Kliptun; ruled by Warlord Acelet
Wuskl: one of the northern nations; located on peninsula west of Holdom

Groups:
Bendel: one of the three major slave cartels; based on island southeast of Malldan
Caishan: one of the three major slave cartels; based on Wuskl
Celshen: one of the prominent families in Celel
Entell: one of the prominent families in Celel
Hukel: one of the prominent families in Celel
Setell: one of the prominent families in Celel
Zangan: one of the three major slave cartels; based on island east of Celel

Other:
Coopa: title of authority among religious followers of Gultten
Garthong: gother bonded to Jack
Gother: flying lizard; indigenous to Nesting Mountain north of Hathra
Great Northern Mountains: mountain range bordering the northern coast of the continent
Great Southern Desert: desert bordering the southern coast of the continent
Gultten: demon god
Lavdoric: language, the common tongue
Mangotten Marsh: marsh south of Gredune

Made in the USA
Charleston, SC
31 December 2015